ALWAYS REMEMBER

Also by Mary Balogh

ALWAYS REMEMBER

A RAVENSWOOD NOVEL

MARY BALOGH

Berkley

New York

BERKLEY
An imprint of Penguin Random House LLC
penguinrandomhouse.com

Copyright © 2024 by Mary Balogh
Penguin Random House supports copyright. Copyright fuels creativity, encourages diverse voices,
promotes free speech, and creates a vibrant culture. Thank you for buying an authorized edition of
this book and for complying with copyright laws by not reproducing, scanning, or distributing
any part of it in any form without permission. You are supporting writers and allowing
Penguin Random House to continue to publish books for every reader.

BERKLEY and the BERKLEY & B colophon are registered trademarks of
Penguin Random House LLC.

Library of Congress Cataloging-in-Publication Data

Names: Balogh, Mary, author.
Title: Always remember / Mary Balogh.
Description: New York : Berkley, [2024] | Series: A Ravenswood novel
Identifiers: LCCN 2023013949 (print) | LCCN 2023013950 (ebook) |
ISBN 9780593638385 (hardcover) | ISBN 9780593638392 (ebook)
Subjects: LCGFT: Romance fiction. | Historical fiction. | Novels.
Classification: LCC PR6052.A465 A78 2024 (print) | LCC PR6052.A465 (ebook) |
DDC 823/.914--dc23/eng/20230327
LC record available at https://lccn.loc.gov/2023013949
LC ebook record available at https://lccn.loc.gov/2023013950

Printed in the United States of America
1st Printing

Book design by George Towne

ALWAYS REMEMBER

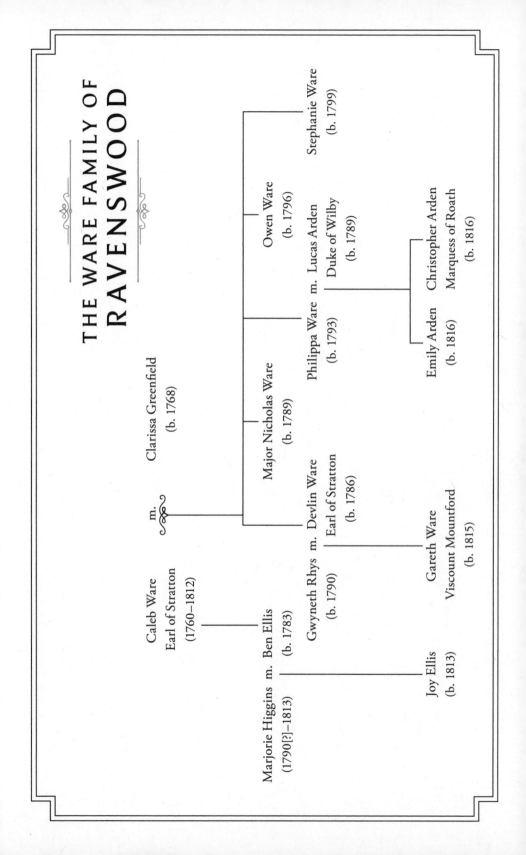

THE WARE FAMILY OF
RAVENSWOOD

Caleb Ware
Earl of Stratton
(1760–1812)

m.

Clarissa Greenfield
(b. 1768)

Marjorie Higgins m. Ben Ellis
(1790[?]–1813) (b. 1783)

Gwyneth Rhys m. Devlin Ware
(b. 1790) Earl of Stratton
(b. 1786)

Major Nicholas Ware
(b. 1789)

Philippa Ware m. Lucas Arden
(b. 1793) Duke of Wilby
(b. 1789)

Owen Ware
(b. 1796)

Stephanie Ware
(b. 1799)

Joy Ellis
(b. 1813)

Gareth Ware
Viscount Mountford
(b. 1815)

Emily Arden
(b. 1816)

Christopher Arden
Marquess of Roath
(b. 1816)

CHAPTER ONE

S ummer had settled over southern England in a most agreeable manner, with long days of warm sunshine, gentle breezes, and just enough rainfall to help the crops yield a bountiful harvest and to keep trees, lawns, and pastures fresh and green. Flowers bloomed in colorful abundance, whether wild over hedgerows and walls, in ditches and meadows, or cultivated with loving care in gardens and beds.

The English, of course, could never quite relax into full enjoyment of such a perfect summer. How long could one expect it to last, after all? There would always be pessimists squinting off to the west, whence most weather approached, nodding sagely as though they could see something beyond the bent horizon invisible to everyone else, and predicting that they would pay for such a perfect spell. Even the optimists were ready to admit it could not last forever, and in that at least they were bound to be right sooner or later.

The Ware family of Ravenswood Hall in Hampshire, the inhabitants of the village of Boscombe just across the river from it, and residents of the surrounding countryside became especially anxious when June passed into July and there was still no break in the beautiful weather. For it seemed impossible that it could last a whole month longer. Yet a continuation of the perfect weather was all they asked for. They would not be greedy.

There was to be a grand fete in the neighborhood on the last Saturday of July, and everyone looked forward to it with an almost sick longing. For eight long years had passed since the last one. The Ravenswood summer fete had once been an annual event and for most people their very favorite day of the year, even including Christmas. It had offered feasting and music and dancing and varied contests and entertainment for all ages from the middle of the morning until late at night. The weather had always cooperated with bright sunshine and blue skies and the gentlest of breezes and warmth without searing heat. *Always*. Ask any old-timers and they would tell you it was so. How everyone *hoped* the eight-year break would not destroy that string of good fortune. It might rain with their blessing on the Sunday following the fete, but please, *please* let the sun shine on the Saturday.

Eight years ago the fete had come to an abrupt and horrible end in the middle of the grand ball with which the day's festivities always culminated. Devlin Ware, Viscount Mountford at the time, son and heir of the Earl of Stratton, the genial and well-loved owner of Ravenswood, had come upon his father engaged in a blatantly improper embrace with a lady guest out in the temple folly on top of the hill close to the ballroom. But instead of keeping his shock and outrage to himself until it could be dealt with privately at a more appropriate time, Devlin had confronted his father very publicly outside the open French windows of the ballroom, in the sight and hearing of his family and virtually every neighbor for miles around.

To call it a shocking scene would be a severe understatement.

It had ended in disaster for the Ware family and in intense embarrassment for everyone, even neighbors and village folk who had no reason to be embarrassed. Except that they had always set the Wares of Ravenswood upon some sort of pedestal. They had seemed the perfect family, virtuous and happy among themselves, amiable toward all, impeccably well mannered, unfailingly charming leaders of the community. They had always been generous about sharing their home and the spacious park surrounding it for community events that ranged from the extravagant grandeur of the summer fete and the joyful warmth of the Christmas party and ball to the fun of the Valentine's treasure hunt and tea and the impromptu and less formal invitation to public days, when everyone was welcome to enjoy the beauty of the park for picnics and walks.

Everything had changed after that night. The guest who had been caught with the earl, a supposed widow and newcomer to the village, had disappeared overnight. Devlin had left abruptly the following morning with his elder half brother, not to be seen again in the neighborhood for more than six years. Clarissa, Countess of Stratton, who had always been warm and hospitable, the perfect hostess, had withdrawn into her home and into herself and was rarely seen in public except at church on Sunday mornings. Her sons Nicholas and Owen had left soon after their elder brothers, one to begin his career as an officer with a prestigious cavalry regiment, the other to attend boarding school. The elder daughter, Lady Philippa Ware, a happy-natured beauty sparkling on the edge of womanhood, had become suddenly subdued and eventually almost a total recluse. The youngest child of the family, Lady Stephanie Ware, only nine years old at the time of the fete, had kept mainly to herself and her family and her governess except for her involvement with the youth choir at the church.

The Earl of Stratton himself—handsome, openhearted, and genial—was the only one among them who had carried on as though nothing untoward had happened, as though he had not been exposed in the most humiliatingly public manner imaginable as an almost certain adulterer and a probable philanderer on a larger scale. Everyone knew, after all, that for most of his married life he had spent the spring months of each year in London for the parliamentary session, while his wife and children remained in the country. After the incident at the ball, several people admitted to having always felt uneasy about that arrangement. Was it realistic, they asked themselves, to have expected that their earl would remain celibate during those lengthy separations from his wife, when London abounded with members of the *ton* eager to amuse themselves at the myriad entertainments of the Season?

Life as usual after the catastrophe had not lasted long even for the earl, however. He had collapsed at the village tavern one evening while he drank ale and chatted jovially with his neighbors. According to those neighbors, he had been dead before he hit the floor.

The biggest change the catastrophe of that summer fete had brought to those who lived in the village and countryside around Ravenswood, however, had been the complete cessation of all the social activities for which the earl and countess had opened their home since their marriage more than twenty years before. The countess had organized and hosted those events, and the earl had paid for them. No longer. Open days, two or three times each week, had never officially been canceled, but they had come to an end anyway.

At first no one had wanted to intrude upon what was obviously a difficult time for the family. And who wanted the embarrassment of coming accidentally face-to-face with one or more of them and having to *say* something? After a while, it had seemed just too awkward to go back there.

Then the earl died.

Two years had passed after his death before Devlin, the new Earl of Stratton, returned home, looking very different from the quiet, pleasant, essentially unremarkable young man his neighbors remembered. He had come home, at the age of twenty-eight, looking dour, even morose, and rugged and battle-scarred. He had purchased a commission in a foot regiment after leaving home and had gone to Portugal to fight in the Peninsular Wars. His elder half brother, Ben Ellis—his elder, *illegitimate* half brother, that is—had gone with him, nominally as his batman. The allied armies had fought their way across Portugal and Spain and over the Pyrenees into France until Napoleon Bonaparte surrendered and abdicated as emperor after the Battle of Toulouse in 1814. Devlin had sold out then, the wars apparently over, and come home. Ben had been married and widowed during the six years they had been gone, and brought an infant child home with him. He had not stayed at Ravenswood. He had purchased the manor of Penallen by the sea thirty miles away, spent a year or so renovating it, and finally settled there with his daughter.

The new Earl of Stratton, meanwhile, so forbidding in looks and manner, had surprised his neighbors. At a tea his mother had dutifully arranged to welcome him home, he announced that Ravenswood would once again be open for public days and social events, and he carried through on his promise almost immediately by offering the ballroom for an upcoming assembly. It had been a great blessing to the villagers, for the assembly rooms above the inn were small and cramped and always so congested on those evenings that it was difficult to find space in which to dance. There was to be a difference, however, from the old assemblies at the hall. At Devlin's suggestion, the planning was done not by his mother but by the landlord of the inn and his wife, with the help of a committee of villagers. Those who attended paid an admission charge to cover costs incurred. The present earl's only contribution was the venue.

It was *not* a sign of meanness on his part. Quite the contrary. Everyone was delighted by the new arrangement, even though it had involved them in a great deal of work and some small expense— or perhaps for those very reasons. Older people remembered the time when it had always been that way, when they had all participated in organizing their own entertainments, and the involvement of the Wares of Ravenswood had been minimal. They had done it again during the years following the great upset at the hall, even if it had been a bit halfhearted, as though they had feared somehow offending the family by ignoring them and carrying on with their lives as if the Wares and Ravenswood itself did not exist.

The social life of the neighborhood had been altogether more robust and cheerful in the two years since Devlin's return. Everyone had continued to have a hand in their own individual and communal activities, but also Ravenswood had become a warmer, happier, more welcoming place than it had ever been. The Earl of Stratton had married at Christmas a few months after his return, and the wedding in the village church had been a joyful occasion for all. For the bride had been Gwyneth Rhys, daughter of Sir Ifor and Lady Rhys of Cartref, the estate adjoining Ravenswood to the east. Sir Ifor was the church organist and conductor of the various village choirs, and both he and his wife were much beloved by everyone who knew them.

Lady Philippa Ware, at the advanced age of twenty-two, had finally gone to London with her mother the following spring for a come-out Season and had met and married the heir to a dukedom. Before the year was out, Gwyneth, Countess of Stratton, had given birth to a son, Gareth, Viscount Mountford. Lady Philippa, now the Duchess of Wilby, had been delivered of twins, a girl and a boy, early in the spring of this year.

The Ware family had moved forward from the dark, gloomy years that had followed the last summer fete. They seemed happy with one another again and open to their neighbors and friends. A new generation was in the nursery. And now the transition was to be complete with the resumption of the annual summer fete and its busy entertainments for all.

Not all the events would happen at Ravenswood itself. Some would center upon the village green. The day would begin there, in fact, in front of the church instead of on the terrace outside the hall. The maypole dancing would happen on the village green, a more appropriate setting than the lawn before the house. And the green would be surrounded by the various booths and stalls at which the villagers and their children would be enticed into parting with their pennies. Other events—especially those needing more space, like the children's races, the archery and log-splitting contests, and the baking, needlework, and wood-carving competitions—would take place as before at Ravenswood. The evening ball would of course be held in the west wing of the house itself. The ballroom there was the only room for miles around large enough to hold all who would attend.

But everything depended almost entirely upon the weather.

The family at Ravenswood was as eager as anyone else for the resumption of the annual fete. They were already busy with plans for those parts of it that were to be their responsibility. But it was still a few weeks away, and they had other, more imminent pleasures to occupy their minds and their time.

Owen was already home after his second year at Oxford, but he was expecting a friend and fellow student to join him for a few weeks. Nicholas—Major the Honorable Nicholas Ware, that was— had been granted a few weeks' leave from his regiment, which was a part of the occupation force stationed near Paris. He was to spend those weeks at Ravenswood with his family, whose members had not seen him since before the Battle of Waterloo last year. Lucas and Philippa, Duke and Duchess of Wilby, were coming with their young twins all the way from Greystone Court, the ducal residence in Worcestershire. And Ben, who had at first sent word that he would stay home at Penallen for the summer, had changed his mind and was coming with his daughter after all.

Viscount Watley, Owen's friend, would not be the only guest from outside the family. Lady Catherine Emmett was a longtime friend of Clarissa, Dowager Countess of Stratton, though they had seen each other only rarely since meeting during a London Season when they were both young brides. They had met again last year when they were in London. Lady Catherine's niece, Lady Jennifer Arden, with whom she lived, had become a close friend of Philippa, and then Philippa had married Jennifer's brother, and suddenly they all seemed like one family—very much to the delight of the two older ladies. Lady Catherine and Lady Jennifer had accepted an invitation to spend as much of the summer as they could spare at Ravenswood.

It was going to be lovely to have all the family at home together again. However, the situation would not be perfectly ideal, for Lucas and Philippa, as well as Lady Catherine and Lady Jennifer, were in mourning for the old Duke and Duchess of Wilby, who had died within an hour or two of each other on the night following the christening of the twins back in the early spring. They had been Lady Catherine's parents and Lucas and Jennifer's grandparents. It would not be entirely appropriate, then, for them to participate in all the festivities of the fete. However, as Lucas had explained in his correspondence with Devlin, it was important to his wife that they spend a few weeks at her girlhood home. She would enjoy showing off her children to family, neighbors, and friends. And both of them needed a break after the busy months of settling into their new ducal roles. They would take pleasure from their visit and simply abstain from any activity that did not feel appropriate—dancing at the ball on the night of the fete, for example.

Lady Catherine, in her reply to Clarissa's invitation, said much the same thing. She and Jenny needed some cheering up, she had explained, and she really did not believe her mother and father would expect them to live in unrelieved gloom and isolation for a whole year. One could mourn just as sincerely with light and laughter, after all, and the memory of good times with her parents.

So the Wares of Ravenswood and the families in the village and the countryside enjoyed the unusually near-perfect summer weather they were having and hoped it would continue through July and possibly even beyond. Hoping was all they could do, of course, since no one could control the weather.

It was everyone's fervent wish that this year's fete would be the happy beginning of a new annual tradition.

CHAPTER TWO

B en Ellis was on his way to Ravenswood. He sat comfortably
with his arms folded across his chest, watching his daughter
play with her dolls on the carriage seat across from him and pon-
dering the issue that had been plaguing him for several months
now. He had never been a ditherer. When a decision needed to be
made, he considered all the options, made his choice, and acted
upon it. But suddenly he had become a ditherer, and he was not at
all happy about it. It felt like having a hive of bees buzzing inside
his head.

The basic question and its answer were not the problem. He was
ready to marry again, and the sooner he did it the better it would
be. Joy needed a mother. Having a father who doted upon her was
not enough for her. Nor was having the kindly, grandmotherly nurse
Ben had employed and a houseful of servants who watched out for
her and indulged her probably far more than they should.

His daughter needed a *mother*. And brothers and sisters. Soon.
She was already three years old. And he needed a wife—or perhaps

wanted was the better word. He had liked being married, belonging exclusively to one woman, having her belong to him. Mutual affection and comfort, shared lives, a shared bed, regular sex—it was a way of life that had satisfied him, and he wanted it again. No one could take Marjorie's place, of course, but she was gone and he was still here. And he was still young at thirty-three. He was invited with some frequency to the homes of his neighbors and occasionally returned the favor, but he felt awkward attending social events alone. He felt even worse entertaining alone. He needed a partner, and Penallen needed a mistress.

He had purchased the property from Devlin soon after their return from the wars. It had been sadly neglected in their father's time. He had considered the house too small for his tastes and too shabby and damp for his comfort. It was too close to the sea for the late earl's liking. He had hated the perpetual smell of salty air and even fish when the wind blew in a certain direction. He had never seen the appeal of gazing out at the endless expanse of the sea. Ben, on the other hand, had always loved Penallen and dreamed of what he would do to improve it if it were his.

Now it *was* his, and the most pressing of those improvements had been made, not the least of which had been replacing all the heavy curtains and nettings that had covered the front-facing windows with lighter draperies that could be drawn back during the daytime to fill the house with light and reveal the view across his own lawns and the public cliff walk and down over the village nestled on the shore at the base of the cliffs to the waters of the English Channel beyond. The nettings had been permanently removed.

The issue plaguing his mind was not *whether* he should remarry. It was *whom* he should marry.

It might have been expected that in such a small rural neighborhood he would have trouble finding even one eligible woman. But that was not the issue either. He had been presented instead with an embarrassment of riches in the form of three women. *Three.* But try as he would, he could not narrow that number down even to two. Reducing it to one was virtually impossible, and he was driving himself slowly insane. One day he would convince himself that he had made a definite decision, only to wonder the following day—or the following *hour*—if maybe one of the others would suit him better.

His dithering struck him as being horribly arrogant, as though he considered himself God's answer to a single woman's prayer and expected that any one of the three would trip all over her feet in her eagerness to become Mrs. Ellis of Penallen. That mental image of himself appalled him. It was just as likely that one or all three would be outraged at his effrontery in considering them.

He was, after all—to use the plain English word—a bastard. The bastard son of the late Earl of Stratton, to be exact. It was true that he had been brought up at Ravenswood Hall thirty miles away with the earl's legitimate family, that he now owned Penallen, which was not exactly a mansion but was a manor of considerable size and dominated the skyline above the village. Nevertheless, he was a bastard, a fact that might well deter any respectable young woman to whom he offered marriage. And if not her, then her parents.

He had tried making a choice based upon that possibility. Which of the three was most likely to ignore the blight upon his name and accept him anyway? There was no way of knowing.

It had been an easy decision the first time. Marjorie had been his woman—he had never called her his mistress—for more than two years before he discovered that she was with child; six months with child, actually. She had not told him and he had been as blind as a bat and as stupid as an ox before he saw her in profile one day when she had not seen him, her hands behind her hips, flexing her spine backward. He had married her the very same day and had never regretted it.

He brought his mind back to the present. Their daughter, his and Marjorie's, was manipulating the arms of the larger of her two dolls so they could hug the woolen cat and she could murmur endearments to it in a higher version of her voice. It was an awkward procedure, as the black, white, and orange cat with its round, startled-looking eyes, which had been knitted by his younger sister Stephanie as a Christmas gift last year, was larger than the doll.

After a moment the cat pulled sharply and rudely away from the doll's fond embrace and bounced about the carriage seat opposite, mewing loudly, pausing briefly to kiss the cheek of the doll, perhaps in apology, and leaping right over the head of the other, smaller doll before settling flat on its belly on the seat and licking one paw with lapping sounds that came from Joy's mouth.

"Naughty kitty," she scolded in the voice of the bigger doll. "Lie still. Time for your nap. No stories for you today. You been bad."

His daughter had been slow to talk, using single words and a pointing finger long after Ben had thought she should be saying more. He need not have worried. Suddenly whole sentences had started to pour from her mouth, and soon after they had been largely intelligible even to people other than himself.

She came out of her imaginary world now as she glanced across at him. She still did that frequently, even though two years had passed since her mother died and her whole world and security had come to depend upon her father alone. She needed at all times the reassurance of knowing where he was. He smiled. She did not like her make-believe world to be invaded by adults, though, and could become very self-conscious, even irritable, if she was made suddenly aware that her nurse or her papa was within hearing distance.

"Are we there yet, Papa?" she asked in her own precise little voice.

"Not quite," he said. Thirty miles was not a very long journey, but to a child even a five-mile stretch could seem endless. "We will be there for tea."

She yawned noisily, grasped the cat by one incongruously long ear, jumped down from her seat, and climbed onto his lap. She curled against him while his arms came about her.

"Tell me a story about Mama," she said.

She would never have any conscious memories of her mother, of course, just as he had almost none of *his* mother, but he tried to keep Marjorie alive for her as much as he could. He told her one of her favorites, of the time when an officer, all decked out in pristine scarlet coat with gold lace and silver facings and buttons, had demanded his washing from her and proceeded to curse her when she told him it was not ready. But Marjorie had interrupted him, her dunking stick waving before his face, the sleeves of her dress rolled up above her elbows to display her reddened, muscular arms.

You shut your mouth right there, sir, she had said, *or I will wash it out with this here soap. When you bring your washing to me, you take your turn with everyone else, even if you are King George of England. I told you it would be ready tonight, and I meant tonight. Does this look like tonight, with the sun almost directly above your head?* She had pointed skyward with the stick before shaking it in his face again. *Go away, now. Shoo. I have work to do even if you do not. Sir.*

Unfortunately Ben could not imitate her broad Cockney accent.

"And he went," he told Joy, "as meekly as a newborn lamb. And everyone who was standing around listening applauded and Mama curtsied to them like a princess, waving her stick like a wand."

"Even if you are King George of England," Joy said, giggling with glee. *"Shoo."* They were always her favorite words from the story. She hugged her cat with one arm while pressing its ear against her mouth with the other hand, turned her face against his waistcoat, and was asleep within moments. Ben felt the familiar ache of love for her, his own flesh and blood, born of two bastards—the word he had been called more than once in his life, and Marjorie too.

Not that Marjorie had known for sure that that was what she was. She had never known either parent but had grown up in the grim, bleak setting of an orphanage in a poorer part of London. She had married a boy from there when she was about sixteen—she had never known either her birthday or her exact age. Her husband had taken the king's shilling soon after and been sent off to the Peninsula as a private soldier. Marjorie had gone with him, having won the regimental lottery to determine which wives could accompany their husbands and which must remain behind in England. And so she had gone there and done her part by becoming a washerwoman, and her feet had been set on the path that would eventually cross Ben's. It was strange how life could be like that. The odds against their ever meeting had been enormous. He had usually done his own washing, but on one occasion, when the army had been marching for days and it had got a bit out of hand, he had taken it to the nearest washerwoman and asked if she had time to do it for him.

He did not think of himself as a man of strong passions. He had not been in love with Marjorie, though he had cared deeply for her. He was not in love with any of the three women he was con-sidering as his second wife. There were other considerations more important to him than romance. He *was* capable of loving with all his heart. His love for his daughter was total and unconditional. He and his wife had named her Joy quite deliberately. She was theirs, their own legitimate child, an important concept to two orphans. But he had always been Ben Ellis. Not Benjamin or Benedict. No middle name. No mention of the name *Ware*. Just Ben Ellis.

Joy was his very own, as she had been Marjorie's. She bore his name—as had his late wife. She had been the joy of their hearts.

When he had been invited to Ravenswood to spend part of the summer, he had excused himself at first. He had already given up a few weeks of the early spring to travel north for the christen-ing of Pippa's twins and had remained longer than he intended for the funeral of the old Duke and Duchess of Wilby, grandparents of Pippa's husband. He had come home to Penallen at last, dream-ing of settling permanently there in his new home and neighbor-hood, of supervising the work on his farm all summer and through the harvest, of choosing a bride, of proposing to her and arrang-ing a wedding, perhaps soon after the harvest or maybe closer to Christmas.

But then he had been faced with the dilemma of having no clear and obvious choice of bride, but rather *three* eligible and very equal possibilities. He turned his head to gaze out through the car-riage window and saw the familiar landmarks that told him they would be at Ravenswood within half an hour or so. Good. Perhaps the bees would take a nap inside his head once he arrived. Perhaps by the time he returned home, he would have made a clear and firm decision.

All he wanted was an ordinary woman, though he meant no offense by that word. Quite the contrary, in fact. He certainly did not want anyone of high social rank, into whose world he could never quite fit—just as he had never quite fit at Ravenswood despite the efforts the countess and his half siblings had always made to treat him as a son and brother equal to themselves. They all genuinely loved him, he knew, just as he loved them.

But there had been the little things, or not so little, perhaps. He had been sent to a good school at the age of twelve, just as his half brothers had, and received an excellent education there. His father had been eager to send him to Cambridge when he was eighteen. His half brothers, however, had been sent to a different school, where most of the pupils were sons of the aristocracy or the upper crust of the gentry. Devlin had gone to Oxford to further his education and now Owen was there. Nicholas had had a commission purchased for him in a cavalry regiment in which all the officers were sons of elite British families.

Ben was not looking for outstanding beauty in a bride either. Character was of far more importance than looks. Marjorie had been a tall, strong woman with a broad, round face and wavy light brown hair she had worn ruthlessly scraped back over her head and twisted into a tight bun. Her hands and arms had been powerful and permanently reddened from all the hours they spent in her washtub, scrubbing and wringing clothes filthy with mud and blood. She had not been pretty, just pleasant looking. She had been a satisfying lover, a comfortable companion, a devoted mother, and a good woman.

Mrs. Collins was the childless widow of a fisherman who had done well enough for himself to leave her a small cottage in the

village down by the shore and enough money to support herself,
though there was probably no surplus to spend upon luxuries. She
was a quiet, seemingly sensible woman, who nodded to him pleasantly at church each Sunday and often handed Joy a sweetmeat to
suck upon during the sermon.

Miss Green, one of the numerous children of an impoverished
gentleman from Gloucestershire, had been offered a home and employment as companion by her maternal great-aunt, Miss Gibbons,
who lived a mile or so west of the village. Miss Green was an unassuming young woman, though neither dull nor unintelligent. Ben
had been in company with her a number of times at various church
functions and evening gatherings at the homes of his neighbors and
had been in conversation with her on one or two of those occasions.

Miss Atwell was the schoolmaster's eldest daughter and helped
her father out a few days a week by teaching some of the slower
learners their letters. She was a serious-minded young woman, but
she obviously cared about children and had a way of drawing the
very best out of them. She had lifted Joy onto her lap at one church
picnic while she told a story to a circle of older children sitting on
the grass before her. She had smiled at Ben as she carefully handed
over his sleeping daughter when reading time ended, with the hu-
morous remark that she must be an interesting reader indeed if she
so easily put children to sleep.

Which of the three would suit him best? Mrs. Collins? Miss
Green? Miss Atwell? Which would make the best mother for Joy?
With which one could he imagine himself living in some content-
ment for the rest of his life, even if they both lived to be eighty?
Which one did he most fancy sleeping with?

There was no clear answer.

He would allow himself these few weeks away from home to

relax with his family. Joy was excited about seeing the babies, her cousins—Devlin and Gwyneth's Gareth and Pippa and Lucas's Emily and Christopher. She was also eagerly looking forward to being made much of by the family, particularly her joint favorites, Uncle Owen and Aunt Stephanie.

He bent his head to kiss the soft, unruly curls on his daughter's head. She made sounds of sleepy protest and pressed the cat to her face.

"We are there," he said after the carriage had passed through Boscombe and rumbled over the bridge that spanned the river between the village and Ravenswood. It was now climbing the slight incline of the drive, which passed between flowering meadows on either side and the few sheep that grazed there, and up between freshly scythed lawns above the ha-ha to the house itself.

Joy yawned hugely before sitting abruptly upright on his lap, wide awake and eager to leap down from the carriage the moment it drew to a halt and the door was opened and the steps set down.

The front doors at the top of a tall flight of steps had opened and Devlin and Gwyneth had come outside, smiling in welcome. Stephanie was close behind them. She came hurrying down the steps, her arms spread wide, as Joy squealed and bounced on Ben's lap and lifted the cat to wave one of its paws at her aunt.

The following day another carriage drew close to Ravenswood, though this one was coming from the east rather than from the south.

"Clarissa and I felt an instant liking for each other," Lady Catherine Emmett was telling her niece. She thought a moment. "It was actually more than just liking, though. Sometimes one meets someone and senses immediately that that person will be a close friend, almost as though one had known her before though clearly it is impossible. In a previous lifetime, perhaps. It would be very convenient, would it not, to have the sort of religion that believed in such a thing?"

"Reincarnation?" Lady Jennifer Arden said.

"That is the word," her aunt said, raising one ringed finger. "I felt just that with Clarissa the first time we met during a London Season when we were both young brides. And I knew she felt the same way. Have I ever told you that by some incredible coincidence our weddings were solemnized at the same hour on the same day in the same year but in different places? We did not see a great deal of each other after that Season until last spring, but we always corresponded regularly and still do."

Yes, Jennifer had heard it all a number of times before. But it was inevitable when one lived with someone that one heard—and told—some favorite stories more than once or even twice. She had enjoyed watching the friendship of the two older ladies blossom last year when they had met again in London. Clarissa, Dowager Countess of Stratton, had been there for the come-out Season of her elder daughter, Lady Philippa Ware.

"It was exactly how I felt when I met Pippa," Jennifer said. "Her daughter and your niece. Perhaps there is something in that reincarnation theory, Aunt Kitty. Maybe we reincarnate in groups and somehow recognize one another when we meet again in the new life."

They both chuckled at the absurdity of that notion and for a few moments were content to watch the English countryside through the carriage windows.

"He was not nearly good enough for her," Lady Catherine said after a while. "The earl, Clarissa's husband, I mean. He was extremely good looking and charming and sociable. He was the center of attention wherever he went and was widely liked and admired. Clarissa was beautiful and charming herself, but she always seemed to move in his shadow. Other women openly envied her."

"Except you," Jennifer said, smiling.

"Well," her aunt said. "It seemed to me that it ought to have been the other way around. Other men ought to have envied *him*, and perhaps a few did. But he somehow chose to eclipse her, and I did not think that well done of him. Your uncle and I were friendly with them before Clarissa stopped going to London every year for the Season, but I never succumbed to his charm. It was clear to me from the start that he liked women rather too much, that he had a roving eye. I always suspected he was a womanizer. I do beg your pardon, Jenny, for such plain speaking."

Her niece laughed. "I have been twenty-five years old for three weeks, Aunt Kitty," she said. "It is unlikely that at my age I will succumb to a fit of the vapors when I hear such a word."

Her aunt patted her hand. "I recall the letter I had from Clarissa soon after the birth of Devlin," she said. "She ought to have been over the moon with happiness in those early days of new motherhood, and on the surface she *was*. But I knew her well enough by then to be able to read between the lines. The earl, her husband, had just brought a three-year-old child home with him from London and explained that the boy was his son, conceived before he fell in love with Clarissa and married her. He told his wife that the child was the unfortunate result of a youthful indiscretion during the brief spell when he was sowing some wild oats, as most men do before settling down. It had happened the one time only, he assured her, and never since or ever again. But the mother had recently died and he had not had the heart to send the boy to an orphanage. He had brought him to Ravenswood instead, sure as he was that his generous, warmhearted, and beloved wife—I am perhaps adding some of my own words here, Jenny—would forgive him and open her arms and her heart to the motherless child. Which, of course, Clarissa did. Her terrible pain pulsed through every word of that letter, however. I suspected then that he would never be faithful to her or totally honest with her, and that she would never confront him on it."

"That child was Ben Ellis?" Jennifer said. It was not really a question. She had heard the story before, and she had met him on two separate occasions, once in London last year at Pippa's wedding to Luc, her brother, then this spring at Greystone for the christening of Luc and Pippa's twins and Grandmama and Grandpapa's funeral, which had followed close on its heels. He must be in his early thirties by now, the illegitimate son of the late earl, whom her aunt had heartily disliked. Jennifer did not have any clear picture in her mind of Mr. Ellis, though she knew she had spoken with him a few times. It seemed to her that he was a very ordinary man and not the sort people did notice or remember. Unlike his father, apparently. Yet he had had the good fortune to be raised in a noble household with a stepmother and stepbrothers and sisters who accepted him as part of their family. They had, after all, brought him with them to that wedding at Arden House, and Pippa must have invited him to the christening this year. Jennifer hoped he was grateful.

She did remember that he had a young daughter, who had been born somewhere in Portugal or Spain during the wars. The mother had died before they returned to England. Actually Jennifer had more memories of the child than of Mr. Ellis himself. She was a little wisp of a thing with large blue eyes and a mop of unruly fair curls. She had patted Jennifer's knee after the wedding, pointed at Jennifer's wheeled chair, which she used because she could not walk, and asked if she could come up for a ride. Someone—one of the Wares? Mr. Ellis himself? No, it had been Susan, Jennifer's young niece. She had come to invite the little girl to play in one corner of the large drawing room with the other children. And away the child had gone, tripping along beside Susan, her ride forgotten.

But not forever. At the christening this spring, she had patted Jennifer's leg and smoothed a hand over her knee while asking again for a ride on the chair. Her language skills had developed in the months since the wedding. She had even said *please*. It was Stephanie Ware that time, Pippa's younger sister, who had whisked the little one away with an apologetic grin for Jennifer. So the child—she was *Joy* Ellis, Jennifer recalled—still had not had her ride on the wheeled chair. Jennifer wondered if she would be at Ravenswood this summer with her father.

"He must be a constant reminder to Clarissa of her husband's infidelities," her aunt was saying, still talking of Ben Ellis. "And I do not doubt they were plural, Jenny. But the audacity of the man! Her firstborn, their son and heir, had just been born. She was given no advance warning of the arrival of his other son, or even of the boy's existence. Can you imagine how she must have felt? Actually it defies imagination, does it not? It is perhaps— No. There is no *perhaps* about it. It is *undoubtedly* wicked of me, but I was never more delighted than I was when I heard of the earl's sudden death. Dear Clarissa, I thought. Free at last. But Ben Ellis must be a permanent millstone about the neck of the family even now that his father is gone. Though that is probably unfair of me. Why *should* the son suffer for the sins of the father, after all? He seems to be a pleasant enough young man."

Jennifer hoped the journey would not last much longer. Her right leg—the twisted one—was aching terribly, but there was not enough space between the seats for her to be able to move or stretch it. Her back was aching a bit too from being tipped to one side whenever she tried to set her aching right foot flat on the floor, a near impossibility even at the best of times. Her right leg was shorter than the other, and thinner and weaker. But she would not breathe a word of her discomfort. She never did. It was bad enough that she had to suffer. She did not need to make anyone else suffer with her.

They were on their way from Amberwell in Lincolnshire to Ravenswood Hall in Hampshire. Invitations had come from both Gwyneth Ware, Countess of Stratton, and Clarissa, the dowager countess. Clarissa had been eager since last year to have Aunt Kitty come to stay, but of course the invitation this year had included Jennifer too. She was, after all, Pippa's sister-in-law as well as Aunt Kitty's niece. Her aunt lived with her. Jennifer was effectively crippled as the result of a lengthy childhood illness that had almost killed her before leaving her permanently maimed.

She was looking forward immensely to the visit, especially to seeing the babies, her niece and nephew, who would no longer be the newborns she remembered from a few months ago. She and her aunt had been a bit dull at Amberwell lately, the fact that they were in mourning having forced them to curtail their social activities in the neighborhood. It had also prevented them from going back to London during the Season. Both of them genuinely mourned, Aunt Kitty in particular, for Grandmama and Grandpapa had been her mother and father and she had loved them dearly. It had been hard to ward off the spells of depression that had sometimes descended upon them, though, no matter how hard they were determined to remain cheerful.

Jennifer, with memories of last year when she and her aunt had spent a couple of months in London, found it hard this year not to make the comparisons and not to feel sometimes that she was still nursing a bruised heart. For a brief spell last year happiness had blossomed and hope along with it. Neither had lasted. Ever skeptical and ever cautious—what man, after all, could really want or love a thin, plain-faced, crippled woman past the first blush of youth—Jennifer had resisted falling in love with the Honorable Mr. Arnold Jamieson, who had been young and handsome and attentive and well born. And impoverished. The only thing surely that could make Jennifer attractive to such a man was her considerable fortune. She had known reality from the moment of their first meeting at a ball, where she had set herself up as a spectator.

She had enjoyed his company and his attentions for a while anyway. And, to his credit, he had never denied that her fortune was the main factor that had encouraged him to seek her acquaintance. When it had come to the point, however, she had refused his marriage proposal. Ever since then her mood had alternated between pride in herself for not grasping what at best might have been a tolerable marriage and sorrow that she had not taken a chance on the slim possibility that it might have brought her some happiness.

She was not suffering from heartbreak, she told herself in her more sensible moments. That was really a silly, theatrical notion. It was just that her heart sometimes ached, and the dull routine of their days at Amberwell while she and her aunt observed their year of mourning could do little to distract her. She was determined to shake off her gloom during the next few weeks, however, and then return home with a renewed cheerfulness of disposition. She had spent years cultivating it. Most of her life, in fact. It ought not to be impossible to retrieve it. *Smile and the world will smile back,* her father had told her once when she was still a very young child and making a slow recovery from her mysterious and painful—and frightening—illness. It had become something of a mantra with her. At the very least, if one smiled the world would not be dragged down into one's own darkness.

"The last time we changed horses," her aunt said, leaning closer to the window on her side to peer ahead, "we were told we had one and a half, maybe two hours to go. We must surely be close. Your leg must be aching, Jenny. I never know how you are able to impose such quiet patience upon yourself. You never complain."

"Would having a tantrum help?" Jennifer asked with a smile.

"Probably not," her aunt said, flashing a smile of her own. "I would pretend to be asleep. Or I would burst into tears and make you feel even worse." She turned her attention to the window again. "Oh, look. We are coming up on a village. Do you think it may be Boscombe? Surely it must be. Cross your fingers and eyes, Jenny. I will cross my toes."

It was indeed Boscombe. The carriage skirted the village green before crossing a stone bridge over a river and then passing between wrought iron gates that stood open and proceeding up a slight slope toward a stone mansion with a vast central block flanked by two equally imposing wings. There were sheep grazing in meadows colorful with wildflowers to either side of the carriage road and cultivated lawns at the top of the rise.

"I am *so* looking forward to these few weeks," Lady Catherine said. "I have been promising both myself and Clarissa for years that

I would come for a visit, but I have never actually done it until now. More than anything else at present, though, I crave a cup of tea."

More than anything else, Jennifer wanted to stretch her leg and foot.

Their approach had been observed. The front doors opened even as the carriage drew to a halt at the foot of a tall flight of steps. The earl and countess—Devlin and Gwyneth—stepped out first, but Clarissa, the dowager countess, was right behind them, and Luc and Pippa stepped around all three and came hurrying down the steps, their faces alight with welcome.

Luc swung Aunt Kitty down to the terrace, ignoring the carriage steps despite her shriek of protest, and hugged her tightly while Pippa leaned into the carriage and reached for Jennifer's hands.

"I know, I know," she said. "It is not me you wanted to see. Or even Lucas. But we will have to do for now. The twins are still fast asleep in the nursery, the wretches. We have been quite unable so far to teach them that it is really not the best of good manners to sleep through the arrival of special guests. Oh, it is *so* good to see you, Jenny."

She leaned farther into the carriage and hugged her sister-in-law, and for the moment Jennifer forgot the pain in her leg and foot.

CHAPTER THREE

B en was smiling and shaking his head as he left the nursery two days later and closed the door behind him. He was quite happy at least for the moment to escape the noise and bustle within. He had spent an hour with Joy, a *quiet* hour since the three babies as well as Idris and Eluned Rhys's had been having their afternoon naps in adjoining rooms. Ben and his daughter had spent the time slapping paint onto a large piece of paper mounted on a low easel, the only rule seeming to be that each color they applied had to be brighter than the one before.

Then the babies had woken almost simultaneously, and adults had arrived on the scene as if by magic. Presumably one of the nurses had sent a servant down to inform them that the children were awake. Ben had been abandoned in favor of prospective new play-mates. He had also been left with the task of cleaning up the painting area. Now all the adults were talking at once, or so it seemed, and the children were all noisily at play.

Devlin and Gwyneth's Gareth was standing precariously propped against a low table, banging a wooden spoon on it and laughing while Stephanie knelt behind him, hands spread to catch him should he lose his balance, as he almost inevitably would. Pippa was on the other side of the table, talking to Steph while she jiggled a rather cross Emily on one hip. Emily was the twin who never seemed to want to go to sleep but, having done so, was never too happy about waking up again. Christopher, the other twin, was sitting on the floor vigorously shaking a wooden rattle and laughing gleefully every time Gwyneth tried to dissuade him from sucking on it. Joy was bouncing up and down for all the world as though there were springs attached to the soles of her shoes as she demanded that Owen get down on all fours to give her a ride on his back.

Ben did not believe he would be missed, for a while at least. He could have gone down to the drawing room to join the other adults, who were probably still there, enjoying some quiet relaxation after seeing off their visitors—Sir Ifor and Lady Rhys and Idris and Eluned and their baby. But he decided instead to step out into the courtyard around which the four vast wings of the house had been built. He would indulge in a bit of welcome solitude in the rose arbor there for a while. Or rather, he thought with a sigh, he would probably sit there and ponder the letter that had been awaiting him at Ravenswood when he arrived three days ago. He had come here with the idea of clearing out his head over the problem of too many prospective brides, but now there was this new problem to set the bees buzzing worse than ever.

It was nothing, he had told his curious family after he had broken the seal and read the letter while they stood around watching him. It was just a brief note from an old schoolfellow who had not realized he no longer lived here.

But in reality it was *something*. Something that had shaken his world to its foundations for those first few dizzying moments while he had assured himself that it was just a silly and rather cruel prank and no doubt he would toss it onto the fire after he had looked at it more closely. But it was still in his pocket two days later, and he had looked at it and read and reread it a number of times. He still had not burned it or otherwise dealt with it. He had not answered it.

There were not many opportunities to spend time alone at Ravenswood. Not now that he was a guest here, anyway, with a child to look after and amuse. He was always surrounded by family and guests. Not that he was complaining. It was all very pleasant, and he was glad he had come. But occasionally he craved some time alone. He had grown accustomed to his own company at Penallen. And he needed to think clearly about this infernal letter.

He stepped out through a door that led directly from the east wing, in which the nursery rooms were situated, into the courtyard and stood for a moment under the shade provided by the peaked roof over the pillared cloister, which ran about the inner perimeter of the courtyard. He drew in a deep breath of fresh air perfumed with the scent of roses and feasted his eyes on the bright, sunlit lawn beyond the shade and upon the sparkling water droplets that formed a rainbow above the fountain in the rose arbor.

He was about to step out into the sunshine when his eyes focused upon the still figure of a man standing under the roof of the cloister directly across from him, outside the west wing. He was that burly footman or servant or assistant or whatever he was called who was assigned exclusively to the care of Lady Jennifer Arden, Lucas's sister. The man carried her heavy wheeled chair up and down stairs, in and out of doors, on and off carriages, and then carried her to sit in it. She had suffered some debilitating illness when she was a young child, and it had left her crippled. Sure enough, her chair stood empty beside the man, which presumably meant that he was about to return to the house for her. Perhaps she too intended sitting in the arbor for a while. Ben would have ducked back inside before she arrived, but he could see that it was already too late. The man had caught sight of him and had turned his head rather sharply to glance to his left.

Ben looked in that direction too and saw what the man was looking at. Lady Jennifer Arden was walking in the shade over there with the aid of heavy-looking crutches. She moved with an awkward, bobbing gait. She would *not* be pleased to be seen by a near stranger, Ben thought with a grimace. He felt deeply embarrassed himself. But it was impossible now to duck back indoors and pretend he had not seen her, for her man's sharp glance seemed to have warned her that they were no longer alone. She stopped walking and looked across the courtyard directly at Ben.

Damn and blast, he thought as he stepped out into the sunlight and strode with a boldness he did not feel across the grass toward her, skirting the rose arbor as he went. Why must one's behavior always be dictated by good manners, though? She would probably have been as relieved as he if he had scurried away.

"We had the same idea, I see," he said when he was close enough not to have to raise his voice. "Fresh air and the seclusion of the cloisters after a busy afternoon of visiting."

"But it was a very pleasant afternoon," she said. "Gwyneth's family are lovely people. I love their Welsh accents. I look forward to hearing Sir Ifor play the organ at church."

"He can bring tears to your eyes," he said. "*Happy* tears." She had not moved since she spotted him. It must be uncomfortable for her standing there in one place, too embarrassed to continue her ungainly walk but not close enough to her chair simply to sit down. "I did not realize you can walk," he said awkwardly.

"If you call it walking," she said. "But I like to take some exercise whenever I can—against the advice of both my aunt and my physician."

Her aunt, Lady Catherine Emmett, her father's sister, lived with her. They seemed very fond of each other.

"I will leave you to continue your walk, then," he said. "I beg your pardon for having disturbed you. I did not realize you were out here."

"No one else knows I am here either," she told him. "But please do not leave on my account. You came out for some air and some time to yourself, and I have finished my walk for today. I will go to my room and rest for a while, something Luc and Aunt Kitty believe I am doing now." She nodded toward her silent footman, who wheeled her chair toward her.

"Perhaps we could both sit in the rose arbor for a while," Ben said. "This fine weather could break at any moment and should be enjoyed while we have it." He could have bitten out his tongue as soon as he had made the suggestion—purely out of good manners. What if she accepted? What the devil would they talk about?

She looked out into the courtyard after she had sat down in her wheeled chair and handed her crutches to her servant. "This courtyard exudes beauty and peace," she said. "Yes, Mr. Ellis, do let us sit for a while. Will you wheel my chair there, if you please? Bruce, I will not need you for a while."

The man inclined his head and disappeared.

And there went his half hour or so of solitude, Ben thought ruefully as he wheeled the chair close to the fountain and the trellises loaded with roses around it and sat on a wrought iron seat. And there too went his chance to ponder his letter and decide once and for all what he was going to do about it. Damnation! Of all the people currently at Ravenswood, Lady Jennifer Arden was the one with whom he least wished to find himself alone.

He was not sure why. She had done nothing to provoke his discomfort. He had grown up in an aristocratic house as a member of the family, after all. He was accustomed to mingling with people from their world, though he did not really identify with it. The fact that Lady Jennifer Arden was the sister and granddaughter of a duke and a woman of privilege and probable wealth ought not to bother him. He was not intimidated by her looks. She was not a ravishingly beautiful woman or even particularly pretty. She had a narrow face, distinguished by prominent cheekbones, a straight nose, and a firm jaw—a proud, aristocratic face, its classical lines somehow accentuated by the fact that she always wore her dark red hair smooth and shining over the crown of her head, though it was dressed in softer curls at the back.

She was rather thin. And crippled, of course. It occurred to Ben that perhaps it was that last fact that made him uncomfortable. He always felt self-conscious whenever he was in her presence, wondering what he would say to her if he had to say anything at all, and how he would behave. He was afraid he might be overhearty. Or oversolicitous. No one else treated her any differently than they would if she were perfectly able-bodied. He had kept his distance from her in the past couple of days without fully realizing he was doing it. He had done the same thing on previous occasions when they had been in company with each other. He had spoken with her, but never at any length.

Now politeness had trapped him into being alone with her and forced to make some sort of conversation. He felt self-conscious, not least because *she* was going to be alone with *him*, and she must surely be uncomfortably aware of the fact that he was not really of her world, that he was not a legitimate member of the Ware family. He did not even bear their name.

"I beg your pardon if you have found my daughter's behavior offensive," he said. "I have tried to explain to her that your chair is not a novelty vehicle invented to give rides to a child. But . . . Well, she is three years old and—"

She surprised him by laughing and holding up a staying hand. "Mr. Ellis," she said. "I have two nephews and a niece in addition to Luc's babies—my sister's children. Each of them in turn had to have rides on my chariot when they were infants. Sometimes I had more than one of them at a time on my lap. Once, I can remember, all three of them climbed aboard until my brother-in-law took pity on me. But I was never offended. Quite the contrary, in fact. It feels good to be a favored aunt when I cannot actually romp with the children. I have been charmed by your daughter's requests for a ride. She is as light as a feather on my lap, you know, and sits very still. She has the prettiest curls. Please do not forbid her to ask again."

"It is kind of you to call her demands *requests*," he said. "She inherited the curls from her mother, who always hid her own in a ruthlessly tight bun."

"That must have been a shame," she said.

"It made practical good sense," he told her. "She needed to keep it out of her face. The weather was often very hot in the Peninsula, and she was a washerwoman."

There was a brief, startled silence. Or so it seemed to Ben. She was too well-bred to show it openly.

"She went to war with her first husband," he told her. "He was a private soldier with the foot regiment in which Devlin was an officer. The wives of the enlisted men had to compete in a lottery to be permitted to go, but those who won a place were expected to make themselves useful. There was always a great need for washerwomen."

"You were her second husband, then?" she said.

"Third," he said. "The other two died in battle. It was a common thing during the wars. Most of the women stayed with the army once they were there, and many married multiple times. Marjorie died when the regiment was fighting and slogging its way over the Pyrenees into France with the rest of the army. The conditions in the mountains were appalling and the weather was brutal. Winter was coming on. She was tough but not tough enough after she took a chill."

Why the devil was he telling her all this? They were not the sorts of things one told a lady. He had not talked much of his years in the Peninsula even with his own family, and he was sure Devlin had not either. Or Nicholas. Was there a sort of defiance in his telling, as though he were thumbing his nose at any preconceived ideas she might have of him? As though he were telling her he was not ashamed of who he was or whom he had married? It had never occurred to him to be ashamed. It had never occurred to him either that he might be carrying a grudge against the world or some part of it. It was not a pleasant thought that perhaps he was. He ought to be making light conversation about the roses and the sunshine. How had this started anyway? With her comment on Joy's curly hair?

"I am sorry about that," she said. "Did she leave a family behind in England?"

"None," he said—and his thoughts touched by natural association upon the letter in his pocket. "She never knew either of her parents or anything about them. She grew up in an orphanage in London. She married a fellow orphan when she was about sixteen."

"I believe, Mr. Ellis," she said, "she must have been very fortunate to meet you after being widowed for the second time. You did not put her child in an orphanage."

He gazed at her in some shock. "She is my child too," he said. "She is ours. She was the joy of our lives."

"Joy," she said, and smiled. "How lovely. You chose the name quite deliberately."

And that was it for *that* topic. Unsurprisingly, he was not feeling any more comfortable with her despite the beauty of their surroundings and the normally soothing sound of the water gushing from the fountain and the heady summer scent of the roses. Perhaps the only thing to do was confront his discomfort head-on.

"Do you walk every day?" he asked her.

"I try," she said. "I made the resolution soon after the passing of my grandparents earlier this year that I would make the effort, that I would boost my energy and spirits by doing something each day to make myself stronger and more healthy. More active. More . . . cheerful."

She was always cheerful. It was something he had noticed about her when he met her last year—though there had been the exception of the days following the death of her grandparents this year, of course. He had noticed her cheerfulness again after her arrival here with her aunt. She almost always spoke with smiling animation. Her eyes frequently sparkled. She gave the impression of perpetual happiness. But it had occurred to him more than once that surely no one could be *that* cheerful all the time. She least of all. The dreadful and crippling illness she had suffered early in her life continued to affect her. She was more or less confined to a chair. She was unmarried, probably as a result of that fact. He estimated that she must be in her early to mid-twenties. He believed she spent most of her life at a country home with only her aunt for company. She might have legions of friends in the neighborhood, of course. Lady Catherine Emmett was certainly a sociable woman and was always cheerful herself. Yet . . .

Well, he had found himself wondering if Lady Jennifer Arden's habitual brightness of manner was something of a mask behind which the real person hid. It was none of his business, of course. Besides, did not all people wear masks to varying degrees? Were there any people who opened themselves up fully to the scrutiny of the whole wide world without keeping at least bits of themselves hidden safely away inside?

"Has life been depressing for you in the last few months, then?" he asked. Lucas and Pippa had lived at Amberwell with her for a few months after their marriage and had intended going back there after the christening of their twins. But the death of the duke had made it necessary that they remain at Greystone to assume their new duties as Duke and Duchess of Wilby.

"A little confining and monotonous," she admitted after thinking about it for a moment. "A mourning period ought not to be like that. Not, at least, for elderly people who lived long, full lives. It ought to be full of happy reminiscences and laughter instead. Many people would look upon me with horrified disapproval if I said that aloud to them, of course. It would suggest that I did not care. I did. My aunt feels the same way, even though my grandparents were her *parents*."

Silence—not of the comfortable sort—threatened to descend upon them again.

"Will you ever be able to walk without your crutches?" he asked.

"Alas, no," she said. "For many months when I was a child I was confined to my bed. My legs were paralyzed. So was the rest of me for a shorter while. I recovered my general health over time and the paralysis went, but it left my right leg bent out of shape and my foot and ankle twisted. The leg did not grow to match the other." She smiled. "I suppose I am blessed to be a woman. A long skirt hides a multitude of sins. I was given the crutches to help me move very short distances with the bad leg raised out of the way. It is a convenience for which I am thankful. But it does not enable me to *walk*. My right leg soon aches too much when I have to hold it off the ground. But my physician is strongly of the belief that I will do further damage by trying to walk on both legs. He has warned me not even to try. I do it anyway. Sometimes the longing to stand upright, on both feet, to see the world as others see it, is quite irresistible. And sometimes I just need to defy the wisdom of those who love me. Love can occasionally be a bit smothering."

Her cheeks were flushed, Ben saw. Undoubtedly she was as unaccustomed to talking about her disability as he was to speaking about his years in the Peninsula. But yes, he decided, her habitual cheerfulness was definitely something that concealed a deeper anguish. It was actually admirable that she made the effort to walk, hopeless though it seemed and against the explicit orders of her physician. He guessed she did not wish to impose her disappointments and frustrations upon the family that loved her. So she bore them alone and exercised her little rebellions in private. Yet she had confided some of them to him. Just as he had confided some of himself to her. It was easier sometimes to talk to near strangers, of course, and he and Lady Jennifer Arden were essentially just that.

He should have left it there. He should perhaps have suggested that they go back inside, especially as the sun was shining down directly upon them and she was not wearing a bonnet. But he continued speaking. "There must be other ways to experience movement and to feel alive and free," he said.

"Must there?" She smiled again.

"Have you ever ridden a horse?" he asked.

"No!" She laughed. "Of course not."

"Driven a gig or any other one-horse vehicle?" he asked.

"No." She laughed again.

"Learned to swim?" he asked.

"Good heavens, no."

"Worn any sort of brace on your leg or any specially designed shoe or boot on your foot to bring the length of your affected leg more in line with the other?" he asked.

"Enough!" She was still laughing. "I am *coddled*, Mr. Ellis. Loved. Held very dear. Protected. Encouraged to rest, to avoid any great exertion. Only when I go to London for parts of a spring Season do I get to go places and do things, though my aunt is forever fearful that I will overexert myself and suffer a relapse. Last year I actually attended a ball and a garden party and visited a number of galleries. I was even at Almack's the night my grandfather suffered his heart seizure—the day before Luc married Pippa. But . . . no. The answer to all your questions is no. Here I sit, and here I will probably sit for the rest of my life, though not as a permanent fixture in the Ravenswood rose arbor, I hasten to add. It is not so very bad, you know. One adjusts to the realities of one's life."

He did not believe her. Not entirely, anyway. There was a certain wistfulness in her efforts to walk.

"Perhaps in the next few weeks while we are both still here," he said, "I can look into ways of bringing something new and challenging into your life to help lift your spirits."

What the devil was he suggesting? From being uncomfortable with her crippled state, he was now to wage a one-man crusade to save her? He was embarrassing himself. It would serve him right if she gave him a sharp setdown.

Her eyes sparkled at him instead—and fine eyes they were too. They were light brown, chocolate with cream stirred into it. "So, by the time I return to Amberwell, I will be able to ride my own horse and drive my own carriage and swim like a fish and walk elegantly without my crutches?" she said. "Perhaps even waltz at the ball on the evening of the Ravenswood fete? But no, alas. That at least will not be possible. I am in mourning."

It was not a sharp setdown, but she was laughing at him nevertheless.

"I beg your pardon," he said, straightening up on the seat. "I did not mean to mock you."

"I did not take your suggestions as mockery," she told him. "You are a dreamer, Mr. Ellis. So am I, though I believe my dreams are more of the airy variety while yours are more practical—even if they *are* impossible to bring to reality. I would find life insupportable, I believe, without dreams."

She raised her hands palm-up to the sky, and he noted the thin wrists and the long, elegant fingers with their perfectly manicured nails. She raised her face too for a moment, her eyes closed. She inhaled slowly.

"Thank you for suggesting that we sit here for a while, Mr. Ellis," she said. "I was not really ready to go back indoors when you came outside. I was disappointed when I thought I must. This little interval has been heavenly. However, I will go inside now if you would be so good as to push my chair or send Bruce to my assistance."

He was being dismissed. But with tact and kindness. She had a lady's way of smoothing out awkward moments and rough edges. He stood and moved behind her chair. He must be very careful to stay as far away from her as possible for the remainder of the time they were both here. She must consider him an idiot at the very least.

"I have never been allowed to drive any conveyance," she said. "I daresay Luc and Aunt Kitty would have a fit apiece if I so much as suggested it. Would you, Mr. Ellis?"

"Have a fit?" he said. "I do not expect I would. I would not know how."

"Shall we try it one day?" she asked. "Do you have a suitable conveyance here?"

"Yes," he said. "Are you sure, though?"

She laughed. "You are not going to turn craven and back out now, are you?" she asked him.

"No," he said. And he laughed too. "But please do not spring the horses the first time."

"The *horse*," she reminded him. "You said a *one*-horse vehicle. I promise. I will wait until the second time."

He felt a bit dizzy as he wheeled her chair inside and found that her servant was waiting a short distance away to take her wherever she wished to go. What the devil had he suggested? Or was it she who had suggested it? Had it been merely a joke? Lucas and Pippa would have his head. So would Lady Catherine Emmett.

Probably Devlin too.

CHAPTER FOUR

Jennifer used her crutches to move from the door of her room to the chaise longue near the window and propped them beside it when she sat. The guest rooms were in the east wing, below the nursery. There was a panoramic view to the east, mostly of rolling grassland that stretched far into the distance before being broken by a line of hills, which apparently formed the boundary between Ravenswood and Cartref, the home and estate of Sir Ifor and Lady Rhys.

There was one noticeable man-made feature between the house and the hills, apart from the crisscrossing footpaths and slightly wider riding and carriage paths. Two long, parallel rows of poplar trees stretched diagonally away from one of the paths. She guessed there must be a secluded walking area between the rows, a place to stroll at one's leisure, perhaps with a book in hand. It was a modest activity she could never hope to enjoy.

But she shook off the self-pitying thought. She *was* able to sit in that lovely courtyard with sunlight beaming down on her and the sight and smell of roses all around and the soothing sound of water spraying from the fountain. How very fortunate she was. Luc had married into a good family. He had wed the perfect wife too. Pippa was not only Jennifer's sister-in-law but also her dearest friend. She had been that even before Luc began to court her. Sometimes life really did shower blessings upon a person.

The whole of the Ware family was amiable, in fact, and warm and welcoming. But there was also Mr. Ben Ellis, who was *not* a Ware by name though he was nevertheless an integral part of the family.

He was the sort of man one tended not to notice. In physical appearance he was very . . . well, ordinary. He was tall, with broad shoulders and a sturdy build. He had darkish brown hair, which he kept short and neatly styled. His face was pleasant but not out-standingly handsome. He dressed just fashionably enough that one did not notice exactly what he wore. He was quiet without being silent, serious without being morose, well mannered without being either ostentatious or obsequious.

It all added up to . . . ordinariness.

Jennifer wondered if it was deliberate. Did he *choose* to go un-noticed? He was the illegitimate son of the late earl but had been part of the earl's family since he was a very young child, according to Aunt Kitty's account. He must have been accepted with kindness by the countess—a remarkable fact. Both she and Mr. Ellis's half brothers and sisters treated him with affection—as he treated them. They all doted upon his daughter. But he had never been given his father's name. Had there been other subtle or not-so-subtle details that had set him apart? One of them, of course, had not been subtle at all. When his father died, it was Devlin Ware, Mr. Ellis's *younger* brother, who had inherited the title and Ravenswood and, presumably, other properties and a fortune too. There would have been no choice in that, of course. Mr. Ellis was *illegitimate*.

Jennifer had scarcely noticed him until today. She *hoped* that had nothing to do with his illegitimacy. She hoped she had not dismissed him as a person of no account because he was by far her social inferior. But she could not be sure. So many of the judgments one made about other people were unconscious. She had clear memories of meeting every other member of the Ware family last year in London. They had all been at Arden House for Luc and Pippa's wedding. She had remembered too the little curly-haired girl who had wanted to sit on her wheeled chair with her and go for a ride. But she had recalled Mr. Ellis, if at all, only as the father of that child, the man who was connected with the Wares but was not really one of them.

What a very strange encounter that had been between the two of them out in the courtyard. It had been almost bizarre. She had been horribly embarrassed to be discovered walking there two-footed on her crutches. She was always careful not to be seen by anyone except Bruce. She had done a mental inventory before going out there after the Rhyses had left, and it had seemed to her that everyone was accounted for. Those who had not still been in the drawing room when she left were on their way up to the nursery, the babies now being all awake. Mr. Ellis had not figured in that inventory. She could not remember if he had said he was going with the nursery group or if he had remained in the drawing room. Or whether indeed he had been there at all during the visit of the Rhyses.

To do him justice, he had been quite willing to leave the court-yard so she could have it to herself again. He had undoubtedly been as embarrassed as she. But somehow—she could not remember who had suggested it—they had ended up sitting together in the rose arbor. And there they had talked.

That had been the most bizarre part.

She had told him about her illness and about her bent leg and twisted ankle and foot. It was incredible. She *never* talked on the subject with anyone else, even her closest family. It was horrid and embarrassing and not at all genteel. And then she had listened to his wild ideas on how she might . . . oh, not overcome her disabil-ity, but find ways to add more mobility and independence and va-riety to her life. Not to mention exhilaration. By riding. Upon a horse's back, if you please. By swimming. In water, where she would sink like a stone. By wearing some contraptions on her leg and foot to help her walk better—or run and leap and twirl. The man was mad.

Oh, but the longing his ridiculous ideas had aroused in her!

He had also told her something of himself, and she wondered if he had set out deliberately to shock her. If he had, then he had certainly succeeded. She knew that Devlin had been a military of-ficer during the Peninsular Wars. She had probably known too that Mr. Ellis had gone with him, though as a civilian rather than as a fellow officer. He—Mr. Ellis, that was—had married a washer-woman, who had grown up in a London orphanage and before she met him been married and widowed twice, both times to common soldiers. Joy, that little girl who was such a delight, was the product of his marriage.

He was like someone from a different world. Someone who had

made himself virtually invisible in her world, not by hiding but by being very . . . ordinary.

She had asked him to take her out one day in a conveyance she might conceivably drive herself. At least that was what she had implied—*Shall we try it one day?* No, she had done more than imply it.

And he had agreed.

Was *she* mad too? She could never drive a vehicle. Even though it might appear as though all the driving was done with the hands, and there was nothing wrong with hers, in reality the feet surely had much to do with it too. They had to brace the body while the driver pulled upon the ribbons to slow the carriage or stop it or change direction. Without two serviceable feet she would be at the mercy of the horse, which could jerk her overboard with one wrong move. She did not have two serviceable feet.

He would probably forget the whole thing. Deliberately. And she was certainly not going to remind him. In fact, she was quite sure she would avoid either looking at him or being near him in the coming days if she could possibly do so without being obvious about it. Mr. Ellis made her intensely uncomfortable. She was not sure why—though a few possible reasons had suggested themselves just this afternoon. There was a certain otherness about the man. A differentness. She was adept at making conversation with all sorts and degrees of people from her own world. Even servants and tradespeople. There was no reason she should not be able to chat amiably with him too. He had, after all, grown up in a noble household—*this* household—and been raised as a gentleman.

These thoughts were spinning in her head and she was not sorry when a light tap on her door interrupted them. It opened slowly and soundlessly, and a head peered around it.

"Ah, good," Philippa said, pushing the door wide and stepping inside. "You are not asleep. Am I interrupting anything? But I do not see a book on your lap."

"I am relaxing and enjoying the view," Jennifer told her with a smile as she indicated the window with a sweep of her arm. "Do join me, Pippa. Is there a cultivated walking path between those two long lines of trees? They must have been planted by people. Nature is not nearly so neat."

"There is," Philippa said. "It is a lovely wide, grassy alley, bordered by the trees you can see, with benches set at intervals along it. At the far end there is a glass summerhouse, though you cannot see it from this window. It is a very pleasant retreat when one wants to be quiet and alone with one's thoughts or a letter or book—or a special someone. Speaking of which, I simply must take Lucas there one day before we go home." She laughed and batted her eyelashes at Jennifer. "The Rhyses are delightful people, Jenny, are they not? We are so very fortunate in our nearest neighbors."

"You are indeed," Jennifer agreed as her sister-in-law settled into an armchair adjacent to the chaise longue. "Devlin might never have met Gwyneth if they had *not* been your neighbors."

"Now *there* is a thought," Philippa said. "How random an adventure life can be. I cannot imagine either one of them married to anyone else."

They went on to talk comfortably with each other for half an hour or longer.

B en was sitting on a bench just inside the stable doors the following day, breathing in the comforting, familiar smells of horse and hay and manure while he stitched around the edges of a cushion he had fashioned out of an old haversack. It had done duty as a pack for his belongings in the Peninsula and since then as a back carrier for Joy. He'd had it fitted with a metal frame and had holes cut and bound in it to accommodate her legs so she could sit snugly and safely inside while watching the world go by over his shoulders. It was no longer needed for that purpose. He had removed the frame, recut the shabby but still tough fabric, and made a cushion of it. It was stuffed with clean straw to make it thick and firm but with some give to it too.

He had become adept with a needle while in the Peninsula. A man could not carry many clothes with him there, and those he did have were forever popping buttons or sprouting holes and split seams and unintended tears both minor and major. He had never allowed Marjorie to do his darning and repairs for him though she had protested on more than one occasion. She had had enough work of her own to do.

The cushion was part of his plan of restitution, if that was the right word. His apology, then, though only he knew there was anything to apologize for and he would not ever make it verbal. He had come to the conclusion that his reason for avoiding Lady Jennifer Arden in the past, though it had been unconscious, had definitely been her crippled state. It had made him uncomfortable and self-conscious for some inexplicable reason. So he had allowed himself to believe that she was a bit cold and arrogant and he did not like her. She was neither of those two things, and there was nothing to dislike about her. She made an effort to be cheerful with everyone. She was not a whiner. She did not use her disability to demand sympathy and attention and service from everyone around her. He had even heard her say *please* and *thank you* to that burly, very silent attendant of hers.

It was *not* well done of him to be uncomfortable with her disability. It was not his. It was hers, and she handled it with quiet dignity. He would still prefer to keep his distance from her, for she remained at the opposite end of the social scale from him despite his upbringing. But restitution had to be made for the sake of his conscience. Hence the cushion. And hence the other idea he intended to propose a bit later, after Joy woke from her afternoon nap.

In the meanwhile, as he stitched, his mind wandered yet again to his letter. He still had not done anything about it. He would really like to discuss it with Devlin, but something made him hesitate. Dev was his brother and closest friend, but he had only ever seen Ben as a member of his own family despite the difference in their status, even down to their last names. It was doubtful that Devlin had ever given much thought to Ben's mother or the life she had lived or the family that had been hers. He had almost never spoken of her with Ben. Perhaps he had thought to be tactful, to refrain from reminding his brother of the disreputable half of his identity. Perhaps he thought Ben was ashamed and wanted to forget. Perhaps he even thought Ben *had* forgotten. When Devlin had been banished following the great debacle at the summer fete eight years ago, he had been surprised that Ben had chosen to go with him and wanted to know why he was doing it. It seemed not to have occurred to him until Ben told him that the discovery of their father's infidelities and philandering ways might be even more of a blow to his elder brother than it was to him.

Ben's father, the late Earl of Stratton, had always assured his firstborn son that the affair with his mother had been a serious relationship, that he had loved her deeply and would have married her if he had not been constrained in his choice of bride by the necessity of marrying his social equal. He had claimed still to love her even after her death. He had told Ben that he would always hold her memory close to his heart, that there had never been any other woman in his life except his countess, Ben's stepmother. Ben had believed him wholeheartedly as a boy and ignored any doubt he may have felt as he grew older. Devlin's denunciation of their father at that ball had come as a terrible shock to Ben, suggesting as it did that his mother had been no more to his father than a casual whore he had used for his pleasure, one of countless many.

Now Ben had a letter in his pocket from a man who claimed to be his elder brother, his elder half brother, the legitimate son of Ben's mother and her husband. The letter was signed Vincent Kelliston. Mr. Kelliston explained that his mother had fled her marriage when her son was five years old and gone to London, where she came under the protection of the Earl of Stratton and later gave birth to another, bastard son. He had actually used that word in the letter—*bastard*.

My father was undeniably a brute, he had written.

> *I do not blame her for running away. I always wondered why she left me behind, but I did not doubt she had good reason, and who was I to judge her when I did not know the exact circumstances? Why my father did not make any effort to go after her and find her and bring her back home, I did not know either. She would have been almost impossible to find, of course. She changed her name.*

Vincent Kelliston's father had died recently, and his son considered it time that the two half brothers make each other's acquaintance at last. He did not explain how he had found Ben or even knew of his existence.

Ben's father had claimed to know nothing of his mother's background, and Ben had believed him. Eventually, of course, he had understood that his father was probably quite uninterested in his mother as a person and had never bothered to question her about herself and her past. She had meant nothing to him beyond the obvious service she provided.

Discovering these bare bones of her history—if Vincent Kelliston was to be believed, that was—was shocking to Ben. Part of him had wanted to dash off as soon as he read the letter to meet this apparent brother of his, who lived in Kent, and discover all there was to be known. Another part of him had wanted to tear the letter to shreds, drop them into the nearest fire, and forget he had ever seen it. What Pandora's box was it likely to open? Or was there more family in addition to this brother waiting to meet him, willing and eager to embrace him as one of their own? Kelliston had made no mention of anyone but himself. Perhaps he was the only one. He must be at least six years older than Ben—close to forty, then, or even past it. He had made no reference to a wife or children.

Since the first shock of the letter and the teeming thoughts and hopes and doubts that had crowded his mind, Ben had been mentally paralyzed with indecision—just as he had been for the last few months over a different issue, the choice of a second wife. It seemed unlikely that any other members of Kelliston's family, if there were any, *would* welcome the illegitimate son of the disgraced woman who had abandoned husband and child and fled, only to give birth to another man's child—another man's *bastard*—a year or so later.

Very unlikely.

But the two questions that had plagued his mind the most were *how* and *why*? How had Vincent Kelliston found him? How had he even known there was someone to find? And why did he wish to acknowledge the connection with Ben? Was it credible that he would want to meet and welcome his mother's *bastard* son, conceived after she ran away and abandoned him to the mercies of a brute of a father? Was it not far more likely that he would hate that brother with a burning passion?

Ben simply could not decide what to do. If he replied to the letter, what exactly would he say? If he did not reply, would he be forever sorry? Or would there be more such letters? Half of his identity had always been a total blank to him. He had yearned all his life to *know*. Yet he had been forced to accept the likelihood that he never would. There had been no way to trace his mother beyond the discreet nest his father had set up for her.

What would Devlin advise? Or Mother? Or Owen or one of his sisters? Or Nick, who would be here in the next day or two? Should he gather them all and speak to them as a group, perhaps? See what they had to say or suggest? This was the worst time for such a private family consultation, however. There were visitors in the house and one more was expected—Owen's friend from Oxford. And the summer fete was looming large on the horizon and was already occupying much of the time and attention of Gwyneth and Mother and Devlin. They were not organizing the whole thing, of course, as Mother used to, but there was still plenty to do.

At least the letter had relieved his mind of that other dilemma. Since the day of his arrival he had spared hardly a thought to his three prospective brides. Maybe it was a good thing. Perhaps while he was not consciously thinking of the decision he must make, it would make itself, and by the time he returned home he would know exactly to which of them he would pay court.

He finished sewing the cushion just as Joy came bursting into the stables. He had left her asleep in the nursery, though her nurse had promised to bring her out here to him when she awoke. He was planning to take her with him into the village. He wanted to call at the smithy to have a word with Cam Holland, but afterward he would take his daughter to the coffee room at the inn for a glass of lemonade.

She bounced two-footed across the floor toward him.

"Did Nurse bring you out?" he asked her.

"Aunty Steph," she said. "She is out by the fence, but there are no horsies in the paddock to watch. Uncle Owen's friend has come. He is nice."

"I suppose he would be if he is Uncle Owen's friend," Ben said, setting the cushion on the bench beside him and getting to his feet to take her hand in his. "Do you want to come to the village with me? For lemonade after I have run my errand? Shall we ask Aunt Steph to come too?"

"Ye-e-es," she cried, and snatched her hand away to dash back out into the sunshine and across the stable yard to the paddock fence.

Stephanie was still leaning on it, gazing at the empty space beyond as though she had not even noticed there were no horses there. She turned her head to smile down at Joy when his daughter tugged on her skirt and told her about the intended treat.

"So Watley has arrived?" Ben said.

"What?" she said, looking briefly up at him before turning her attention back to the paddock. "Oh. Yes. Owen is happy."

But Stephanie was not, Ben could see. "What is the problem?" he asked.

"There is none," she said.

"Was he not polite to you?" he asked.

"Who?" she said. "Owen? Oh, you mean Viscount Watley? He was. Yes. Of course he was."

"But you dislike him," he said.

"Of course I do not dislike him," she said. "I do not even *know* him. But oh, Ben, he is the most handsome man I have ever seen in my entire life. How can I ever go back into the house?"

The problem might not be obvious to anyone who had not known Stephanie all her life. At seventeen, she was large—both tall and generously built. She had a round face, with cheeks that glowed with youth and good health. Her hair was golden blond and might be called her crowning glory except that she always wore it in a heavy double plait about her head and had flatly refused to have it cut or even trimmed since she was a child. She had always seen herself as fat and ugly. As a child she had waited with waning hope for her baby fat to go away, as everyone had assured her it would. It never had.

"Steph," Ben said, setting an arm about her shoulders. "You are beautiful."

She made the puffing sound of contempt she always produced with her lips when anyone said things like that to her.

"If you could see yourself as others see you," he said, "you would know the truth of that."

It *was* true too. Oh, there would always be people who would see her as she saw herself. Unfortunately physical size, especially for a woman, was something by which beauty or its lack was often measured. But even largeness could be beautiful, especially if it housed a fit and beautiful person. Steph was lovely, a ray of light in a world that was often dark. Yet when she looked in a mirror all she saw was her size.

"You are Lady Stephanie Ware," he reminded her. "Owen's sister. And Dev's and Pippa's. Nick's too. And mine."

"You are my aunty," Joy said, tugging again at her skirt.

"So I am," Stephanie said, and laughed. "What a wonderful thing to be. Did you say I am invited to the village too?"

"For lemonade," Joy told her. "Papa is taking us."

"Then I am definitely coming," Stephanie said, taking one of Joy's hands while Ben took the other.

Everyone, Ben thought, had their troubles. It was not a very profound or original thought, but sometimes one forgot and became absorbed in one's own woes to the point of self-pity.

Even the sisters and granddaughters of dukes had their troubles. Sometimes big ones.

With which troubles he was about to interfere.

"Uncle Owen's friend is like a story prince," Joy was saying as she tripped along between them. "Maybe he will marry a princess."

CHAPTER FIVE

B en had inspected the old gig before making the cushion. As far as he knew, it was rarely used. He had made sure it was in good repair, that the seats were comfortable and would offer the proper support, and that the footboard was firm and not too far distant from the seats. The cushion was what he hoped was a solution to one problem that had occurred to him—the fact that Lady Jennifer Arden's right leg was shorter than the left and that her right foot was twisted and no doubt sensitive to any undue pressure put upon it.

But the gig would not fulfill all her dreams. She also wanted to walk. However, the way she was trying to do it now just did not work and would not no matter how much she tried. The illness and the damage it had done had happened when she was a child and must surely now be irreversible. Her leg muscles, maybe her back too, must ache unbearably after her attempted walks. Yet she persisted—against the direct advice of her physician and family, it seemed.

One could not help but admire her.

One could not help also sympathizing with her family. They loved her dearly. He had observed that last year in London and again at Greystone. He had seen it here. She had almost died of her illness, which had apparently been a mystery to all the experts her father had summoned. It had left her crippled, or as close to being crippled as made no difference. It was understandable that they protected and coddled her and tried to prevent her from doing further damage to herself.

Just occasionally families could be one's worst enemy. Especially loving families.

He spent half an hour at the smithy in Boscombe, talking with Cameron Holland, who had taken over most of the work from his father during the past year or so.

Cam frowned and sounded very dubious indeed after Ben had explained his idea. "You mean like a kind of *cage*?" he asked.

"Well." Ben frowned back. "Sort of, I suppose. Something to brace the leg and hold it steady while weight is placed on it."

"But not to *straighten* it," Cam said. "I would not dare try that, Ben, besides its surely being impossible anyway. Is there such a thing as a league of physicians—associated with a league of lawyers? They would have me hanged or at the very least transported for life if something went wrong, as something surely would. Her brother might be Lady Philippa's husband, but he is also a bloody *duke. His Grace of Bloody Wilby.*"

"No," Ben said. "Not to straighten the leg. Merely to hold it steady, to give it some support. Is it a mad idea? Is it possible?"

"Yes to the first," Cam said. "No to the second. It would be grand if it did work, though, wouldn't it? Does she know you're here spouting madness on her behalf?"

"No," Ben said. "And another thing, Cam: The deformed leg is shorter than the other. There would have to be something to make it the same length."

"Ah, well that's an easy one." Cam's frown disappeared to be replaced by a grin. "We just pull hard on it, Ben, you and me."

Ben grimaced and rubbed one knuckle over his forehead. "I was thinking maybe a boot with ankle support and an extra thick sole?" he said, making a question of it.

Cam stared at him. "It would weigh a ton," he said. "We would need a cobbler."

We?

"I'll trot over and have a word with John Rogers," Cam said. "He is always complaining that almost the only work he gets these days is dull stuff, like replacing worn-down heels and stitching uppers that have sprung loose from their soles. I'll see what he thinks of a real challenge."

"It *is* madness, is it not?" Ben said. And really, why the devil was he even here doing this? Just because he felt guilty for cringing from her disability? Or because he had had a brief glimpse of hope and hopeless determination when he had looked across the courtyard to see her lurching along on her crutches? He had always been a dreamer and a problem solver, but he had never entertained the delusion that he was a miracle worker.

"Utter insanity," Cam said cheerfully. "Come back down here tomorrow or even later today, and I'll tell you what John says—though I would dare predict it will be nothing more constructive than a mouthful of profanities. I'll tell you something, though, Ben. We could do nothing whatsoever without the lady's consent and cooperation. She would have to come here and let us have a look at what we would be facing. A *lady*, Ben. A *duke's* sister. Think about it. Would you get her to agree in a million years?"

"Maybe in a million and a half," Ben said. "I'll see you later, then, Cam. I'm sorry to have disturbed you. You were busy."

"I was," Cam said with an exaggerated sigh. "But you have got me thinking and wondering now, Ben, damn your eyes. I usually try to avoid doing either. It keeps life simpler."

Ben had left Stephanie and Joy out on the village green. There were—unusually, despite its name—some ducks bobbing about on the duck pond: a mother with a row of ducklings following her in a line. Joy was lying on her stomach on the grass close to the water, her chin propped on her hands. She was totally absorbed in watching while Stephanie sat beside her, her arms hugging her updrawn knees.

He stood and watched them for a few minutes until Stephanie turned her head and saw him. She said something to Joy, who jumped to her feet and bounced across the green toward him.

"Duckies, Papa," she said, pointing back to the pond. "All in a row. Can we go for lemonade now?"

"We may indeed," he said, taking her hand in his and smiling at Stephanie, who seemed to have recovered from her earlier discomfort at discovering that their new guest, Viscount Watley, Owen's friend, was the most handsome man in the world. Or, in Joy's words, a storybook prince.

Jennifer's spirits had indeed lifted with her stay at Ravenswood, as had her aunt's. Their days were filled with busy, interesting activities and good company, with conversation and laughter, with visits to and from neighbors, with the frequent presence of children, mostly babies, who were held and rocked and talked to and played with by everyone. She marveled at the warmth and soft weight and plump cheeks of her nephew and niece and held them, one in each arm, whenever she had the opportunity. They were at the most adorable stage of babyhood.

Joy Ellis had finally had her ride on the wheeled chair, sitting very still and prim and light as a feather on Jennifer's lap, but then shrieking with glee and tipping back her head to laugh upside down at Jennifer as Owen wheeled them sedately about the perimeter of the drawing room, at rather more speed around the adjoining music room, and almost recklessly fast along the wide corridor beyond it while making the sounds of a trotting horse. The child charmed Jennifer utterly when they were back in the drawing room by saying thank you and raising puckered lips to her for a kiss before Owen snatched her up, set her astride his shoulders, grasped her hands, and went galloping off with her back out into the corridor while the child's father shook his head and laughed.

After a few days there was new company to enjoy. Jennifer had met and liked Major Nicholas Ware last year in London before he returned to Belgium and the Battle of Waterloo, which had been fought soon after. Fortunately he had survived and had sustained no serious injury. She had no previous acquaintance with Viscount Watley, Owen Ware's friend. He was an extraordinarily handsome and charming young man who invited everyone to *please* call him Bertrand. He told them all one afternoon as he bounced Luc and Pippa's twins on his knees that he was a twin himself and, like Christopher, the younger of the two, with a sister half an hour older than he.

"It is a ghastly weapon fate has put in your sister's hands, lad," he had told a chuckling Christopher while Emily blew a bubble and clapped her hands. "She will never let you forget."

They went to church on Sunday morning, and Jennifer was enthralled by the organ music played by Sir Ifor Rhys. He wheeled her chair closer after the service to show her the soaring pipes, the multiple keyboards, the long rows of wooden pedals, and a great deal else. He described the instrument with pleased animation for all of fifteen minutes even after Joy Ellis had joined them and been lifted up onto the bench beside him with one of his arms about her to hold her safe. Lady Rhys and Aunt Kitty came to their rescue at last, though Jennifer had enjoyed every moment. His enthusiasm and his rather thick Welsh accent were utterly endearing.

Jennifer was very glad she had come to Ravenswood. But one morning she was feeling a bit weary after several busy days and craved some quiet time alone. She could have gone to Cartref with Aunt Kitty and the dowager countess to have luncheon with Sir Ifor and Lady Rhys. Mr. George Greenfield, the dowager's brother, was coming to take them, and Gwyneth and the baby were going too. Or she could have gone a longer distance with Luc and Pippa and the twins to visit Mr. and Mrs. Greenfield, Pippa's maternal grandparents. She had been invited both places. But she pleaded the need for a quiet morning, and no one had argued. That was one thing she particularly liked about Ravenswood and the relaxed way Devlin and Gwyneth played host and hostess. There was always company to be had and places to go. But nothing was regimented. Nothing was demanded.

She was sitting on the terrace outside the ballroom in the west wing, feasting her senses upon the park that stretched beyond it. To her right and not far distant from the house was a hill with a stone folly in the form of a Grecian temple at the top, framed by trees on the north slope. She had been told there were seats inside with views out through the tall columns. It must be lovely to sit up there, looking down, but she was not going to demand that Bruce carry her. Ahead was rolling grassland dotted with trees, some of them surely quite ancient. A driving path wound its way through the parkland and past the lake in the distance. There was an island on the lake with trees and what looked like another, smaller version of the temple on the hill. The park had been carefully designed to look natural, she could see, though of course it must need constant attention by an army of gardeners to prevent nature from running wild. She breathed in the varied scents of greenery and listened to the songs of mostly unseen birds.

Oh, how she loved the countryside, much as she sometimes craved a few weeks in London during the spring months when it teemed with company and busy social activities.

As far as she knew, she was the only one at home. Those who had not invited her to join them on their pursuits were busy with their own. Devlin had gone to confer with the leader of the orchestra he had engaged to play at the ball on the evening of the fete. Stephanie had gone with Pippa and Luc to visit her grandparents. Owen, Bertrand, and Major Ware were out riding.

Riding. The word brought back memories that made her smile. *Riding. Driving. Swimming.* She laughed softly as she remembered that odd conversation with Mr. Ellis in the courtyard. Impossible dreams, all of them. They had nevertheless aroused in her an old, restless yearning and had brought on the ever-present danger that she would slip into depression. She would not allow it to happen. She would *not* give in to self-pity. There was *so much*, especially this summer, to cheer her spirits and make her glad and very thankful to be alive.

How she longed to ride and swim and walk and dance and run up hills and down dales, her arms spread to the sides, her face turned up to the sun. She must always keep those impossible dreams strictly to herself, however. Aunt Kitty, Luc, Pippa, Charlotte—they would all be upset if she shared them because they would feel helpless to do anything to make them come true. She knew they would all give her the earth and the moon and stars if they could.

One of the French windows that extended the length of the ballroom opened behind her and she turned her head to smile at Bruce, who would be bringing coffee and no doubt some of the Ravenswood cook's freshly baked biscuits or muffins. But it was not Bruce. It was Mr. Ellis, who had been avoiding even as much as eye contact with her since their last encounter—as she had with him. The memory of what they had shared that afternoon in the courtyard was embarrassing, to say the least. She had neither been back there nor walked on her crutches since except to move short distances on one leg inside her room. But it was foolish of her to have stayed away for she doubted he had been back there either.

"Ah. You *are* here," he said. "I had to search high and low for your manservant."

"Was he hiding?" she asked with a smile. "I have been sitting here quietly admiring the view."

"I thought you might enjoy a drive about the park," he said, coming to stand beside her chair. "I can fetch anything you may need and bring the gig around here."

Oh. She looked up at him warily. He had sought her out deliberately in order to offer to give her a tour of the park? In a *gig*? In a small vehicle, that was.

"And by a *drive*, Mr. Ellis, you mean—?"

He grinned at her suddenly and transformed himself into a surprisingly good-looking man. No, his good looks were not a surprise. The fact that he was also attractive *was*. She had not noticed before, and she did not particularly wish to notice now. She felt self-conscious enough with him as it was.

"I mean," he said, "that I may want to sit back and enjoy the scenery for part of the drive while you take your turn at the ribbons."

No one had ever suggested such a thing to her before him. The only carriages in which she had ever ridden were of the solid, ponderous type that had a coachman up on a box in front. Even her aunt never drove herself. Or Charlotte, as far as she knew. Women tended not to, even perfectly able-bodied women.

"Are you not afraid of being tipped into a ditch?" she asked him.

"No," he said. "There are no ditches in the park to be tipped into. I might get tossed into the lake, I suppose, but I will take my chances on that. The gig has two large wheels and is constructed in such a way that it would take considerable effort to tip it. The horse I have chosen does not know the meaning of the word *gallop*, or whatever its equivalent is in horse language. Anyway, I will be seated right beside you, and I have a strong instinct for self-preservation. I have a young daughter to raise."

"Where *is* Joy?" she asked.

"She jumped at the chance to go with Pippa and Lucas to visit her great-grandparents," he said. "Or *step*-great-grandparents, if there is such a relationship. They always spoil her quite shamelessly, as they did me when I was a child. They are good people. Steph has gone too."

And the little girl adored Stephanie.

"Do you have the courage to drive, Lady Jennifer?" he asked her.

"Is it very difficult?" she asked.

"Almost impossible," he said. "But you will have an expert instructor in the seat next to you."

"And a modest one," she said.

"That too." He looked down at her and awaited her answer. And strangely it was not so much the fear of taking the ribbons of the gig into her own hands and thus taking control of the whole vehicle that made her hesitate, but the thought of sitting beside Mr. Ellis for perhaps half an hour or longer. What would they talk about? It was a question she never asked herself in any type of social situation. Why now, then? Besides, they would be traveling about the park, and she would be trying to drive the gig herself. There would be no necessity to make conversation.

"I will need a bonnet and gloves," she said. "And perhaps a shawl or a spencer. It is not quite as hot today as it has been, is it? My maid will know what to choose. Bruce will lift me into the gig."

He turned back to the ballroom doors. "Give me ten minutes," he said.

She was going *driving*. Without the usual company and support of a member of her family. In a small one-horse vehicle she would be expected to drive herself. She would actually be able to *move herself* from place to place. The excitement of it was almost overwhelming, though why had no one thought of it before now as a possibility for her? Why had *she* not thought of it for herself? Why had she accepted her limitations, her essential immobility, so meekly? But perversely, she wished suddenly that she could send a message after Mr. Ellis to inform him that she had changed her mind. She would far prefer to continue sitting quietly here, breathing in the peace and beauty of her surroundings. It was why she had chosen to remain at home, after all. She *could* send a message. There was a bell on the table beside her. She could ring it and Bruce would come. He never went out of earshot of her bell when she was not in the company of other people or within reach of a bell rope that connected with the servants' quarters.

She left the bell where it was and waited. Though not for long. Bruce soon appeared with her bonnet and spencer. They would have been easy to choose, of course. Everything was black. As she was tying the ribbons of the bonnet beneath her chin, a gig turned the corner from the front of the house, Mr. Ellis at the ribbons.

Oh dear. It was too late now to change her mind without making herself look like a dithering coward.

But what in heaven's name was she *doing*?

CHAPTER SIX

❧

The gig looked very smart to Jennifer and more than a bit intimidating. Its body was sky blue and gleamed in the sunshine. The black leather seats shone with a fresh polishing. An equally shiny leather hood was folded over the back. The two large wheels, without a speck of dust or dried mud upon them, gave a solidity to the whole and convinced her that Mr. Ellis had spoken the truth and it really would be fairly safe to try her hand at the ribbons. Though the horse, its brown coat brushed to a smooth sheen, looked disconcertingly large.

Mr. Ellis got out of the carriage, but it was Bruce who lifted her from her chair and set her down on the nearer seat and made sure the hem of her dress rested neatly on the tops of her shoes before stepping back out of the way. It would be almost impossible to fall out, Jennifer decided. The arms of the seat wrapped reassuringly about her sides. Mr. Ellis had come around the vehicle, a gray bundle in one hand.

"You will need to brace both your feet against the footboard if you are to take the ribbons," he told her. "Try setting your right foot against this. I believe it will help."

He was holding a cushion. He propped it now against the footboard in front of her, and it was large and heavy enough to stay there. He did not touch her, and Bruce, who was hovering beside her chair, did not come to her assistance. She set her left foot against the board and her twisted right foot against the cushion, which she found to be firm but just soft enough to be comfortable. She could brace herself with both feet, she discovered, without having to lean to her right side.

"It is perfect," she said. "Where did you find it?" It was not the sort of cushion one would expect to see adorning any furniture.

"I made it," he told her. "Out of an old army haversack and some fresh straw. I learned to use a needle and thread when I was in the Peninsula."

"Really?" She smiled at him as he came back around the gig, took the seat beside hers, and gathered the ribbons into his hands.

"Indeed," he said. "There is more to me than just my handsome face, you know."

She laughed out loud. She would not have suspected this man of having a sense of humor, though there had been flashes of it before. "Ah," she said. "That is reassuring."

He chuckled too, and they were on their way.

"It was not an impulsive idea to come in search of me this morning, then?" she said. "You had it all planned? The gig is clean and sparkling and the horse is perfectly groomed. And you made a cushion especially for me."

"You wish to be independently mobile," he said. "Making the effort to walk with your crutches is admirable but less than fully satisfactory, I suspect. I am sure you would love to fly like a bird. I cannot fashion wings for you, I am afraid, but I *can* give you an opportunity to discover how to move yourself quickly and easily from place to place without relying upon others to carry you everywhere or push you in your chair or drive you in a carriage."

"You are suggesting that I could drive a gig *alone*?" she asked.

"Why not?" he asked in return.

"Getting in?" she suggested. "Getting out? Getting stuck? Having a runaway horse?"

"There is a perch that can be attached to the back of most gigs," he told her. "Where a groom can sit."

"Bruce," she said.

"Has no one ever suggested this to you before?" he asked.

"No." She laughed. "I am taken from place to place in very safe carriages. To be fair, no one in my family drives a gig either. My aunt prefers to be driven in a closed carriage or a barouche. So does my sister, though of course she has the three children as an excuse. Luc and my brother-in-law and my cousin, Aunt Kitty's son, prefer to ride when they are alone or drive their curricles."

He was taking the gig northward beside the west wing, then past the stables and carriage house on the north side, and then back along the east wing. Just before the drive reached the downward slope to the river and the village beyond, narrower carriage paths branched off to the left and right, scenic drives for those who had no particular place to go but wished to enjoy the air and the beauties of the park, Jennifer supposed. Mr. Ellis took the path to the right, the one that led to the lake. He had not yet offered to let her drive, but that was the apparent object of this outing.

Jennifer had been watching his hands on the ribbons, especially as he made the turns. And she was reminded somewhat of the kite Sylvester, her brother-in-law, made last year in London with two of the children. She had watched them fly it in Hyde Park one breezy morning and had noticed how they held on to the stick about which the string was wound. It had not been a passive holding just to ensure that the kite did not blow away, never to be seen again. Rather, they had maneuvered the string to change the direction of the kite, to catch the wind, to fly higher or lower. Even with her young niece it had seemed to be an instinctive thing. None of them had watched their hands but had kept their eyes on the kite.

"Do you have to think about what you do with your hands when you hold the ribbons?" she asked.

"No," he said as he brought the gig to a halt. "But perhaps I did when I was a lad. I cannot recall."

She turned her head to look at the wheel on her side. "If I had these on the sides of my chair," she said, "I would be able to propel it myself. Well, perhaps not these exact wheels. My arms would not be long enough. Besides which, my chair would look ridiculous. You expect me to take the ribbons now, do you?" She was feeling absurdly nervous—and excited. Just like a child being offered a rare and daring treat.

"You will be quite safe," he assured her, handing them to her. "I am right here beside you, though I do not suppose you will need me. Just use soft hands. Do not clutch the ribbons or jerk on them. You will not need to maneuver them, except if we make a sharp turn onto a different path. The horse will know at other times to stay in the center of the path."

"How absurd that I am twenty-five years old and have never done anything like this before," she said. And without knowing quite how she did it, she must have given the horse the signal to start. It trotted obediently forward, taking them westward past the corner of the house, below where she had been sitting a few minutes ago, and then past the hill with the temple on top and off in the direction of the lake. And *she* was the one causing the movement. She listened to the clopping of the horse's hooves and the crunching of the wheels on the graveled path while she felt a slight breeze move against her face, and she laughed in sheer delight.

"Who needs to be a bird?" she cried.

"You see?" he said. "I could jump out and you would still be perfectly safe."

"Please do not," she said hastily. "I might be discovered a few days hence a few hundred miles west of here and still headed straight for the horizon."

After a few minutes she relaxed sufficiently to take her eyes off the bobbing rump of the horse in order to glance from side to side, between the trees to her left to the fields beyond, over rolling lawns and copses of trees within the park and even a few artfully placed flower beds, to the lake coming up ahead. And she enjoyed the fact that the path was not perfectly flat and did not move in an arrow-straight line, but took them over slight rises and down gentle dips and turned with the contours of the land. The ribbons did not have to be maneuvered on the slight bends, he had said, but her hands told her otherwise. It was indeed an instinctive thing, though.

Why on earth had she never thought of this as a possibility until Mr. Ellis suggested it? Why had no one else? Was it because everyone saw her as a delicate creature, even an invalid? She was *not* delicate and she was *not* an invalid. She was a perfectly normal woman who just happened to have one twisted leg and foot that, combined, made it impossible for her to walk. And, incidentally, her feet were perfectly braced against the footboard. Both of them were, though the left was far stronger than the right, of course. It seemed to Jennifer that perhaps her back would not ache after she returned to the house as it sometimes did when she had been walking with her crutches or sitting too long tipped slightly to one side.

The pathway did not run very close to the bank of the lake, she was relieved to discover as they drew closer. There was a wide, grassy verge as well as a few sturdy trees between it and the bank. Nevertheless, Mr. Ellis directed her to stop before they proceeded further.

"How do I stop?" she asked, but she was doing it even before he could warn her again not to clutch the ribbons too tightly or jerk upon them. The horse halted obediently. It was the mildest mannered of creatures.

"I am quite in love," she said with a smile, and turned her head to find that Mr. Ellis had a slightly startled look on his face.

"With the horse," she explained, horribly embarrassed. He really was rather . . . attractive. He was a man with a physical presence one could not simply ignore—whatever she meant by that. But she had ignored him without even trying until a few days ago. She just had not noticed him. This was confusing.

"Ah," he said. "For a moment I thought perhaps you had discovered my charms to be irresistible. Have you ever ridden in a boat?"

"Last year," she said, willing herself not to blush. "At a garden party in Richmond. My brother rowed me on the River Thames." And then someone else had taken her back out there, though she preferred not to think of Mr. Jamieson. She had *no* desire to feel her spirits plummet again. "It was a wonderfully exhilarating experience."

"I cannot offer the Thames," he said. "But there are boats in the boathouse over there, and it is but a short distance to the island. There are chairs and cushions in a shed behind the temple pavilion. Would you like to go there?"

All her self-consciousness was back, but it had a far more real cause now than embarrassment over what *she* had just said about the horse and the joke *he* had made about his charms. How did he propose to get her from here to the boat and from the boat to the little pavilion? And then back again?

"I did not bring my crutches," she said.

"May I offer my services?" he asked. "If I promise not to drop you in the water, that is?"

Bruce's touch was always quite impersonal. She never felt embarrassed with him. He had been with her for years, since she was fifteen. He was the only man who ever carried her from place to place, with the occasional exception of Luc and Cousin Gerald. The very thought of allowing a virtual stranger to do it shocked and embarrassed her. But the sun was shining, the air was warm without being oppressively hot, the water sparkled invitingly, and the day felt very special—the day she had sprouted wings by driving a gig at a pace some people would surely consider laughably slow. And Mr. Ellis was an amiable companion and quite unthreatening despite that joke and her admission to herself a few minutes ago that he was rather attractive. He really was just a very ordinary man. A *kind* man too. There was no reasonable explanation for the discomfort she always seemed to feel with him.

"Oh dear," she said.

He took those two words as agreement and hopped out of the gig to stride toward the boathouse, which seemed a very long way off to Jennifer. She felt suddenly very alone with the gig and a potentially runaway horse—which proved what a dangerous beast it was as soon as she loosened her hold on the ribbons by lowering its head to nibble on the grass beside the carriage path.

Oh dear, she thought again a few minutes later as Mr. Ellis, having slid a small rowboat into the lake water and tethered it to a post on the bank, came striding back toward her.

Oh dear.

This was *not* the best idea he had ever had in his life, Ben thought ruefully as he strode back from the boat to the gig, where Lady Jennifer Arden waited, looking apprehensive and downright severe in black. It certainly had not been part of his original plan, which had been to let her drive sedately around the park and return to the house half an hour or so later, perhaps an hour if they slowed or stopped occasionally to admire a particular view. All the lifting in and out would be done by her servant.

But now look what he had gone and done. It was not simply a matter of getting her in and out of the gig. He was going to have to get her to the island and back. And while there he was going to have to sit beside her and—with no moving scenery around them—*make conversation*. As he had in the courtyard a few days ago.

It occurred to him suddenly that she probably ought to have some sort of chaperon with her, even if only her maid. This was probably not at all the thing.

But, damn it all, she had lit up like a candelabrum full of candles when he handed the ribbons to her and clucked for the horse to start moving again. She had fairly burst with suppressed excitement as she drove the gig along a path a blind horse could have traveled without any guidance at all and at a pace little faster than a leisurely jog. She had reminded him a bit of his daughter when she was given a treat. Lady Jennifer had taken enormous pleasure from something so very simple.

And like the prize ass he was, he had wanted to prolong her happiness, even enhance it, by rowing her over to the island of all places. He had always loved it, perhaps more than any other spot in the park. He had thought it would be the perfect place for romance—though remembering that now intensified his discomfort.

He tethered the horse to a tree lest it take it into its head to turn around and amble back to the stables, leaving him, Ben, to have to carry the lady all the way back to the house like some modern-day Hercules.

"You know, Mr. Ellis," Lady Jennifer said as he turned back to her. "I do believe I can walk to the boat if you will give me the support of your arm."

"Do you wish to try?" he asked.

But of course he still had to lift her down from the gig. He did it as quickly and impersonally as he could, set her down on her left foot, and drew her right arm firmly through his left. She was quite tall, he discovered, only a few inches shorter than he. She leaned heavily upon him, her shoulder pressed to his arm when she walked upon her right foot and away again when she used her left.

He had not known when or how—or whether—he was going to broach a certain subject with her, but he decided there was no time like the present. He had enough other things to dither about.

"I have been talking with the blacksmith and the cobbler in the village," he told her. "Neither possesses a magic wand to straighten a twisted leg and foot, but both are agreed that it may be possible to brace your leg sufficiently to allow you to trust it with more of your weight and to build a shoe soft enough for comfort but firm enough, especially about the ankle, to support your foot. And with a sole carefully designed to the shape of your foot and thick enough to lift it so that your right leg will match your left in length. Both believe they can produce such a brace and shoe within a week or so.

They are certainly eager to try. I daresay they would work night and day on the project."

The scheme sounded even madder than it had before as he described it—at great length.

She had stopped walking, halfway between the gig and the boat. She turned toward him, her weight apparently balanced on her left foot and the toes of her right, a look of what Ben could only interpret as mingled chagrin and outright horror on her face.

"You have been *discussing* me with the village *blacksmith* and the village *cobbler*, Mr. Ellis?" she asked. "Without my consent? And, presumably, without the permission of either my brother or my aunt?"

"I have," he admitted.

Her nostrils flared. Her lips thinned. He waited for the explosion of wrath he could almost see building to a crescendo within her. She opened her mouth, drew breath, paused, and closed her mouth again. But she continued to glare at him.

"Why?" she asked at last. The single word was like a whiplash.

"You want to walk and run and dance," he said. "And fly."

"*None* of which I can do or can ever do," she said curtly. "Do you believe *you* are the one with a magic wand, Mr. Ellis? And do you think I have spent the twenty years since illness struck me down moping and pining for the moon when the moon is going to stay up in the sky regardless? I am not a *victim*. I am not *helpless*. I am not a *project*. We all yearn for the impossible from time to time. For the moon. That does not mean we cannot live productively and even happily with what *is* possible. The earth. Most of us can dream our dreams while also living our reality. I neither need nor appreciate your crusading zeal."

"And some of us," he said, stung by her scorn, "will continue to bang our foreheads against a stone wall even when moving along it might lead us to a gate to take us through to the other side. Do you still wish to go to the island?"

He willed her to say no. He was angry—unjustifiably so—and embarrassed and humiliated. And guilty. Worse, he had infuriated and embarrassed and humiliated *her*. He had stepped way out of line. Her problems were not his to solve.

She turned her head to look at the boat and the island and the pavilion framed by trees. A small white cloud had just moved off the face of the sun, and sunlight came beaming warmly down on them.

"Yes," she said curtly. "I do."

She walked the rest of the way with his assistance, and he lifted her into the boat very gingerly. It would be the last straw if he tipped it and got her wet. He took his place across from her and picked up the oars. The sunlight was sparkling on the water, and her lips, shaded by the brim of her black bonnet, curved into a smile, though doubtless it was not for him. He must be the blackest of villains in her estimation.

"It is a very short distance to the island," he said. "Shall I take you around it before we land?"

"Yes, please," she said. She set her hands neatly in her lap, one on top of the other, palms up, and took one good look around before focusing her eyes upon him.

"When I asked you *why*," she said, "you told me it was because I want to walk and run and dance. But that did not really answer the question. Why would you clean and polish that gig and groom the horse and make a cushion to brace my foot? Why would you go into the village to discuss me with the blacksmith and the cobbler? I am nothing whatsoever to you, Mr. Ellis, except that my brother happens to be married to your half sister. We scarcely spoke to each other when we met last year or earlier this spring at Greystone. Some people are uncomfortable with my . . . disability and avoid me. I am accustomed to such a reaction and am no longer hurt by it. I assumed—if I thought about it at all—that you were of their number."

"That is not true," he assured her, not entirely truthfully. Not truthfully at all, in fact. And he would wager she was still hurt by such behavior in others. Who would not be?

"Why?" He frowned and thought about it. "I think the need to find solutions to practical problems is built into me. I was the steward here for a number of years, and now I have my own property and farm to manage. I see problems, but instead of daunting me they actually invigorate me. For where there is a problem, there is almost always a solution."

"You were the *steward* here at Ravenswood?" she asked, her eyebrows arching upward in surprise and making her look very aristocratic. Was it just occurring to her that she was spending an hour or so with a sort of *servant*?

"I was," he said. "The longtime steward was looking to retire, and I begged my father to allow me to train with him and then take over the position myself. I was eighteen at the time, and my father wanted to send me to Cambridge. Academic studies for their own sake did not particularly interest me, however. Running things, organizing them, staying abreast of new ideas, keeping everything working smoothly, spotting problems and solving them, seeing opportunities and taking them, making everything gradually better, more efficient, more productive and prosperous—those things *did*. Interest me, that is."

She gazed wordlessly at him as the boat circled around the back of the island, keeping well away from the shore. There was a sort of beach there with a gentle slope extending quite a way into the water—a favorite bathing place when he and his brothers and sisters were young. It was easy to get a boat hung up in the shallow water, however. He knew. It had happened to him once or twice when he was a boy.

"My father granted my request, though reluctantly, and only after I had pestered and begged him," he said. "He retaliated by insisting upon paying me a full salary, which I neither needed nor wanted, but he never treated me in any other way as a servant. Nor did any other member of the family. I just happened to be the brother who ran the estate."

She removed her gaze from him and looked around. "What a very beautiful place this is," she said. "I am so glad I came here—to Ravenswood, I mean. It is just what Aunt Kitty and I needed. I am sorry I snapped at you a little while ago, Mr. Ellis. It is just that I realized that if the blacksmith and the cobbler were indeed to work upon some contraption to help me walk better, they would not be able to do it sight unseen, would they? They would need to see and probe and measure—just like a dressmaker. The very idea is appalling."

"Yes," he said. "I can understand that, Lady Jennifer. I am sorry. It was a bad idea. At the very least I ought to have told you what I wished to do. But I decided to talk to them first to discover if what I had in mind was even remotely possible. I will apologize to them for involving them in something that was none of my business, though both are very well aware that you must be consulted before they can proceed in any way at all. You need not fear that either one of them is blabbing the story all over the neighborhood. They are rather awed by the fact that your brother is His Grace, the Duke of Wilby."

"Would it work?" she asked, looking directly back at him. "Could it *possibly* work?"

"There is only one way to find out," he said. "Unfortunately."

He pulled the boat in to the bank before the pavilion and glanced over to see that the horse, shaded by the branches of the old oak tree to which he had tethered it, was still contentedly nibbling on the grass. He tied the boat to a post and got out to hurry back to the storage shed behind the pavilion to fetch two chairs and tuck a heavy cushion under one arm. He set up the chairs inside the little temple and went back to carry her from the boat. She set one arm about his neck and for a moment their eyes met.

It was *not* a comfortable thing to be carrying a woman who was essentially a stranger and feeling her warmth and feminine curves and smelling her light floral perfume. Especially when one considered the fact that socially they were universes apart. And—

But he was *not* going to start finding her attractive. Good God. The very thought could bring him out in a cold sweat. His life was quite complicated enough as it was.

An ordinary woman, Ben, he reminded himself silently. That was what he wanted more than anything else in his second wife. It was time to start thinking again about the three very ordinary women he was considering, though the description sounded a bit insulting.

He set her down on one of the chairs and arranged the cushion beneath her right foot. Her ankle was twisted inward, he noticed, while her foot was angled downward. It must be difficult or even impossible for her to set her heel flat on the ground.

"Very few people have ever thought to do that for my comfort," she said. "You are kind, Mr. Ellis. Thank you."

He took the seat beside her, feeling tongue-tied again. He did not look forward to having to carry her back later. This whole excursion had been presumptuous of him and far more intimate than he had intended or wanted. He was not sure her brother would be best pleased if he learned of it—though, to be fair, Lucas had never treated Ben any differently than he treated Pippa's other brothers.

Perhaps that was because he had never had any reason to treat him differently. Ben had never before carried off his sister quite literally to a secluded, romantic island on a lake.

CHAPTER SEVEN

J ennifer relaxed into her chair, her right foot comfortable on the cushion. The roof of the temple pavilion shaded them from the direct rays of the sun, though the view on three sides was restricted only by the stone pillars that supported the roof. She could see water all around and green grassland stretching beyond. In the distance was the hill with its larger temple and the west wing of the house jutting out beyond it. She had driven herself all the way from there to here. How very clever of her!

She felt free and lighthearted. It was warm here but not hot. Her black garments did not feel oppressive as they sometimes did in the summer heat. But she removed her bonnet and dropped it beside her chair before smoothing her hands over her hair and lifting the curls at the back. She could drive herself from place to place. And she *would* do it. She was going to purchase a gig of her own after she returned home. She would make sure it had a perch at the back so Bruce could accompany her for extra security if she was going more than a mile or two from the house.

It was Mr. Ellis who had opened up this possibility for her. He had challenged her and then taken the time and made the effort to clean and polish the gig until it looked almost new and to choose and groom a suitable horse. He had even made a firm cushion for her foot. She had never known a man who could use a needle and thread. He had done all that to make it possible for her to be sitting here now. He had also gone into the village to confer with the blacksmith and the cobbler about the possibility of making some kind of leg brace and specially designed shoe or boot to help her walk more easily with her crutches.

But why?

She was not fully satisfied with either of the explanations he had given her. Perhaps it was just because he was a kind man. She could have seen that kindness for herself before now if she had chosen to open her eyes. He was a wonderful father to his motherless little girl. It was clear that to the child he was everything in the world that was care and safety and love. And he saw to her needs without fuss or needless possessiveness. He simply loved her.

There was something very appealing about a devoted father. Jennifer thought briefly of her own. He had spent countless hours at her bedside when she was ill, reading to her, telling her stories designed to take her mind off her pain, or simply sitting there holding her hand or smoothing back the hair from her brow. And then her mother had died giving birth to the child who would have been Jennifer's brother, and her father had changed. He had begun to do so even before Mama's death, as though he had felt some premonition. But he had been a wonderful father. It had taken her a number of years to look back beyond the terrible pain of his unnecessary death—he had been riding recklessly, something he *never* did, as though he no longer cared about remaining alive and present for his living children.

She became aware after a few minutes that they had been sitting in silence. It did not feel uncomfortable, however, for Mr. Ellis somehow contrived to go largely unnoticed whenever he was in company. He did not talk a great deal, though he never looked bored or morose. He really was a very nice man. A bland word, that— *nice.* But it fit him. He *was* nice. Was *he* finding the silence comfortable, though? She turned her head to look at him. He did not return her gaze, a sure sign, perhaps, that he was *not* comfortable. It would not be surprising. She had unleashed the full force of her anger on him a short while ago. She had apologized, but was it enough? Had he felt that she was treating him more like a servant than as an equal?

Was he an equal?

He had grown up here at Ravenswood. His father, the late Earl of Stratton, had wanted to send him to Cambridge. Was that where his half brothers had gone? But no. She did not know about Devlin, but Owen was at Oxford. And Major Nicholas Ware had probably not gone to either one. He must have been the son designated at an early age for a military career and had taken up his commission soon after finishing school. Mr. Ellis had taken the position of steward of the estate—at his own request, he had told her. His father had even paid him a steward's salary. He had gone with Devlin to the Peninsula, but not as an officer—or as an enlisted man, for that matter. He must have gone as his brother's servant or batman.

No one, not even Pippa, had ever explained to Jennifer quite how Mr. Ellis fitted into the family. All she really knew was that he was the illegitimate son of the late earl but had grown up here—though not with his father's name. He was still dear enough to the legitimate part of the family, however, to have been invited to the wedding last year and the christening this spring—and here for part of the summer. Everyone doted upon his daughter. His role in the family did not have to be explained, perhaps. It had evolved over all the years since his father brought him here. How old had he been then? Had Aunt Kitty told her?

"How old were you when you were brought to Ravenswood, Mr. Ellis?" she asked.

His head jerked rather stiffly toward her, and she knew that indeed he had not been feeling comfortable with the silence. "Three," he said. "My mother had just died and my father brought me here."

About the age his daughter was now, then.

"Do you remember your mother?" she asked, hoping he would not find the question too intrusive.

He sat back in his chair and sighed. "It is curious," he said, "that one can live night and day with another person for three years yet have no clear memory of any of that time. It makes me wonder if Joy would remember me if I were to die today. It seems incredible that she might forget, but it would very probably happen. It happened to me. I have snatches of memory—a bit of a scene here, a whiff of a scent there, the inflection of a voice somewhere else, a hint of laughter and song. A sense of being enfolded in . . . warm security. But none of those fleeting impressions will form themselves into a clear image or a concrete memory. I believe she loved me and cared for me. I believe my father was part of my life with her. He must have been. I came here willingly enough with him when he brought me. I can recall sitting on his lap in the carriage. Why is it I remember that but not anything before it?"

Poor child, Jennifer thought. And she realized as she lifted one hand from the arm of her chair that she was about to reach across the distance between them to squeeze his hand. She caught the impulse in time and closed her fingers about the chair arm again.

But what a precious thing memory was. She had been eleven when her mother died, twelve when her father had his fatal accident. They were terrible memories she often wished she could erase. But at least she had clear mental images of them as they had been. She remembered what they had looked and sounded and even smelled like. She remembered how they had loved her and Charlotte and Luc. One tended not to think of memory as a gift until it was not there when one needed it. Mr. Ellis had no conscious memory of his mother or her love for him.

"My stepmother—actually I call her Mother and almost never really think of the step relationship," he said. "She was wonderful to me, all things considered. Her own firstborn—Devlin—was just a few weeks old when I arrived. I can only imagine how she must have felt. But I can remember being rocked on her lap, being sung to, being kissed. I believe I must have cried a lot in those early days. It is strange how my memory began then—after I came here, or actually while I was on the way here. I have never, ever heard Mother refer to me as her stepson. She is a very special lady."

Yes, Jennifer thought. Aunt Kitty had chosen her friend well. But it was a chilling image—the little boy crying for his dead mother in the arms of his father's wife.

"What do you know of your mother's family?" she asked, and then wished she had not. If his mother had been his father's mistress, it was very possible that her family, if she had any, had disowned both her and the child she had conceived out of wedlock.

"Nothing," he said in a voice grown suddenly harsh. "I do not know who they are or where they are or if any of them exist. My father could tell me nothing. I suspect he was never interested enough to ask."

He squinted across the water toward the house in the distance, and Jennifer could feel agitation coming from him in invisible waves, though he said no more. His mother had been only a casual mistress to the late earl, his words implied. He had not been interested in her as a person. It must hurt immeasurably. That woman, that casual mistress, had been his *mother*, about whom he knew nothing.

"I am sorry," she said. "I ought not to have asked. It is none of my business."

But he turned toward her suddenly, an almost fierce look on his face, and drew breath to speak before shutting his mouth with a distinct clacking of his teeth. He drew breath again a few moments later.

"I have had a letter—" he said, and stopped abruptly. She heard him swallow.

"About your mother?" she asked.

He reached inside his coat and withdrew a folded piece of paper she assumed was the letter he had referred to. He tapped the edge of it a few times against his thigh before his hand stilled.

"It was waiting for me when I arrived here last week," he said. "The writer claims to be my brother."

Jenny's hands gripped the arms of her chair. *Not* a brother on his father's side, she guessed.

"He says he is the son of my mother and her husband," he told her, the words jerking out of him as though he had just finished running a long distance and was still breathless. "He says his father was a brute of a man and she ran away from him, leaving her son behind. He was five years old at the time. He says that to his knowledge his father never made any effort to discover where she had gone or to go after her to bring her home. He died recently, and the son—Vincent Kelliston—thinks it is time he and I became acquainted."

Ah. Kelliston. K-*Ellis*-ton.

He was tapping the edge of the letter on his leg again.

"Have you written back to him?" she asked.

"No," he said quickly. "I do not know what to say or whether to say anything."

A new brother he had never known existed. His mother's son by an abusive marriage she had fled. None of which he had known before he read that letter last week.

"How do I know his story is true?" he asked.

"Why would it not be?" She frowned.

His eyes, deeply troubled, gazed back into hers. "If he is her legitimate son," he said, "the one she abandoned when he was still a very young child, why would he seek an acquaintance with the bastard son she had with a lover? Is it not the very last thing any normal man would want?"

She could see his point.

"But why else would he have written?" she asked.

He continued to stare at her before shaking his head as he shrugged and looked away. "I do not know," he said.

"What do your brothers and sisters and your . . . mother say about it?" she asked.

He shook his head again. "I have not told them or anyone else," he said. "Until now. I told them the letter was from an old school friend."

Jennifer gazed back at him. His head had dropped. He was looking at the ground between his booted feet. Why her, when he had talked to no one else about his letter? Because she was a stranger, perhaps, and it is sometimes easier to confide in a stranger than in a relative? Because she had asked about his mother's family and this troubling letter had leapt to his mind?

She could understand why his brothers and sisters and the dowager countess might be the last people in whom he would feel he could confide. They had always been good to him and accepted him as one of their own, he had just told her, but . . . Ah, but had they ever thought about the pain he must always have endured at having had one half of his identity amputated, so to speak? With the best intentions in the world, had they thought the least said about his mother and the irregularity of his birth, the better? Perhaps a well-meaning tact on their part had made it impossible for him to speak openly with them about the yawning gap in his personal history. Or perhaps any reference to the sordidness of his birth was abhorrent to them.

"Will you allow me to read the letter?" she asked, turning one hand palm up on the arm of her chair.

He looked up at her. "Sometimes," he said, "I blurt out things I ought to keep to myself and instantly regret not doing so. For some reason it seems to happen more with you than with anyone else. I wish I could eradicate the last few minutes. I do beg your pardon, Lady Jennifer. I had no business speaking to you about such . . . unseemly matters."

She smiled. "If you wish," she said, "I will erase the last few

minutes from my mind and recall today only as the memorable occasion when I first drove a gig and brought myself—with some help
from you—to surely one of the most beautiful spots in all England.
It *is* that, is it not? Or I can read your letter and perhaps offer an
opinion. You can rely upon my discretion. I will make no mention
of its contents or even its existence to anyone else."

"I must be the most troublesome man you have met in a long
while," he said. "Perhaps ever."

She laughed. "Oh no," she said. "I will not have you believe
that. You have revived my dreams, Mr. Ellis, and it is always a good
thing, perhaps even an essential one, to dream. Indeed, one of my
dreams has already come true. I drove myself here—well, partly
anyway. It is something I intend doing again and again, though,
despite the anxiety my family is sure to feel and express quite vehe-
mently. Sometimes it is good to unburden oneself to a person who
has a sympathetic ear even if that person is unable to offer any constructive help or advice. I seem to remember unburdening myself
to you in the courtyard back at the house. I was embarrassed at the
time, but . . . Well, here I am as a result of something I said then.
Here I am feeling happy about the incredible sense of freedom bringing myself here has given me."

He sighed, hesitated, and handed her the letter.

B en lowered his chin to his chest and closed his eyes.
Why her? Why Lady Jennifer Arden of all people? In the
courtyard a few days ago he had told her about Marjorie when he
almost never talked about her with anyone else. And now, after
keeping silent about his letter, even though he was surrounded by

his closest relatives, all of whom loved him, it was *she* he had told about it. It was she who was now reading it.

He had brought her here, for the love of God, because she had been happy in the gig and he had wanted to prolong that happiness.

Good God!

She was taking her time about it even though the letter was only half a page long. Perhaps she had nothing to say. Perhaps she was waiting patiently for him to look up again so she could give the thing back. He looked up.

"I can understand why the letter has upset you, Mr. Ellis," she said. "It is brief and terse. It restricts itself to facts. But very few facts. It arouses far more questions than it answers."

She handed him the folded letter, and he returned it to his pocket.

"You are right," he said. "But it does not matter. I will ignore it."

"It *does* matter," she said. "For the unanswered questions will surely gnaw at you for the rest of your life. If you do not ask them, that is. Or if Mr. Kelliston does not write again or come in person to answer them."

"I do not understand why he wrote in the first place," he said. "Why does he wish to make himself known to the bastard son of the mother who deserted him when he was little more than an infant? If, that is, what he says is true. But if it is not . . . Well, why?"

"He knows you are the son of the late Earl of Stratton," she said. "He knows, or believes, that you live here at Ravenswood, which is reputed to be one of the grandest, most prosperous estates in England."

"All the more reason to hate me," he said.

"Or—" She hesitated. "May I ask a personal question? Did your father leave you anything when he died?"

"I own Penallen," he told her without explaining if it was a cottage or a manor or a mansion. "I purchased it from Devlin for a fair price. It comes with a farm. I have an independence besides that." He actually had considerably more than just an independence. His father had transferred to him the money he had settled upon Ben's mother after he married. That money had been wisely invested and had grown over the years to several times its original value. His father had paid him a good salary while he was steward here, most of which he had saved. He had also left Ben a sizable portion in his will.

"Perhaps," she said, "Mr. Kelliston believes you are wealthy, Mr. Ellis. Or that the Ware family at least is wealthy."

He frowned. "You think greed is his motive, then?" he asked. It was what he had suspected, though Kelliston had said nothing in his letter about his own circumstances.

"I have no idea," she said. "Perhaps he is simply alone and lonely and longs for someone who is related to him. If he had an abusive father, perhaps he has been shunned by all who might have been his relatives and friends." She shrugged and looked ruefully at him. "It is impossible to know from just that one letter. You do not feel you can discuss it with anyone in your family here?"

He shook his head. "They are accustomed to thinking of me as one of them," he said. "I expect they would say, if asked, that we have a shared identity and a shared history. But *their* identity includes the Greenfield side of the family—Mother's side. They have always been good to me. They are good to my daughter. But they are not my full-blood relatives. My family here probably does not understand that what is identity and history to them—enriched by knowledge of and acquaintance with blood relations on both sides—does not fully apply to me. They would not understand why this letter has so disturbed me. They would not understand—" He made circles in the air with one hand.

"—the emptiness that is the missing half of yourself," she said softly, and he was jolted by the accuracy of her understanding. "You have never spoken of it to any of them?"

"Never. Not to anyone." Though that was not quite true. He had spoken his truth to Marjorie, aware even as he did so that her pain was far greater than his. She had not known either of her parents or anything at all about them. "But I do not want to give the impression that they are insensitive. They cannot understand if I have never explained, can they? And I have never done so. I would find it almost impossible now."

Devlin, who had always been both courteous and kind to Marjorie, had never understood why Ben made her his regular and exclusive companion in the Peninsula when she was not particularly pretty or obviously attractive and had twice been the wife of a common soldier. And she had spoken with a sometimes almost unintelligible Cockney accent. He had been astonished when Ben married her, even though Ben had told him she was with child. He had even offered to pay her a substantial sum and find her a decent, steady man from the ranks willing to marry her. There were always soldiers eager to marry any newly widowed woman.

Suddenly Ben felt horribly embarrassed again. Why on earth had he opened himself up to this woman of all people—someone of impeccable, and impeccably noble, lineage? "You must be feeling trapped here with me," he said. "You must be longing to go back to the house."

"Must I?"

She smiled at him with what looked like genuine amusement, and he was uncomfortably aware of her femininity. Her dark red hair was a gorgeous color, a bit brighter than her brother's. It must look breathtakingly beautiful when it was let down. Her hand, which rested on the arm of the chair beside his, was slender, her fingers long and elegant and perfectly manicured, though her nails were short. And there was something about her face, about the perfect classical lines of her profile. Actually it was not perfect. Her upper lip curled ever so slightly and provocatively upward, and he wished he had not noticed. The inappropriateness of his having brought her here unchaperoned weighed down on him again. Her very safety and reputation depended upon him and his self-control. And to have talked to her of such things . . . Well.

"But this has been the happiest day—or part of a day—I have spent in a long while, Mr. Ellis," she said. "I thank you for it. You have made me feel carefree, and you have filled my head with dreams I seem to have stopped dreaming in recent years. You have also *spoken* to me, *talked* with me. Do you sometimes find it a bit tedious to make endless and essentially meaningless conversation with people just so silence may be averted and the social norms observed?"

"But the weather and one's own health and that of everyone else one has ever known provide an endless variety of observations to enliven conversation," he said.

They both laughed while she reached out that elegant, very pale-skinned hand and patted his arm rather sharply in a mock scold. Then she blushed and withdrew the hand to rest on her lap.

"You needed someone in whom to confide," she said. "I am glad you chose me, even if it was only because I am neither a relative nor a close friend. I am, however, a good listener, and sometimes that is what a person needs more than anything. I do not suppose you really expect me to offer you a definite solution to your dilemma. Indeed, you would probably resent my trying to tell you what to do. I will not try. But I will ask you one question, which you may feel free to leave unanswered. How will you *feel* if you simply ignore your letter and never hear from Mr. Kelliston again?"

"Extremely relieved," he said. "It would mean, would it not, that he is not sincere about wishing to meet his long-lost brother?"

"Then perhaps that is what you ought to do," she said.

"Or," he said after thinking about her question for a few moments longer, "you may be right in what you said at the beginning of our conversation. Not knowing may gnaw at me for the rest of my life."

Her hand came up as though to touch him again, but it paused above the arm of her chair and then clasped it.

"It would feel like cowardice to do nothing," he said. "When I was a boy I used to beg and beg my father to tell me about my mother—just as my daughter begs me now to tell her about hers. I gladly do it for Joy. I *want* her to know her mother even though it will never be a physical knowing and she will never have conscious memories of her. I tell her stories of my own experiences with Marjorie, and I tell her what she told me of the orphanage where she grew up. I even tell her of the boy, a fellow orphan, she married when she was about sixteen and followed to the Peninsula as an army wife. But my father had nothing to tell me except that my mother was beautiful and he loved her and would have married her if he had not been obliged to choose a bride who was his social equal. Does that mean, I wonder, that he did not even know she was already married? *If* she was, that is. All my life I have longed to discover more about her. Now I am shying away from the possibility of doing just that."

"Why?" she asked him.

"Perhaps because I do not trust what Kelliston has told me," he said. "Or perhaps because I fear what I might learn. It already feels almost unbearable. She was *married*. She had another child. She abandoned him. In the absence of facts or real memories, I realize I have always made an angel of her. And I have always been the center of her universe."

She had been a real person, his mother. She had, after all, lived for many years before he was even born. There were the husband and the son she had had with him. But who else? What of the larger picture? Who had her parents been? Had there been—or *were* there—sisters and brothers, aunts, uncles, cousins? Grandparents? All the supporting cast of characters that make up most families? But *where had they been* while his mother suffered and then fled? She had run *away* from them rather than *to* them.

"Perhaps there is a whole family of Kellistons in Kent," he said. "Though it is not they who would concern me, is it? Perhaps there is a whole family of my mother's—name unknown. But what would they think of the bastard son to whom she gave birth after leaving her lawful husband? Is it even remotely possible they would open their arms to me? I think not."

She did not answer him, and he marveled again that he was sitting here on the island under the sheltering roof of the pavilion, talking of things he had never spoken aloud before, even to his father. To Lady Jennifer Arden of all people. No matter what she said about this being a happy day, she must wish him in Jericho. Yet she had said she was happy that someone was *talking* to her rather than simply making polite conversation.

"Perhaps," he said, "I am afraid to find out the truth. There is something in the old adage about sleeping dogs."

"To embark upon a quest," she said. "Or not. *To be or not to be.* Poor Hamlet. Many readers, I know, find his eternal indecision vastly irritating. I have always felt deeply for him. Why do many of the most important questions in life not have neat and obvious answers? Like the sum of two and two."

But he knew what the right answer was. He had known it all along but had just not wanted to know. He had grown accustomed to the dull ache of the emptiness that was the one half of his identity. He did not want to disturb it now for fear of what he might uncover. He also feared trusting the letter only to discover that it was a cruel hoax. But all the time he had known that he must and *would* send an answer. An answer composed of a vast list of questions, he suspected.

"I am sorry I have not been able to offer any real help," she said.

"Oh, but you have," he assured her. "You have no idea. Just to be able to *tell* someone and to have someone else read the thing have meant a great deal to me. My head has cleared out. I have a letter to write."

She smiled at him with a soft and genuine smile that had nothing to do with her habitual cheerfulness. Or so it seemed to Ben. She was twenty-five years old, she had mentioned earlier. She ought to be married with children by now. Surely only one factor had prevented it from happening—the small matter of a childhood illness that had left her effectively crippled. Though not, by God, as debilitated as everyone around her seemed to believe. She had *one* deformed leg and foot. But why should they blight the whole of her life?

She was still smiling at him.

"Thank you," he said.

"May I drive the gig again, Mr. Ellis?" she asked. "Not straight back to the house, unless you are eager to return immediately, but beyond the lake. Is there a circular route? If I merely follow the carriage path, or encourage the horse to follow it, will I eventually drive us back to the house—from the east?"

"You will indeed," he said, getting to his feet. "Let me carry you to the boat before I put the chairs away, and then we will resume our epic journey."

She laughed. "For me it *is* epic," she said. "You have *no idea* how it feels to convey myself from place to place, even if I *do* need a gig and a horse and your guidance to make it possible. *And* Bruce to lift me in and out."

He bent to pick her up after she had tied the ribbons of her bonnet beneath her chin again, and she wrapped her arm loosely about his neck. It was a proximity he could have done without, but he was the one who had brought this on himself. He tried to pretend he was the burly Bruce.

He had better *not*, he told himself firmly, start finding this woman attractive—or rather, to be honest with himself, *continue* to find her attractive. Kind as she had been to him, they were still at opposite ends of the social scale.

CHAPTER EIGHT

The family and their guests spent the evening together in the music room next to the drawing room. Tonight they had decided upon music as well as just conversation. Gwyneth played her harp and sang a few Welsh songs to her own accompaniment. She got to her feet when young Viscount Watley—Bertrand—remarked that the harp must surely be one of the most difficult instruments in the world to play.

"Come and try," she said, indicating the chair behind the harp with a sweep of one arm. Her eyes twinkled at the dismayed expression on his face. But he got gamely to his feet while Owen chuckled.

"Sometimes in this house, Bert," he said, "it is wise to keep one's thoughts to oneself."

Bertrand sat and drew the harp to rest on his shoulder. He spread his hands on either side of the strings without touching them.

"Now what?" he asked, laughing.

"Now you sweep your fingers over the strings, looking elegant as you do so, and produce heavenly music," Lucas said. "And do not forget the pedals."

Bertrand plucked a few strings at Gwyneth's direction before grinning at her. "I believe I might in time, with a great deal of effort and practice, produce *noise* from your harp, Lady Stratton," he said. "But I will leave the music making to you. And you must confess that you have the unfair advantage over me of being *Welsh*."

"He is an extraordinarily handsome young man," Jennifer heard her aunt murmur to the dowager countess beside her. "Tall, dark, and handsome. *And* charming. If you and I were just twenty-five or thirty years younger, Clarissa."

"We would probably fight over him and not be friends any longer, Kitty," the dowager murmured back. "Better to stay the age we are."

And the two of them actually giggled like the girls they no longer were. Jennifer found herself smiling too. They had been so enjoying each other's company during the past week.

Stephanie played the pianoforte, a far grander instrument than the one in the drawing room, though she warned those who had not heard her before that her playing might be described as competent at best. She said much the same thing before she sang to her brother Nicholas's accompaniment. She claimed that her voice was better suited to singing in a group. She was a member of a youth choir Sir Ifor Rhys conducted. They had won prizes at more than one Welsh arts festival, or *eisteddfod*—she spelled out the word for Aunt Kitty and looked toward Gwyneth to make sure she had it correct.

"But I seem to recall, Steph," Devlin said, "that you have a solo part in a piece your choir is currently practicing."

"A very *small* solo part," she said, her face and neck turning quite red, poor girl.

She actually had a sweet and pure soprano voice.

Jennifer sang to Lucas's accompaniment, and then Gwyneth and Nicholas sang two duets. They were very good, though they did make a false start with the first one, to general laughter, when, as Nicholas explained, Gwyneth took off like a galloping steed and he like a plodding mule. Apparently the two of them had been close friends when they were growing up, and Jennifer wondered if the general expectation had been that they would marry each other when they grew up. Nicholas was a ruggedly good-looking man. He apparently resembled his father to a remarkable degree. But Gwyneth had married Devlin, the elder, dark-haired brother with the nasty scar slashing across his forehead and the top of one cheek, and the two of them seemed very happy with each other.

Bertrand played Bach on the pianoforte. He played with a talent quite equal to Gwyneth's on the harp. He declined Aunt Kitty's request for an encore, however. He seemed to be a remarkably modest young man.

The arrival of the tea tray put an end to the music, and not long after, the gathering broke up. Aunt Kitty and the dowager countess declared their intention of having a reasonably early night after a busy few days and went upstairs together. The men all withdrew to the billiard room. Gwyneth and Stephanie went off to the ballroom, late as it was, to work out some detail they had discussed over tea concerning the evening ball at the upcoming fete. Philippa asked Jennifer if she should ring the bell for Bruce.

"Or we can stay here for a while and talk," she suggested as an alternative. "It is not very late and it is comfortable here. Are you enjoying your stay, Jenny? I felt a bit guilty when we drove off this morning to visit my grandparents, and some of the others went to Sir Ifor and Lady Rhys's for luncheon. The men all had other plans, and so you were left alone. It felt like abandonment even though you insisted that a quiet day was just what you most needed."

"It was a lovely day," Jennifer assured her, "though not at all what I had planned. I drove myself all around the park in a gig and went over to the island in a rowing boat and sat in the shade of the temple there and dreamed of walking and running and riding and swimming. And flying."

Philippa laughed and patted her arm. "You are such *fun*, Jenny," she said. "What did you *really* do? I hope Bruce took you outside for some fresh air. It was lovely today, a bit cooler than it has been but very pleasantly warm nonetheless. Grandpapa had Christopher outside sitting on the grass, pulling it out by the fistful and trying to eat it, as he does with everything. Joy ran around barefoot, pretending to be a bird flapping its wings, and Emily actually *laughed* at her when Joy swooped down and tickled her stomach. Poor Emmy. She is so determined much of the time to be cross. Tell me what you really did."

"I drove the gig," Jennifer said. "I actually held the ribbons in my own hands and *drove*. The horse was obliging enough not to bolt with me or rear up and scare me half to death. And we went all about the park, going toward the west and returning from the east, with a stop at the island on the way to relax and enjoy the beauty of our surroundings."

Philippa looked at her, still not sure she was not being teased. "*We?*" she said.

"Mr. Ellis and I," Jennifer said. "He believes I ought not to be compelled to spend my life immobile in my chair or on my bed except when there is someone to carry me or push me from place to place. He cleaned and polished the gig until it looked shiny and new, though I daresay it is not new at all. He chose a docile horse. And oh, Pippa, best of all, he made a cushion out of an old haversack I daresay he had when he was in the Peninsula and stuffed it with straw and sewed it together himself. And he set it against the footboard of the gig to give extra support and comfort to my right foot and make my right leg more or less match my left in length. He took me out this morning and let me do the driving."

Philippa gazed at her in amazement until she relaxed back in her chair and smiled. "Oh, yes," she said. "That is *just* the sort of thing Ben would do. He never saw a problem that he did not have to solve. I can remember when the head came right off Stephanie's favorite doll one day and Papa tried to comfort her by assuring her in his usual jocular but helpless way that it could be glued back on. But she was inconsolable because the head could be *moved* but would no longer be able to do so if it was glued. Ben just picked up the doll and the head and disappeared without a word. He brought them back not long after, all one piece again—with a movable head. But, Jenny, what gave him the idea not only that you *could* drive the gig but that you would *wish* to?"

"I did. He came upon me walking in the cloister out in the courtyard one afternoon," Jennifer said while Philippa's eyes widened. "I do it as often as I can, you know, though I tell no one— except Bruce, of course. I use my crutches and *both* legs and feet. I am not very successful at it and never will be, alas. But I am also stubborn. Mr. Ellis and I were both horribly embarrassed when he discovered me doing that. But we sat awhile in the rose arbor, and I believe I must have told him how I dream of walking and running

and leaping and flying. He asked me if I drove or rode or swam."
She laughed. "And then he went off and prepared that gig, without
a word until he found me on the terrace outside the ballroom this
morning and offered to take me driving. Or, rather, he offered to
let *me* take *him* driving."

Philippa was looking pensive. "I have just realized something,"
she said. "Forgive me for not understanding it before now. A person can be smothered by love—genuine love, which quite desperately wants to shield the loved one from being hurt. Is that how
everyone—including me—has always treated you, Jenny?"

"Oh, I do not complain," Jennifer assured her without denying
it. "For I know I *am* loved. I am surely one of the most blessed
people alive. My little rebellion has been for me alone and not as
a defiance against those who love and protect me. I have never
dreamed— Well, yes, I have actually. I have *dreamed*. But I have
never expected to have greater mobility. Do you remember that
morning last year in Hyde Park, Pippa, when my sister's children
flew the kite they had made? I was so very envious. Not only of the
kite but of *them*, dashing about on the grass, taking their ability to
run so much for granted—*as they ought*."

"How well done of Ben to have made it possible for you to drive,"
Philippa said. "Without a word to anyone. Will you now have a gig
of your own?"

"Yes," Jennifer said. "Aunt Kitty will have a fit. So will Luc,
I daresay. But yes. I am going to purchase my very own gig and
horse, and I shall tool about the countryside with them, and everyone will pronounce me an eccentric. I shall have a perch for the
back of it—Mr. Ellis says it is possible—and Bruce can travel with
me when I go more than a mile or so from home."

Philippa clasped her hands to her mouth and smiled at Jenny over the top of her fingers. "I am so *glad*," she said. "And I shall tell Lucas so if he grumbles to me."

"But not yet, please," Jennifer said, holding up one hand. "There is something else, Pippa." Actually, there was more than one thing, but there was just one for which she needed to enlist the help of her sister-in-law. Was she really considering it, then? It was surely utter madness and would involve her in an embarrassment worse than any she had ever experienced before.

"You had better say it now that you have started," Philippa said, reaching out to pat her hand and then squeeze it. "I will not tell anyone else if you would rather I did not. Even Lucas. *Especially* him, in fact. Goodness, he is your *brother*, and he would wrap you permanently in cotton wool to keep you safe if he could. Does this too concern Ben?"

"I need you to come into the village with me," Jennifer blurted. "To the blacksmith's. And the cobbler's."

Philippa tipped her head to one side and looked inquiringly at her friend. "The blacksmith?" she said. "Cam Holland?"

"Is that his name?" Jennifer said. "He believes it may be possible to make some sort of brace for my right leg. *Not* to straighten it or constrict it in any way, but to hold it steady while I try to walk. And the cobbler believes it may be possible to fashion some sort of shoe or boot that will give extra support to my ankle and raise the level of my foot so that I will not bob so much from side to side when I walk."

Philippa was frowning again. "You went and *talked* to Cam Holland?" she said.

"No, Mr. Ellis did," Jennifer told her. "I am afraid I went for his throat—though not quite literally, of course—when he told me. I was *furious*, and he did apologize. I almost demanded that we return to the house immediately—he was about to row me over to the island at the time—though I did not. I recognized the goodness of his intention though it enraged me that he had discussed me with those . . . *men* without a word to me in advance. I would *of course* have said no."

"As you ought," Philippa said, looking angry herself. "I am ashamed of my own brother. How *could* he?"

"But then I got to thinking," Jennifer said. "Pippa, what if it is possible? What if with a bit of help I find I can *walk*? Still with my crutches, of course. I would never expect to walk without their aid. But with two legs that are somehow the same length and strong enough with all the supports that I can put the same weight on my right leg as I put on my left? I will surely die of embarrassment if I go to consult those two men, however, for they would have to see my leg and foot, would they not, and measure them? But I will surely die if I do not at least find out if the dream can become reality. Oh, what foolish exaggeration. I shall not *die* in either case. But I cannot possibly go there with Mr. Ellis for an escort, and I cannot possibly tell Aunt Kitty or Luc or anyone else. You are the only one I *can* ask."

Philippa stared at her, speechless.

"*Will* you come with me?" Jennifer asked. "You have not seen my leg and foot either. They are not a pretty sight. But—"

Philippa's hand squeezed hers again. She even laughed. "*Of course* I will come," she said. "What an adventure. And a splendid secret. Cam Holland has a sister—Sally. She is a couple of years older than me, but we were always friendly as girls. Shall I ask her to come too? Would you feel happier to have *two* women to lend you support?"

"I think I would," Jennifer said.

"But I wonder what on earth possessed Ben," Philippa said. "He has not fallen in love with you, has he, Jenny?"

"Good heavens, no." Jennifer could feel the color rise in her cheeks. "He just felt sorry for me when he saw my sad attempt to walk, that is all."

"I beg your pardon," Philippa said. "I sometimes forget that Ben is— Well, never mind."

I sometimes forget that Ben is our illegitimate brother. That was surely what she had been about to say. But she had been right to think of it. Mr. Ellis was not a Ware. He was the son of the late Earl of Stratton and a married woman who had fled her husband and left behind another young son—if that letter was to be believed, and Jennifer could not think of any reason why it would not be.

Mr. Ellis was aware of his differentness. His manner toward her, Jennifer, had shown her that he was as aware as she of the vast social gap between them. He was good-looking. He was kind. He was a very good father. He was . . . attractive. She had felt it today when they were together. She thought perhaps he had found her a little bit attractive too. But it was *not* a feeling either one of them was going to encourage. Any sort of . . . *romance* between them was out of the question.

"By your own admission, Pippa," she said, smiling, "Mr. Ellis is a man who cannot see a problem without seeking a practical solution."

They were interrupted when Lucas opened the music room door and peered about it before stepping into the room.

"I just tiptoed into our bedchamber, Phil," he said, "so as not to wake you. Then I discovered you were not even there. Or in the nursery, where the twins are both fast asleep, I might add." He grinned at his sister. "Have you solved all the world's problems between you?"

"Only half," Jennifer said. "We have left the other half for tomorrow."

"Are you ready to go up?" he asked, coming up behind her and squeezing her shoulders. "I'll carry you."

"Thank you, Luc," she said.

G wyneth had planned a picnic at the lake for the family and some friends from the neighborhood for the following afternoon. In the morning, however, everyone went about their various pursuits, and Ben was free to sit at the desk in the library and write the letter he had been composing in his head all night during lengthy waking periods and even while he slept.

Joy had gone down to the church with Gwyneth and Stephanie. Sir Ifor Rhys was going there too so Steph could practice the solo part she had in one of the pieces the youth choir was to sing for the opening of the fete, and Gwyneth was always happy to see her father. Joy had gone because she had a bit of an obsession with the organ, and Gwyneth had promised that Sir Ifor would almost certainly allow her to play on the keyboards for a little while.

Ben had jotted down a list of questions the previous night before he went to bed. He had added more when he got up. And really, he thought as he drew paper toward him now and dipped the quill pen into the ink, he was going to have to write in numbered points. His writing master at school would probably have sentenced him to a week of detentions if he had done such a thing in a class assignment while the art of letter writing was being taught. But there were so many questions that he was afraid some of them might get lost in the density of a lengthy paragraph.

He got stuck immediately on how he should address the man who had written to him. Mr. Kelliston? Vincent? Mr. Vincent Kelliston? Sir? Brother? He settled for Kelliston alone and began his letter. *Dear Kelliston . . .* Why did one address a stranger as *dear*? he wondered. Who had made it a rule of polite letter writing? It was odd, to say the least. But he must not procrastinate or allow his mind to wander. He had decided yesterday that he would write, that he *must* write, and this morning he had been presented with the perfect opportunity.

He was not going to hide his doubt or his skepticism. He began the letter with it, in fact. Why would any man wish to communicate with the bastard son to whom his mother had given birth after leaving her husband and abandoning *him*?

Thirty-one more questions followed that first. *Thirty-two* in total. Ben sat back in his chair when he had them all written down and clearly numbered. At least they would show his brother that he was not so pathetically pleased and grateful to have his existence acknowledged that he was going to fall into any emotional trap the man had prepared for him. What would it be? That his father had drunk or gambled away any money or property or business he might have possessed and Kelliston needed a small loan to get back on his feet? At the age of forty or so?

Ben hated his skepticism. And he hated his hope and the soreness about his heart that felt as much physical as it did emotional. He wished Kelliston had not written at all. Though no, of course he did not. That was not what caused the soreness. It was his fear that when his hopes were dashed, as they surely would be, the pain would be worse, *far* worse, than the emptiness had always been.

Except that it could not possibly be worse. At least pain was *something*. Emptiness was *nothing*.

He finished the letter, made sure the ink was dry before folding and sealing it, and set it on the tray in the hall with the outgoing mail.

He wondered if that was the last he would ever hear of the matter. Part of him hoped it was. But . . . how had Lady Jennifer phrased it yesterday? *The unanswered questions will surely gnaw at you for the rest of your life.*

Yes. They would. He rather feared that if Kelliston did not write again, he would find himself impelled to go in pursuit of the man and the answers to his thirty-two questions.

And this involved Joy too. So far in her life, only one quarter of her history was available to her. Although he told her stories of her mother, Marjorie had grown up as an orphan with no knowledge of her parents and no possible way of tracing them. Joy's father was half a Ware and half . . . something else.

And now that something else was opening up like the tiniest of buds that might wither to nothing or transform itself into some sort of bloom. A rose? A dandelion? But both had their beauty and were surely more to be hoped for than a shriveled bud.

He went back into the library to tidy the desk and return Kelliston's letter to his pocket. The door burst open behind him before he could do anything else and Joy dashed in, flushed and excited and babbling a half-intelligible tale of playing the organ and Aunty Steph and Aunty Gwyneth and Aunty Eluned clapping and Sir Ifor telling her she could be a great musician one day if she worked and worked at it and Aunty Eluned taking them to the shop, where Joy helped her pick out the prettiest wool with which to knit booties for the baby, whom Uncle Idris and Lady Rhys were looking after at home. Only a parent would have been able to decipher that single-sentence account of her morning, Ben thought.

"You will be very fortunate, Ben," Gwyneth said from the door-way, "if you do not find yourself having to purchase an organ when you return to Penallen."

He grimaced and then grinned as he swept Joy up into his arms and she patted his cheeks and beamed at him. "Perhaps you can persuade Aunt Gwyneth to show you her harp sometime," he told her while Gwyneth laughed and disappeared. "But first, if you are going to be wide awake enough to enjoy the picnic this afternoon, it is time for a nap."

CHAPTER NINE

Y ou must be feeling exhausted, Jenny," Philippa said softly as
she leaned into the barouche, her arms folded along the top of
the door.

Jennifer was seated with her back to the horses, ready to depart
for the lake. It would not be at all surprising if she was weary, but
instead she was looking forward to the picnic and felt full of energy.
Guests were already arriving. A few had just driven by on the carriage path on the far side of the lawn, the one she had driven yesterday in the gig.

Mr. Ellis had already gone to the lake to help some servants
unload a wagon of food and crates of drink and large blankets to
spread on the grass—and Jennifer's wheeled chair. He had also
volunteered to arrange chairs for those who would prefer a higher
perch. Devlin and Gwyneth had also gone on ahead, on foot, with
Gareth bouncing on his father's arm after an early nap. Devlin
wanted to make sure all the boats were out of the boathouse with a

proper complement of oars. Gwyneth wanted to be sure the hampers were properly arranged.

Most of the family was also going to walk to the lake, since it was not a vast distance away. Devlin had arranged for the barouche to take Jennifer, but she suspected his mother and Aunt Kitty were quite glad of the excuse to ride with her.

The two of them sat side by side now on the forward-facing seat, chatting busily with each other, but Aunt Kitty overheard Philippa's softly spoken words.

"Why would Jenny be exhausted, Pippa?" she asked. "She is made of sterner stuff than to wilt after a short ride into the village this morning to call upon your friend and her mother at the blacksmith's. I was delighted to see her go with you. She has had far too few outings since poor Mama and Papa passed in the spring. She told me you had a lovely visit."

"We did," Jennifer said, and she and Philippa exchanged twinkling smiles. If her aunt only knew! If *everyone* only knew. They would probably have her locked away in some sort of asylum. She ought to be cringing with remembered embarrassment. Instead, all she wanted to do was laugh. She felt more lighthearted than she had in a long time—well, since yesterday morning anyway. "I very much enjoyed meeting Sally Roberts and her mother, Mrs. Holland."

And she had enjoyed meeting Cameron Holland, the large, impressively muscled blacksmith, and Mr. Oscar Holland, his father, who had described himself as being more or less retired, while his son rolled his eyes and shook his head. She had enjoyed meeting Mr. Rogers, the cobbler, and Mr. Taylor, the carpenter. And Dr. Isherwood too. He had been summoned after the first half hour or so at the insistence of Mrs. Holland, who had warned that His Grace, the Duke of Wilby, and his lordship, the Earl of Stratton, would surely have the lot of them clapped up in jail if they did not seek professional advice or at the very least consult a medical man.

The smithy, with its outer doors firmly locked against the scrutiny of the outside world, had soon been very crowded indeed. Yet everyone had sworn, when the doctor had raised the issue before they all dispersed, that everything that had happened during the past hour must remain strictly confidential.

"Not one whisper," Cameron Holland had added. "Not even to Alan, Sal." His sister was married to the village schoolmaster.

"Not even Alan," she had said. "I shall merely tell him I had a very pleasant visit with Mama and Lady Philippa and Lady Jennifer Arden."

"Her Grace of Wilby," Mr. Holland had said, correcting his daughter.

"And I will not say *one word* to Lucas or Lady Catherine Emmett," Philippa had said, laughing. "Or anyone else at the house. I do not fancy having my head bitten off."

She probably should be exhausted, Jennifer thought now. But she was not.

Stephanie was hurrying toward the barouche. "May I ride with you?" she asked the ladies within.

"But of course," Aunt Kitty said. "We have an empty seat just waiting for you."

"There is room next to Jennifer," her mother said. "But would you not prefer to walk with all the other young people?"

"I would rather ride with Jenny," Stephanie said, climbing into the barouche and shutting the door firmly without waiting for Philippa or the coachman to do it for her.

She had come out of the house a few minutes ago hand in hand with Joy Ellis and beaming happily, Jennifer had observed. But then Owen had come out right behind them with his friend, and already the two men were on their way to the lake, Joy between them, clinging to a hand of each as they counted to three before lifting her high into the air for a giant jump forward before beginning the count again. She was shrieking with exuberance. Luc was on the terrace cuddling Christopher, who still looked sleepy after his nap, while Nicholas held Emily and was whispering in her ear and making her bounce and laugh. They were waiting for Pippa to join them.

Under normal circumstances, Jennifer suspected, Stephanie would have been perfectly happy to walk to the lake with her siblings and the young children. She would have enjoyed herself every step of the way. But the presence of Bertrand Lamarr, Viscount Watley, had changed all that. It was not because he was either unkind or insensitive. He was absolutely neither. He had looked apologetically at Stephanie when Joy abandoned her to take his hand while demanding the jumping game he and Owen had apparently played with her yesterday. He had smiled and asked Stephanie if she was coming too. But she had shaken her head, muttered something while gesturing vaguely toward the barouche, and then come hurrying toward it. Poor girl. She was obviously smitten by the young man's dark good looks and charm but was also totally intimidated by him.

It sometimes hurt to be seventeen.

"Ah, there goes George," the dowager countess said, raising one hand as her brother, Mr. George Greenfield, went riding along the lower path. He saw them and stopped to lift his hat and wave it at them.

"Are you coming?" he called. "I'll wait down here and give you my escort. The carriage paths in Ravenswood Park are bristling with brigands, I have heard."

"But we will feel perfectly safe with you, Mr. Greenfield," Aunt Kitty called back as the barouche moved off and Stephanie waved to her uncle.

Jennifer wondered if she would have a chance to talk with Mr. Ellis this afternoon. She wanted to know if he had replied to his letter yet, or if he ever would. She wondered if he would be surprised—and perhaps a little offended?—to discover that she had taken the initiative this morning and gone to the smithy with Pippa without either informing him or asking if he would like to accompany them.

Just as he had done to her a couple of days ago, of course.

B en had always loved picnics at the lake. Sometimes they had been just for the family. Occasionally they had been for the community at large, and crowds would come to mingle and play and ride in the boats, even to swim. They had come to be fed a sumptuous fare of picnic foods, to listen to music played by an orchestra from the pavilion on the island, and to bask in the warmth of the welcome Mother and Papa had lavished upon them all.

Papa.

Ben rarely thought of his father by that name these days. He rarely thought of him at all, in fact. Not consciously anyway. He was still too hurt by the realization that he had loved an illusion—an essentially selfish man, whose affection for his family, though real, had not been enough for him. Whose insatiable appetites, particularly for women, had overshadowed his duty to his countess and their children—including his firstborn son, who had clung far too long to the myth that his mother had been the love of his father's life, not just one of a long string of mistresses.

He did not wish to think of his father even now. And when he overheard Colonel Wexford greeting Nicholas in his booming military voice with the observation that Nick was the very spit of the old earl, Ben winced inwardly and wondered how his brother felt about the fact that in looks and personality he did indeed resemble their father—tall, fair-haired, well built, handsome, confident, cheerful, charming. There were so many similarities. But Ben remembered how Nick had wept out in the Peninsula when they received the news of their father's death. Devlin had refused to react at all and had never referred to the matter again, though their father's passing had made him into the new Earl of Stratton. He had made no plans to return home either. As far as Ben knew, he had written to no one, not even his mother. Ben was thankful he did not resemble his father, except perhaps, as some people had told him, in the square firmness of his jaw and the shape of his nose when viewed from certain angles. There was enough of a resemblance, he supposed, to prove at least that the late earl *was* his father.

But these were *not* thoughts to be having on a picnic day.

This was neither an intimate family gathering nor a vast community event. It was an afternoon entertainment for family and close friends and neighbors. George Greenfield was here from Mother's side of the family, Uncle Charles and Aunt Marian Ware with Cousins Susan and Clarence from the Ware side. The Rhyses had come. So had Colonel Wexford with his sister and his daughter, Ariel. David and Doris Cox were here, invited largely, Ben suspected, because they had young children who were favorite playmates of Joy's. His daughter had discovered that she could not actually play very much yet with the babies, much as she adored them. Baron and Lady Hardington were here with James Rutledge, the younger of their two sons, and Barbara, their unmarried daughter.

There had been some discussion over whether the Rutledges should be invited. Several years ago there had been some unpleasantness between them and Lucas, who had been the Marquess of Roath at the time and quite unknown at Ravenswood. He and James Rutledge had been fellow students at Oxford, and he had been invited to spend Easter with James's family. His visit had been cut short, however, by an incident about which Ben knew tantalizingly little. It had had something to do with Pippa, however. James had taken exception to whatever it was, and Lucas had taken himself off abruptly the very next day. Then, of course, he met Pippa again in London last year and married her before the Season ended. Devlin, who obviously did know the whole story, had asked if it was likely to be embarrassing to either Pippa or Lucas—or to James Rutledge and his parents for that matter—to come face-to-face again at the picnic. They had both assured him it would not be and had pointed out that if James or Lord and Lady Hardington felt differently, then they would simply not come.

Besides, Pippa had added, it would be foolish to avoid the meeting since it was bound to happen at some time. At the fete next week, perhaps? It would be tedious for them all to be dodging one another there all day long. Why not meet at the picnic, then?

Ben was talking with James when Lucas and Pippa arrived at the lake with Nicholas and the twins. After greeting a few people and raising a hand in acknowledgment of others, they came toward Ben while James half turned away, perhaps hoping he had not been noticed.

"James," Pippa called. "How lovely to see you again. It has been an age. I will not ask if you remember Lucas. How could you forget? How could any of us forget?" She smiled at him and patted his arm. "Will you listen to him for a few minutes?"

James sighed, and the two former friends eyed each other warily.

Ben moved away. This was none of his business. He hugged Aunt Marian and Cousin Susan and chatted with them and Uncle Charles. Joy came dashing over and scrambled into his arms in order to smile at her Ware relatives and shake her head vigorously when Uncle Charles asked if he might snip off one of her curls to cover his bald spot. Ben hoped there was not going to be any sort of scene between the two men, but when he glanced back, he saw that they were shaking hands while Pippa was patting James's arm again. Lord Hardington, who had joined the group, was beaming genially at them all while Lady Hardington, at his side, was holding Christopher and laughing as he tried to pull off her necklace. All seemed to be well, Ben thought.

The picnic proceeded merrily. The guests appeared to be enjoying themselves. Indeed, it was quite like old times. Devlin was a very different sort of host than their father had been. One did not know at every moment where he was. One did not constantly hear his voice and his laughter. But there was a quiet warmth in Dev's manner that made his guests feel welcome and comfortable. Gwyneth was as charming as Mother had ever been, but livelier, more filled with laughter.

Everyone mingled with everyone else, though there did tend to be a division between the older people and the younger. The former stood in groups or, more often, sat in circles. Sometimes a few of them would take a walk, along beside the lake or up onto the slight rise of land to the north of it, from which vantage point they would have a panoramic view over the park and the fields beyond. The younger people were a bit noisier and more boisterous. They got up a game with a large ball that had been unearthed from the boat-house, a game that involved the participants forming a circle with one person in the middle attempting to dodge the ball that was being hurled at his or her legs. There was much shrieking and laughter.

The babies and children found their own amusement, often—especially in the case of the babies—in the arms of various willing adults, including the men. Colonel Wexford drew all attention his way when he let out a bellow of mock outrage as Gareth grabbed a fistful of the curled mustaches of which the colonel was inordinately proud. Joy flitted from the babies to the Cox children, with whom she played energetic games of hiding and chasing as they darted about, getting under everyone's feet without apparently tripping or otherwise annoying anyone.

The boats were in constant demand, especially after the ball game was over. Barbara Rutledge and Ariel Wexford were currently standing on the bank of the lake with Owen and Bertrand, waiting for the boats to come in so they could take their turn. David Cox and Ben were up to their knees in the shallow water a little way from the boathouse with Cox's three children and Joy, who were splashing around with a gleeful disregard for how wet they were getting themselves and their fathers. Five-year-old Olwen went staggering off to her mother, soaking wet and howling, after losing her balance and going right under for a fraction of a second before her father hauled her back up into the air. Eight-year-old Philip pretended to swim with a vigorous flailing of his arms, though his feet still anchored him to the bottom. Three-year-old Andrew jumped up and down, shrieking with glee at his sister's misfortune and splashing water into Joy's face. She gasped and reached for Ben. He lifted her up and laughed with her after she had caught her breath and cleared her eyes. But they had to get out and dry off. Gwyneth was signaling that it would be time for tea in a few minutes, and it looked as though almost everyone was discovering a ravenous appetite.

Ben wondered how on earth he could have expected when he removed his boots and stockings earlier and his coat and waistcoat too as an extra precaution that the worst damage he could do to himself was get the bottoms of his pantaloons wet. He was *soaked*. Even his hair was dripping.

"I'm c-c-cold, P-p-papa," Joy said, burrowing against him as he hurried her toward the boathouse, though there was not much warmth to burrow *into*.

"We will soon get a towel around you," he said. He had had the forethought when he arrived earlier to take a pile out of the boathouse and stack them on the bank.

He set her down on the grass, wrapped a large towel about her, rubbed her vigorously, including her hair, and picked her up again. "Into the boathouse with you to get dressed," he said.

He was glad he had brought extra undergarments for her. He wished he had brought a dry shirt for himself—not to mention pantaloons. But what he had on would dry quickly enough in the sunshine, he supposed.

"I want to go play with Olwen and Andrew, Papa," Joy said as they came out of the boathouse, her chills forgotten.

"You are not ready for tea?" he asked.

"Ye-e-ess," she shrieked, but she dashed off anyway to find her friends. She would have tea with them.

And they feasted. For a while there was a mere murmur of sound as they all did justice to the banquet of both savories and sweets. But inevitably hunger was satisfied and voices rose again in conversation. People mingled again and the walks and boat rides and games resumed.

Only one person had done no walking or riding all afternoon. No moving about at all, in fact.

From his seated position on one of the blankets in a group with James and Barbara Rutledge, Clarence Ware, Ariel Wexford, and Stephanie, Ben looked at Lady Jennifer Arden. She was seated in the shade cast by the branches of an elm tree, as she had been from the start. She had not been neglected. There had always been one or two or even three people with her, squatting or kneeling or sitting on the grass close to her and conversing with her. She had been her usual cheerful, spirited self throughout, listening and talking with animation and a look of real interest on her face.

Miss Wexford, the colonel's spinster sister, who had kept house for him for as far back as Ben could remember, was with her now, as were George Greenfield and Bertrand Lamarr. She looked as if she was enjoying their company.

But damn it all, she wanted to walk and run and dance.

Just the simple pleasure of driving the gig yesterday at a very sedate pace had given her a pleasure that had seemed quite in excess of the activity itself. She had been transformed from a cheerful, sociable, dignified aristocratic lady into a warm and vibrant, somehow beautiful young woman. An *attractive* woman. He wondered if anyone else here saw those things in her or ever had seen them. Perhaps her aunt or her brother? Or Pippa, who was her friend?

Surely he was not the only one who was aware of her essential unhappiness.

He ought to stay away from her. Good God, she was the *sister* of the Duke of Wilby, and all the outside guests would be very well aware of that fact. They would also be perfectly well aware of exactly who he was. No one—none of these people here—had ever treated him any differently from the way they treated the other members of the family. But that did not mean they were unaware. He had never even considered courting any of their daughters or sisters and putting that awareness to the test.

Not that he was considering courting Lady Jennifer Arden. But some might think it presumptuous of him even to single her out for conversation. Perhaps he was being oversensitive, but he had always preferred to keep his distance from anything that might be even mildly controversial.

He wanted to speak to her, however. He wanted to tell her he had written to Vincent Kelliston. He thought she would be pleased. He also wanted to apologize again for the terrible indiscretion of discussing her case with Cam Holland and even involving John Rogers. He wanted to assure her that he would go to the smithy early tomorrow to instruct the two men to forget what he had said and on no account to tell anyone else, though he did not believe either man would need to be told that.

Miss Wexford was moving away from Lady Jennifer, and George Greenfield was answering a question Mother had asked him from his other side—she was sitting a few feet away with Lady Catherine Emmett and Lady Rhys. Bertrand had been hauled away by Owen to row a boat. A quick glance showed Ben that Joy was dancing what might possibly be a waltz with Cousin Clarence while Stephanie appeared to be la-la-la-ing the music and Olwen Cox jumped up and down, clapping her hands and awaiting her turn.

Opportunity had presented itself and the temptation was too great to resist.

"Lady Jennifer," he said as he approached her, and she smiled at him. "Would you care for a change of scenery? I believe your chair will move quite smoothly on the carriage path. There is a narrower footpath that branches off it and goes right around the other two sides of the lake. I am almost certain it is wide enough for your chair."

"Perhaps, Ben—" Mother said, lifting a staying hand as she turned her attention away from her brother.

But Lady Jennifer forestalled her objection. "A change of scene sounds quite *heavenly*, Lady Stratton," she said. "And if the footpath proves to be too narrow and rough, well, then, we will just have to turn around and come back."

Mother looked dubious, Lady Catherine Emmett, who perhaps *did* understand some of her niece's yearnings, twinkled at her, and Ben bore her off, hoping the wheels on her chair were durable enough to take her over the footpaths all the way around the lake. He hoped too that all the picnic guests were not gazing after them, aghast at his impudence.

"Let the adventure begin," she said when they arrived at the oak tree to which he had tethered the horse yesterday. There was laughter in her voice.

Ben smiled. An adventure indeed.

CHAPTER TEN

The carriage path was well maintained, as Jenny remembered from yesterday. Her chair moved quite smoothly along it. She hoped it was going to be possible to go along the narrower footpath that branched off it at the southwest corner of the lake. She had not noticed the path yesterday, but at that time, of course, she had been concentrating upon driving the gig.

The footpath was indeed wide enough and well enough maintained that they could turn onto it and move ahead without any great difficulty, though it must be a long way to go all about the lake. Poor Mr. Ellis would have sore arms tomorrow. The path was bordered on the side away from the lake by a variety of low bushes and a few well-placed flower beds. At the northwest corner there was a pretty little open-fronted grotto with a thatched roof and hanging baskets at its corners overflowing with multicolored sweet peas. Flowerpots on the ground beneath them brimmed with blooms. There was a wooden table inside with benches pushed against it.

It was a little piece of rural paradise, Jennifer thought. She had seen a few people stroll this way along the northern path, including Aunt Kitty and Mr. Greenfield, but she would have had no idea what she was missing if Mr. Ellis had not offered to bring her here. The air was fragrant with the scents of the flowers. No one else was strolling the paths now. Probably the picnic fare upon which they had all feasted had made them content just to sit and relax.

"I did not notice any of this from the gig yesterday, or even from the boat," she said. "How unobservant of me. But these paths are meant to be walked and enjoyed with all the senses, not just admired from afar." Bees hummed all around them but were far more interested in the flowers than in the two humans who were admiring them.

"The park was very well designed," he said. "At first glance it may appear to be little more than open, green countryside, though *tamed* countryside. And that was intentional. Nature at its most unspoiled can be very soothing. But there are areas of enhanced loveliness, like this path around the lake, and the poplar walk to the east—you may have observed it through the window of your room—or even the courtyard at the center of the house. They concentrate the attention upon how astonishingly beautiful individual flowers or beds and flowering bushes can be. It is possible for nature and art to work together in a pleasing harmony."

The sun was sparkling on the lake water. Nicholas was out there in one of the boats with Ariel Wexford, the colonel's daughter.

"It must be hard work pushing my chair," Jennifer said. "Shall we sit in the grotto for a while? I hope you will not get blisters on your hands."

They had not spoken a great deal since they left the far side of the lake. It had not been an uncomfortable silence, however, for she had been drinking in the sights and sounds and smells of the park around her, and he had probably needed all his breath to push her chair.

"If you see me in the coming days wearing fat white mittens on both hands," he said as he stepped inside the grotto, moved back one of the benches, and wheeled her chair inside, "you will know that you were correct." He turned her chair slightly so that she could look outward with ease, and sat on the bench at the other side of the table. "I am sorry I have no wine to serve you. Or even lemonade."

"I ate and drank my fill not an hour ago," she said, removing her bonnet and setting it on the far end of the table. The air felt deliciously cool on her head. "Why is it that food tastes so much more appetizing outdoors than in?"

He was wearing his coat over his shirt, she noticed, but neither a waistcoat nor a neckcloth. She wondered if his shirt had dried before he pulled the coat back on. He must have felt very uncomfortable when he stepped out of the water with his little girl, dripping wet. He had probably not expected to be soaked, since the water where the children had played was quite shallow. He had obviously not brought any dry clothes from the house with him. Jennifer had felt quite breathless at the sight of him, feet bare beneath his pantaloons, his shirt transparent with wetness and clinging to every impressive muscle in his chest and arms.

She had fully amended her earlier impression of him. There was nothing ordinary about Mr. Ben Ellis. Not about his person and not about his looks. He was actually quite gorgeous—though no one else ever seemed to notice. He had indeed perfected the art of going largely unnoticed. She was sure it must be deliberate. He had mingled with the guests today. He had smiled and made conversation and offered plates of food and fetched drinks. But it had all been done unobtrusively. She had been left with the impression that everyone liked him but almost no one really *knew* him. She had no idea how he did it.

"I have been hoping all afternoon to have the chance of a word with you," she said. "You will never guess what I did this morning."

"Let me see." He folded his arms on the tabletop. "Your secret is out, alas. You went with Pippa to call upon Sally Holland—Sally *Roberts*, I should say—and Mrs. Holland. It was brave of you to go, though I daresay you did not have to suffer the embarrassment of seeing Cam. He would have been in the smithy working. And I must apologize again, Lady Jennifer—"

"But I *did* see him." She laughed as she interrupted him. "I went specifically to see him, in fact. I took Pippa with me, and she suggested asking Mrs. Roberts to join us. I daresay she asked her mother to come too, and Mrs. Holland brought *Mr.* Holland. A full family gathering."

Mr. Ellis leaned back on the bench, visibly grimacing. "I *am* so sorry," he said. "What did I start with such careless disregard for your privacy?"

"But I am the one who started it," she said. She was enjoying herself enormously. "Well, perhaps not quite. You may rightly claim credit for that, I suppose, but I continued it. The smithy is rather large, is it not? Yet this morning it seemed quite crowded with all the Hollands in it as well as Mr. Rogers, the cobbler; Mr. Taylor, the carpenter; and Dr. Isherwood, the village physician. And Pippa and me, of course."

He gazed at her, openly aghast, and Jennifer laughed again.

"It was a scene worthy of farce," she told him. "Mrs. Holland insisted upon running for a very large pink blanket and making a sort of tent of it to guard my modesty, but everyone had a look anyway and made a comment and pointed and gestured, every bit as though I were some sort of new *farming* machine that needed adjusting. It was all so impersonal it was hardly even embarrassing. And then Mr. Rogers was sketching and the others were all looking over his shoulders and stabbing fingers down onto the paper making suggestions and disagreeing and raising their voices to be heard over everyone else. That was when Mrs. Holland insisted upon sending her son running to fetch the doctor."

"Good God." He groaned and pressed his palms to his eyes.

"To cut a very long story a little shorter, Mr. Ellis," she said, "the verdict was as I expected. My leg and foot can never be straightened or lengthened to match my left leg. But they all knew *that* as well as I did even before they started, and Dr. Isherwood strictly forbade anyone to try—not that anyone had suggested such a thing. There is little hope that I will ever walk much better than I do now, which is almost not at all. Certainly I will never be able to discard my crutches to engage in a footrace about this lake or to waltz in a London ballroom. But I take encouragement from those two pairs of words—*little* hope and *much* better."

She paused to smile at him, but he still had his palms pressed to his eyes. He was shaking his head slightly.

"The leg brace will not work at all," she said. "The idea has been abandoned. The shoe will not solve every problem. But with a shoe carefully made to fit the curve of my foot and raise it a few inches, there may be a possibility that I can walk in some fashion. Better than I can now, anyway. Dr. Isherwood suggested that a single crutch for my right arm, carefully made so that it will not easily slip from my grasp, might actually work better than *two* crutches since it will brace the side of me that needs bracing. Though he did make me promise that I will consult my own physician before making extensive use of any of these inventions, which the other men are quite convinced they can produce within the next week. I did tell them about the cushion you made for me and explained how the combined firmness and softness of it worked well for my foot. I do not want an iron sole on my shoe that weighs half a ton, after all. Imagine if I were to step upon someone's foot."

He rubbed his palms over his eyes before folding his arms on the table and looking at her. "Curse me for being an interfering busybody," he said. "It must have been excruciatingly distressing for you, Lady Jennifer. And I suppose *that* is a vast understatement. Only to be told that there is little hope of success. I do not even know how I can ask your forgiveness."

"Oh, but I enjoyed myself enormously," she told him, reaching out one hand to rub his arm. "They were all so *earnest* and so eager to do something for me, Mr. Ellis. And even if what they produce helps just a little, it will be a gigantic something to me. I do not expect miracles. Dr. Isherwood was surprised, though, that none of the grand physicians who have tended me most of my life have suggested anything that may actually *help* me. They have merely murmured soothing words and assured me that I am a brave woman but that I must relax and allow those who love me to look after me. But what I realized at the smithy this morning—and what I began to realize yesterday when you came to suggest that I drive the gig around the park—is I have been a passive participant in my own immobility for years when really all that is wrong with me is that I have *one* useless leg."

She realized suddenly that her hand was still on his arm and slid it away, hoping he had not noticed.

"At the *very* least," she said, "you have shown me that I need not be entirely helpless. I can drive myself about in my own gig."

"I daresay," he said, "you can be driven anywhere you want anytime with a simple request or command."

She leaned back in her chair. "No," she said, frowning. "Please do not do that, Mr. Ellis. Do not do what everyone else in my life has done since that wretched illness came calling on me. Anytime *you* want you can get to your feet and propel yourself wherever you wish to go, whether it be across a room or on a five-mile walk, you can mount a horse and ride. You can drive yourself in any sort of vehicle. You do not have to enlist the help of anyone. Even with a gig I will have to be lifted in and lifted out—unless, that is, I can become more effective on my crutches. But I want more than what I have always had. I do not want the rest of my life to depend totally upon servants and family members. I want at least *some* independence. Do you wonder why Mr. Taylor was at the smithy too this morning? The carpenter?"

"Curiosity?" he said. "He lives above the smithy. Probably all the commotion under his feet brought him down."

"No." She laughed. "He was sent for. When you took me driving in the gig yesterday, you gave me a wild idea. You explained that the large wheels made the vehicle safe and stable, almost impossible to tip over. I made a joke about having them fixed to the sides of my chair so that I could propel myself about. But afterward I could not stop thinking about it. I asked Mr. Holland what he thought. Neither he nor his father was very encouraging. They said it would be impossible to change the size of the wheels on my chair. But they sent for Mr. Taylor anyway, and he knew something about Bath chairs and a few other chairs that might be similar to what I had in my mind. And they were at it again—all the men excited and talking at once and sketching a new chair that might work for me—something with which I could propel myself forward and back and even perhaps in different directions, though *that* idea sent them into a frenzy of argument and discussion and more sketches. And it would have to be something I could stop in the event that I suddenly found myself at the top of a steep hill with the prospect of becoming a screaming missile hurtling toward the bottom."

At last he was laughing. She joined him.

"So they are going to design a new chair for you?" he asked.

"Yes," she said. "They did not believe this chair could be adapted. But such is their enthusiasm that they are convinced they can have a new one ready before Aunt Kitty and I return to Amberwell. It may not work at all, Mr. Ellis, and even if it does, it may be a monstrosity and is bound to be more cumbersome than this chair and more difficult for poor Bruce to haul about. I do *not* expect miracles. But oh—" She stopped and bit her lower lip and stretched both hands across the table without realizing she was doing it. "It feels so wonderful to dream on the outside of myself instead of always just deep on the inside so that other people will not pity me over the impossibility of it all. No one called me an idiot or looked at me as though I had sprouted an extra head. Not even Pippa or Mrs. Holland, who seems to be a very sensible sort of woman. She is the one who thought of the necessity of my having a way to stop the new chair once I had set it in motion."

He took both her hands in his and squeezed them. His hands were large and strong and warm, rather as she had expected them to be. She looked down at them, and something in her very absurdly envied his daughter, who could grasp these hands whenever she wished—and walk right into his arms. And be safe and at home and happy.

"I wonder," he said, "if I have unleashed a monster on the world.

Perhaps people should be warned to stay clear of English roads and lanes if you happen to be in the vicinity." He grinned at her, but then suddenly looked embarrassed and released her hands. "If you ever learn to swim, people will have to be warned to stay far away from lakes and the sea."

Jennifer, feeling uncomfortable at his closeness, looked away toward the lake. Idris Rhys was in one of the boats now with his wife. Bertrand, Viscount Watley, was on the island with Barbara Rutledge. He saw them in the grotto and raised an arm to wave to them. They both waved back.

"I have talked about nothing but myself since we arrived here," Jennifer said. "What of you, Mr. Ellis?"

"Thirty-two questions," he said.

She knew exactly what he was talking about. "Numbered points?" she asked.

"Yes. I have atrocious letter-writing skills," he said. He was still looking out at the lake while drumming the fingertips of one hand on the tabletop. "I will see what he has to say, if anything."

"Have you told anyone else?" she asked him. "Any of your family?"

"No," he said. "They would not understand."

"Are you sure?" The Wares seemed to her to be an exceptionally close and loving family.

"No." His fingers stopped drumming. "Of course I am not sure. Though actually I *am*. I know they *would* understand. What I am not sure of is whether I want them to. The relationship between them and me would change."

They would no longer see him as quiet, contented, reliable Ben, but as *vulnerable* Ben. He would find that hard to bear, she thought. He had lived all his life here hidden away inside himself, counting his blessings, adoring his father until he could no longer do so, but always hurting because he was different, because he did not quite belong, because he did not know *where* he belonged. All of which he believed his family did not understand.

"They would feel sorry for me," he said.

"And that would never do?" she asked softly.

"No," he said, getting abruptly to his feet, pushing back the bench with the backs of his knees as he did so. He went to stand in the doorway, his shoulder propped against the beam that held up the roof on one side. "It would not. There is nothing for them to feel sorry about. Though I do regret confiding in you yesterday. I did it impulsively, and I wish I had not."

"I was unable to tell you *what* to do, of course," she said. "But I do believe that speaking to me helped you clarify your thoughts, Mr. Ellis, and put an end to your procrastination. So please do not be sorry. You and I have no relationship to be changed by what you have told me. And I do not pity you. Why should I? You have made what seems to me a good life, and I know you appreciate it. You have your own home and your daughter. You are an excellent father. We all have things missing from our lives, things that could drag us down into deep depression if we allowed them to. It is the nature of living. There is no such thing as the perfect life or happily ever after. And listen to me delivering this inspiring sermon to an audience of one."

He turned his head to smile at her before looking back across the lake.

"Your audience of one *is* listening to you," he said. "What is missing from your life, apart from the ability to walk and run and fly? Though they are big enough things in themselves, bigger than the missing half of my identity. What else is missing? You said yesterday that you are twenty-five years old. But you are unmarried. Have you never wanted to be? Surely as the granddaughter of a duke and as a woman of some wealth, if I guess correctly, you have had offers."

Oh goodness. No real gentleman would dream of asking her such a thing.

"Look at me, Mr. Ellis," she said, and waited until he had turned his head. "I am thin. I pass my days on a bed or a sofa or chair. I occasionally have relapses into spells of muscle pain. They can last for days or sometimes even weeks. I am neither pretty nor beautiful. My hair is of a color that is never, ever in fashion. But I am wealthy—*very* wealthy—and well born. I am *Lady* Jennifer Arden. My brother is the Duke of Wilby. *Of course* I have had offers. But why would any man want to marry me?"

"You imply that the answer must be your money and your rank in society," he said. "People, both men and women, marry for those reasons all the time. But they are not necessarily the *only* reasons. Often there are affection and attraction too, or at least the hope of companionship. Have you never been tempted to accept any of the offers?"

"Yes," she said, smiling rather bleakly. "Last year when I was in London with Aunt Kitty. When I met Pippa and *she* met Luc. Yes, I was tempted. He was handsome and had a perfect physique. He was elegant. He was charming and attentive and full of vitality. He was of good birth and breeding. He did not deny that his primary reason for seeking my acquaintance was my money—his father had frittered away a fortune. But he claimed to like me, even to love me. I had no real reason to doubt him. And I believed I was in love with him."

"You *believed*?"

"Yes," she said. "How can one know for sure? What *is* romantic love, after all? I refused his marriage offer, and my heart ached terribly afterward. Sometimes it still does. Though of course, hearts do not literally break."

"Why did you refuse him?" he asked.

"He never stopped smiling," she said. "He had lovely white teeth. He had a dazzling smile. But I do not believe I ever saw him without it. Except after I had said no."

"Perhaps," he said, "he will yet prove the constancy of his affections."

"Doubtful," she said. "He married a considerable heiress from Bristol shortly after Christmas."

"Ah," he said. "Then you did the right thing."

"Yes," she said. "Oh, look."

She nodded toward the lake, where his daughter was seated in one of the boats with Stephanie while Clarence Ware rowed.

Mr. Ellis raised one arm, as did Jennifer. The child waved both arms.

"Papa," she screeched. "Look at me."

"I see you." He laughed and lowered his voice. "I am very thankful that both Clarence and Steph are strong swimmers."

"And you?" Jennifer asked. "Do you have any plans to remarry, Mr. Ellis?" He had a home of his own by the sea, a sizable manor, apparently, with lovely views. There was farmland too. He had a daughter. And he was still a young man, in his early thirties, she would guess.

"Yes." He grimaced. "It is one reason why I decided to come here this summer when I had originally planned to stay home and settle in more fully there. I had hoped to choose a bride by now—pending her acceptance of my offer, of course. I am always very aware that any woman I do ask may say no, as you did to your smiling swain. I must remember not to smile too much. However, I cannot decide among three possible candidates. Reason it out as I may, I can arrive at no clear answer."

"Three?" She gazed at him in some amazement. "There are *three* women you would like as a wife, Mr. Ellis, but you cannot choose among them? Perhaps you should set up a harem."

He winced. "I know it seems incredible," he said.

"And do you *love* all three?" she asked.

"If you speak of romantic love," he said, "I agree with what you said earlier. Since it relies entirely upon emotion, it is surely a poor measure by which to choose a potential life partner. I seek other things, Lady Jennifer—comfort, companionship, someone of unassuming, dignified demeanor. Someone who will take firm but quiet command of the household. Someone who will be a good mother to Joy and our future children. I am sorry. A list of attributes does not convey what it is I hope for. I do not look for anyone of outstanding beauty or obvious attractions or superior birth or wealth. I want someone—"

"Ordinary?" she suggested when he could not seem to find the word he wanted.

"To match myself," he said. "Yes."

It was strange, Jennifer thought, that until a couple of days or so ago she would have agreed that indeed he was a very ordinary man, so much so that a person rarely noticed his existence. But now she knew he was very far from being ordinary. Of course, perhaps no one was if one had the time and opportunity to get to know them in rather more depth than a few social conversations could reveal.

"Were you in love with your wife?" she asked him.

He gazed out at the lake again, empty of boats at the moment.

"No," he said after some hesitation. "My feelings for Marjorie went deeper than that. I chose her at first because, being in the Peninsula during the war, constantly moving with the army from place to place, I felt the need of— Forgive me. I sometimes forget to whom I speak."

"—a woman," she said, completing the thought for him.

"Yes," he said. "But I was never one to avail myself of the services of . . . a whore. My mother was one, and I believe I loved my mother. I believe she loved me. Marjorie was a widow. She was hardworking and spirited, but she kept much to herself. She took no nonsense from men who treated her with less than the respect she demanded. She never flirted. When I asked her and she said yes, I believe we both understood that it would be for the long term and an exclusive relationship, though there was no question of marriage. She saw me as a gentleman and far above her expectations. I never thought of her or described her as my mistress. I did not love her. I just needed her and liked her. When she found that she was with child, she did not tell me. She explained afterward that she had assumed I would cast her off once I knew, and the prospect of being alone again saddened her. When I *did* find out—I was an incredible slowtop—I went and found the regimental chaplain and we were married that same day. Joy was born less than three months later. I am not sure I realized fully just how much I cared for my wife until I no longer had her. Though I did tell her when she was very ill and dying that I loved her, that I would never forget her, that I would never let Joy forget her. And I was speaking the truth. Love grows within a good relationship. It is finding and nurturing that relationship that is the tricky part. I wish I could know with which of the three women, all of whom I like and respect, I could build that sort of marriage again."

"But you did not think of any of those things when you chose your first wife," she told him. "You looked, you liked, you offered, and you did not even think about relationships or marriage until circumstances drove you into matrimony—though I do not suppose anyone would have expected you to marry her. Even she did not."

"Am I overthinking this choice, then?" he asked her.

Poor man. He had loved and lost, and now he did not know quite how to make his way forward into a settled and contented future. Which described her too to a certain degree, she supposed. She had rejected her last, best chance of a happy life as a married lady, perhaps even as a mother. And now what? Learn to walk and propel herself about in a wheeled chair and in a gig? Perhaps even learn to swim? Would any of those things, or all of them, be enough?

It was a question that frightened her, though that might be too strong a word. She was twenty-five years old. It was still a youthful age for a man. But not for a woman. It established her firmly upon the shelf. She was a *spinster*. Ghastly word.

"We are in danger of making each other very maudlin, Mr. Ellis," she said. "Should we continue on our way? It is a good thing, perhaps, that we have been spotted here by quite a few people or your family and my aunt and brother would surely be sending out search parties by now."

"I suppose we have been gone rather a long time," he said, pushing his shoulder away from the beam. "I beg your pardon. I never talk to anyone else the way I talk to you. I suspect you can say the same of me."

He came inside and bent down to pick up her bonnet, which had fallen unnoticed to the floor. He handed it to her without first straightening up, and suddenly their faces were very close. She gazed into his, which was not ordinary at all, and he gazed back. She could feel the heat of him, and she could feel her own heat and a desperate longing. A mere few inches separated their mouths, and more than anything else in her life, she believed, she wanted him to close that gap. She wanted to know . . . She wanted . . .

He jerked upright and went to stand behind her chair while she pulled on her bonnet and tied the ribbons beneath her chin.

Neither said a word as he wheeled the chair back out into the sunshine and then returned to place the benches neatly against the table. They set out along the northern path beside the lake, back to the picnic site and the safety of other people.

"If it will make you feel any better," he said a few minutes later, "I am quite sure you made the right decision last year. You distrusted the man's smile. It may seem like a very trivial reason for doubt, but one should always trust one's instincts. Something—someone—will come along for you one day, and you will be glad you waited. And incidentally, your hair color may never be fashionable, but it will always be glorious."

She laughed, though she was very glad he was behind her chair and could not therefore see her blinking furiously to clear her blurred vision.

"As for you, Mr. Ellis," she said, "if you cannot decide among three women, then perhaps you have been right not to decide at all. One day a fourth woman is going to come along, and you will no longer be in any doubt that she is the one you have been waiting for."

"And they all lived happily ever after," he said.

They both laughed, and the horrible awkwardness of that totally unexpected moment of awareness and desire in the grotto was put behind them.

His daughter was dashing along the path toward them while Devlin, holding one of Luc and Pippa's twins, watched her from farther back. She skipped the last few yards.

"Papa," she cried. "Did you see me in the boat? Cousin Clarence said I was almost too heavy to row. He is silly."

"I saw you," Mr. Ellis said, such tenderness in his voice that Jennifer blinked her eyes again. How *fortunate* the woman was going to be who . . .

He had stopped pushing her chair. And the child, without any hesitation, as though it was the most natural thing in the world to do, climbed up onto it, and beamed up at Jennifer as she burrowed in beside her. Jennifer wrapped one arm about the child and drew her closer.

"I ride back with you," she said, and puckered her lips for a kiss.

CHAPTER ELEVEN

❧

Olwen Cox told Joy during the picnic that there was a litter of six puppies on the farm adjoining their own. The Coxes had confirmed the story. So had Stephanie, who had been told of them at choir practice by the granddaughter of the owners of the farm. The puppies were too young to be separated from their mother yet, but the farmers were in active search of good homes for all six after they were weaned. There were already two other dogs on the farm in addition to the puppies' mother.

Joy wanted to see those puppies—with a certain purpose in mind, Ben suspected. He had been promising for some time that she might have a dog as soon as she was old enough to participate in its care. Stephanie was interested too. Nicholas proved quite agreeable to her persuasions, and off they went the following morning, Joy squashed between them in the gig.

"Just to take a look," Stephanie said as Ben waved them on their way.

"Just to take a look, Papa," Joy said, beaming at him.

"Just to take a look, meaning *I want one, please, please, Papa, and I will have a major tantrum if I do not get one,"* Ben said cheerfully as he and Devlin made their way back to the carriage house to inspect the archery equipment that had been stored there since the last summer fete and was almost certain to need some attention before it could be used again this year.

"I predict she will not need to throw a tantrum," Devlin said. "She appears to have an accommodating papa. You are contented at Penallen, then, Ben?"

"I really am," Ben told him. "It is the right size for me and it is in exactly the right place. I doubt I will ever tire of looking out over the sea and breathing in the salt air through open windows. I have some good neighbors, a few of whom are becoming real friends. And it is not very far from here."

"I am glad to hear that is important to you," Devlin said as they inspected the bows to discover which of them had warped or grown brittle since the last time they were used.

Ben looked curiously at him. That was a strange thing to say. It was important to Dev too, then? "It is to me," he said. "And it is to Joy. All her known family apart from me are here or at least come here for visits, just as I do. Are you intending to string the bows today?"

"No," Devlin said. "We will leave that until a day or two before the fete. We had better give the arrows a look, though. We do not want them flying off in unpredictable directions even when they have been aimed at a bull's-eye. Some people used to bring their own equipment, of course, and may do it again this year. I wonder if Matthew Taylor will still be as invincible as he used to be. Eight years is a long time. Can it possibly be that long, Ben? Though in some ways those fetes we looked forward to so eagerly and worked so hard for seem a lifetime ago. Like something that happened to other people."

"They were good times," Ben said.

"They were," Devlin agreed. "Shall we take a walk out to the poplar alley and do some measuring and marking?"

The archery contests had always been held there, well away from the house and a safe distance from where most people would be wandering and participating in the myriad entertainments of the day. No one would have enjoyed having to duck arrows.

"I miss you, Ben," Devlin said as they walked. "I miss Pippa too, of course. And Nick. And Owen, though he does still come home for lengthy spells over the holidays. I suppose it is the inevitable result of growing up, which we all desperately wanted to do during our childhood and youth. Adults were always telling us that childhood is the best time of life, but of course we never believed them. We will probably tell our own children and grandchildren the same thing."

"You are the one who was designated to remain here," Ben said. "The rest of us have naturally scattered or soon will to find our own places of belonging. I have found mine."

Devlin gave him a sidelong glance. "And you are happy," he said.

"I am," Ben told him again. "Though I still miss Marjorie."

"She was a good woman," Devlin said.

"Yes." There seemed to be a hint of concern in Devlin's voice and manner—concern that Ben, though older than he, was one of the siblings who had been forced to seek out his own home and way of life while Ravenswood and all it entailed was his, Devlin's, by right of the fact that he was their father's eldest *legitimate* son. It would pass to Gareth after him and then to *his* eldest son and so on down the generations. Perhaps Dev understood better than Ben had realized.

"Do you remember the letter that was awaiting me when Joy and I arrived here?" he asked.

"The one from your old school friend—who did not know after all this time that you now live at Penallen?" Devlin said.

Ah. He had recognized the lie, then, had he?

"It was from a man called Vincent Kelliston," Ben told him. "He claims to be my brother. My *half* brother. He claims that we had the same mother, who was married to his father, a brute of a man. She ran away from both of them to go to London, where she met *my* father. Kelliston senior died recently, and the son wants to establish some sort of communication with me. That was about the sum total of what the letter said."

They were at one end of the alley, which, to Ben's experienced eye, looked as if it could do with a good mowing, though it was undeniably lush and green. No doubt it would be made perfect for the fete. Sunlight was glinting off the glass windows of the summerhouse at the far end.

Devlin was frowning when he turned his head after a short silence. His eyes looked troubled. "Ah, Ben," he said. "Do you believe it is the truth?"

"Why would he say it if it were not?" Ben asked.

"Does it *matter* to you?" Devlin asked.

"It does," Ben told him. "Whenever I asked Papa to tell me about my mother, and I did ask over and over when I was a child and even a few times when I was older, he could never tell me anything except that she was beautiful and he loved her. And I believe *could* is the correct word. It was not that he *would* not tell me. He was not interested in her as a person, Dev. She was just a— She served only one function in his life."

"You do not know that for sure," Devlin said. "He felt a real affection for a large number of people. Perhaps he really did love her."

"She was his *whore*," Ben said harshly. "She was without real identity as a person. She was without a story. Without a history. He did not care enough to discover *who* she was. Yes, it matters to me. I long to restore the dignity of those things to her even though she is long dead. She was my *mother*. I do not even *remember* her. But I will always remember that she loved me."

"Good God." The troubled look in Devlin's eyes had intensified, and he took a step forward suddenly and caught Ben up in a tight hug. Ben stood frozen for a moment. He could not remember such a thing happening before. He and his father and brothers had always treated one another with affection, but the brothers had almost never *hugged*. Yet now—God damn it!—Ben was gulping and fighting tears.

"I blame myself so much," Devlin said. "I have always avoided any mention of your mother or of your unique position in this family or the fact that your very name is different from ours. I meant it as a mark of affection. Of acceptance. You are my *brother*, dash it all to hell. I have always assumed you wished to avoid any mention of your origins. That was almost *criminal* of me. She was your mother, half of yourself and your own history. Good God, can you ever forgive my . . . *denseness*, Ben? What was her *name*?"

They *had* talked about his mother, Ben remembered, eight years ago when Devlin had wanted to know why Ben insisted upon leaving home with him and accompanying him to the Peninsula. But it had happened just the once, at a very emotional time for both of them.

"Jane," Ben said. "At least, that was the name she gave Papa. Jane Ellis. Yet, according to the letter, her surname must have been Kelliston. Maybe Jane was not her real name either. It is a very simple name, is it not? Jane Ellis. Just like mine: Ben Ellis. At least Joy has *Marjorie* between her two names."

"What have you done about the letter?" Devlin asked.

"It left me with far more questions than answers," Ben told him as his brother took a step back but continued to give him his full attention. "Not least of which is *why* he wrote to me. If Mother had run away and abandoned you years ago and had then had a bastard child with a lover, would *you* want to have anything to do with that bastard now, Dev? I was tempted to ignore the letter, but I have sent off a reply with thirty-two questions, all in point form so none of them are lost. I should have added a thirty-third. I ought to have asked him my mother's name. The next move is his now. Lady Jennifer Arden believes I did the right thing."

"*Jenny?*"

"Sometimes," Ben said, "it is easier to talk to a stranger than to one's own family."

Devlin closed his eyes and clenched them tightly for a few moments. "I deserve that," he said when he opened them again. "To my shame, you are right. I am sure you remember how out in the Peninsula I would never, ever talk about the family and what had happened here. And after I came back I had a very hard time talking to the people I had always loved most dearly but was convinced meant nothing at all to me any longer. Gwyneth was my savior. She flatly refused to let me get away with *that* attitude, Ben. Good God.

One is not supposed to have favorite siblings, and I love all of mine. But you have always had a special place in my heart. You must know that."

"Yes," Ben admitted.

"Then do not be an ass any longer," Devlin told him. "And I will do my damnedest not to be one either. *Talk* to me. I will not let you get away with not doing so any longer, in fact."

Ben's mind touched upon Cam at the smithy and the cobbler and the carpenter and what they were all apparently busy doing or trying to do. But this was not the time to raise that particular issue. Besides, it was not just his secret.

"Are we going to stand here all morning and leave our measuring tapes neatly wound up and unused?" he asked.

They spent more than an hour measuring distances and marking the places, a little more than halfway along the alley, where the targets would be set up and those, less than halfway along, from which the archers would let their arrows fly. They decided where the alley would be roped off so that spectators could stand close enough to have a good view but far enough back to be safe from errant arrows.

It was a good long while before they finished and returned to the house.

Meanwhile, Lady Jennifer was preparing to go for a drive with her brother. Owen and Bertrand had gone fishing with Colonel Wexford on the colonel's land. James Rutledge was to join them there. Most of the women were in the ballroom, finalizing plans for the ball, in particular the floral decorations. Lucas was taking his sister for a drive in Devlin's curricle over the crest of the hills that formed the border between Ravenswood and Cartref. There were some spectacular views to be had from up there, they had been told.

"You trust my driving skills, do you, Jen?" Lucas asked as he turned the curricle up into the hills. He grinned at her before giving his full attention to the road that climbed ahead of them.

"Of course I do." She patted his arm. "I will keep in mind that you have a wife and two young children for whom to live. Besides, I never heard of you being a reckless driver."

"I have been assured," he said, "that this road is well maintained and wide enough along its whole length to be perfectly safe despite appearances. The fact that for a while the hills fall away quite steeply on both sides accounts for the sense of danger one gets. It makes the road seem like a ribbon when really it is not. When we get there, imagine that there are hedgerows on either side instead of empty space."

Jennifer laughed. "Then we might as well have driven along a country lane," she said. "We came for the views, did we not? I think I would love to drive a gig over here."

It was his turn to laugh, as though she had made a joke.

Already Jennifer could see the square, varicolored fields surrounding Cartref like a patchwork quilt to their right and the massive east and south wings of Ravenswood way off across the park to their left.

"Jenny," Lucas said after a minute or two of silence while she looked and he concentrated on his driving. "Are you happy at Amberwell, just you and Aunt Kitty alone together?"

"Fortunately we share a deep affection," she said. "We are comfortable with each other. We laugh at the same things. We enjoy doing the same things."

But she sometimes wondered if her aunt had somehow become trapped into living with her. Cousin Gerald, her son, was still unmarried and had hinted a few times that he would like to have his mother back home or at least living in the dower house he kept ready for her close by. And surely Aunt Kitty would go more often to Ireland to visit Cousin Beatrice, her daughter, and her son-in-law and grandsons if she did not feel obliged to stay at Amberwell with her niece. She always said it was because she dreaded the boat journey to Ireland. But while Jennifer knew that to be true, she was not convinced it was the real reason.

Why was it, she wondered, that she had only recently become aware of her total dependence upon the members of her family? It had been unavoidable while she was a child. But she was twenty-five now. Most women her age were married with children and settled in their husbands' homes. She, on the other hand, had become a lifelong burden upon others. And therefore a burden to herself.

Did she have Mr. Ellis to thank—or blame—for opening up her eyes to the reality of her life and dependence?

"I am so glad you came here to Ravenswood," Lucas said. "I have missed you. So has Phil. The two of you became firm friends very quickly last year, did you not?"

"Yes," she said. "It happens that way sometimes."

"We would love to have you live with us at Greystone," he said. "I know you are attached to Amberwell and are happy there. But I am your *brother*, Jen, and Phil is your friend—and your sister-in-law. Emmy and Chris are your niece and nephew. I know Greystone seems a bit more austere than Amberwell, and it has never been your home. But it was Grandmama and Grandpapa's, and now it is ours. Even in the few months we have been there, we have made it into *our* home. At least, Phil has. I merely approve and enjoy, though she makes no change without first consulting me. We can make you happy there, Jen. And you will make us happy. You will never be in our way or we in yours. You may have your own suite of rooms and be as private there as you choose to be."

"Oh."

He had taken her by surprise. The offer had been made back in the spring, it was true, but it had not been pressed on her then. After Luc and Pippa married last year, they had come to live at Amberwell, and Aunt Kitty had planned to move to Greystone to be with Grandmama and Grandpapa, her parents, who were aging and ailing. But they had both died while everyone was at Greystone this past spring for the christening of the twins. And suddenly it had been necessary for Luc and Pippa, the new Duke and Duchess of Wilby, to remain there, and poor Aunt Kitty had been forced to change her plans yet again and return to Amberwell with Jennifer. She had first come there more than a decade ago, after her brother, Lucas and Jennifer's father, died suddenly in a riding accident only a year after their mother died in childbed. Luc himself, heir to the dukedom, had been borne off to live with his grandparents so he could learn all he would need to know when he succeeded to the title. Jennifer had remained at Amberwell, and Aunt Kitty had raised her.

Poor Aunt Kitty, Jennifer thought again, though she was not accustomed to thinking of her aunt with pity. She had given up years of her life to her niece's care, with never a word of complaint. Now it must seem there was no way out for her.

"Do you want to take some time to think about it?" Lucas asked, easing the horses to a halt. "Just *look* at this, Jen. The view fairly take's one's breath away, does it not? Though the hills do not look particularly high from down there."

"I so hate being a burden," she said, something she *never* said aloud, for saying it would only make her seem more of a burden. Now she had said it.

He patted the back of her hand and then slid his fingers around into her palm and squeezed. "You are never that," he said. "You must never even *think* of yourself that way. You are my *sister*. I love you more dearly than I can say."

"I know," she said. "I am the most fortunate of mortals. Luc, do you think I could ever walk—even slowly and clumsily? Or ride or drive or swim? Or fly?" She laughed as her eyes alit upon a pair of birds too distant to identify as they flew high on the Cartref side of the hills.

"All your life you will have a host of people only too happy to take you wherever you wish to go," he said. "All you have to do is ask. You *know* that. And you are never, ever a burden. We all admire your courage and your ever-cheerful disposition."

He had not answered her questions. Or actually, perhaps he had. He had been tactful enough not simply to say no.

"I drove a gig the day before yesterday," she told him. "All around the park down there. Several miles altogether. I can see the eastern part of the carriage path from up here. But we went west first, all the way past the lake and then around to the line of the trees and lower hills in the north. It was really not difficult. I felt safe and exhilarated. I felt happier than . . . Well, than almost any time I can remember. I felt *free*."

She had not intended telling him. Not yet anyway. And she was sure Pippa would have kept her promise not to tell either. Of course his mind focused upon just one word out of all she had told him.

"*We?*" he said.

"Mr. Ellis cleaned and polished the gig to look like new," she said. "He groomed a quiet horse until its coat gleamed. He sat beside me the whole way while I held the ribbons, and I felt perfectly safe. Oh, and he made a big cushion, which is firm but with a slight softness to it, to brace my right foot against the footboard. My body felt quite balanced as I drove."

Again he seemed to hear only the one small detail.

"*Ben Ellis?*" he said. "He will answer to me for this. By God he will. He could have got you killed, Jen. At the very least he might have caused serious damage to your leg."

"Serious damage has already been done to my leg," she told him. They both seemed to have forgotten the views to either side of them. "Nothing is going to change that, Luc. But it has occurred to me recently that I have allowed one leg—not even both—to blight my whole life. Why should I be forever immobile except when someone is obliging enough to carry or wheel or drive me from place to place? I will never be *normal*, but even if all I ever do to help myself is drive a gig, I will have done something to fight back against a— a *stupid disease.*"

He did not seem mollified. Indeed, it looked to Jennifer as though her brother was whipping himself into a rage.

"Whatever gave him the idea?" he asked. "The *insane* idea. He just came upon you one day and offered to provide you with a gig and horse *and* a damned cushion, and bore you off as soon as all our backs were turned? It was the morning we went off to the Greenfields, I suppose, and Aunt Kitty and my mother-in-law and Gwyneth went to Cartref. How *dared* he? I do not care if he is somehow special to the family here, Jen, just because his damned father got him on one of his whores. He is *not* welcome to put dangerous, insane ideas into my sister's head."

Oh goodness!

"Perhaps we should move on," Jennifer suggested, and he shook his head as though to clear it before giving the horses the signal to start again. "And I would appreciate it, Luc, if you would watch your language in my hearing."

"I beg your pardon for that," he said. "But really, Jen—"

"No," she said. "It is my turn to speak. I shared my dreams with Mr. Ellis when we were sitting together in the courtyard one afternoon. He listened, but not just with sympathy over the fact that absolutely none of those dreams can ever come true. His thoughts took a more practical turn, and he started to think up ways of making some small reality of at least a few of them."

"You have dreamed of riding and driving and . . . *flying*?" he asked her, darting her an incredulous glance. "But you are always so *contented*, Jen."

"Because dreams are for oneself," she said. "If you were confined to a bed or a chair for the rest of your life, would you not dream dreams like mine? Even while being cheerful about the realities of your situation, which could be far worse than they are?"

"He ought at the very least to have consulted me first," Lucas said. "And so I shall inform him."

"Why?" she asked. "I am twenty-five years old, Luc."

"You went off with him yesterday during the picnic for an awfully long time," he said. "I was about to go in search of you. But—"

"But it was to Mr. Ellis alone that it occurred that perhaps I would like to move from the spot where I had been sitting since the start of the picnic," she said. "Not that I expected anyone to think of it. I am *not* complaining. I had company the whole time and was enjoying the outing enormously. But the footpath about the lake is a feast for the senses. I would never have seen it if he had not taken me, for I could not be driven there."

The curricle was descending the northern ridge of the hills to the lowlands of the park where Jennifer had driven herself a couple of days ago.

"Jenny," Lucas said. "You are not starting to fancy that man, are you? Or he you? You must be aware that you would be a huge feather in his cap."

"Because his father got him on one of his whores?" she said.

He winced. "It was unpardonable of me to say those words aloud," he said. "It was probably unpardonable even to think them. I was angry—which is no excuse, I grant you."

"I do not *fancy* him," she said, and surely she spoke the truth. "And he does not fancy me. Why should he? Even apart from my condition, I am about the last person he would consider courting. I would be a constant reminder to him of what he knows all too well. When he took a wife in the Peninsula, he chose a twice-widowed washerwoman, who grew up in a London orphanage. Now he is actively considering three candidates from the neighborhood of his own home for his second wife. One qualification they all have is lowly birth, or at least not high enough on the social scale to make him conscious of his own illegitimacy. You do him a terrible injustice, Luc, when you suspect he is looking to fulfill his social ambitions through me. Please stop suspecting it. I *like* him. Surely I can enjoy a mild friendship with a man without arousing speculation and alarm among my relatives and his."

"I beg your pardon," he said, though he did not sound convinced. "But I *will* have a word with him, Jen. I do not like it that—"

"Then you will need to know everything," she said with a sigh, and proceeded to tell him about the shoe and the crutch that were being designed for her. And the chair. None of which might be successful or even mildly helpful to her. But oh, if she could just wheel herself from one part of a room to another without having to enlist help or tell herself that she was quite content to remain exactly where she was for hours on end. And if she could just walk a few yards every day or so on both feet without lurching awkwardly from side to side and jarring her hip and her back.

If she could just . . .

Fly.

CHAPTER TWELVE

I t rained the following day.

It started with a light drizzle at first light, when most people were still asleep, and turned to a steady rain by breakfast time, when it became the general topic of anxious conversation for miles around. The summer fete was less than a week away. Was there any hope that the hot, sunny weather would return now that it had broken? In *Britain*?

By early afternoon the rain had become a heavy downpour.

But everyone continued with their daily lives. What else was one to do?

The youth choir practiced in the church. Stephanie went, of course. Owen insisted upon giving her a ride in the closed carriage he and Bertrand were taking to Charles Ware's home, where they were going to work on their archery skills with Clarence and a few other young men in a large empty barn.

"You *cannot* turn up at the church dripping like a drowned rat, Steph," Owen said when his sister tried to insist that she would take an umbrella and walk, as she always did. "What is wrong with you these days?"

Such was the insensitivity of the brother next to her in age, who had used to try to reduce her to hysterics by playing practical jokes on her, usually in the form of *creatures*, like the dead mouse he had once dropped at the bottom of her wardrobe. He had never succeeded but had sometimes yelled ignominiously himself when he thrust a foot into one of his boots only to find that it was already inhabited by the frog he had put in *her* boot, or when he awoke in the night to find the spider he had left in her bed taking a shortcut to wherever it was going across his face.

"Nothing at all," she said in answer to his question, accepting the carriage ride with sullen ingratitude.

"I believe your sister dislikes me," Bertrand said after they had set her down outside the church and she ran inside without a word of farewell to either of them.

"Eh?" Owen said. "Steph? Nonsense, Bert. Why would she not like you? Other girls fall all over their feet in their eagerness to get close enough to be noticed. It is enough to make any other fellow doubtful of his own charms. Steph is just weird."

"Lady Stephanie is a very . . . *nice* person," Bertrand said, putting a little emphasis upon the one word, perhaps to suggest that he did not mean she was also a bland person.

"You had better get Brad Danver to show you how to hold the bow and shoot the arrow," Owen said. "He can hit the target nine times out of ten. I have even seen him hit the bull's-eye once or twice, though I daresay those shots were pure accident. My brothers used to say I could not hit the broad side of a barn from twenty feet away, and it pains me to admit they were not far wrong. But a fellow must try. There needs to be a few people willing to take on

Matthew Taylor. And there may be a few girls to impress. Speaking of which, Ariel Wexford has grown into something of a beauty. I remember the time when her teeth were three times too large for her face. To be fair, I suppose mine were too for a time."

The dowager countess and Lady Catherine Emmett went to Cartref despite the rain. Clarissa was in charge of the needlework and wood-carving and baking contests at the fete, but in the spirit of changed times she had decided to work with a committee of ladies, which included Lady Rhys; Mrs. Proctor, the village dressmaker; and Miss Wexford, the colonel's sister. They spent the afternoon drinking tea and planning the displays and the judging and prizes without going off on too many conversational tangents.

Nicholas spent the afternoon out in the stables, cleaning and polishing his equipment and checking and grooming his horse. He was on leave, of course. But he had been a military officer for almost eight years, and certain habits were ingrained in him. And rain was always the worst inducer of rust. The head groom's young son watched wide-eyed from a distance, and occasionally Nicholas would smile at him and beckon him closer to show the lad what he was doing and explain why he was doing it.

"You want to be a soldier when you grow up?" he asked.

"I do, sir," the boy replied. "In your regiment, sir," he added earnestly.

Devlin and Lucas were in the village, paying a call upon Cam Holland, Matthew Taylor, and John Rogers. Cam had summoned the other two to the smithy so that one visit would suffice for all. Ben was not with them. Lucas had had a talk with him, however, and had made it clear that he was *not* pleased. His sister was precious to him, he had explained to Ben. She was *fragile* for obvious reasons. He and the rest of his family had been at pains to give her all the help and support she could possibly need in the difficult life she must live, and she had accepted reality long ago and learned to live a moderately active life and remain cheerful despite her handicap. It was unkind, even cruel, to raise her hopes with wild and unrealistic schemes that must inevitably fail and remind her more than ever of all that was missing from her life.

"Do you believe, then," Ben had asked quietly, "that she was unaware of those things before I . . . interfered?"

"That is not the point," Lucas had said, tight-lipped. "You had no right. You *have* no right. My aunt and I know better than anyone else here or in Boscombe what is good for Lady Jennifer Arden, and I would be obliged if you would refrain from *interfering* further. You used the right word there."

"Does the *anyone else* you refer to include Lady Jennifer herself?" Ben had asked. But he held up a staying hand before Lucas could answer. "Forgive me. That question was out of line and I will not interfere further. But I would beg you to consider something she may have been at pains to hide from you all these years. She has *dreams*."

"She also knows, as most sensible and intelligent people do, that dreams are vastly different from reality," Lucas had said. "A sane person does not even try to blend the two."

"Perhaps." Ben had nodded. "I am sorry. I know your anger stems from your love for your sister. I am sorry I have trodden upon your feelings."

So Ben had taken Joy to see the collie pups again and choose the one she wanted—for of course she wanted one so desperately she had hardly been able to catch her breath when telling him about them yesterday, in particular the littlest one, which squeaked and was *so sweet, Papa.*

They went from there, slightly damp, to the Coxes' farm for Joy to practice running a three-legged race with Andrew Cox, who was her own age. It was an unfortunate pairing, however, as Joy could not seem to understand the concept of matching her long, springy stride to Andrew's slower, more steady steps. She was surprisingly good at the egg and spoon race, which the children ran with old billiard balls David Cox had reshaped to resemble the real thing. While the Cox children spent most of the practice time chasing their oval balls across the floor, Joy dashed for the finish line, only occasionally slowing to juggle her egg securely back into the bowl of the spoon without touching it and only once actually dropping it—to her great chagrin.

Ben would have taken her home after the practices were declared over for the day and lemonade had been drunk and a plateful of biscuits covered with pink icing had been consumed. His daughter and the Cox children had other ideas, however. They wanted to *play*.

"You are quite welcome to leave her here for a while if you wish," Doris Cox said to him in a quiet aside. "I have to go into the village in a while to get a few things from the shop. I have been assured that the rain has not made the road impassable. I will be happy to deliver Joy safely back home. The children love having her. They quarrel less among themselves when she is here."

So Ben returned alone to Ravenswood and stayed in the stables with Nicholas, helping him by cleaning his sword so that not a speck of rust would mar its shine. He put a keen edge and point on the blade and slid it gingerly back into its scabbard after his brother had cast an experienced and critical eye over it.

"I suppose," he said, "you did this a time or two for Dev when you were in the Peninsula with him, though I know you were his batman only in name."

"I did," Ben said. "Are you still happy with life in the military, Nick?"

Nicholas shrugged. "It is the life that was always intended for me," he said. "It is what I know and what I do. On the whole it has been good to me."

It was not a ringing endorsement. Nick had been quieter than usual since coming home, though not unhappy. He had matured from the eager, exuberant boy Ben remembered best.

He had been through innumerable skirmishes and sieges and battles during the Napoleonic Wars, culminating in the Battle of Waterloo last year. He had survived them all. He had no visible scars, though he did walk with a slight limp as the result of one wound that had come very near to killing him. The surgeon to whom he was carried had wanted to take off his leg, but Ben, normally quiet and pacific in nature, had threatened the man with painful consequences, the least of which was death, if he so much as glanced at a saw.

Ben had deserted Devlin for a whole month after that to remain with their severely injured and gravely ill brother and flatly refused to allow him to die.

Since last year Nicholas had been stationed in Paris with the occupying forces.

"Life is quiet here," Nicholas said. "One forgets just how quiet. You do not miss the bustle of army life, Ben?"

"Not at all," Ben said. "I have some good memories, mainly of the camaraderie. I also have a few very sad memories, which will always linger. I have moved on, though. I love Penallen. It is home."

Nicholas nodded, understanding in his eyes. Like Devlin, he had been visibly surprised when he first met Marjorie, who had been Ben's woman for several months at the time. He had approved, though, when Ben had not hesitated to make an honest woman of her after he discovered that she was with child.

"You are an honorable man, Ben," he had said, squeezing his brother's shoulder the first time they met after the deed was done. "And I admire you for it."

"I had better brave the rain and go inside," Ben said now. "I daresay Joy will be home soon, and she will be needing a sleep."

"This rain will do wonders for the crops," Nicholas said. "Dev must be pleased. I'll be in soon too."

Jennifer was in the library, writing a long letter to Charlotte, her sister. Philippa had sat with her for a while, reading a book, but she had gone up to the nursery a short time ago to see if the twins were awake after their nap. She had not returned, so she was no doubt feeding them and playing with them.

Jennifer was in the middle of describing the picnic for her sister's amusement when the door opened and Mr. Ellis's little girl came bursting inside before stopping abruptly.

"Where is Papa?" she asked.

The last Jennifer had heard of him was that he was taking his daughter to see some newborn puppies and then play with the children at the Cox farm. "Have you lost him?" she asked, smiling. "Perhaps he is in the drawing room or has gone to the nursery, looking for you."

"No." The child's curls bounced as she shook her head vigorously. "Not there. I looked. I looked in his room too, but he is not there. Where is he?"

"Did you not come home with him?" Jennifer asked.

"No," Joy said. "I stayed to play with Olwen and Andrew, but

Philip called me a pest and his papa made him stand in the corner and then say sorry. I don't like him. He is eight."

"Ah, that would explain it, then," Jennifer said, cleaning her pen and setting it down beside the blotter. "Eight-year-old boys sometimes think they are vastly better than boys and girls who are three or four."

"Yes," Joy said. "Olwen poked her tongue out at him and crossed her eyes but her papa did not see. I came home with her mama, but I cannot find Papa." Her lower lip wobbled. She looked to be on the verge of tears.

"Well," Jennifer said. "I tell you what. You come and sit down safe in here with me, and I will ring for a servant, who will surely find your papa in no time at all."

"Yes," the child said. But instead of sitting down on the chair Jennifer had indicated, the one Philippa had vacated a short while ago, she wriggled between the desk and Jennifer's chair, climbed up onto the footrest and from there onto Jennifer's lap, where she sat very still and upright.

Jennifer rang the bell on the desktop. Unsurprisingly, it was Bruce who answered the summons. "Bruce," she said. "I believe Mr. Ellis is in the house somewhere, though apparently he is not in the drawing room or the nursery or his own room. Would you find him, please, and inform him that his daughter is in the library with me?"

"Right away, my lady," he said, and left the room, closing the door quietly behind him.

"I wanted Papa to tell me a story about Mama," Joy said, still sounding close to tears.

She was tired, Jennifer realized. She had played with her friends through her usual naptime, and now she had come home weary and wanting her father and a sleep.

"Would you like to snuggle against me until he comes?" Jennifer suggested, setting her arms loosely about the child.

"Yes," the little girl said, and tipped sideways to do just that. "I wanted Papa to tell the story where Mama says *shoo* to the rude man and he goes away and everyone claps and Mama curtsies."

"If he was very rude," Jennifer said, "I daresay I would have clapped for your mama too."

"He *was* rude," Joy said. "He said *right now* and Mama shook her stick at him and said *shoo* and he went." She yawned hugely. "I don't have my cat."

"Your cat?" Jennifer said.

"I want my cat," Joy said. "Aunt Steph made him for me."

Ah. A toy cat.

Bruce tapped on the door before opening it. "Mr. Ellis is nowhere to be found in the house, my lady," he said, "but one of the chambermaids saw his carriage return awhile ago when she was upstairs. He must be outside somewhere, perhaps in the carriage house or stables. Shall I send someone to look?"

Jennifer glanced down at Joy. "I am sure he will be inside soon," she said. "But, Bruce, will you do Miss Ellis the favor of going to the nursery to find the toy cat I believe she likes to hold when she sleeps?"

"Certainly, my lady," he said, and disappeared again.

"Mama *loved* me," Joy said, looking up. "Her hair was like mine."

"Of course she loved you," Jennifer said. "And her hair must have been very pretty."

"Yes," Joy said, and launched into an involved and barely intelligible account of a race in which she ran fast because that was what one was supposed to do in a race but Andrew ran slowly, just like a tortoise, so they both fell down but she was the one who got scolded because Andrew was crying even though there was not a single cut or scrape on his knee or anywhere else. There was another story—or was it the same one?—about eggs that were not eggs, because they would all get broken and the hens would cry, but were balls that looked like eggs but Philip sulked because they were ruined even though his papa explained that they were old balls that were no longer any good for billy.

It must have been a three-legged race she had run so incompatibly with Andrew, Jennifer decided. Old billiard balls must have been used instead of real eggs for the egg and spoon race. The children must have been practicing for the upcoming fete.

"You smell nice," Joy said. "Mama smelled nice too because her arms were always in her washtub. Papa told me."

Bruce returned with the cat, a large knitted feline with round, startled eyes and floppy ears that looked more rabbitlike than catlike. But it was obviously the right creature. Joy sat up and reached for it and clasped it to her chest.

"Thank you," Joy said to Bruce before curling against Jennifer again, hugging the cat, and holding one of its ears to her mouth.

Jennifer kissed the soft curls on top of her head and willed the child to find her lap and her arms comfort enough for the sleep she so obviously needed. *Is there any greater joy?* she wondered, and smiled to herself at the unintentional pun. She had held her niece and nephews when they were younger and Luc's babies more recently, but it had never been quite like this. This child had been a bit frightened when she first came into the library because she could not find her father. Now she was relaxed and very warm. She was already asleep, in fact. Jennifer closed her own eyes and rested her head against the back of her chair, hoping selfishly that Mr. Ellis would not come too soon to take his child.

This.

Oh, just *this*.

It was at the heart of all her dreams but pushed so deep that she rarely admitted it even to herself. She was twenty-five years old and crippled with a grotesquely deformed leg. She had had chances even though she could never promenade in Hyde Park, dressed in the latest fashion and spinning a lacy parasol above her head, pretending that she was not preening before the admiring eyes of gentlemen. She could never twirl in a London ballroom, watching the candles in the candelabra wheel above her head and lowering her eyes to the handsome face of her dancing partner, who watched only her, admiration glowing in his eyes.

She had had chances, nonetheless. Her position in society as well as her wealth were attractions she *did* have. One or two of the offers might have led to tolerably contented marriages. Last year she had actually fallen more than halfway in love with one of those suitors, though not all the way. She had been attracted to him. She had wanted him desperately. If only he had not smiled so incessantly . . .

She wanted to be wed. She wanted companionship, the sense of belonging in a social world that valued married women a thousand times more than it valued spinsters. She wanted . . . intimacy. But oh, more than anything else in the world she wanted *this*. A child snuggled trustingly against her, warm, comfortable, and asleep.

But more even than that, she wanted a child who was hers, who was always with her, who would always seek her out for comfort and security. Who would call her Mama.

But in the absence of all that, she would enjoy this moment

while it lasted. She held Joy on her lap, safe in the circle of her arms, and dreamed.

B en went first to the nursery, where he found Pippa playing with the twins but no Joy.

"Bruce, Jenny's attendant, came looking for you a short while ago," Philippa told him. "We were to inform you if you came here that Joy is in the library. He came back a few minutes later for the cat I believe Steph knitted Joy for Christmas last year."

"She sleeps with it," he said, returning with a wink the wide smile with which Christopher had greeted him. "Thank you, Pippa. I'll find her."

Who was in the library with his daughter, apart from Lady Jennifer Arden? he wondered as he hurried downstairs and into the south wing. Joy had probably been as cross as a bear when she arrived home after a busy, sleepless afternoon and he was not waiting at the door to sweep her up into his arms.

He opened the library door and peered around it. Lady Jennifer Arden was sitting in her chair behind the desk, upon which were spread what looked like a couple of pages of an unfinished letter, with a quill pen beside them and an ink bottle with its lid off. She was no longer writing, however. Her head, fallen slightly to one side, rested against the back of the chair, and his daughter was cradled in her arms. One of Joy's arms was wrapped about her cat while her other hand pressed its ear to her mouth. Both were asleep.

He stepped closer, expecting that Lady Jennifer's eyes would open since he had not made any effort to keep silent. There was a half smile on her lips, softening the classical lines of the aristocratic features in her narrow face. The curls at the back of her head had been pushed upward to give the effect of a dark red halo. She looked at peace, and his embarrassment at having so imposed upon her time when she had clearly been busy with her letter faded.

She was beautiful.

Joy looked right in her arms. For the merest moment he felt a pang of regret that Marjorie had missed all this with their child, who had been not quite one year old when her mother died. But there was no point in brooding over what could never be.

He walked slowly around the desk, intending to ease his daughter from Lady Jennifer's arms. Though that would probably wake them both, he thought, and he was curiously reluctant to do that. He nudged the blotter and the letter back from the edge of the desk with the side of his hand so he could rest his palm flat on the wooden surface. He grasped the back of the chair with his other hand. And he gazed down at the two of them. His heart ached, though not with sorrow. He did not know the cause.

Lady Jennifer's eyes, dreamy with sleep, fluttered open. The corners of her mouth lifted into a fuller smile.

And he lowered his head and set his mouth to hers.

It hardly qualified as a kiss. He did not part his lips or increase their pressure against hers. Her lips did not move at all. It did not last longer than a few seconds, but by the time he raised his head he was fully aware of what he had just done, though he was not yet as consumed with horror as he no doubt would be soon.

Her smile had faded. Awareness had returned to her eyes. But she still did not move. And Joy slept between them. They gazed at each other. It did not occur to Ben to say anything. Perhaps it did not occur to her either.

And she was dear to him. A woman who in every imaginable way was as unattainable as the moon. An impossibility. Except that she was here, holding his sleeping child, still relaxed in the fading shreds of sleep, and she was very dear.

He kissed her again. A real kiss this time, though not in any way a passionate one. He parted his lips, her own trembled open, and they both pressed slightly into the embrace, tasting each other, sharing the warmth of mouths and longing. Any moment now, he thought while he touched the tip of his tongue to that slightly up-turned upper lip of hers and ran it lightly across the soft, moist flesh within, his mind was going to jump into action. So was hers.

Meanwhile, and very consciously, they lived this moment.

There was a soft sigh of contentment, a thin arm curled about his neck, and a sleepy voice spoke. "Papa."

And he ended the kiss and smiled down at his daughter, whose eyes were still closed.

Lady Jennifer kept her head against the chair back.

"You could not find me?" he asked. "I was in the stable with Uncle Nick. Shall we go up to the nursery?"

"No," Joy said, and sighed and snuggled. "I stay here."

His eyes met Lady Jennifer's, a mere few inches from his own. Her lips looked soft and moist. There was a flush of color in her cheeks.

"She can stay," she murmured. "Please let her stay."

He straightened up and moved to the window behind her chair to stare out across the rain-soaked lawn to the ha-ha and the meadow beyond and the river and village in the distance. There was silence behind him after some sleepy lip-smacking from Joy and a few soft, soothing murmurs from Lady Jennifer.

And *now* what had he gone and done?

CHAPTER THIRTEEN

Jennifer stayed very still and relaxed for the sake of the child, who had not fully woken when she sensed her father's presence and was now sleeping again, her little body soft and warm.

Jennifer did not know where Mr. Ellis was, though she did know he had not left the room. He was out of her line of vision. She could not hear him either. She could not hear pages of a book being turned. She guessed he was looking out at the rain, which was the only thing she *could* hear as it pelted against the window panes. She hoped he was not looking at her.

She closed her eyes.

She had been kissed.

And she wondered if a kiss was always like that. Not just the physical sensation of lips meeting, of warm breath against the cheek, of a face so near that one was obliged to close one's eyes. Not just a quickening of the breath and a glow of warm affection. But all-encompassing. Humming and singing through the blood and everything that was the self—body, mind, heart, and spirit. Was it always thus? Or was she being silly and naïve?

She had been kissed, and she had *no idea* if it was always like that. Or usually. Or rarely. Or virtually never.

She had been kissed, and it was *like that*. Except that she could not define what *that* was. Or even exactly what it was like. Sometimes there were no words, even in one's mind.

She moved her tongue along the flesh behind her upper lip, but there was no lingering taste of him there. He had been gentle. So gentle. She had somehow expected a kiss to be fierce—at least a kiss that left one feeling as though the world had stopped for a moment before turning again, but not quite as it had before.

She had been kissed and she wanted to weep. But . . . with sorrow? Partly, perhaps. But not entirely. Partly she wanted to weep with joy.

She had been kissed. At the age of twenty-five.

And she doubted it would ever be repeated. Not with this man or any other. It had probably been a kiss of light affection because she had fallen asleep with his daughter in her arms. But no, that was not right. The first kiss could perhaps be interpreted that way, but not the second.

He was an impossibility. For so many reasons she could hardly sort them in her head. He was the illegitimate son of the late Earl of Stratton, though he had had the good fortune—perhaps—to be raised at Ravenswood with the earl's legitimate family. But he was still illegitimate. Some people would not scruple to use another word. It ought not to matter. But it did and it would. He had no real interest in her anyway despite the kiss and some sympathetic concern, which had been aroused when he saw her trying to walk.

He intended to remarry, but he very deliberately did not want to choose any woman from his father's world or that of his half brothers and sisters. And he was not looking to increase his fortune. He seemed content with what he had—and with his home close to the sea. He did not want to live like an impostor or as a social climber in the world in which he had grown up.

She guessed that wherever he was in the room, he was mentally composing some sort of apology for that kiss. She did not want to hear it. She did not want him to be sorry. She was going to have to live her life on the memory of those two brief kisses, and she did not want to know that he regretted them. They would become a part of her dreams, but not the dreams that had never been real and very probably never would be. This had been real, though it would fade into something indistinguishable from a dream.

I remember being kissed, she would tell herself down the years. *I will always remember . . .*

Luc and Pippa would share kisses every day through their lives together, as would Charlotte and Sylvester. Mr. Ellis would share kisses with whichever of three women he chose to marry—probably sometime soon. And through all those years Jennifer would remember a pair of kisses. She did not want him to be sorry. She would not expect him to remember, but let him not be sorry.

She did not want to be pathetic, but . . . *Please do not let him be sorry.*

The little girl twitched and fussed in her arms after a while. "Papa?" she murmured sleepily, and then sat bolt upright on Jennifer's lap. "Where is Papa?"

"I am here," he said, and was back beside the chair, smiling at his child and bending to lift her into his arms. She wrapped her arms about him and her legs too and kissed him on the cheek.

"Philip was made to stand in the corner," she said. "He said I was a pest."

"Did he indeed?" Mr. Ellis said. "You were behaving like an angel and just out of the clear blue sky he called you a pest?"

"He would not let me play with his toy soldiers," Joy said, "so I told him he was mean."

"Ah," her father said.

"Olwen poked her tongue out at him," Joy added. "And crossed her eyes."

"And Philip was the one who was punished," Mr. Ellis said. "It sounds about right. He is the eldest, poor boy. Did he say sorry to you?"

"Yes." She patted his cheeks with her palms.

"And did you say sorry to him?" he asked.

"No." She shook her head firmly. "He was mean."

"They were his soldiers," Mr. Ellis said. "And he said no. How many times did he say it?"

She thought for a moment and then held up three fingers. "This many."

"Three times?" he said. "And each time you heard him say it?"

"Yes," she said. "He was mean."

"When you ask me for something and I say no and you ask again, what do I tell you?" he asked her.

She thought. "Once is enough," she said.

"And here is a new one for you to remember," he said. "Three times is too many. Perhaps next time you see Philip, you can say you are sorry?"

"Yes," she said.

"Good girl. Now, you have a *Thank you* to say," he told her, and she turned in his arms and beamed down at Jennifer, her hair wildly tousled, her cheeks flushed from sleep.

"Thank you," she said. "Are you Aunty Jenny? Like Aunty Steph and Aunty Pippa and Aunty Gwyneth?"

"I would love to be," Jennifer said.

"Thank you, Aunty Jenny," Joy said.

"I believe Lady Jennifer has a letter to finish writing," Mr. Ellis said. "Shall we go and see if we can find you some tea even though it is very late?"

"Yes," she said, and then laughed gleefully and pointed at Jennifer's lap, where the cat was sprawled, looking startled. "Cat wants to stay."

"I believe he would soon miss you and start mewing piteously and disturbing Lady Jennifer," her father said, and bent to take the toy from Jennifer's hand.

For the first time since he had come back into sight he looked at her. Their faces were close and their fingers were almost touching around the knitted cat.

"Thank you," he said, and she smiled.

He left the room with his child, who waved to Jennifer over his shoulder, and he closed the door quietly behind them.

She did not know for what he had been thanking her. She swiped her forefingers beneath her eyes. She was not going to cry. Good heavens she was not. Someone else might come into the room at any moment. She pulled her unfinished letter toward the edge of the desk, picked up her pen, dipped it in the ink, and tried to remember what she had been telling her sister. Since she wrote that last word she had fallen all the way in love with a little child and she had been kissed. Her world had shifted.

But she was being thoroughly silly. And yes, pathetic.

She read through the last, unfinished sentence she had written—and continued. She described her wondrous trip all around the lake in her chair, making it sound as if all the picnic goers had accompanied her en masse. She described the movement of her chair in the passive voice so she would not have to say who did the pushing—*my chair was pushed all about the perimeter of the lake* . . .

She still did not know what he had thanked her for. But he had not said he was sorry.

There was some new excitement at Cartref the following day when Dylan and Angharad Howell, Eluned Rhys's brother and his wife, arrived in the rain with their four children. They had come from Wales to spend a few weeks and had timed their visit so they could attend the fete, which was fast approaching. Fourteen-year-old Mari and ten-year-old Huw were drawn into the youth choir by Sir Ifor, who assured them that they would learn the songs in no time at all, even if they did not already know them.

Stephanie assumed the role of elder sister to Mari in particular and set out to make the girl feel at home. Huw and eight-year-old Glyn were content to become their Uncle Idris's shadows and follow him about the farm, especially after the rain finally stopped, pausing to climb a few trees and play with the dogs along the way, especially if their father was with them and the two men got into long, boring conversations about farming.

Marged, aged four and named for her grandmother, became Joy's particular friend during their first meeting on the day the rain stopped, when Lady Rhys, Eluned, and Angharad paid a call at Ravenswood and brought the youngest child with them. Indeed, the only thing that would reconcile the two little girls to parting when the ladies were ready to leave was the promise that a return visit would be made the very next day.

It turned out to be a much better day weather-wise, still a bit cloudy but warm and dry. And the clouds were quite unthreatening, Bertrand observed at breakfast. They were merely passing by and minding their own business as they went. He and Owen were going to help Nicholas set up the archery targets in the poplar alley if the grass was not too wet, and then they were going to string a couple of bows and practice their skills, since both had entered the archery contest.

"Though if Matthew Taylor is even half as good as he used to be," Owen said to his friend, "we do not stand a chance, Bert. He was always a joy to watch, unless you were a contestant, I suppose. I never was. I was only twelve at the last fete. He used to bring his own bow, and carried his arrows in a quiver on his back—a bit like the archers a person can see on those medieval tapestries. And he could pull out an arrow, set it to his bow, and shoot straight into the bull's-eye faster than you could blink. Then, before your eyes caught up with what had happened, another arrow was already on its way. I never could work out how he did it."

"You are filling me with despair," Bertrand said, grinning. "We had better get out there and practice."

Gwyneth, Stephanie, and Philippa were going to Cartref. All the babies were going too. So was Joy, who took both her dolls with her since Marged had not brought any from Wales.

"I will give her this one to play with," Joy told Ben before she left, holding up the larger of the two dolls, her favorite. "I will play with this one." She indicated the smaller doll.

"That is very noble of you," Ben said.

"Yes," she agreed, though he was not sure she knew the meaning of the word *noble*. "She is my friend. She is—" She looked down at her hand, spread her fingers, and then held them all up before bending her thumb into her palm. "This many."

"Four years old," he said.

Lady Catherine Emmett, Lucas, and Lady Jennifer Arden were going into Boscombe. Nothing had been said—not in Ben's hearing anyway—about why they were going there, but it did not take any great genius to guess. There had been a bit of an atmosphere at Ravenswood for the past few days, nothing a stranger would have detected, perhaps, but something that had been quite noticeable to Ben. He had even feared that Lady Jennifer might have complained to someone about that kiss, but he dismissed the possibility as soon as it came into his head. No, she would not have done that even though he had not apologized. Not yet anyway, though he knew he must. He could not quite say that in the past day and a half there had been no opportunity whatsoever to have a brief, private word with her. But none of those moments had felt right. Perhaps none ever would. In the meanwhile, they were back to avoiding any sort of closeness with each other, including eye contact. And now everyone else seemed to be colluding in that effort.

Perhaps he ought to leave Ravenswood, Ben had thought last night as he lay in bed while sleep eluded him. Go home to Penallen. Relieve everyone from the embarrassment of his presence here. But he had quickly rejected the idea, attractive as it had seemed when it first occurred to him. Joy was enjoying herself very much indeed, and even more so with the arrival of Marged Howell at Cartref. He could not deprive her of that enjoyment merely because he felt uncomfortable.

He spent the morning with Devlin. They were seeing to the leveling of the stable yard and the setting up of the stone blocks upon which the great logs would be placed for the log-splitting contest. There were six contestants, including Cam Holland, close runner-up eight years ago and an even more formidable physical specimen now than he had been then as a result of all the years he had spent at the anvil in the smithy. He *was* eight years older than he had been then, however, and the oldest of all the contestants. Six massive logs, as identical in size and shape as they could possibly be, were lined up in one corner of the yard next to two even larger ones. The six were for the preliminary heats, the larger ones for the final round between the two contestants who split their logs in the shortest time during the heats.

"This was always the most popular contest of the day," Devlin said. "I wonder if it still will be, with everyone having to come up from the village to watch it. There will be a lot going on there too."

"I would wager on it," Ben said. "And people will be coming here for the other contests too. The archery used to be almost as popular as the log splitting. They will come in droves, Dev. Especially after such a long time."

His final words seemed to hang in the air between them as they lapsed into silence.

"He used to love the fetes more than anything else," Devlin said, going very close to where he had never gone before. He never talked about that fete eight years ago and the disastrous way it had ended. He never talked about their father. Neither did Ben.

"He loved people," Ben said. "And people loved him."

"Damn," Devlin said. "Damn, damn, damn."

"Ben." It was Mother's voice. She was just stepping into the stable yard from the carriage house. "I could use your advice if you are not too busy here?" She looked inquiringly at Devlin.

"I believe we are finished for now," Ben said. "How may I help you, Mother?"

"I am trying to visualize the courtyard as it will be for the fete," she said. "But I need some advice. Let me show you what I have in mind."

"Certainly," he said, and they made their way through the carriage house and out into the north cloister of the courtyard, leaving Devlin behind.

She had decided to set up the display tables for the needlework and baking contests in the courtyard this year instead of down by the lake, where they always used to be.

"I cannot quite decide," she said now, "if the tables should be set up along the cloisters in order to leave more room in the court-yard for all the people who will come to view them, or whether they should be set on the grass just outside the cloisters. If it is a sunny day, as we all fervently hope it will be, the displays may be in deep shadow beneath the cloister roof, and that would be unfortunate."

"It would," he said.

She had needed to find him and bring him here to confirm what she already knew was the only sensible place to set up the tables?

"Yes, of course," she said. "Well, that is settled, then. Thank you, Ben. Shall we sit and relax for a little while in the rose arbor? It has been a busy morning. I had forgotten how much needs to be organized for the fete, even though this year I am responsible for only a small fraction of what I used to do."

Ah, Ben thought as she led the way to the arbor and sat close to the fountain before smiling at him and indicating the wrought iron sofa close by. So *this* was why she had lured him here. It had been a slim excuse, but here he was.

"How lovely it is," she said, "to have all my family around me. I miss those of you who have left to begin new lives elsewhere, though it is inevitable, of course, with the passing of time. Why do children have to grow up? It is hard to believe that even my baby is seventeen years old and on the very brink of womanhood. You are happy at Penallen, Ben? Joy is such a delight."

"She is," he agreed. "And I am happy, Mother. I always thought of Penallen as my dream home. I was very fortunate that Devlin was willing to sell it to me."

"He wanted to *give* it to you," she said, "or at least let you have it for a token amount. But your pride would not allow it, and I respect you for that. I wish I could have known your wife. I believe you were very fond of her."

"I was," he said. But, much as he would have loved to bring Marjorie home with him, there was a part of him that wondered how it would have been possible. She would have been dreadfully uncomfortable in a place like this, and his family would not have known quite how to deal with her. With the best intentions on both sides and all his efforts to be a bridge between them, he could not imagine that it would have worked. Even Penallen might have been too much for her. He really did not know where they would have made their life together. He did not often make this admission to himself—not consciously anyway—but he made it now. He and Marjorie had fit each other's worlds only in the context of the army in the Peninsula during the war.

"It has been well over two years," Mother said. "Do you ever think of remarrying, Ben?"

"Yes," he said. "There are two or three women near Penallen I have been considering."

The relief she felt at his words was all too obvious in her facial expression. "I am so glad," she said. "A new marriage will be very good for both you and Joy. Tell me about these women. *Plural*, Ben?"

He told her briefly, and she looked even more pleased.

"And so you are having difficulty choosing," she said. "Poor Ben. They all sound very suitable, both as wives and as potential mothers."

Very suitable. She did not have to explain what she meant by that.

"Yes," he said.

She beamed at him. "Ben," she said. "I have always, always loved you as I do my own children. Indeed, I do not think of you all as *them* and *you*. I loved you from the moment your father brought you to Ravenswood, such a sad, bewildered little boy, who climbed onto my lap and cuddled against me as soon as I held my arms open to you. I always will love you. You will always be my son. I hope you realize that."

Oh, he did. And he could see the sincerity in her eyes and hear it in her voice. Her eyes even brightened with tears as she gazed at him. He also understood what she was really saying and why she had concocted a rather lame excuse to draw him here, where she could sit and talk privately with him for a few minutes.

She loved him and he was as dear as a son to her. But he was *not* her son. He was the son of a woman her husband had bedded and impregnated without also marrying her, and that fact made all the difference. *Not*, amazingly, to her feelings for him. But to what his expectations needed to be. He was *not* a Ware of Ravenswood. He was Ben Ellis.

He must not even *think* about courting the sister of the Duke of Wilby.

But he was not going to force her to spell it out to him. He loved her too. Very dearly.

"I hope," he said, "you will come to Penallen to help plan my wedding as mother of the bridegroom when the time comes. Before Christmas, I hope. If I can persuade someone to marry me, that is."

"Ben!" she said, laughing. "You must be the biggest matrimonial prize for miles about Penallen. I would be surprised if each of the three women you described to me is not holding her breath in the hope that she will be the chosen one. And there are probably a few more than just those three eligible women of whom you are not even aware. I will arrange the grandest of wedding celebrations for you, and I will be as happy as mother of the bridegroom as I was at Devlin's wedding and Pippa's—mother of the *bride* in her case, of course. I can hardly wait. How happy you have made me."

She got to her feet, waited for him to stand, and hugged him close.

"I suppose I do not tell you often enough, or perhaps ever," he said. "But you are the very best mother a man could ever want."

Yet he wished he could have rephrased that somehow. For he could not forget the mother he could not remember—a strange emotional muddle for a man to bear through his life.

She patted his arms. "*Some* people have work to do, and I am one of them," she said briskly. "Go away, Ben. Thank you for your advice."

CHAPTER FOURTEEN

Jennifer was sitting on the terrace outside the ballroom again. She loved it there, the seclusion of it, the sense of being a part of the serene, unspoiled natural world that was spread before her. The other ladies were taking tea in the drawing room with some afternoon callers, but Jennifer had excused herself. She was weary after her morning in the village.

The terrace turned out to be not so very secluded a place after all, however. Less than a quarter of an hour after she had been wheeled out there, Stephanie and Mr. Ellis came around the corner from the front of the house with Joy and two of the children who had come from Cartref for the afternoon. None of them came to disturb Jennifer, but Stephanie and Joy waved and called out cheerful greetings as they passed to make their way up the hill nearby. The two older girls disappeared inside the temple folly and remained there, the only sign of their presence an occasional burst of girlish laughter. The younger girls chased each other around the outside of the temple and in and out of the pillars for a while, shrieking and chattering, while Mr. Ellis stood just outside watching them. He must have suggested that they try rolling down the hill, for they stood at the top of it jumping up and down and clapping their hands while he strode to the bottom and turned back toward them. It was a game that lasted several minutes while they took turns rolling and he caught them and set them back on their feet and brushed the excess grass from their dresses before they dashed back up to roll again.

Jennifer did not resent the intrusion upon her quiet time. The children were enjoying themselves, the sun was winning the game of hide-and-seek with the clouds, which had still been quite heavy this morning, and . . . well. And there was Mr. Ellis to gaze upon as he played with seemingly endless patience with his daughter and her friend.

He must know she was here though he had not acknowledged her on his way to the hill. He had neither looked toward her nor *not* looked, if it was possible for both to be true. His family had got to him, Jennifer thought a little sadly. Just as her family had got to her. Oh, not with any sort of blazing scold or firm ultimatum. They were very well aware that she was twenty-five years old. Mr. Ellis was probably in his thirties. But when she made the second visit to the smithy in Boscombe this morning, it was Luc and Aunt Kitty who had accompanied her, like two loving jailers. There had been no mention of Mr. Ellis.

There was something terribly appealing about an attentive fa-ther, she thought with a sigh. The little Welsh girl had not been in proper position for her most recent descent of the slope and had come to a sprawling halt close to the bottom. Mr. Ellis scooped her up when she started to wail, took a look at one of her knees be-fore rubbing it and talking to her until her tears stopped and she giggled. He dried her face with a large white handkerchief before putting it back into his pocket and lowering a hand to ruffle Joy's hair as she completed her own roll and wrapped both arms about one of his legs. He took them around the base of the hill after that, still carrying the one little girl, and Jennifer could hear them a few minutes later chattering and laughing as they scrambled up the wooded back side of the hill to the temple.

Jennifer had a book open on her lap. She had been looking forward to a quiet read, all too rare since she came here. But she had not turned a single page since the interruption. She did not mind. There was always time for reading. At home there were often long stretches of time when there was little else to do, and she had all the leisure time she needed to lose herself in the pages of a book.

The group at the temple came back down after about an hour, and this time they came directly toward the terrace.

"I hope we have not disturbed you too much, Jenny," Stephanie said. "I know you were looking forward to some time alone. This is Mari Howell. Lady Jennifer Arden, Mari. And this is Mari's little sister, Marged. There are two boys between them in age, but they stayed at Cartref."

"Aunty Jenny has a magic chair," Joy said after Jennifer had greeted the two girls. "It has wheels. I have rides on it with my aunty."

"If there were wings on it too," Stephanie said, laughing, "you would never have the chair to yourself, Jenny. I am taking the girls up to the turret room on top of this wing. We could see it from outside the temple on the hill, and I told Mari what a splendid place it is to go to talk or play or simply gaze, since there are windows facing in every direction. I know it looks a bit odd perched up there on the edge of the wing, for all the world like a giant raindrop that never dries up, but I think it is my favorite room in the house."

"There are lots of cushions," Joy said. "We throw them."

"There are," Stephanie said. "And we are going to have a fierce cushion fight. You will have your peace and quiet back, Jenny. And, Ben, there is no need for you to come with us unless you have a burning desire to be attacked by four females armed with a few dozen cushions. I will look after Joy."

"Aunt Steph will be in charge, then, Joy," he said.

"Yes," she said, and she and Marged darted off through the ballroom hand in hand while the older girls followed at a more sedate pace.

Mr. Ellis remained. He had still not looked at Jennifer. But how did she know that when she had not looked at him either?

"It must be lovely up in the temple," she said before the silence could become too awkward.

"It is," he said.

And awkwardness threatened again.

"Would you like to go up there?" he asked. There was a sort of tightness to his voice, as though the words had been dragged out of him.

She looked fully at him and wondered how she could ever have considered him *ordinary*. His dark hair was slightly windblown—he was not wearing a hat. There were a few blades of grass clinging to his pantaloons and his coat. He looked . . . Well, *attractive*. Maybe even gorgeous.

"Now?" she asked foolishly. "But no. It is impossible. The hill is too steep for my chair."

"I will carry you," he said.

Oh. Her lips formed the word, but she did not say it aloud. It was too far and she was too heavy. He had been avoiding her, either because he deeply regretted what had happened in the library a few days ago or because his family had been having a word with him. Or both. And she had been avoiding him for basically the same reasons.

He was looking steadily at her now, an unreadable, flat sort of expression in his eyes.

"Will you?" she said.

He nodded and bent over her chair. She had time only to hook one arm about his neck before he lifted her and strode off with her in the direction of the hill. Neither of them spoke until they were halfway up it.

"I must weigh a ton," she said.

"Not at all," he told her. "A ton and a half, maybe, but definitely not a ton."

His flashes of impassive humor always took her by surprise. And he was half smiling, she saw. He was also breathless. There were lines fanning out from the outer corners of his eyes. They would surely become permanent as he aged. His good nature would be written on his face. She had a sudden image of his grandchildren crawling all over him as he sat in his fireside chair sometime far in the future, and there was a certain foolish pang in the knowledge that she would not know him then. Except perhaps in a rare gathering of the Ware and Arden families. Would she feel the pang then too? Or would she look upon him with indifference? Would she remember that it was because of him she could travel about freely in her gig and move herself from room to room in her chair and . . . And *walk*?

The temple was larger than the one on the island. The open front was held up by tall, slender stone columns, but Jennifer could see even before she was set down that they did not impede the view. Perhaps they even enhanced it by offering some framework through which to see it. There was a wide sofa against the back wall and a deep armchair on either side of it. There were lots of cushions and a couple of blankets piled on a table beside the sofa.

He set her down on the sofa and put one of the larger cushions on the floor as a rest for her right foot. He stood to one side of her.

"The hill does not seem very high from down there," he said. "But the view from up here always amazes me."

She could see the corner of the west wing of the house, though not the onion-shaped turret room on top of it where the girls had gone. Not without stooping down or moving closer to the outer edge of the temple, anyway. There were a few glimpses of the river through the trees ahead, and most of the village beyond them was fully visible. She could see the smithy, where she had been this morning. Farmland, like a patchwork quilt of fields bordered by hedgerows, all in various shades of green and brown, stretched ahead and to either side. The parkland below and the lake to her right were serene and lovely.

"It really is quite breathtaking," she said. "I thought I would only ever see the temple from below and imagine the view as it must be from up here. Thank you for bringing me."

He sat on the chair to her right, leaning forward, his forearms draped over his spread knees. "Lady Jennifer—" he said. He stopped when she held up a staying hand.

"Please," she said. "Please, *please* do not say what I believe you are about to say. I do not want to hear that you are sorry." She bit her lower lip, and he stared at her. "I do not want you to be sorry. I want to live with the illusion that it was spontaneous, that it is something you will remember with some fondness, as I will. I do not want my memory of it to be spoiled by the knowledge that you are sorry."

Oh goodness. She was making such an abject idiot of herself, and all over something so slight that it might not even be definable as a *kiss*. And perhaps he had not been about to apologize. Perhaps he had been going to make some mundane comment about the view.

"I regret it," he said, "only because it ought not to have happened. We are of different worlds, Lady Jennifer, and I ought not to have crossed the invisible line I *did* cross as soon as I sat with you in the rose arbor and concocted the mad idea that you could possibly be far more mobile than you ever have been except in your dreams."

"It was *not* a mad idea," she said. "I have driven a gig. It may sound to you as trivial a thing as a kiss that was not really a kiss. But to me it was an enormous something. I felt as free as a bird. And perhaps I will have a chair in which I can move myself and a way of walking that is more . . . *possible* than what I have now. Perhaps I will even *swim*."

"It *was* a kiss," he said softly. "It was not trivial."

Ah. She smoothed her hands over the skirt of her dress before turning them over and gazing at her palms. She had not wanted that said aloud either. It made her want to weep.

"Look," he said, and he moved a little farther forward on his chair. "Let us be real. Early in my life I learned how to be part of this family and Ravenswood itself without being *of* either one. Fortunately for me, there were never any serious romantic entanglements with anyone who visited here or anyone from the neighborhood with whom we mingled socially. I was twenty-five when I left here with Devlin. In the Peninsula I was fortunate enough to marry a woman who suited me and brought me considerable happiness. Now I have my own home by the sea and am about to choose a second wife from a stratum of society that will perhaps blend with my own and bring us both contentment. There has been no need for the alarms that have been sounded here in the past several days, though with a very genteel lack of noise and fuss. There has been no need *for either of us.* You are possibly the last woman on this earth I would consider wooing and wedding. You are, to put it succinctly, the sister of a *duke.* You are *Lady Jennifer Arden.* And I am the last man on earth *you* would consider marrying. Although I am a son of the late Earl of Stratton, I am also—again, to put it succinctly—a bastard."

She held up her hands, palms toward him, as though to push him away. But when he stopped talking, she curled her fingers into her palms and lowered her hands to her lap again.

"You are quite right, of course," she said, smiling at him. "But are you perhaps overdramatizing? There is no danger, is there, that we might ever consider such a thing?"

"The danger seems real to my family and yours," he said. "They are very alarmed."

"They are being foolish," she said.

"Are they?" he asked. "We did spend a few hours alone together, driving about the park in the gig and sitting on the island, when none of them were here to protest or insist upon accompanying us or at least sending a chaperon with you. During the picnic, we did disappear together and did not return for upward of an hour."

"But everyone knew where we were going. And we were seen," she said. "By several people."

"Yes," he said. "Sitting together inside that very romantic little thatched grotto. And in the library we did kiss. And if the first one took you by surprise—took us *both* by surprise—the second one did not. Either of us could have avoided it. Neither of us did. Yes, Lady Jennifer, there *is* a question of where the relationship between you and me might be leading. And here we are again, sitting up inside the temple alone together."

Jennifer was starting to feel a bit annoyed, perhaps because she still wanted to weep. "There is a world of difference," she said, "between liking each other's company and being interested in each other's lives on the one hand and considering *marriage* on the other."

"That world of difference can contract to nothing in a heartbeat," he said. "Sometimes marriage can pounce."

"Is that how you felt about your first marriage?" she asked, and he frowned and recoiled slightly before recovering his poise. But he did not answer the question. "You were trapped into it?"

"There was no entrapment," he said. "We had been together for some time and by free and mutual consent. I put the child in her. She made no scene about what had happened. There was no hysteria, just the quiet expectation that as soon as I knew I would put her from me. There was no trap. I married her."

Jennifer felt the sharp stabbing of something—pain? longing?— deep in her abdomen and recognized it as mingled desire and envy. *I put the child in her.* She was jealous of a dead woman. And how on earth had they ended up going off on this tangent?

"I thank you for all you have done for me, Mr. Ellis," she said. "For the ideas you have put into my head, some of which are being acted upon. Thank you for talking to me and listening to me. Thank you for recognizing my longing at the picnic to *move* and for taking me all about the lake. Thank you for—giving me the memory of a kiss. And for bringing me up here. I have only ever thought of you as a pleasant person, you know, as something close to a friend, though we have not known each other long enough, nor will we ever, to refer to what is between us as a *real* friendship. Any idea of a courtship between us is absurd. It had not crossed my mind until Luc and Aunt Kitty each had a serious talk with me. Just as it had not crossed yours until your family became alarmed. As you said earlier, we are of different worlds, and it would not have occurred to us to cross the barrier between. The summer fete is the day after tomorrow. Aunt Kitty and I will perhaps stay here for a week or a bit longer after that. I daresay you will soon be thinking of returning to your home. Between now and then it will not be difficult to stay away from each other and put everyone's groundless fears to rest, will it?"

"When Gwyneth and Nicholas were growing up," he said, "they were the best of friends for years. As thick as thieves. Sometimes almost inseparable. The general expectation in both families and for miles around here was that they would eventually marry and live happily ever after. Yet as they grew closer to adulthood and understood that expectation, panic apparently set in. They were *friends*, not sweethearts. Nick was about to go away to take up the commission our father had purchased for him, and he was excited about moving into his adult life. My guess is that Gwyneth had been nursing a secret passion for Devlin for quite a while, and I knew Devlin had felt a passion for her for years—but would make no move because he thought our brother loved her. Nick and Gwyneth sorted it all out between themselves shortly before the last fete, eight years ago, and all might have ended happily there and then if the fete had not ended so calamitously. I do believe Devlin and Gwyneth found each other on that day—and lost each other the next when Dev was forced to leave."

Jennifer gazed at his lowered head.

"My point is," he said, "that friendship between a man and a woman—or a boy and a girl in Nick and Gwyneth's case—is not always easy. Other people invariably misconstrue it and complicate their lives."

"So even the slight friendship we have must be renounced in order that appearances be kept up?" she said.

He shrugged and sighed aloud. "There were other people at that picnic apart from our families," he said. "I was very careful during all my growing years and early adulthood at Ravenswood never to be the subject of gossip and never to make people uncomfortable with their knowledge of just who I am. Now it is possible there are the stirrings of gossip and speculation—and scandal."

She had been right, then. His perceived ordinariness had been a carefully cultivated image. Taking up the position of Ravenswood's steward instead of going to Cambridge when he was finished with school was a part of it. So was going away with Devlin as his nominal batman. He had never allowed himself any serious sort of romance while he lived here. When he had discovered in the Peninsula that his Marjorie was with child, he had married her the same day to ensure the legitimacy of their child.

He was not ordinary, she thought. He was as far from being ordinary as the south pole is from the north. And she was very much afraid that her feelings for him were such that there was going to be some pain in her future, after she was back home.

"What happened at that fete?" she asked. "I know *something* did, but it has never been explained to me."

"I daresay Pippa has told Lucas," he said. "But neither of them has told you? Our father had brought a woman from London and set her up in a cottage in Boscombe. She told some story about being a widow needing somewhere quiet to live. All his children, including me, had been carefully shielded from his many indiscretions down the years, though Mother had known of them, and our aunts and uncles too. But he had stepped over a line by bringing his latest woman here, and Dev came upon them together on the night of the ball. Right here, in fact. But they were not sitting here, sedately admiring the moonlit view. Dev could have waited until the next day to confront our father in private. Instead he chose to make a very loud scene, during which our father tried to escape by returning to the ballroom. He only made things worse, for Dev—and poor Gwyneth—followed him down and the whole thing became wretchedly public on the terrace outside the ballroom, where your chair stands now. The ball ended abruptly, and Devlin was banished. He and I left early the following morning and did not return until six years later, two years after our father's passing. We came home after the Battle of Toulouse, which we assumed at the time was the end of the wars."

"I am sorry," she said. "It must have been particularly hard on you."

He looked up at her and laughed briefly, though without any apparent humor. "You understand that, do you?" he said. "That far from being the love of his life, my mother was just one of a string of whores with whom he amused himself all his adult life?"

"You cannot be sure of that," she said. "He brought you here,

Mr. Ellis. He raised you with the children of his marriage. He treated you as one of them. He might have made other arrangements for you and put you out of his mind and his life."

They were silent for a while.

"Lady Jennifer," he said then. "This is a cruel twist of fate."

"What is?" she asked.

"Through the course of my life," he said, "I have had a number of friends and a larger number of friendly acquaintances. None of the former have been female, and only a few of the latter. I have cultivated a few friendships near Penallen but have avoided any with women. I have hoped—I hope—that friendship will grow as a result of marriage. But you and I could be friends right here and now, could we not? I mean real friends, who speak openly to each other upon any subject on earth, including those topics that live in the heart and are usually closely guarded there. Yet we must stay away from each other. We are not in love. We are not even thinking of marrying each other. But we must consider appearances anyway. I will make arrangements to leave here early next week—on Monday or Tuesday. That will make everyone happy."

"Except me," she said, and then wished she had not spoken aloud. As a couple, they were an impossibility—whether as friends or something else. They had both acknowledged that. She had not needed to say what she just had and so add a link to the invisible chain that was trying to bind them together.

He surged to his feet and went to stand between two of the pillars for a silent minute or two, looking out. He turned toward her then and stood looking down at her. She could not see his face clearly. He was like a silhouette, backlit by the sun over his left shoulder.

"Damn it," he said irreverently. "Damn it all to hell."

And he came and sat down beside her on the sofa. For a few moments he propped his elbows on his knees and pushed his fingers through his hair. Then he turned and set one arm about her shoulders and touched the fingers of the other hand to the underside of her chin.

"Damn it," he said again, and kissed her.

CHAPTER FIFTEEN

It was a very different kiss from the two in the library. Those had been sweet and affectionate, with perhaps a bit of yearning mixed in. This was hot and urgent—on *both* their parts—and ultimately despairing. It did not last long. She was clutching the lapel of his coat, he realized when he lifted his head.

"I can hear the echo of a few words I ought not to have uttered in your hearing," he said. "I beg your pardon."

"Granted," she said. "I am twenty-five years old, Mr. Ellis. You are what?"

"Thirty-three," he said.

"If we were both . . . normal human beings," she said. "If I could walk as other people do and if you were a legitimate son of your father, would anyone in your family or mine or anyone in this neighborhood be alarmed and jump into protective action if we went on an open carriage ride together *within the park*? Or if we took a stroll about the lake during a picnic, when for most of the time we could be seen or even joined by family or fellow guests?

Even as I am, would there be any feeling of consternation if I had done either of those things with . . . let us say Major Ware?"

"What-ifs are not usually very constructive," he said.

"My point is," she told him, "that given our ages, we have not done anything even remotely indiscreet since we both came here. We have spent some time in company with each other. That, surely, is the whole purpose of a social gathering. *This* is a social gathering—your family and mine spending a few weeks together here because my brother married your sister last year and my aunt is a long-standing friend of the dowager countess."

"But I went and had that talk with Cam Holland when I had no business doing so," he said.

"Yes," she said. "And I might have rebuked you—as I did. I might have sent word immediately to Mr. Holland that I would have no need of his services, now or ever, thank you kindly. I did not do it. I went instead to talk to him myself, and I took Pippa with me. That whole matter was an issue that became mine, Mr. Ellis. I am a grown woman, and a woman, moreover, with a mind and a voice. I used both. I am becoming increasingly annoyed to find that you and I—*both* of us—are treated differently from other people by our families. I am coddled, as though I were still the child I was when I fell ill and was quite incapable of managing my own affairs. You are treated as an equal as long as you do not behave like one. If we wish to be friends while we are both here at Ravenswood—which will not be for very much longer—then why should we not be? I do not need permission from my brother or my aunt. You do not need permission from anyone at all."

She was still holding on to his lapel. He still had one arm about her shoulders. They were gazing directly into each other's eyes as she spoke. And Ben felt the rather bizarre unexpectedness of what was happening. Just a very short time ago he had thought of Lady Jennifer Arden as a bit on the haughty and unapproachable side and even as unattractive. He had thought of her as someone to be avoided whenever possible because she made him uncomfortable.

"If we wish to be friends," he said softly. Was that what they were to each other? If they were perfectly honest? But yes, it was and they *were*. They seemed to be attracted to each other too—sexually attracted, that was. But it was not the only thing between them, and even that was not raging lust. It could be controlled, even suppressed, as it must be. Any sort of romantic relationship was impossible for them. He could not bed her without marrying her, and marriage was totally, one hundred percent out of the question—for both of them. He did not even want it. Neither did she. It would strand them both between two worlds and bring them nothing but ultimate misery. There could be no middle ground.

"Yes, friends," she said. "Pippa is my friend, perhaps my dearest one. But she also has Luc and the babies. And she is here to spend time with her whole family, whom she sees only rarely, and with neighbors she has known all her life but not seen for some time. Her days are taken up with all the people who are dear to her— including me. Everyone here has become my friend too, to a greater or lesser degree. I am very well blessed to find myself in such amiable company. But you are somehow different from them all, Mr. Ellis. I find myself eager to talk with you. *With* you, not just *to* you. I want to tell you about my morning in Boscombe. And I want to know what has happened about your letter. I want to learn something of your home by the sea. I want to tell you what Luc and Pippa have asked me to do. I want to drive the gig again, with you giving a sense of security from beside me. I want to stop at a few other places in the park we did not stop at the other day. I want to sit in that summerhouse at the end of the poplar alley with you. I want your little girl to run to you as she does when she has not seen you for a while and then climb up on my chair as if it was the most normal thing in the world to do and call me Aunty Jenny. I do not want to *avoid* you or have you avoid *me* simply because our families are worried that at any moment we are going to blurt out an announcement of our betrothal and plunge them all into deep crisis."

He sat back on the sofa, his arm along the back of it, and her hand slid away from his lapel. But after a moment she too settled back against the cushions and tipped her head sideways to rest against his shoulder. It did not feel exactly like friendship. Not *just* friendship anyway. But she was right. They were mature adults quite capable of choosing their own companions and deciding for themselves what was appropriate between them and what was not.

"The fete is the day after tomorrow," she said, "and that is somehow suggestive of the end of summer or at least the end of my stay here. And of yours. There will be just a week or so left after it. I believe I would regret looking back and realizing that for the final days here, including the day of the fete itself, you and I avoided each other, purely because our families were terrified of what might become of our friendship."

One week. Two at the longest. He guessed that in the future they *would* avoid being in the same place at the same time—especially after he married. For there was something between them that was not just friendship. But in the meantime . . .

"What we need to do," he said, "is not keep our friendship a secret. If we do, then it becomes unnecessarily clandestine and uncomfortable."

"If I could," she said, "I would run down the hill hand in hand with you right now, whooping with exuberance. Alas, I cannot do it."

They laughed together, their faces turned toward each other, and he noticed how white and even her teeth were, and how sparkling her eyes, and how pretty she was when she forgot her mask of dignified cheerfulness. She was happy. She had burst free of the mask. And he felt a pang of yearning. How he would love the chance to make that expression on her face and the happiness behind it habitual.

"Have you had any reply to your letter yet?" she asked.

"No." He turned his face to the view beyond the pillars. "It is a bit soon, I suppose, though not perhaps for a man eager to establish some connection with a half brother he has never met. My guess is that I will not hear at all. If his goal was to benefit somehow from my connections and perceived wealth, he might have been daunted when he read the long list of questions I asked. Question number seventeen, for example, asked if the fact that I am a landowner of independent means influenced his decision to write to me."

"Ouch!" she said. "Did you really ask him that? Well done."

Perhaps. Or maybe with such blunt questions he had offended Vincent Kelliston and squashed any possibility there might have been of meeting the only relative on his mother's side of whom he had ever been made aware.

"What will you do if he does not write to you?" she asked.

He sighed. "I long to be fully settled at last at Penallen," he said. "So far there has always been something to draw me away just when I was getting into a happy routine there, sometimes for weeks at a time—as now. I long to immerse myself in my life there, to be at peace, to have my own identity quite distinct from other, outer influences. I long to be . . . *at home* to stay. Yet I very much fear I am going to be spending a week or two of the autumn in Kent seeking out the man who says he is my half brother, checking the truth of his story, filling in at least some of the missing details, finding out if there are any other relatives there. Even if there are, of course, they almost without a doubt will want nothing to do with me. But if that is where my mother grew up and lived until after she was married and had a son, then I want to see it. I want to get a sense of her. I want her to have a history that did not simply begin with my birth and end with her death three years later. That history is mine too. I am her son, even though I was conceived out of wedlock six or seven years after she had her legitimate child. I need to adjust my image of her. I have always pictured her as being very young, perhaps not much above twenty when she died. But she had a *five-year-old child* even before she met my father."

"You will take your daughter with you?" she asked.

"Yes, of course," he said. "Where I go, Joy goes too. I have never spent a night away from her. Giving her a sense of security is my primary concern and will remain so while she is still a child. Besides, my history and her grandmother's history are hers too. I can do nothing to expand Marjorie's story beyond the little I know of it, the little *she* knew of it, but what I can do I will."

"You will continue to tell Joy stories about her mother," Lady Jennifer said, smiling at him. "She loves to hear how her mama stood up to all those fighting men, even the more arrogant of the officers, who must have been very intimidating. Was she really as bold as you describe her?"

"Oh, indeed," he said. "I would not give Joy a false image of her mother. What I tell her is all she will ever have of her, and it must be the truth. Marjorie was a quiet, dignified woman. She was not coarse and vulgar, as so many of the regiment's wives were. But she would not allow anyone to treat her with disrespect. She told me once that none of those privileged, entitled, spoiled officers, with their gold and silver lace and their white breeches and pristine scarlet coats and boots they could see their faces in, would be able to do without the washerwomen and the batmen and cooks and baggage carriers and sergeants and corporals and men in the ranks and everything and everyone else that made up the army. Within twenty-four hours, she told me, they would be helpless and blubbering for their nannies. She spoke to even the most obnoxious of them with respect, but she always insisted that they say *please* and *thank you* to her—and pay their bills promptly. That was something many of them were not accustomed to doing."

She laughed again. "I wish I could have met her," she said.

That would have been interesting. He doubted Lady Jennifer Arden would have been able to decipher one word in ten of Marjorie's very Cockney speech. Though Marjorie would have been speechless with awe if she had come face to face with Lady Jennifer. And she would have stood with her hands on her hips, her lips compressed into a thin line, a martial gleam in her eye, as she steeled herself to assume a courage she did not feel.

"What happened in the village this morning?" he asked.

"Ah." She looked out at the view for a few moments. Ben's arm along the back of the sofa brushed against her neck. "Mr. Rogers has made me a very smart pair of shoes. They are a combination of black, tan, and cherry-colored leather and very noticeable. Deliberately so. He explained that since people will look at my feet anyway, the best plan is not even to attempt to hide them but to do just the opposite. I so *liked* that idea. The shoe for my left foot is a perfect fit and very neat and comfortable. It was also a surprise. I did not realize he would make me a *pair* of shoes. The right one is not quite finished. He understood that adjustments would almost certainly be needed, and he waited for me to try it first. Raising the sole to lengthen my leg is not by any means the only thing that has to be done if the shoe is going to be of any use to me. It also has to accommodate the shape and angle of my foot and ankle—it will be a boot more than a shoe, by the way. The adjustments will be minor. He believes they will be done so the finished pair can be delivered tomorrow for me to try out here."

"Goodness," he said. "You will be able to dash from venue to venue at the fete, then, will you?"

"If it pleases you to make mockery of me, Mr. Ellis, please do not let me stop you," she said—and giggled. It was definitely a giggle, not a ladylike laugh. "Mr. Holland has made a sturdy crutch, with leather straps for my right arm to slide through. He believes it will help me walk without the necessity of a second crutch. My left side does not need one, he says. I am inclined to believe him, though the thought of being without my other crutch makes me a little nervous. A feeling I fully intend to fight."

"You are hopeful, then?" he asked.

"I am hopeful," she said. "But I am without unrealistic expectations. And both men reminded me of my promise to consult physicians at home and in London before I use either the shoe or the crutch for any length of time. I will *not*, alas, be dashing from the house to the village and back again during the fete—or waltzing at the ball. Luc and Aunt Kitty promised faithfully that they would insist upon the consultation with physicians. But they have agreed that they will not stop me from trying the shoes. This is going to be a painful learning experience for them too. I must be patient with them."

He turned his head to smile at her.

"And the chair?" he asked.

"I can see that Boscombe is a community of artists," she said. "Mr. Taylor is a very skilled carpenter. The chair is beautiful. It is also comfortable and the perfect fit for me. It has wheels large enough and positioned in such a way that I can turn them myself. It still needs work, however. There has to be some mechanism beneath it to allow me to turn it in various directions and to stop it and to lock the wheels when I wish it to stay in one place. It will be heavier than my present chair, though Mr. Taylor has chosen materials that are as light as possible. Oh. And there is even a holder into which I can slide my crutch."

"It will be ready before you return home?" he asked.

"Almost certainly," she said. "I am so looking forward to having it, though it is going to lack one feature I considered essential. It will not take to the skies, alas, and fly me from place to place."

He loved the way she could turn her sense of humor upon herself. He loved the way she could dream and hold on to reality at the same time. Yet the pressing forward with possibilities, limited as they were, was something new with her, he realized. Until very recently—until their talk in the rose arbor in the courtyard, in fact—it seemed she had resigned herself to the limitations others had imposed upon her, those others being the people who loved her and the apparent experts on her condition. In the short time since that talk she had woken to the possibility of taking charge of her own life—and her own friendships. She seemed very different from the dignified, ever-cheerful aristocrat he had met last year in London and this spring at Greystone.

"Am I forgiven, then?" he asked.

"By me?" She sat upright on the sofa and cocked her head to one side as she turned to face him. "Why would I need to *forgive* you, Mr. Ellis? When I came here, I was in low spirits and trying to deny it. I was determined to be cheerful so no one would know and so maybe I could deceive myself. I had been depressed for some time, perhaps since last year when I was in London and rejected what might well be my last marriage offer. Then Grandmama and Grandpapa died and all our planned living arrangements changed. Luc and Pippa would not be returning to Amberwell with me after all, so Aunt Kitty was compelled to come back to live with me instead. Then I turned twenty-five and woke up to the realization that I had lived for a quarter of a century and had only more of the same to look forward to. Then my lack of gratitude depressed me more. How dared someone who has so much be dissatisfied?"

She sat back again and rested her head against his arm.

"You brought sunshine blazing into my life, Mr. Ellis," she told him. "You reminded me of the importance of dreams and the equal need to let them out into the light to bring hope and some fulfillment no matter how small. You reminded me that I *am* twenty-five, fully adult and capable of making decisions about the course my life will take. Luc and Pippa can no longer come to live with me, but I *can* go and live with them. They have even invited me and assured me that they both *want* me to live at Greystone. I believe them. I love Amberwell. It has always been home. But insisting upon staying there for no other reason than that will only show a lack of willingness on my part to step ever forward into new adventures. If I move to Greystone—*when* I move there—Aunt Kitty will be free to do what she wishes with the rest of her life, which I am quite sure she longs to do, kind and loyal and affectionate though she has always been to me."

"So you are going to move," he said.

"Yes, I am." She turned her head and smiled at him. "And in a very real way, Mr. Ellis, I have you to thank for it all, for what has been a much-needed . . . revolution in the way I look at my life and my future. I am going to *move* in far more than just one way. I am going to move in every way I can for the rest of my life—from one home to another, in the gig I am going to purchase, in my chair, in my shoes, and on my crutch. Perhaps even through water. I might even ride one day, though at the moment I cannot imagine I will ever want to. But I will never say *never* again. If you feel guilty about what you set in motion during our conversation in the rose arbor, Mr. Ellis, please stop doing it. I will always remember how you brightened and changed my life."

He had been right, then. That half hour they had spent together really had been a pivotal moment in her life. He could forgive himself for going to speak with Cam without her knowledge.

"And you have kissed me," she said softly. "I will always remember that too. My first and only kisses."

Oh, God!

But they were about to be interrupted.

"Pa-pa-a-a."

"Je-e-enny."

The two voices called almost simultaneously from somewhere outside—Joy's and Stephanie's.

Ben got to his feet and went to stand between the pillars at the entrance of the temple. They were on the terrace outside the ballroom, one on each side of Lady Jennifer's chair. Idris Rhys's young nieces were with them. So were Owen and Bertrand.

"Up here," Ben called, raising an arm.

"Is Jenny there too?" Stephanie cried. But it seemed to be a rhetorical question. All of them were coming toward the hill without waiting for his answer.

"We are about to be invaded," Ben said over his shoulder.

"Papa," Joy shrieked as she climbed. "We had a cushion fight and Aunty Steph and Mari were winning because they are bigger. But then Uncle Owen and Uncle Bert came and they were on our side and Mari joined us too and we piled the cushions on Aunty Steph and beat her. I sat on her."

"The odds certainly sound to have been against her," he said as his daughter dashed past him and scrambled onto the sofa to sit beside Lady Jennifer.

"We did not know *where* you had gone," she said. "Your chair was empty."

"Did Bruce carry you all the way up here?" Stephanie asked after toiling to the top.

"No," Lady Jennifer told her. "Your brother did. I guessed the view from up here must be splendid, but I did not expect ever to see it for myself. He is very kind."

"Ben is?" Stephanie said. "Oh, he has always been the kindest person I know."

She was looking flushed and a little disheveled, Ben thought. She had had a strenuous afternoon. Steph was always kind toward children and indulgent with them. But . . . *he has always been the kindest person I know.* She had been talking about him. What a lovely compliment.

She scurried past him and went to sit on the other side of Lady Jennifer. Meanwhile, the younger of the Welsh girls was rolling down the hill again, shrieking to be caught by Owen or Bertrand.

"It is time for the girls to return to Cartref," Stephanie said. "Owen and . . . Bertrand are going to take them." She always had noticeable difficulty getting that man's name past her lips, Ben had noticed. Poor Steph.

"I will carry you back down," he told Lady Jennifer.

But she had glanced at Stephanie and perhaps come to the same conclusion as he had. "I think Stephanie might enjoy a bit of quiet relaxation and a chat with me up here, Mr. Ellis," she said. "She can go down ahead of me when we are ready to return to the house and call Bruce."

Ben nodded. "Come along, then, Joy," he said. "Your friends will be leaving. We will wave them on their way."

But his daughter was not listening to him. She was frowning intently up at Lady Jennifer. "Everyone has a mama," she said. "Mari and Marged have one. Gareth has Aunty Gwyneth, and Emily and Christopher have Aunty Pippa. Olwen and Andrew and Philip have their mama. Even Aunty Steph does. But I don't. I *had* a mama and I love her and she loves me, but I will never see her and she will never see me."

Oh, good God, where was this coming from?

"You do not have a little girl," Joy said. "Or a little boy. Nobody calls *you* Mama."

"No," Lady Jennifer said. "No one does."

Ben closed his eyes.

"Can I call you Mama?"

Lady Jennifer did not reply immediately. The little girl on the hill was shrieking again and Owen was shouting. The older girl was telling her sister it was time to go home. Ben was wishing a hole would open at his feet so he could drop through it. At the same time, he wanted to snatch up his daughter and fold her so far into himself that she would never again feel the absence of a mother in her life. What the *devil* was he doing here at Ravenswood when he should be at home, choosing . . .

"Just for pretend while we are here, before we both go home?"

Lady Jennifer said, her voice very gentle. "I think that would be lovely, Joy."

"I do too," Joy cried. "Mama." She laughed with glee.

Ben swallowed and turned back to the temple. "Time to go," he said, reaching out a hand for hers. She came skipping toward him, smiling sunnily, though she dashed past him to have one more roll down the hill.

"Catch me, Uncle Bert," she shrieked.

Ben strode down after her without looking back.

Chapter Sixteen

O h goodness, that was touching," Stephanie said. "Were you
embarrassed, Jenny?"

"Only in the sense that your brother was within earshot," Jennifer said. "He tries hard to be everything in the world to Joy, and
he tries equally hard to keep her mother alive in her memory. But
indeed I *was* touched. I will ask him in private if he will find it offensive to have me allow his daughter to call me Mama, but if he
has no objection, I do not."

Oh, but she was more than just *touched*. She was smitten. Upset. Bereft. She could not come up with just the right word.

"I was happy to find you up here," Stephanie said. "I felt sorry
earlier when we were on the way up here and you were sitting alone
on the terrace with your book that I could not simply invite you to
come with us. It must be awfully frustrating to be unable to get up
and dash off to do whatever takes your fancy. Yet you are always so

cheerful about it and such a good sport. I am filled with admiration for you. You are quite my idol."

"Now I am touched anew," Jennifer said. She was someone's *idol*? "But when you have been like this since you were a very young child, you know, you have learned to adapt your life accordingly. Besides, if I was always bemoaning my lot and complaining that I cannot do what others do, I would succeed only in making my own life a misery and that of everyone around me insupportable. Recently, however, I have been making an effort to find ways to make myself more mobile. I did not walk up here, of course, but when an offer was made to bring me, I did not refuse, as I normally would, on the grounds that I am too heavy and it would be too much to ask—even if I had not asked. I came, and the view is every bit as glorious as I thought it would be. This has been much more enjoyable than sitting on the terrace reading."

"It was Ben who offered to bring you," Stephanie said. "He is lovely, is he not? When Devlin left here so abruptly right after the last fete, I thought my heart would break. I was only nine years old. I was terribly upset that Ben was going too, but it was Dev I thought I could not live without. In many ways, though, it turned out to be Ben I missed more. There was a sort of empty ache where he had been. I think we all depended upon his sturdy, calm presence far more than we realized. He was always *there* and always ready to help in any way a person needed, even if it was no more than his silent, supportive presence. I felt terribly sad for him when he came home with Joy tucked inside his greatcoat and clinging to him. If anyone deserved happiness, it was Ben. But his wife had died."

"Yes," Jennifer said.

She had been fond of Stephanie ever since meeting her in London last year, though it was Pippa, closer to her in age, who had become her particular friend. Stephanie was an endearing mix of affection and youthful energy, but she also suffered from a terrible lack of confidence in her own attractions. She was the one, it seemed to Jennifer, who was enjoying this summer at Ravenswood the least of them all. And it was all because of one person. Owen's friend Bertrand Lamarr, Viscount Watley, who was a remarkably handsome young man, though he also had the charm and character to enhance his looks.

"Tell me what has upset you," she said, patting Stephanie's hand.

The girl looked startled. "Upset me?" she said. "Nothing has—"

"No," Jennifer said, squeezing her hand before letting it go. "Do not deny it, Stephanie. I am your friend. And I can be very discreet. The game you were engaged in with the children in the turret room was ruined, was it?"

Stephanie lowered her chin and examined first the backs of her hands and then the palms before curling her fingers into them and dropping them to her lap.

"It was not ruined," she said. "The other girls enjoyed themselves enormously. Owen was the plague of my life when we were children, or would have been if I had not given as good as I got. But children now adore him. He has a gift with them. Joy and Marged were soon shrieking and giggling more than before, and Mari was bright and flushed with laughter. She was dazzled by both men. They all turned on me, and I fought back ferociously because that was what the game was all about. The game was not ruined. I laughed as hard as everyone else. And when it was over, all three girls hugged me and laughed with me and Owen told me I was a good sport and . . . Bertrand gave me his hand to help me to my feet and smiled at me."

"You cannot just . . . *like* him?" Jennifer asked. The poor girl had a hard time even saying his name.

"He has a twin sister," Stephanie said. "He says she looks very much like him. So she is tall and slender and dark and beautiful. Her name is Estelle. They must turn heads wherever they go. Yes, I *like* him. Of course I do. How could anyone not? But I do not like him looking at me. He is polite and very . . . *nice*, but . . . Oh, what must he think when he looks at me, Jenny?"

"I am not privy to his thoughts," Jennifer said. "But I am quite sure he is happy to be as friendly with you as he is with everyone else." That would be no comfort to the girl, of course. "He is an agreeable young man."

"Yes," Stephanie said. "He is."

Jennifer took her hand again. "Love can be a wretched thing," she said. "I know."

She had been wretchedly in love with Arnold Jamieson last year. The fact that she no longer was did not negate the pain she had lived with for months afterward and even to a degree until very recently. It had been real and terrible and a very closely guarded secret. Now she thought she might well be in for more wretchedness after she returned home from here, though not over Mr. Jamieson this time. For friendship was not always *just* friendship.

"I *hate* being the ugly one in the family," Stephanie said with sudden passion. "And I hate being so abject about it. I want to be able to say, if only to myself, *Here I am. This is me, and I am comfortable and happy with who I am. Take me or leave me.* But it is easier said than done."

"Because the words themselves are not enough, are they?" Jennifer said. "One has to *believe* them right through to the depths of one's soul. But I am going to remember your words. If one can say them and mean them, then one's esteem for oneself and one's beauty and value as a person will be unassailable."

"Do you feel unlovable too, then?" Stephanie asked, her eyes moving over Jennifer. "But you are so slender and elegant and beautiful, and you are always so cheerful and sensible and wise. Do you feel unlovable because of your *leg*?"

"And do you feel unlovable because you are not as slender as a reed?" Jennifer asked.

"Silly, is it not?" Stephanie said after staring at her for a few moments. "I have tried not to be fat. I am not a glutton. When other people eat cake, I often merely drink my tea."

"We can become obsessed with a part of ourselves we consider imperfect," Jennifer said. "In our minds it becomes the whole of ourselves, and we believe that it is the only thing people see when they look at us. I am far more than my twisted leg."

"And I am more than my fat," Stephanie said. "Or perhaps I should say I am *less*."

They both collapsed with laughter.

"I like you so very much, Jenny," Stephanie said.

"The feeling is mutual," Jennifer assured her, patting her hand once more. "I am older than you are, Stephanie. I do not lay claim to any great wisdom, but I do have a bit more experience of life than you. I have discovered the overwhelming value of friendship. I am not saying it quite makes up for the sort of romantic love most of us dream of—the sort that Luc and Pippa have or Devlin and Gwyneth, but maybe it is unwise to believe that a good relationship

between a man and a woman must be the stuff of romantic dreams
or not worth having. If Owen's friend was a very ordinary-looking,
pleasant young man, would you have been happy when he spoke to
you or invited you to walk to the lake with him and your brother?
Or when he came with Owen to the turret room and threw cushions at you until you were down and then offered his hand to help
you to your feet? Would you at least be willing to be his friend?"

"But Viscount Watley is not ordinary looking," Stephanie said.

"Poor man," Jennifer said. "Are you going to hold that particular handicap against him for the rest of his stay here?"

Stephanie laughed. "I should take pity on him and be his friend,
then?" she asked.

"Why not?" Jennifer said. It was a rhetorical question.

"Is Ben *your* friend?" Stephanie asked, and Jennifer was not at
all sure it was just a casual question.

"Yes," she said. "Yes, he is."

Fortunately Stephanie was not looking directly at her. Perhaps
if she had been, she would have seen the tears that had sprung to
Jennifer's eyes.

"Perhaps you would be good enough," Jennifer said, "to go back
to the house now and ask Bruce to come up here and fetch me."

"I will," Stephanie said, jumping to her feet. But before she left
the temple she bent swiftly over Jennifer and kissed her cheek.

Jennifer sat and waited—and thought of a lonely widower coming home from the wars with his young child, little more than a
baby at the time, tucked inside his greatcoat.

Her friend.

And she thought of that child a few years later gazing earnestly
at *her* and asking if she might call her Mama so she would not be

the only child of her acquaintance here who had no one to call by that name.

And she looked out over the parkland.

Ben sat beside Lady Jennifer Arden at dinner that evening for the first time. He would not have done so now despite the fact that they had agreed earlier to be openly friendly toward each other, but she was already seated, and she looked up at him with a welcoming smile and patted the empty place beside her as he passed. It was as clear as any verbal invitation. She spoke to him while everyone else took their places and there was a buzz of voices all around them.

"If my allowing your daughter to call me Mama is hurtful or offensive to you, Mr. Ellis," she said, "then it is still not too late for me to suggest to her that I would prefer to remain Aunty Jenny. She will, after all, soon have someone else she can call Mama for the rest of her life. But if it is all the same to you, I am happy for her to play make-believe for as long as she and I are still here at Ravenswood."

Her voice was earnest and she was looking intently at him, almost as though she were pleading with him not to say no. That scene up in the temple had been bothering him ever since it happened. He ought to have put his foot down right there and then and insisted that Joy apologize for embarrassing Lady Jennifer.

"I did not reprimand Joy at the time because the request was made to you, not to me," he said. "But I *was* horribly embarrassed on your behalf. You truly do not mind?"

"I do not," she said. "I feel honored."

"Then thank you," he said.

The soup was served, and conversation became general, as it

usually did when they dined *en famille*. Inevitably it focused mainly upon the fete the day after tomorrow. Although preparations at the house were not nearly as frenzied as they used to be, when Mother organized every detail and her children and servants were her cohorts and worked almost as hard as she, nevertheless there was still a great deal to do. All the contests must be organized and the displays set up, including all the needlework and lace making and baking and wood carving that would be delivered in a constant stream tomorrow if they had not already been brought today. Everything must appear to advantage before the judging began. There was also the evening ball, the sole responsibility of Ravenswood.

Uncle George Greenfield, who was dining with them, as he did quite frequently these days, changed the subject by asking Lady Jennifer about her visit to the village during the morning. She told everyone what she had told Ben in the temple earlier.

"The shoes will be finished by tomorrow," she said. "But the village will be a hive of activity by then, and so will Ravenswood. I will leave them where they are until Monday. And then you may all expect to see me striding about the house on my own two feet with some support from my single crutch."

"It is a deuced shame you are going to have to wait all that time, though, Jenny," Owen said. "I rather fancied the prospect of seeing you dashing all about the village and park the day after tomorrow."

"I would be delighted to drive you to the cobbler's in the morning," Nicholas told her. He winked. "A one-way journey, of course. You can walk back."

"That is very kind of you—I *think*," she said, laughing. "But everyone will be busy and does not need one more thing to do. I can be patient for a few more days."

"But why should you be, Jenny?" Nick asked. "It seems to me you have been patient all your life."

"I would have a giant tantrum if it were me," Owen said. "Forget patience."

Lady Jennifer laughed again.

"In all seriousness," Gwyneth said from her place at the foot of the table, "it really would be a shame if one of our guests was neglected over something so important just because we were too busy planning a fete. I daresay Mr. Rogers would be perfectly willing to come here tomorrow morning if he were asked. He could bring your shoes, Jenny, and make sure they fit properly and are comfortable. He could watch you walk in them and make any further adjustments that are needed. How long would it all take? An hour at the longest? I really do not believe he would consider it an imposition. He has been known to complain that the work of a cobbler is generally dull and routine. Devlin, what do you think?" She looked along the table, her eyebrows raised.

"But Jenny would need a suitable space and some privacy, Gwyneth," Lucas said. "Apparently she walked on her crutches out in the cloisters here a few times—without a word to either Aunt Kitty or me, I might add, knowing very well that we would have done our best to dissuade her. But the courtyard is going to be a busy place for the next couple of days. The ballroom and the terrace outside it will be too. And most of the other rooms in the house."

"Gracious," Mother said. "Ravenswood is not so small that we cannot find a private space for Jenny to try out a new pair of shoes, is it? How about—"

"The gallery," Ben suggested.

It was above the ballroom in the west wing and stretched the whole length of the wing, though it could be partitioned off into four smaller salons when occasion demanded. It was never much used in the summer. In the winter, on the other hand, it could be a marvelous playground for children. And for adults it provided a place to walk when snow and ice or even simply rain and bitter winds discouraged them from going outside.

"It is upstairs in the west wing," Mother explained.

"But Jenny cannot—" Lady Catherine said.

"Her chair could be wheeled all the way to the bottom of the staircase next to the ballroom," Ben said. "She could be carried up. There are comfortable seats up there. And she *will* be walking."

"The whole length of the gallery?" Owen said. "Will it be long enough for her? We will have to go and see this, Bert. All of us must. You could charge admission, Jenny."

"I would hasten to explain, Jenny," Philippa said, "that Owen sometimes believes it is his mission in life to tease and torment other people."

"Only family members and close friends, Pippa," Owen said. "Be fair now."

"I think ten guineas apiece is a fair price," Lady Jennifer said, laughing. "*Not* to admit you or anyone else to the show, Owen, but to keep you all away. Do you *really* believe Mr. Rogers would be willing to bring my shoes here, Gwyneth—and the crutch from the smithy? And stay long enough to make sure they fit properly and I can actually use them?"

"I would remind you that I am lord of the manor here," Devlin said, his eyes twinkling at her. "He will come if the Earl of Stratton himself summons him, or even if he simply *asks* him, which I am far more likely to do. He is also very aware of the fact that your brother is His Grace, the Duke of Wilby. He is suitably awed. It *is* rather a grand title to have. I am quite envious."

"But I hate to be a bother to anyone," Lady Jennifer said.

"I cannot think of anything that would be less of a bother," he assured her. "I will send him a note first thing in the morning—with a liveried footman. That always impresses people."

"I will come to the gallery with you, Jenny," Lady Catherine said.

"No, Aunt Kitty," Lady Jennifer said. "You are going to be busy all day planning the displays with Lady Stratton and Lady Rhys, and I know you are vastly looking forward to it."

"But—" Lady Catherine said.

"Phil and I will come to the gallery with you, Jen," Lucas said, interrupting. "I can carry you up and then make sure you do not overexert yourself."

"Baron and Lady Hardington have invited you to luncheon, Luc," Lady Jennifer reminded him. "You are to take the babies with you—at the express request of Lady Hardington."

"I will send word—" he began.

"You most certainly will not," she told him. "I refuse to be a nuisance to anyone or to upset anyone's plans for the day. I have told you all that I can wait until Monday."

"I have no particular plans for tomorrow," Ben said, "beyond taking Joy to see her puppy early in the morning and making sure everything is ready to set up for the races on the front lawn. That will take me no longer than an hour or so in the afternoon. I can take you up to the gallery, Lady Jennifer, and remain with you there."

All attention swung his way, and he was sure he did not imagine the brief moment of silence.

"Oh, *will* you?" she asked, turning toward him, her eyes shining, her cheeks glowing. "It would be very fitting. You, after all, Mr. Ellis, were the one who started this whole business of my walking shoes by suggesting to me once upon a time that dreams can sometimes be helped along with a bit of practical thought."

"And courage," Philippa said. "Ben supplied the one and you the other, Jenny."

There was another moment of silence, so brief that Ben thought he might have imagined it.

"That would seem to be settled, then," Devlin said. "I will have Rogers sent up to the gallery when he arrives—shall we say at eleven o'clock?"

Stephanie clapped her hands. "I am so *glad*," she said. "It would be horribly dreary for you to have to wait until Monday, Jenny. That is eons away. And of course Ben can carry you up to the gallery. He carried you all the way up the hill to the temple this afternoon when he saw you stuck alone in your chair outside the ballroom while the rest of us were on the way up to the turret room for a cushion fight."

There was no mistaking the silence about the table this time.

"I *do* hope you will be able to walk in your new shoes, Jenny," Philippa said, beaming across the table at her friend. "Even if just for a few minutes each day. What a wonderful feeling it will be for you."

"It will," Lady Jennifer agreed. "But that is quite enough about me. You have entered the archery contest, Owen? And you too, Bertrand? Do you like your chances?"

"Not one little bit," Owen said with a grimace. "Though Bert can at least hit the target most of the time."

"Which is not much of a recommendation," Bertrand said. "I

believe one has to hit the bull's-eye at least once if one is to stand a remote chance of winning. A *very* remote chance even then."

"Joy has entered some of the races," Mother said. "She assures me that she almost never drops the egg from her spoon when she is practicing."

"It is no boast," Ben said.

"Remember that you have taken it upon yourself to gather enough eggs for the race," Mother reminded him. "The hens must do their part in assuring the success of the fete."

"They have been given their orders," he told her.

The conversation remained back on the main topic for the rest of the meal, until Gwyneth got to her feet to lead the ladies from the room.

Ben went with them. It was time to tuck his daughter into bed for the night and tell her a few stories.

His family and Lady Jennifer Arden's were alarmed again, he thought. It was more than a little annoying. Both of them were adults. Good God, he was thirty-three. And both of them were rational beings. Neither was likely to do anything outrageous, like thinking of marrying each other, for example. They were friends. They had decided this afternoon that they would not deny that fact or try to hide it any longer just to reassure their families.

To the devil with them all. Their anxieties were their problem, not his.

"Papa," Joy said after two stories, her voice sleepy as he fluffed her pillow and straightened the covers on her bed and made sure her cat was beside her. "Can Mama come with us to see the puppies tomorrow?"

"Mama?" He frowned.

"My pretend mama," she explained. "Can she come? I want to show her my puppy."

And why the devil not, he thought, quelling his first instinct, which was to say a firm no. Why the devil *not*?

"I will have to ask her," he said. "She may be busy, but I will ask."

She yawned and pressed the cat's ear to her mouth.

CHAPTER SEVENTEEN

After an early breakfast the following morning, the gig was brought around to the terrace outside the front doors. Lucas lifted his sister onto one of the seats while Ben took the other with Joy on his lap, Devlin placed the haversack cushion beneath Jennifer's right foot and handed her the ribbons, and almost the whole family, their faces wreathed in smiles, waved them on their way to visit the litter of collie puppies.

"Mama is *driving!*" Joy shrieked.

It was surely the most bizarre scene Ben had ever been witness to—or a participant in. He had passed on Joy's request to Lady Jennifer in the hearing of everyone else after coming down from the nursery last night, and she had said yes—*if* they could take the gig and she could drive it. They had survived the brief silence that seemed to follow all their public communications with each other. Then Owen had commented that he hoped Jenny did not intend to spring the horses, Stephanie had said she wished she could go too but she had choir practice, and Mother—aided and abetted by Gwyneth—had changed the subject.

So here they were on the descent to the village, Lady Jennifer looking slightly tense as though she expected that the horse might try to bolt at any moment, while Joy clapped her hands and Ben resisted the urge to laugh.

It was a brief visit. They had not brought either Lady Jennifer's wheeled chair or her crutches, so she stayed in the gig while Joy fetched the collie puppy she had chosen to be her own once it was weaned. It was the smallest and liveliest of the litter. It bounced and yipped and nipped in her hands. She laughed as she handed it carefully up to Lady Jennifer, who settled it on her lap, her skirts forming a sort of nest about it, while Joy scrambled up to the seat beside her and Ben stood on the other side ready to catch the puppy should it be in danger of falling. But he need not have feared. Lady Jennifer soothed the little thing with one finger stroking its head and ears while Joy murmured nonsense words at it and tickled its chin. Both of them were totally absorbed in the puppy as it squeaked and licked and nipped at them.

"Does she have a name?" Lady Jennifer asked.

"Cariad. Carrie for short," Joy said without hesitation—it was the first Ben had heard of it. "*Cariad* means *love* where Marged and Mari live. Their mama calls them that all the time. Lady Rhys says it too."

"Carrie is a pretty name," Lady Jennifer said. "I think she may be falling asleep."

"She does that lots because she is a baby," Joy said. "I love her."

"I am not at all surprised. She is adorable," Lady Jennifer said while Ben gazed from one to the other of his girls and felt utter contentment—until he heard the echo of his thoughts almost as if they had been spoken aloud. *His girls?*

"Can we take Carrie home with us when we go, Papa?" Joy asked.

She asked frequently in the hope, he supposed, that his answer would have changed since the last time—or that conditions would have changed.

"She is going to need her mother for a while yet," he told her. "But Uncle Owen has promised to bring her to Penallen when she is ready and stay with us for a few days."

"Ye-e-es," she cried, her face brightening. "He can play with me and come swimming in the sea with us. We can show him the fishing boats and take him to the shop with all the sweets. He can come with us when we take the puppy for a walk."

"Perhaps we will persuade Aunt Stephanie to come too," he said.

"Ye-e-es," she said again. "And Uncle Nick and Uncle Bert? And *Mama?*" She turned her eager smile upon Lady Jennifer.

"Uncle Nicholas has to go back to work soon," Ben told her. "All the way across the sea to France. Uncle Bertrand will be going home next week to see his sister. He misses her and I daresay she misses him. Lady Jennifer will be going home too. So will Lady Catherine and Aunt Pippa and Uncle Lucas."

"Going home is always lovely, is it not?" Lady Jennifer said. "Even when a vacation has been great fun."

The puppy sneezed and woke itself up, and Joy laughed and was distracted. A few minutes later Ben took her to the pen to set the puppy back inside and then to the house to thank the farmer and his wife for allowing them to come. It was time to go and play with Marged and the other children at Cartref, he told Joy. Mrs. Howell had offered to have Joy for the day, since she had been told that all was going to be busy activity at Ravenswood and indeed through-out the village as everyone prepared for tomorrow's festivities. She would be happy to have Joy to keep young Marged company.

Ben drove them there while Lady Jennifer held Joy on her lap and the two of them laughed over the little dog's antics and Lady Jennifer told Joy how good collies were as sheepdogs when they were properly trained.

Joy dashed off hand in hand with her friend into the garden a few moments after the gig had arrived at Cartref. After a brief chat with Eluned and Mrs. Howell, Lady Jennifer insisted upon driving the gig home.

"I think you are showing off now," Ben said.

She turned her head to smile at him before concentrating upon the road again. "I have twenty years of lost freedom to catch up on, Mr. Ellis," she said. "Indulge me, please."

My girls. He could not get the phrase out of his mind. How wonderful it would be . . . But he shook his head. How wonderful it was going to be when he had chosen a bride and married her and settled down with her at Penallen.

Bruce whisked Lady Jennifer away to parts unknown—probably her room—as soon as the gig arrived on the terrace. But Ben found her in the library less than an hour later. Pippa was there too, rocking a sleepily crying Christopher in her arms while Lady Jennifer had Emily on her lap and was amusing her with a few silver bangles that dangled from her wrist.

"Poor Chris," Pippa told Ben. "Those new teeth of his have *still* not pushed through the gum, and he is feeling very sorry for himself. Emmy had hers more than a week ago."

Ben kissed the top of his sister's head and smoothed a hand over his normally placid nephew's.

"Will he be well enough to go with you for luncheon?" he asked.

"Oh yes," she said. "I believe Lady Hardington is more eager to see the children than she is to see Luc and me. Lowering, is it not? She will be only too happy if one of them is in the mood to be cuddled."

Lady Jennifer raised her arm until the sunlight from the window caught the silver of her bangles, and Emily blinked and reached more determinedly for them.

"Am I being a tease?" She lowered her arm so the child could get a good grip.

"There is no sign of Rogers yet?" Ben asked unnecessarily.

"It is only ten minutes to eleven," Lady Jennifer said.

But even as she spoke there was the faint sound of approaching horses, and Ben moved to the window to see who was coming. It was a carriage, but it did not turn onto the terrace toward the main doors. It proceeded along the east wing, presumably to the servants' entrance.

"I believe he is just arriving," Ben said. "Good man. He is eight minutes early. I will take you up, Lady Jennifer. Shall I ring for help with the children, Pippa?"

But before she could answer, the door opened and Lucas came into the room. Emily bounced on her aunt's lap and reached out her arms for her father.

"Well. This is a lovely welcome," he said, picking her up and kissing her plump cheek before settling her on one arm. "A smile for Papa this morning? I think the cobbler is arriving, Jen. Let Phil and me come up to the gallery with you. There is time before we need to leave for the Hardingtons'. And you really ought—"

"*You* really ought to be getting ready to go," she said. "All I am doing, Luc, is trying on a new pair of shoes. It is nothing to fuss about. And I trust Mr. Ellis to take good care of me. He is my friend, after all, as well as the possessor of two strong arms."

That information—probably both parts of it—were doubtless not what Wilby would want to be hearing, but perhaps he had learned some wisdom in the past few days, for he did not argue the point. Instead he was probably counting down the days until his sister—and Ben too—could be safely away from Ravenswood.

They reached the gallery before John Rogers was shown up. Ben was able to settle Lady Jennifer on a sofa partway along the room, opposite one of several long windows that filled the gallery with natural light during the day and offered lovely views over the park and lake to the west. The room was hung with family portraits going back generations. They culminated, Ben knew, in a large canvas painted when Stephanie was a baby about the twins' present age and he was almost seventeen. He had overheard his father asking Mother if she minded having Ben included in the painting. She had sounded quite indignant when she answered.

"Ben has been a member of this family for fourteen years, Caleb," she had said. "As far as I am concerned, he is our son. Of course he will be in the portrait for future generations to see."

So there he was in the family portrait, standing a bit awkwardly half behind his father's head and half behind his left shoulder—fourteen-year-old Devlin had been squarely behind his right—while everyone else was arranged artistically in front of their father, Steph on his lap.

There was a separate portrait of Devlin striking a casual but elegant pose beside his horse, painted when he turned twenty-one. The heir.

"What a breathtakingly lovely room," Lady Jennifer said.

"Yes," he agreed. "It is an indoor promenade as well as just a gallery."

He had not been up here, he realized suddenly, since before he went to the Peninsula with his brother. He had never brought Joy here. And he knew the reason even though he had not thought of it consciously until this moment. There were no portraits of his father anywhere else in the house. Only here. He had always used to think that the family portrait was an incredibly accurate one of his father, who was smiling genially, beaming love upon his wife and children, who surrounded him. It was unusual in that most such portraits depicted solemn, dignified subjects. None of the rest of them had been smiling—except three-year-old Owen.

Ben could not bear the thought of seeing that portrait after his return. He did not want to see it now.

"Are you in any of the paintings here?" Lady Jennifer asked.

"Yes, the family one." He pointed vaguely along the gallery.

"I would like to—" she began.

But they were interrupted by the arrival of John Rogers, who looked a bit awed by his surroundings, and Cam Holland, who grinned at Ben and inclined his head politely to Lady Jennifer.

"My lady," he said. "I came too, bearing your crutch. I hope you do not mind."

"Not at all, Mr. Holland," she said, smiling at him. "Is this whole thing going to work? Or are we going to go down in ignominious defeat?"

"Never say that," he said in mock horror as Rogers unwrapped her shoes and Ben saw them for the first time. "John and I don't know the meaning of those words, do we, John? We cannot have you crippled for the rest of your life just because of one lame leg. If these contraptions do not quite work for you, we will keep at them until they do. You ought to be walking just like everyone else. Like I told you before, I've made you a crutch, because that is what you are accustomed to. But eventually I think you will be able to manage with a cane, provided we give you plenty to hold on to and lean on."

He had been unwrapping his metal crutch with its leather-bound straps and pads while he talked. Rogers more characteristically worked in silence.

"I do not expect perfection, Mr. Holland," Lady Jennifer said.

"Well there, if you will pardon the impertinence, you do not have the right attitude, my lady," Cam said. "A person should always expect perfection and success. I do and John does. Ben too. When he was steward here back in the days of the old earl, I always used to think to myself when he came into the smithy, *Uh-oh, here comes trouble,* though it was my pa in those days who took the brunt of it."

"Was I really such a tyrant, Cam?" Ben asked in some surprise.

"Not a tyrant," Cam said. "Just someone who did not stand for even the smallest suggestion of shoddy workmanship. Here we go, then, John."

Lady Jennifer had said the shoes would be very noticeable. They were that. They had been crafted of three colors of supple, gleaming leather—black, tan, and burgundy—but the colors were not in neat stripes, as Ben had pictured them in his mind, but rather in artistic swirls, which had obviously called for the hand of a master crafts-man. They would certainly draw attention to her feet, but as she had observed to him, that was the whole point. Why try to hide that which could not possibly be hidden? Why not deliberately draw attention to it instead?

"The left one was fine when you tried it on a few days ago, my lady," Rogers said as he fitted it on her foot now. "If you find after wearing it for a while that it is not so comfortable, I will make the necessary adjustments."

"It feels just like a glove that has molded itself to my foot," she said.

Ben watched the right one being fitted and so saw her foot clearly, the ankle twisted inward, the foot bent downward so her heel was much higher than her toes. Both ankle and foot were thin in comparison to the left ones. The shoe—or boot, rather—had been made with what looked like great expertise to mold ankle and foot while raising them and giving them support. The sole had been built in such a way that it would be difficult for her to turn over on her ankle as she walked and thus cause herself further injury. Its essential clumsiness had somehow been made to look almost el-egant.

"I took to heart what you said about the cushion Mr. Ellis made for you, my lady," Rogers said. "I made the inside of the shoe as soft as I could without sacrificing the support you need."

"Thank you," she said, her voice sounding a bit breathless. "I will need a hand up."

"Allow me," Ben said, moving to her left side as the cobbler stepped back and Cam hovered with the crutch in one hand.

She leaned heavily on Ben as she rose to her feet and stood for a moment, seemingly balancing her weight. She reached for the crutch and allowed Cam to show her how to slide her arm through the leather straps and settle it beneath her arm.

"It feels a bit strange and alarming to have no crutch on the other side," she said. "But I must keep in mind that there is nothing whatsoever wrong with my left leg. I will learn to trust it for both strength and balance. In the meanwhile, Mr. Ellis, may I just rest a hand upon your arm, if you please?"

Both workmen had stood back now to watch her. Ben noticed again what he had observed down by the lake, that she was rather tall. She was also standing very upright, deliberately resisting the urge, he guessed, to hunch forward over her crutch. She looked somehow regal in her black dress, with her face pale and set with concentration and her dark red hair gleaming in the sunlight streaming through the window.

She took one step forward with her left foot, clutching Ben's arm tightly, and then another step with her right foot and the crutch. She was breathing heavily. The problem, of course, was not *just* with her ankle and foot. Her leg too was thin and bent backward, so it was some sort of miracle that she could bend her knee. It was never going to be possible for her to balance her full weight over her feet.

She took a few more steps before releasing her viselike grip on Ben's arm. He slid his arm beneath hers and clasped her bent forearm lightly. He took none of her weight but offered the assurance of support should she need it for balance.

"All the little problem areas that gave me trouble a few days ago have gone away," she said. "You are a true marvel, Mr. Rogers. And the crutch is perfect, Mr. Holland. It is far more comfortable and suited to my height than the ones I currently use."

"You may call either of us back at any time, my lady," Cam told her. "In the meantime, keep walking, but don't overdo it. I would not enjoy having to deal with His Grace, your brother, if you do."

"If I overdo the walking, Mr. Holland," she said, "it will be my fault, not either yours or Mr. Rogers's, and so I shall inform my brother. I will not keep you any longer now, even though I intend to walk at least twenty-five more steps along the gallery and back again before sitting down for a rest. I know both of you must have a busy day planned. I thank you for having given up a part of it for my sake. When you have your bills ready, please send them to me, though I am quite sure my brother has directed you to send them to him. Tyrant brothers have to be firmly dealt with. *By me.*"

Both men chuckled as they bowed awkwardly to her and took their leave.

"Are you sure you want to remain on your feet?" Ben asked when they were alone together.

"Perfectly sure," she said. "I cannot believe the feeling of not lurching to my right every time I use my right foot. I am going to *walk*, Ben. Not as other people do. Never without a crutch or a cane, and never without a grotesque-looking boot on my foot. But we are all unique, and this is my uniqueness. I am going to *walk*."

Her eyes blazed into his, and there was color in her cheeks to replace her earlier paleness. The strength of her determination wrapped itself about him. But really he heard one word with far more clarity than all the others. She had called him Ben.

By the time she had counted out her twenty-five steps along the gallery, turned—she had needed to lean quite heavily upon Mr. Ellis's arm to accomplish that—and walked the thirty-two steps back to the sofa where rest and her slippers awaited her, Jennifer felt as if every bone and sinew and muscle and organ and blood vessel in her body was screaming in protest. *Not* pain. There was no specific point in her body she could label with that word. Just . . . discomfort. And a fatigue that went far deeper than mere tiredness. She was not tired. She felt no desire to sleep.

She had held herself very erect through the whole exercise, though the urge to slump forward, especially on the return journey, had been almost overwhelming.

"I am nearly as tall as you, Mr. Ellis," she said—and wondered if he had noticed the horrid blunder she had made earlier, when she had called him Ben.

"I have been muttering a silent prayer of thanksgiving over the fact that you do not tower over me," he said. "That is quite lowering for a man—pun *intended*."

She always loved his flashes of dry humor.

"I must beg you for a few minutes more of your time," she said. "I have to sit down for a while before you carry me back to my chair."

"You are hurting?" he asked.

"I do believe every hair on my head hurts," she said. "In addition to every other part of me. But not really with *pain*. I *will* overcome, however. Not all in a day or even a week or a month. But it will happen."

"Turn," he said, "and I will help you to sit. I will remove your shoes then and help you back on with your slippers."

But there was something else, and she spoke before she had a chance to properly consider.

"Mr. Ellis," she said. "Before I sit, will you please hold me?

Against you, I mean. I have been hugged all my life, but never with my whole body against someone else's. Not since I was a small child anyway."

She heard her own words almost as though they were coming out of someone else's mouth. *Against you . . . never with my whole body against someone else's.*

He hesitated for only the briefest of moments and then grasped her right arm while he took her crutch and propped it against the sofa. She was in his arms then, her body leaning along the full length of his, his one arm about her shoulders, the other about her waist. She set one cheek against his shoulder and turned her face in to his neck. And she thought she might well swoon.

He held her securely but did not strain her to him. His body was warm and solid and very masculine. He smelled of soap or cologne, or perhaps it was his shaving soap. It was not an overpowering scent but simply seemed part of him. She must have caught whiffs of it before now—probably when he had carried her. She slid her arms about his waist and wished this moment need never end. How could she ever, *ever* have thought him an ordinary man, scarcely worth noticing?

She raised her head and tipped it back so she could look into his face. He gazed back, his expression unreadable. Though perhaps that was not quite true. There were endless depths of kindness in his eyes, and she felt tears well into her own.

"Please kiss me," she said. "Kiss me while we are standing like this."

They were words she knew she ought to regret. For they were not fair to him. She was giving him virtually no choice, especially given the kindness in those eyes. But they were words she knew she would never regret as much as she ought. For she was building memories to last a lifetime, and the events of this morning would surely live large in the very forefront of her memory.

She expected the warm touch of his lips, perhaps prolonged for a moment or two. But he did not kiss her immediately. He did not move his arms, very aware as he must be that she might find it impossible to stand alone, especially after she had just admitted to her weariness. But he brushed his nose lightly over her own before turning his head slightly and feathering kisses over her cheeks and her chin and one corner of her mouth. He gazed into her eyes again then before letting them roam upward to her hair and over her face and then kissing her, his lips parting over hers, his tongue moving along the seam until she opened her mouth and it came inside to circle hers and explore every surface. What would it feel like, she wondered, to have him come inside another part of her? She felt a stabbing of raw longing deep inside and along the insides of her thighs and knew she was experiencing real desire, real lust, for the first time.

With a man who was an impossibility. Life could be such a cruel joker.

He withdrew his tongue but did not immediately end the kiss. She leaned into it and into *him*, noting how sturdy and dependable, how *kind*, he was. Though it seemed to her that there was no heat of passion in him, only a gentle willingness to give her what she had asked of him because this was an important, memorable morning for her.

She drew back her head and smiled at him, and it was the hardest thing she had done in the last hour. "Thank you, sir," she said, her tone light, her eyes twinkling. "Now I know what it feels like."

"Turn," he said. "And sit." He was helping her do both as he spoke. Then he knelt down before her and gently eased first the right boot and then the left shoe off her feet before fitting on her slippers. It distressed her that he was seeing her foot in all its misshapen hideousness.

"Ah," she said, flexing her left foot and wriggling the toes of her right as Mr. Ellis packed her shoes back into the wooden box in which Mr. Rogers had brought them. "What bliss."

He came to sit beside her. "They are a possibility, then?" he asked her, nodding toward the box.

"A *probability*," she told him. "More even than that. I am going to progress by slow but sure degrees to Mr. Holland's cane, and the next time I come to Ravenswood I am going to walk the whole length of this gallery to see the family portrait that includes you and then back again. I will maybe even walk all the way to the lake. Or the poplar alley."

She was deliberately exaggerating the possibilities, of course. For having a foot that would not lie flat on the ground and an ankle that would not flex as her left one did and a leg that was not straight would never make walking a comfortable activity. But it was nevertheless a possibility. No, a probability. And more even than that. For she was going to exercise her leg, gradually and sensibly, to strengthen it, perhaps to build it up to more nearly match the left in size if not in length. She was going to put on her shoes and walk in them every single day, even if only for fifty steps.

But oh dear, at the moment everything inside her and on the surface of her screeched in protest against the exertion to which they had just been subjected.

And her spirits were threatening to plummet for a different reason. She tackled the issue head-on.

"Mr. Ellis," she said as she gazed through the window on the other side of the gallery at the temple on the hill, where they had sat yesterday. "Tell me about your three lady loves."

"*Lady loves?*" He laughed. "They might be a bit startled to hear themselves described thus."

She suspected that all three of them would be thrilled. Unless, that was, he had cultivated invisibility as successfully in his new home as he had here and in London and at Greystone. It was altogether possible.

"Tell me about them," she said. "Which is your favorite?"

"Well, that is the whole problem," he said. "They all are."

Was he so undiscriminating, then? But no. She suspected he had no idea how very attractive he was. And though he must know how capable he was of loving, perhaps it had not occurred to him that he was very lovable too. And she suspected that he might also be a passionate man if he would but let go of the iron control he had always imposed upon his emotions. She would wager he could blow the universe to smithereens for both himself and the lady he loved if he would just move beyond his lifelong practice of containing his feelings deep within himself.

"Tell me," she said.

One was the widow of a fisherman. Another was companion to an elderly lady, who was a relative of hers. The third was a schoolmaster's daughter. They all sounded worthy. They would all probably make him a good wife and Joy and his future children a good mother. He would probably live contentedly with any one of them, just as he had with his Marjorie. For his demands did not include deep emotion. Well, they did, but not *passion*. And his loyalty, once given, was as firm and immovable as the Rock of Gibraltar. But oh, Ben . . .

"Well?" He was smiling at her. "Are you going to tell me which I should choose?"

She shook her head. "No," she said, and had to turn her head sharply away when tears unexpectedly welled in her eyes again. Who was she to tell him—or even to *think*—that he ought to hold out for love? For *romantic* love, that was. For a passion to move the earth or explode the universe? Perhaps even if he found it, he would not be happy with it. Perhaps a gentle affection and a quiet contentment were exactly what he needed and what would suit him best. Could one ask more of life in the long term, after all, than contentment?

"Did I say something?" There was concern in his voice.

She shook her head. "I just do not believe I have ever felt more weary in my life," she said. "Would you carry me down to my chair and take me to my room, please, Mr. Ellis? Or go and ask Bruce to come to me?"

"There is a faster way of getting you to your room," he said. "Why carry you down to your chair only to have to carry you back upstairs when we reach the east wing? I will go fetch your chair and wheel you around this floor without having to encounter any more stairs."

"Ever the practical thinker," she said, laughing.

She sat waiting while he went downstairs to fetch her chair and knew she had failed to prevent her spirits from sinking. It was very perverse of her when in many ways this had been the happiest morning of her life. But of course she had done the unthinkable, and now she was going to have to spend weeks, maybe months, fighting the consequences.

She had fallen head over tail over ears over everything else in love with Ben Ellis, illegitimate son of the late Earl of Stratton and one of his mistresses.

And she hated *with a passion* those three blameless women who were probably all waiting with bated breath for him to come home and choose one of them. So that he could live *contentedly* ever after.

She hated that phrase.

Hated it.

CHAPTER EIGHTEEN

Almost everyone within a five-mile radius of Ravenswood Hall heaved a collective sigh of relief when the morning of the fete dawned with a clear blue sky and not a sign of a cloud on the horizon. The air was already warm at six o'clock, when the innkeeper's wife drew the second batch of perfectly baked bread from her oven and Sidney Johnson and a helper laid the maypole on the village green, attached all the brightly colored ribbons, and hoisted it into place. The ribbons fluttered in the light breeze. The Reverend Danver threw open the doors of the church to watch and drew in a deep breath of the lovely fresh air as he made a private bet with himself that Sir Ifor Rhys would arrive before seven to make sure that no dust had settled in the pipes of his organ overnight. He was to play a recital during the afternoon for anyone who wanted to come and listen or merely sit in the pews to rest after a few hours of frolicking in the sun.

At Ravenswood itself, Christopher Arden, Marquess of Roath, woke his nurse early with a demand for attention, preferably breakfast, even though his two new teeth had come through and his fever had dropped before he went to bed last night and it might have been expected that he would sleep longer. He greeted her with a wide smile and flapping hands, and she almost forgave him.

Ben and Devlin were out in the stable yard, setting in place the first two logs for the log-splitting contest later. Nicholas and Bertrand had already gone off to the poplar alley to get everything in order for the archery contest. Owen was still asleep. Stephanie was in her dressing room, vomiting, though she cleaned up after herself and told no one. They would only rally about her and assure her that she would sound like an angel when she sang her solo part with the choir later. Useless words, though she appreciated the sentiment.

Lucas, Duke of Wilby, having just finished making languorous early morning love with his wife, wondered aloud to her if anyone was up yet. She laughed softly and settled her head into the crook of his arm.

"On the morning of the fete?" she said. "Only half the world."

"Mmm," he said. "I would rather be part of the other half."

She sighed. "Me too."

Gwyneth, Countess of Stratton, was awake, though she was still in bed, having promised Devlin half an hour ago that she would stay there another hour, though she had assured him too that she was not feeling queasy. Actually she was, very slightly, but she had decided a week ago, after Dr. Isherwood had confirmed her suspicion that she was with child again, that she would *not* succumb to the nausea she was beginning to feel in the mornings, at least until the fete was well and truly over. She did not have time for such foolishness. Her mind ran determinedly through the daunting list of tasks that must be accomplished today if all was to run smoothly and wondered if she had forgotten anything.

The dowager countess was up and getting dressed even though it was too early for breakfast and she was not expecting her committee to arrive to help set up the displays of contest items in the courtyard and along the terrace for a couple of hours yet. She was trying not to remember the last, disastrous fete and all the ones that had gone before it. She was trying not to miss Caleb. No one ever spoke to her of him, on the assumption, she supposed, that his memory was hateful to her. It was not. She had known him for who he was since very soon after their marriage when she was seventeen. She had loved him anyway. More fool she, perhaps, but love was complicated. She realized that today would be particularly painful— but no one would know. Not even Kitty. Not even her children. Well, let the day begin, and let it end happily for Devlin and Gwyneth's sake and everyone else's. A woman's lot in life was to endure, after all. She had always been good at that.

Ah, Caleb.

Joy turned over in her bed, taking her cat with her. She pressed its ear to her mouth as it stared at the brightening window with its permanently startled eyes, and she muttered words whose images were weaving their way through her dreams—*Papa, Carrie, Marged, Mama. Papa.* She did not wake.

Jennifer *did* wake. It was because her nose was plugged, she realized, and her cheeks and the pillow on either side of her head were wet with tears. What a dreadful humiliation. She could not possibly summon her maid before all traces of the tears were gone. She reached beneath the pillow to find her handkerchief and dried her cheeks and blew her nose. She turned the pillow so she would not be lying on dampness.

She had been dreaming. He had chosen one of the three women, and Jennifer was at their wedding because, bizarrely, it was at

Greystone, where she had gone to live. The woman was seven feet tall and was wearing plumes at least three feet long in her high-piled hair. All the time they were exchanging vows, he had been peering about her arm to stare directly at Jennifer so that his words seemed to be directed at her. She had had that panicked urge, which comes only in dreams, to speak out, to protest when the clergyman asked if anyone knew of any impediment to the marriage, but no sound would come out of her mouth. Instead she jumped to her feet and dashed from the room, her iron boot ringing out like a hammer on an anvil.

Enough, she told herself, and anger came to her rescue. She threw back the covers, swung her legs carefully over the side of the bed, reached for her crutches—not the new metal one but the old ones—and got herself into her dressing room, where she bathed her face in cold water from the jug on the washstand and spoke aloud to herself.

"Enough now. Enough!" If she was heartsick, she had no one but herself to blame. *No one.* Both Aunt Kitty and Luc had tried to warn her, but she had not listened. She had known better. She was perfectly capable of enjoying a friendship with a man without falling in love with him. She had been wrong, and she had *no one but herself to blame.* "Enough," she said again.

She could see in the looking glass on the washstand that there were still red blotches on her cheeks. Her eyes were still slightly bloodshot. Fortunately it was early. Her maid would not bring her morning cup of chocolate for a while yet.

She returned to her bedchamber and stood looking out after throwing back the curtains and opening the window. She leaned on her crutches, her right leg raised, though her toes touched the floor and helped her keep her balance. She felt stiff all over after yesterday's exertions. But that was good. She had something to live for and work toward. She was going to *walk*. And *drive*. And move to Greystone and make a new life there with new neighbors and new friends. And with Luc and Pippa and the babies. Perhaps she would even learn to swim.

And fly.

She laughed softly to herself and watched Nicholas and Bertrand approaching the house from the direction of the poplar alley. They were talking and laughing and in evident good spirits.

She was going to enjoy today. Every moment of it.

Out in the stable yard, Devlin stood back from the great blocks of wood and looked around to make sure everything was ready for the contest, though it was not scheduled for hours yet.

"Have you had any reply to your letter, Ben?" he asked.

"No," Ben said. "Not yet."

"What will you do?" Devlin asked.

Ben shrugged. "Nothing," he said before sighing. "Go chasing after rainbows, I suppose. I will take Joy to Kent after the harvest and see what I can find. Or *whom* I can find, though I cannot imagine that any persons who knew or were related to my mother will want any sort of acquaintance with me. I could not be anything but an embarrassment to them after all, could I? I just need to *know*. Or at least to find out for sure that there is nothing to know."

"I will go with you," Devlin said.

Ben turned sharply to look at him. "There is no need," he said.

"There is." Devlin sighed too. "You are my brother, Ben, and I think you have always been my closest friend. You cannot know how much I leaned upon you during those years in the Peninsula, when *you* came with *me*. I am not sure how I would have done without you. Now I suspect you are going to need me. And there is no point in denying it. I will be going with you anyway."

"Thank you," Ben said after a longish silence.

On farms for miles around cattle were milked and fed, sheep were let out into pastures and horses into paddocks, eggs were collected from chicken coops, stalls and barns were swept out and spread with fresh straw, water was pumped, and numerous other chores were completed so that the farm families could spend the day and even half the night in Boscombe and at Ravenswood with a clear conscience. Life usually plodded along with a routine that was only occasionally broken by a minor social event, even if that was no more than the weekly jaunt to church to listen to Sir Ifor on the organ and to the Reverend Danver delivering his mercifully brief sermons and to stand outside exchanging news and gossip with neighbors for half an hour or so afterward.

But today the annual fete—at least, everyone hoped fervently that it would become an annual event again—was to be celebrated. It would surely be better than ever, as its myriad activities were to be spread between the hall and the village, and many of them had had a hand in preparing it all.

The festivities would begin outside the church on the village green this year with a prayer from the vicar and a few unaccompanied songs from the youth choir, which was famous since it had competed and placed in the top three in several Welsh festivals, or *eisteddfodau*, where the standards were very high indeed. Then there would be the demonstration of maypole dancing by the group that practiced faithfully all year long in Mr. Johnson's barn. And then— the culmination of the morning's delights in the minds of many— there would be the breakfast, to be served at the inn and outside on the green by Jim Berry, the innkeeper, and his wife.

There would be so much going on after that that choosing was going to be a bit of a dilemma. For everyone wanted to see and do *everything*, but it was not possible. Choices must be made.

But at least tonight there would be only one activity, the culmination of everything to which they had looked forward for months past, ever since the decision had been made to revive the summer fete after a gap of eight years. Tonight there would be the grand ball at Ravenswood.

By seven o'clock in the morning there were not many people still in bed. And there were not many who were yawning and dragging their feet, as happened on most other days of the year.

At five minutes to seven Sir Ifor Rhys strode into the church, and the Reverend Danver, who had wagered against himself less than an hour earlier, won his bet. Too bad he had put no monetary value on it. He would have demanded of himself that he pay up. He smiled at his own private and silly little joke.

The final Saturday in July had dawned bright and clear and full of the promise of nothing but pleasure all day long.

They all went down to the village more or less together, though Stephanie had left half an hour before, having assured Devlin when he asked that no, of course she was not nervous.

"Why should I be?" she had asked, doubtless rhetorically.

"She is scared out of her wits," Owen said after she had left.

"Poor Steph," Gwyneth said. "But she will sing like an angel."

"Of course she will," her mother said. "She *is* an angel."

"Not that Mama is biased or anything like that," Nicholas said, grinning.

The dowager countess went in the barouche with Lady Catherine Emmett and Lady Jennifer and George Greenfield, who had ridden early to Ravenswood. A wagon followed with Lady Jennifer's chair and two of the children's nurses. Everyone else walked in a cheerful body together. If they were remembering this day eight years ago, none of them were showing it. The fete was beginning, and they were prepared to enjoy it to the full. Devlin carried his son. Lucas carried Emily, while Nicholas took Christopher, who was sporting two new teeth this morning. Joy was perched astride Ben's shoulders, her hands clasping his chin while his hands held her by the waist.

Boscombe was filling up, or at least the village green and the streets surrounding it were.

"Look, Papa," Joy cried, pointing to the tall maypole standing to one side of the duck pond. And then, "Look, Papa," as she saw all the stalls and booths set up around the perimeter of the green, laden with wares that would be sold from them as soon as the opening ceremonies and the breakfast were done with. She was pointing at one particular stall with its lavish display of bright, garish jewelry.

She spotted Marged Howell then, also astride her father's shoulders, and waved and bounced.

"Stay up there for a while," Ben said, "so you can see Aunt Steph's choir and the maypole dancing. Then you can get down."

It would be perfectly safe for the rest of the day to allow the little children to run more or less wild. Here, where everyone knew everyone else, no child would escape the attention of at least a dozen people at every moment. None would wander off to get lost or fall in the river or get into any real mischief. Parents would be able to relax and enjoy themselves and not feel that they must keep both eyes firmly riveted upon their children at every moment.

It was good to belong to a rural community, Ben thought. Penallen was another such place.

Things were very different than they had used to be. The Reverend Danver stood with his wife outside the church to open the fete instead of at the foot of the front steps at Ravenswood, flanked by the Earl and Countess of Stratton and their children. His prayer, delivered in his clergyman's voice, which reached across the road and across the green so no one had any trouble hearing him, was not prolonged. The youth choir filed out of the church when he was finished and lined up in two rows facing Sir Ifor, who beamed encouragement at them, hummed the starting note, and raised his arms to conduct them. They sang without fault, the first song in unison, the second in three-part harmony, and the third in two parts, with Stephanie's solo to begin and end it.

She did indeed sing like an angel in her sweet soprano voice. She also sang the first part in Welsh, which was a surprise to everyone and drew an enthusiastic burst of applause when the song came to an end, though only very few had understood the words.

"Perfect pronunciation," Dylan Howell said from beside Ben. "Good old Sir Ifor."

"That's my Aunty Steph," Joy was telling Mrs. Proctor, the dressmaker, on Ben's other side.

And then all attention turned to the maypole, where Sidney Johnson was gathering his dancers together and they were taking their ribbons in hand. The two violinists were checking that their instruments were in tune with each other. The women dancers had always worn dresses in different but harmonizing pastel shades, while the men had worn black breeches and waistcoats and shirts to match the dresses of their partners. They had not changed that tradition, Ben was happy to see. The women wore flower garlands on their heads. They were a visual delight even before they started to dance.

The fiddles struck a chord and the dancers were off, circling the maypole in intricate patterns, the women clockwise, the men counterclockwise, taking their ribbons with them, plaiting them together until it looked as though they would be hopelessly tangled, and then miraculously unplaiting them before the dance ended.

"More," a few voices called above the general applause.

"Again," Joy shrieked.

"Again," Marged yelled after her.

But they need not have feared. The dancers always performed three dances, just as the choir always sang three songs. The second dance was fast and furious while the spectators gasped and roared. At every moment it seemed that the dancers must surely collide with one another or hopelessly snarl their ribbons. But with the final chord, everyone was in place and every ribbon flowed free from the top of the maypole to the hand of the dancer who held it.

The third dance was slower and statelier. The dancers smiled at one another and at the people gathered about them as they dipped and weaved past one another. Their audience smiled back and clapped their hands in time to the music—including Joy, who clapped above Ben's head.

"We will be giving lessons after breakfast to anyone who wants to learn to dance about the maypole," Sid Johnson announced after the applause had died down. It had happened at the last fete too. Steph and Pippa and Devlin had taken up the challenge then, Ben recalled. Gwyneth too. She had still been Gwyneth Rhys at the time.

But he did not really want to think of the last fete. He did not want to make comparisons. If this one was to become a new annual tradition, then it had made a cracking good start.

Long tables had been brought out of the inn and set up on either side of the door. Now every inch of them was being covered with platters piled high with food, and people were lining up to help themselves to what looked like a sumptuous feast. Chairs had appeared outside the shops and other buildings around the green and in front of the stalls, which had not yet opened for business. Large blankets were being spread over the grass on the green. The various committees had been busy, Ben could see as he set Joy down and she went running off, hand in hand with Marged and Olwen Cox before he could suggest that he help her fill a plate with food. They were heading directly for Sidney, who was about to have his first recruits, Ben suspected.

"It is a sad day, it is," Dylan Howell said, chuckling despite his words, "when even one's youngest goes dashing off with friends without even a backward glance at her dada."

"It is," Ben agreed, remembering those days when Joy had clung to him at every moment or at the very least had kept him well within her line of vision. It was time he had another baby in his nursery. And another and another. He wanted *children*.

But the thought threatened to bring on the mental turmoil he had been unable to shake off for most of yesterday and last night. Even when he slept he had found himself desperately trying to untangle the mess of his life—which had seemed far worse in his dreams than it was in reality.

His future children had to have a mother. But she was not going to be any of the three women he had picked out at Penallen as possible brides. At least he did not *think* she was going to be any one of them. He might change his mind when he returned home, of course. But he liked them all too much—he *respected* them all too much—to pick any of the three as a sort of second-best choice. He would not marry any of them just because he had decided that he must marry someone so he could have more children soon.

Second best.

It implied, did it not, that there was a *first* best.

But since that was an impossibility, he was stuck where he had been for the past two years, without the stability and comfort of Marjorie, a widower adrift in the world with a young child and wanting more. Wanting that stability and comfort back. Trying not to want more than just that. Trying to quell yesterday's mental torment.

One thing he had always been good at was keeping his life orderly, avoiding anything that might threaten chaos. He suspected that somewhere in the lost memories of his first three years was the terrible anguish of losing his mother and being taken from his home and brought here. His whole life since had been a largely unconscious effort to create order out of the turmoil and keep that order at all costs. A few times his world had teetered, but always he had brought it under control again. Until recently. More specifically, *now*.

He had actually been very close to the contentedly-ever-after life he had craved.

Falling in love had *not* figured in his plans.

It was not that he did not believe in it. He did not have to look beyond his own family to see that it very much did exist. Devlin and Gwyneth were certainly not living contentedly ever after. Nor were Lucas and Pippa. Both couples behaved with perfect good breeding when in company with others, but both were nonetheless and unmistakably alight with . . . *passion.* Romantic, passionate love certainly existed, then. It was just not for him. He did not want it. He never had. He had not been in love with Marjorie, or she with him as far as he knew. But God, he had loved her. He had been happy with her. With her he had found all he had ever wanted, even if he still could not imagine how what he had with her could have survived after the war years.

He took his plate of food to sit on one of the blankets with Idris and Eluned Rhys and the Howells and Sally and Alan Roberts, the schoolmaster.

Lady Jennifer Arden was seated in her chair over by the church with the vicar and his wife, Colonel and Miss Wexford, and Barbara Rutledge. She was her usual smiling self.

Ben wished he could go home tomorrow. He wished *she* could. Every ounce of self-control he had spent a lifetime building and converting into the quiet, stolid Ben everyone knew had been tested almost to the breaking point yesterday. He had thought of her and Joy collectively as *my girls.* He had held her and he had kissed her in the gallery because she had asked it of him. She had not asked lightly, he knew, or flirtatiously or frivolously. She had asked out of a deep need for some normality in her life. She had asked because he was her *friend.*

God damn it all to hell.

He wondered how long it was going to take him when this was all over to piece himself back together and be his normal self, inside as well as out. Outwardly, he guessed—and hoped—no one would see that his world had come apart. How long?

Would it ever happen?

Had the master plan for his life, so carefully constructed, so nearly realized, crumbled beyond repair?

He hoped to God it had not.

With what would he replace it?

CHAPTER NINETEEN

J oy was having the best time ever.

She ate with her friends, but there was no one today to insist they sit down to eat and finish everything on their plates. They were too busy and too excited to eat much. They danced about the maypole with enough other children that each of them had a ribbon—Joy's was bright yellow, like the sun—and most of them followed the instructions, except for one boy who pranced about the pole like a clumsy workhorse, going under when he was supposed to go over and going that way when he was supposed to go this and laughing like a wild thing and thinking he was *funny*. But it was fun anyway, and the pretty lady dancers clapped their hands afterward and told them all they were very clever.

The girls ran around the green with friends from the maypole, hiding among the crowds and jumping out to frighten one another and laughing their heads off. The duckies were not on the pond today. Papa's Uncle George snatched Joy up in the air after she had hidden behind him and swung her about in two big circles while she shrieked, and then he had to do it for Marged and Olwen and Andrew too until he said his old bones were weary and he was so dizzy he could hardly stand and Mama's Aunt Kitty told him he was silly.

By then the stalls all around the outside of the green had been open for some time, and they ran to see what was on them all, squeezing between the crowds to have a good look. There were all sorts of things from the village shop on one table and toys on another, but they were not toys anyone could *buy*. You had to throw balls at targets really far away and knock over three of them—the same as Joy's age—and then the man would *give* you whichever toy you wanted. The girls did not have any money, but they jumped up and down with glee as they watched other people throw and mostly miss.

A man in another booth was drawing pictures of people who sat on a chair beside him and he was ever so good.

"Maybe he will draw us," Marged said, but they still did not have any money and anyway who would take the picture when it was done? They would not *all* be able to have it. Besides, they would have to sit still for a long time, and there was too much else to see.

There were gloves and scarves and shawls on another table, all in bright colors, and some of them would fit little girls. But they were for cold weather and it was hot today. Anyway, that stall was a bit boring.

And then they came to the jewelry stall. There were bright beads and silver and gold chains, all worked into necklaces and bangles and bracelets and brooches and earrings. They stopped there, wide-eyed and enthralled.

Marged's mama—though Marged called her Mam—came up behind her, set her hands on her shoulders, and laughed. "I think we should buy matching sets, Marged," she said, and threw one string of bright orange beads over Marged's head and another over her own. She picked out matching bracelets for them both.

Olwen's mama arrived at almost the same time. "What a good idea," she said to Marged's mam. "Shall we do it too, Olwen? Beads or gold or silver chains?"

Olwen picked the gold.

"You must pick out something too, Joy," Marged's mam said kindly. "What would you like?"

"Oh, you must, Joy," Olwen's mama said. "Something from Mrs. Howell and something from me. You girls are going to dazzle everyone's eyes."

Both mamas were laughing. Marged and Olwen were jumping up and down in their excitement.

"No, thank you," Joy said politely, because Papa had taught her never to take money or anything else from strangers. Not that these ladies were strangers exactly, but they were not her aunties either. And neither of them was her mama. Her own mama loved her, but she was in a place where she could never, ever be with Joy to buy her something and a matching something for herself. Joy could ask Papa to buy her something, but it would not be the same. She wanted . . . she wanted *Mama*.

But of course! She *had* a mama, even if she was only a make-believe one for a little while. She was kind and she always smiled and she always let Joy climb onto her chair and snuggle in with her. She always smelled nice, and she had red hair Joy wished she had too. She had gone with Joy and Papa yesterday to play with Carrie. She could not walk because she had a funny foot, but it did not make her grumpy. Surely there would be nothing wrong with asking Mama for some money. Maybe she would even want to get something matching. Joy looked eagerly toward the church not far off and, sure enough, she was still there, sitting in her chair and talking with a man who had stooped down on his haunches beside her. Joy had seen him before but could not remember his name. She ran over and clambered up onto the chair and sat still on Mama's lap until the man got to his feet.

"The day after tomorrow, then, my lady," he said. "I'll bring the chair over to the hall and you can see what you think."

"I shall look forward to it immensely, Mr. Taylor," Mama said, and then gave Joy her attention. "Are you having fun, sweetheart?"

"Yes," Joy said. "There are beads and glittery things over there, and Marged's mam and Olwen's mama are buying them some and the same things for themselves, and they wanted to get me something too but I said no because Papa said not to take things from strangers and I don't know where Papa is and besides, Papa could not wear beads to match mine, could he?"

"He might look a bit funny," Mama said, her eyes twinkling. "Since I am your honorary mama, Joy, would you allow *me* to buy you some beads?"

"Yes," Joy said, though she did not know what *honorary* was. "And the same for you."

"Let me see if I can draw the attention of someone to push my chair over there," Mama said, raising her head to look around. "Ah, I see Luc over by the maypole."

But before she could raise her arm to attract his attention, Papa appeared suddenly beside them as though from nowhere.

"Is all well here?" he asked.

Joy beamed up at him. "Mama is going to buy me beads," she said, "and the same ones for herself, but she needs someone to push her chair. You do it, Papa."

"I will indeed," he said.

And then they were over at the jewelry stall, the three of them, and they managed to get close, and it felt like pure heaven to Joy as they looked over everything on the table. Mama found a whole lot of rings Joy had not noticed before, little ones that could be made to fit her fingers and bigger ones that could be made to fit Mama's. There were butterflies and birdies and flowers, and soon Joy had a different one on every finger except her thumbs, though she had to take off the blue butterfly and have a green one instead because there was not a blue one that would fit Mama. They fluttered their fingers at each other and laughed.

Mama threw three bright bead necklaces about Joy's neck, and Joy touched them and looked up at Papa with glowing eyes. But he was busy picking out longer ones in the same colors to go about Mama's neck, but first she had to take off her bonnet. It was a straw one today, with a black ribbon to tie beneath her chin. The sun shining through the straw brim made pretty patterns on Mama's face. She laughed when Papa put the beads about her neck. They looked bright and lovely on her black dress. Her cheeks were rosy.

"And three bracelets to match for each of you," Papa said, rummaging on the table until he found what he wanted.

"Oh, six, I believe," Mama said. "Three for each arm."

Joy did not know what six was, but it was three for each arm. One-two-three and one-two-three. And that was six.

Then Mama and Papa argued over who was going to pay for all their treasures, though they were not cross with each other. They were both laughing, but Mama won because she said it was important to Joy and besides, she was not likely to beggar herself.

Joy, with loaded fingers and jangling neck and wrists, thought she must surely burst with happiness. She and Mama *matched*, and

Papa was smiling at both of them and admiring them and telling them they looked like twin princesses.

Joy clambered back onto the chair because Papa had spotted the toy booth and wanted to see if he could win one of the toys for Joy by knocking down three targets. And he did it, and Joy chose a cuddly dog because it had droopy ears and droopy eyes and she just wanted to hug and hug it. Mama had suggested the cloth doll with the bright red hair, and Joy liked it, but she liked the dog better. And then Papa threw more balls but knocked over only one target. He tried again and knocked over all three, and he chose the doll and gave it to Mama, who looked at him with eyes so bright Joy thought for a minute she was crying. But she was not. There were no tears on her cheeks, and she was *smiling*. She must have really, really wanted that doll.

"Thank you, Ben," she said, and Joy thought her papa's name sounded nice when Mama said it.

Mama wanted to go into the church then, where Sir Ifor had started to play the organ—they could hear it from outside—and Joy wanted to go too even though her friends were still not far off, bedecked with jewelry, as she was. She wanted to listen to the organ, and she wanted to be with Mama and Papa, just like Aunty Gwyneth and Uncle Devlin and Gareth when they were all together, and Aunty Pippa and Uncle Luc and the twins. Mama told Papa that he must not feel obliged to remain with them, but after setting her chair at the end of one of the pews, he sat on the pew right beside them, and they all listened to the music along with a number of other people.

Joy did not know words to say what she was feeling so she said nothing. But when she grew up she was going to do just what Sir Ifor did. She was going to fill the whole world and the whole sky and the sun and the moon and the stars with music too big to de-scribe, almost too big to *feel*. Even Aunty Gwyneth's harp could not quite do it. Or the pianoforte in the music room. Or the fiddles playing for the maypole dancing. Only this organ.

She stretched one hand over the arm of the chair until Papa took it in his own, squeezing her rings a little bit, though they did not really hurt. And they were all together—Mama, Papa, and her. But then after a while the music made her eyelids droop. She tried to keep them open so she would not miss a note but then she turned to stretch out her arms to Papa, and he took her onto his lap. She brought her dog with her because she did not have her cat, and she pressed its soft, floppy ear to her mouth and smiled at Mama, who smiled back and took her ankle in a loose clasp. She tried hard to keep awake because this was the best day *ever* and there was still lots more to come and she did not want to miss a minute of it.

S ir Ifor Rhys would continue to play the organ for a while lon-ger. The taproom at the inn remained open for anyone who cared to go in for a pint of ale, though the innkeeper and his wife were no longer there, and there were jugs of lemonade and large urns of tea and coffee on a table outside, free to any persons who cared to help themselves. The maypole had been abandoned, but the ribbons still fluttered invitingly in the breeze and a few children still pranced about it and called to parents to watch them. The various stalls and booths were still open but with greatly depleted supplies and fewer customers. The portrait painter, who was using charcoal today rather than paints, still had a couple of custom-ers awaiting their turn, though he had warned them that soon he would be packing up his things and moving up to the hall, where he would set up again in one corner of the main terrace. Chairs were being returned to the buildings whence they had been brought. The blankets that had half covered the green during breakfast had been folded up and put away.

Most of the remaining planned events were to take place at Ravenswood. Many people had already gone up there, eager to be present for the races and other contests and to look at all the needlework and baking and wood-carving entries and try to predict who the winners would be.

The children's races would be run on the lawn in front of the house just before the three preliminary heats of the log-splitting contest in the stable yard behind the house. The archery contest would follow in the poplar alley and then the final round of the log hewing.

Philippa and Lucas were still in the village, though the twins had gone back to the hall quite a while ago with their nurse and Gareth and *his* nurse. They had been sitting inside the inn, out of the heat, having a chat with James Rutledge and Barbara, his sister. But word was brought to His Grace that the barouche and the wagon had come down from the hall for the convenience of Lady Jennifer. Philippa and Lucas went to find her. She was nowhere to be seen on the green or at any of the stalls, but it became perfectly obvious where she must be as soon as they heard the organ music coming from the open church doors.

They stood at the end of the nave of the church while their eyes adjusted to what seemed like semidarkness after the bright sunshine outside. There was a surprising number of people sitting quietly in the pews, listening, or perhaps merely resting after a busy morning or cooling off from the heat outside.

It did not take them long to spot Jennifer, whose chair was out in the nave, though it had been moved right up against one of the pews. Sitting at the end of the pew, almost shoulder to shoulder with her, was Ben. Her arm reached out toward him. Her hand, they could see, was grasping a little ankle, presumably Joy's. Ben's fingers were resting lightly on three garishly bright beaded bracelets on Jennifer's wrist. Joy must be asleep to be keeping so still. Ben and Jennifer appeared to be engrossed in the music.

Lucas glanced at his wife, his eyes bleak. She looked back and smiled softly at him. They did not say anything. No words were necessary. They waited for the music to end, which it did a couple of minutes later with a decisive chord and a smattering of applause.

Lucas took his wife's hand, something he did not often do in public, and led her toward his sister.

"Jen," he said, keeping his voice low as he bent over her chair. She had identical rows of the cheap bracelets on her other wrist too and three long strands of them about her neck, startlingly notice-able against the black elegance of her dress. She appeared to have a bright ring on each finger too. The child, he could see in one glance, was similarly adorned. And good God, he thought, they looked gor-geous, the two of them, like two exotic birds. Like mother and . . .

Well.

"Oh, look at you two in all your finery," Philippa said, her voice laughter filled but equally quiet. "I am quite jealous."

Joy was waking up and yawning hugely. "Yes," she said, lifting one arm and shaking her bracelets at them. "Mama bought them. And Papa knocked over three things and won my doggie—she waved it at them—and he won Mama's doll too because it has the same color hair as hers. And yours, Uncle Luc."

A large cloth doll in bright, clashing clothes with a shock of scarlet hair made of thick strands of wool sat on Jennifer's lap, cradled in her free arm.

"Are you ready to go back to the house?" Lucas asked Jennifer. "The afternoon activities will be starting there soon, and the barouche and wagon have come for you."

"I am ready," she said. "Thank you, Luc." And she smiled at him with such luminous sweetness that his heart turned over painfully and he wondered what being a brother really meant, and what being head of a family meant. He wondered what being the Duke of Wilby meant. And did those roles ever clash with one another? And where did love fit in?

"We will see you soon, Ben?" Philippa asked as Lucas turned Jennifer's chair.

"Very soon," Ben said. "I have to get all the equipment for the races out of the carriage house."

"I am running the egg race," Joy said. "I am in the race with legs tied together too, but I won't win that because Andrew runs like a *snail* and always forgets which leg comes next."

"I shall cheer for you anyway," Philippa said, laughing.

"Yes," Joy said.

There was time after they returned from the village for Jennifer to go into the courtyard with Pippa and Luc and look at the marvelous displays of embroidery and tatting and knitting and lace along the west side and sumptuous baked goods on the east. They had not been judged yet. That would happen a little later, during the archery contest. But the displays in themselves were a collective work of art, as Pippa remarked to Aunt Kitty, who had come to join them.

"Yes," she said. "Clarissa did not really need her committee for this part of the task at least. She has an unerring eye for pleasing design and display."

The entries had not been placed haphazardly on the tables, wherever space could be found for them. They had been purposefully arranged according to color and shade and texture and design so that the displays flowed from one end of the tables to the other. It was a remarkable lesson in arrangement, Jennifer thought, something she could appreciate when she saw it but would never be able to produce herself.

"I am very glad not to be a judge," she said when they had looked at everything. "How would one decide which items are better than others and which are best of all?"

"With a great deal of dithering and anguish and second and third thoughts," her aunt said. "I agree with you, Jenny. I would not enjoy judging these contests. Now the wood-carving contest is a different matter, as least as far as first prize is concerned. There is one sculpture—Mr. Taylor's—that is far and away superior to all the others. Have you seen it yet?"

"We came in here first," Lucas said. "Unlike you and Jenny, Aunt Kitty, I *could* judge the baking contest—provided I could eat the winners as my reward, that is."

"You would have a stomachache all night," Pippa said, "and it would serve you right."

"True enough," he admitted. "We had better go up and fetch the twins, Phil, so they can come and cheer their cousin to victory in the races—except, presumably, the one in which she is to have her leg tied to that of a snail. Do snails *have* legs?"

George Greenfield wheeled Jennifer's chair out to the terrace and in front of the tables upon which the wood carvings were displayed. Aunt Kitty went with them.

"The sheep and lamb are mine," he told Jennifer. "Whittling has only ever been a leisure activity when the mood is upon me. It has not been a passion, as it is to some other, more talented people. You may, however, make appropriate sounds of appreciation when you see them, Lady Jennifer."

"I see them already, Mr. Greenfield," she said, laughing. "They are charming. And if we all gave up activities we find congenial just because we do not have the talent handed out to the chosen few at birth, then the world would be a duller place and our lives more tedious."

"Thank you," he said. "Those were the appropriate sounds."

They both laughed.

"The sheep and lamb have been carved by a very caring hand," Aunt Kitty said.

"And those sounds were *more* than appropriate," Mr. Greenfield said while Aunt Kitty beamed at him.

But Jennifer had seen the carving to which her aunt must have been referring, though the names of the carvers were not displayed with any of the entries. It was a full-length carving, about three feet high, of a woman standing against the trunk of a tree and gazing off into the distance. What was really remarkable about it, Jennifer thought, was that the woman was ageless and without any distinguishing features to suggest her identity. And though her eyes gazed forward into the distance or into the future, she seemed also to be gazing inward. She was Everywoman, with sadness, endurance, and acceptance etched into every line of her face and body, while yearning and hope looked out through her eyes.

"Oh goodness," Jennifer said, and wondered if, despite the surely deliberate universality of the figure, she was someone Mr. Taylor knew. And loved. She was not his wife. He was a bachelor.

"He will win the archery contest too," Mr. Greenfield said. "No one else will come close. The man is a phenomenon. His parents were our neighbors when Clarissa and I were growing up. His elder brother inherited the land and married and had half a dozen children while Matthew moved here and surprised everyone by becoming the village carpenter."

The lawn in front of the terrace was becoming more and more crowded with people, including what seemed like hordes of shrieking, darting children. It was time for the races.

Jennifer stayed outside to watch, her chair on the terrace by the steps leading up to the front doors. Stephanie was on one side of her, Nicholas on the other. They watched the footraces for the various age groups and the more specialized races that followed. Joy and Andrew Cox did not win the three-legged race for all the reasons Joy had explained earlier. Surprisingly, however, Andrew did beat her and everyone else too in the sack race, having turned from a snail to a hare as soon as he had both his legs back to himself. Joy came in last in that race, mainly because she stopped short of the finish line to help a little girl get to her feet and rearrange her sack after the child had fallen and burst into tears. Joy held her hand as they hopped over the finish line together, a full minute after everyone else. Joy won the egg and spoon race by a mile.

Nicholas went to congratulate her, though it was Ben who swept her into his arms and kissed her—and restored her necklaces and bracelets.

"Are you coming to watch the log splitting, Jenny?" Stephanie asked.

But Jennifer was feeling a bit weary. There was much of the day left. She was looking forward to the picnic tea at which the winners of all the contests would be awarded their ribbons and everyone would feast upon the foods everyone had brought.

Bring enough cold savories and/or sweets to feed your own family, the relevant committee had decreed, the idea being that when all the food was put together there would be enough for everyone and a great variety of delicious dishes among which to choose. In reality, of course, almost everyone had brought enough to feed at least five families.

"I am going to go inside to rest for a while," Jennifer said. "Would you do me the favor of going in and finding Bruce for me, please, Stephanie?"

"Of course," Stephanie said, and bounded up the steps with all the energy of youth even though she had been busy all day.

Crowds still milled around, though some people were making their way back to the stable yard to watch the preliminary heats of the log-splitting contest. It had always been one of the most popular contests of the day, Jennifer had been told. Cameron Holland was favored to win, though the man who had beaten him eight years ago, another blacksmith from a neighboring village, was apparently entered again this year.

A chaise had just driven up from the village, though it did not proceed back to the stables, where the crowds would have inhibited its progress. Nor had it turned onto the crowded terrace.

"Bruce will be here in a moment," Stephanie said, running back down the steps. "He has been sent for. I am off to see the log splitting."

"Thank you," Jennifer said. She must remember to tell him after he had carried her up to her room that he was free to watch the log splitting if he wished and even the archery contest that would follow. She knew that Gwyneth and Devlin had made an effort to see to it that at least some of the servants could enjoy the day along with everyone else. Those who had to work were to be compensated with extra pay and time off.

Two people, a man and a woman, stopped at the foot of the steps and looked up. They were strangers to Jennifer. She did not believe she had met them before, though there was something vaguely familiar about the man. They must be the people who had come in the chaise.

"May I help you?" she asked, and both turned to look at her. The man's eyes took in the wheels on her chair.

"Perhaps, ma'am," he said, doffing his hat to reveal a head of dark hair graying at the temples. "My aunt and I seem to have chosen the worst of all days to come here, but we are reluctant to postpone our errand until tomorrow after coming so far. Are you able to confirm that Mr. Ben Ellis lives here? Is there any chance you can point us in his direction?"

And Jennifer knew, just as though he had spelled it out in words to her.

He had come.

Bruce was descending the steps.

"I will have him fetched," she said to the man, who faintly resembled his half brother. She smiled at the small, elderly lady who was with him.

"Thank you, ma'am." The man straightened up and glanced at his aunt. Both looked tense.

"Bruce," Jennifer said, making an instant decision. "Would you carry me to the library, please, while this lady and gentleman follow us? Find Mr. Ellis then, if you would be so good. He is probably in the stable yard. Ask him to join us there. You may bring my chair in later and leave it outside the door."

He had come, she thought again. His letter had not been a hoax. Mr. Vincent Kelliston had not answered Mr. Ellis's letter with its thirty-two questions because he was coming instead to answer them in person.

CHAPTER TWENTY

A fter putting away the equipment from the children's races and
making sure there were adults to keep an eye on Joy, who was
running around playing with friends both old and new, Ben joined
his brothers and Gwyneth and Bertrand in the crowded stable yard
to watch the log-splitting contest. Pippa and Lucas were there too
with the Rutledges and Idris Rhys and his brother-in-law.

Ben wondered if anyone had thought to ask Lady Jennifer Arden if she would care to come too. She had been sitting on the terrace when he left the front of the house, talking with Stephanie. He
had not wanted to go and ask her himself. It would probably be
better to stay away from her for the rest of today. The last hour or
so in the village had been too . . . *intense* for comfort, even though
Joy had been with them and for much of the time they had sat in
the church, side by side but not touching, and without saying a
word to each other as they listened to the organ music.

"I wonder what the delay is," Nicholas said.

"Colonel Wexford is supposed to be wielding the starting pistol," Devlin explained. "Neither he nor the pistol are in evidence yet."

"Cameron Holland is in the third heat?" Gwyneth asked of no one in particular. "I am going to reserve my cheers until then."

"I am not so sure the lady of the manor ought to be that openly partial, Gwyn," Owen said.

Gwyneth pulled a face at him. "This lady of the manor will be as partial as she chooses," she said. "Though I shall be very gracious to the winners of each heat and the final bout. And I shall cheer just as partially for you and Bertrand later in the archery contest."

Owen winced. "Only if I hit the target," he said. "You would look a bit foolish jumping up and down and yelling your head off if my arrow went sailing a mile wide. There is every likelihood that that is exactly what will happen. It is downright lowering. Next year I plan to enter the footraces. Maybe I can beat a child or two."

"You had better not enter, Owen," Nick said. "Maybe a child or two would beat *you*."

"Owen is not nearly as hopeless as he thinks," Bertrand said. "The widest I have seen his arrows fly past the target is *half* a mile."

"Some friend you are," Owen grumbled.

"Now put a cricket ball in his hand," Bertrand said, "and . . ."

But Ben did not hear the rest of the sentence, though he did know Owen had a bit of a reputation as a deadly effective bowler. Someone had touched him on the arm—Bruce, the attendant of Lady Jennifer.

"Yes?" Ben said.

"Lady Jennifer asks that you join her in the library, sir," the man said, keeping his voice low but probably not low enough. What the devil? Was something the matter with Joy? But *in the library?*

"I will be right there," he informed Bruce, and told his brothers he would be back as soon as he could.

Lady Jennifer was seated in an armchair on one side of the fireplace to the left of the desk, he saw when he opened the library door. She looked her usual elegant self in black, even after a long morning of outdoor activity—except that she still wore the brightly colored beads about her neck and on both wrists as well as assorted birds, butterflies, and flowers on her fingers. Ben stepped into the room and smiled at her even as he became aware that she was not alone. A woman sat in the chair opposite her, half hidden behind the high back of the chair. And a man stood close to the desk. They were both strangers to Ben.

"I beg your pardon for keeping you waiting, Lady Jennifer," he said. He looked from one to the other of the strangers and addressed the man. "It is perhaps the earl or the countess you wish to see? I am just—"

But he felt the faint buzzing of a premonition even before Lady Jennifer interrupted him.

"Mr. Ellis," she said. "May I introduce Miss Delmont? And Sir Vincent Kelliston?"

Ah.

Ben exchanged a measuring glance with the man as the buzzing in his ears became more persistent. Kelliston looked to be in his early forties. He had neatly styled dark hair, going gray at the temples. He was about Ben's own height and a solid figure of a man. He was fashionably though quietly dressed. He was . . . a baronet? Ben turned and bowed to the lady, whom he could see clearly now that he had moved inside the room. She looked small and elderly, though not perhaps past her sixties. Her hair was iron gray beneath the small brim of her bonnet. She was dressed rather drably in gray. Her face looked worn and lined.

"Miss Delmont?" he said, bowing to her. He looked back at the man. "Kelliston?"

"Miss Delmont is my aunt, my mother's elder sister," the man explained. "Aunt Edith. Your aunt too."

"It has been such a desperately long time, Reuben," the lady said. "Thirty years. You were a very little boy when I saw you last and quite adorable. But you do not even remember me, I daresay."

Ben stared at her. *Reuben?* This woman had known him when he was a child? She was his aunt? His mother's sister?

"Reuben?" he said.

"I have startled you," she said. "I suppose you have never used your full name. Janette named you Reuben after our father, hoping, I suppose, that one day he would forgive her and acknowledge your existence. But he was a stubborn man. He never did either. She always called you Ben. It suited you so much better. And it is what your father always called you."

"I—" Ben held up a hand. "Pardon me, please, ma'am. Until a few weeks ago, when I found Mr.—when I found *Sir*—Vincent Kelliston's very brief letter awaiting me here upon my arrival for a visit, I knew nothing whatsoever of my mother except that her name was Jane Ellis, that she was my father's mistress, and that she died when I was three. I still know almost nothing, though some of the facts have already changed. Her name was apparently Janette Kelliston, née Delmont, she fled her marriage and abandoned her son, now Sir Vincent Kelliston, when he was still very young, and she named me Reuben Ellis. All of this is very strange indeed to me. I feel that my very identity has come under siege. Will you sit, Kelliston? May

I pour you a drink? May I have a tea tray brought in for you, Miss Delmont? And for you, Lady Jennifer?"

She held up one hand. "You would probably like me to leave," she said. "If you would be kind enough to summon Bruce . . ."

"I would prefer you to stay," he told her. "If you wish to do so, that is." He was feeling a bit light-headed. He had not been exaggerating when he said that he felt as if his very identity was threatened. Even the little—the almost nothing—he had known of the other half of his heritage had been snatched from him. Even his name . . . Who the devil *was* this Reuben Kelliston? Who *was* Janette Kelliston? Though one thing she had been, presumably, was *Lady* Kelliston. The world seemed to be tilting at an odd angle.

"I will be happy to remain here," Lady Jennifer said as Kelliston turned a chair away from the desk and sat on it and Miss Delmont said that a glass of wine or ratafia if there was any would be very welcome.

Ben took his time pouring drinks for everyone before sitting to face the fireplace. "I hope to get some answers to the thirty-two questions I asked in my return letter to you, Kelliston," he said. "Understand if you will that I know nothing, that I remember nothing from my first three years, and that my father, who brought me here and raised me with the children of his marriage to my stepmother, always insisted that he knew nothing about my mother except her name and the fact that she was his mistress for four years before her death. He knew her as Jane Ellis." At least that was what he had told Ben.

"Oh dear," Miss Delmont said. "He answered none of the letters I wrote during the first year after he brought you here, and he had me turned away the only time I came in person to see you."

Ben stared at her, frowning. Kelliston cleared his throat.

"Perhaps we should explain," he said.

"Yes," Ben said. "I wish you would."

Lady Jennifer had crossed her hands on her lap and was gazing down at them. The bracelets on her wrists and the rings on her fingers looked very bright.

"I have known almost nothing but rejection for most of my life," Miss Delmont said sadly. "It is my dearest wish that I can turn that around, Ben, before I die. I have two nephews . . ."

"Perhaps it would be best if I were to have my say first, Aunt Edith," Kelliston said gently enough. "And then you can tell your story. Unlike you, Ellis, I was five years old when my mother left home. I have some memories of her, though not any of the night when she apparently tried to take me away with her. I remember asking my father a number of times where she had gone and when she was coming home, but I stopped asking after a while. I suppose even at that age I understood that there was a connection between her disappearance and the rages and blows and sobs and even screams I had sometimes heard before she left, though I do not believe I was ever witness to any of those altercations. My father was a drunkard though never a cheerful one. He would become sullen and morose with everyone—and vicious with my mother. He had no friends, or none at least who ever came to our house. As far as I knew we had no relatives except for my father's sister, who came occasionally to visit but never stayed long.

"When I was ten years old, she gave me a folded piece of paper and told me to keep it safe somewhere. It had my uncle's name on it and their address. She told me it was ten miles away. I had a tutor, or rather three in succession. The first two did not stay long. I remained at home until I was twelve. Somehow I had always escaped the worst of my father's drunken wrath. He never struck me. But it occurred to me by that age that there must be some better life some-where else. I left one afternoon while he was in a drunken stupor and walked with my bundle of belongings to my uncle's house, which I reached after dark. He and my aunt took me in, and I lived with them until the age of nineteen, when I married the daughter of one of the partners in the law firm in which my uncle was also a part-ner. I worked there too at the time, climbing the ladder, so to speak."

He paused to drink from his glass.

"It has been a good marriage," he said. "We have five children, two sons and three daughters, ranging in age from nineteen to eight. We were always industrious and reasonably prosperous. My aunt and uncle on my father's side and my wife's numerous family mem-bers have helped me forget the isolation and loneliness of my first twelve years. I blocked the memory of them from my mind and thought I had succeeded. Until, that was, news came that my father had died and I had inherited the title and the property, which was in surprisingly good condition, all things considered. My father's manager had lived in his own home and had gone about his busi-ness without much reference to my father, it seems. He had been in his employment for many years. He continues to work for me now. I did not want to go back there to live. I resisted using the title. My wife was rather delighted with it, however, and so were my children. We were, I was surprised to learn from them, rather crowded in the home where we had lived quite comfortably since our marriage. So we moved."

He twirled the glass in his hand and gazed into the dark liquor within. He took a quick swallow.

"I was determined to keep this story brief," he said. "I apologize. It is not so easy to do. I am keeping both you and Lady Jennifer Arden from enjoying what appears to be a rare day of festivities."

"I have time," Ben said. The log-splitting contest no longer seemed important.

"My wife, who knew my story, told me she had always felt a great depth of sadness in me, rather like a yawning black hole, where my history ought to be," Kelliston said. "My mother, that was, and my family on her side, if there was any still remaining. At the time I did not even know what her maiden name had been. Believe me, Ellis, when I read your letter and your thirty-two questions, I could fully relate to many of them. The blankness of my heritage on my mother's side was almost as total as yours—except that I did at least have a few memories of her. I remember, for example, that she loved me. Though she also abandoned me."

"Vincent," Miss Delmont said in obvious distress. "I believe we—"

"Yes, I know, Aunt Edith," he said. "But at the time of which I speak I did not know. My wife urged me to make inquiries about the other side of my family, Ellis. I resisted her. For one thing, I did not know where to start. One cannot simply open wide one's front door and cry into the wilderness beyond, *Where are my mother's relatives if there are any?* And for another, I had learned at a very young age in that house to stop asking questions, to keep quiet, to let sleeping dogs lie, if you will. But . . . Well, I was back in that house and getting rid of as many reminders of my father as I could. His papers, of course, had to be looked over before they were burned, and I discovered his marriage certificate. My mother's maiden name, I learned, was Delmont. There were people of that name living fifteen miles or so away—in the opposite direction from my uncle's home. My wife discovered that. She also discovered that one of them was Miss Edith Delmont, my mother's elder sister. And so we met."

"All my letters to Vincent after Janette had fled to London went unanswered," Miss Delmont said. "The gifts I sent went unacknowledged. It was hard for me to get away without explaining to my father exactly where I was going and without being properly chaperoned—even when I was well past the age of majority. Any unmarried daughter of his, he always used to say, must live under his full authority just as she would under her husband's if she were married. I managed it only twice, when I convinced a cousin to invite me to stay with her for a few days. But Sir Richard Kelliston would not receive me or allow me to see my nephew. Both times I hid in a hedgerow and stayed there for hours, but I never caught so much as a glimpse of any boy. I understood later that on the second occasion he had already run away from home. By that time I had lost *both* my nephews. And my sister was dead."

"Miss Delmont," Lady Jennifer said. "Would you like Mr. Ellis to refill your glass?"

"Oh," she said, looking down into the empty glass in her hand. "No, thank you, my dear. But that was very tasty and reviving."

Ben got to his feet to take the glass from her hand. "May I order some tea for you, Miss Delmont?" he asked.

"No, thank you. But I wish you would call me Aunt Edith," she said, looking wistfully up at him. "You could never quite get your tongue around my name when you were a child. I was something like *Aunty Ethith*. And sometimes there was an extra *-ith* at the end."

"I wish I could remember," he said.

"Sir Richard Kelliston was a gloriously dashing young man," she said as he resumed his seat. "My father assumed when he first came calling after a local hunt ball that I was the one who had caught his eye. I was ten years older than Janette, who was barely seventeen at the time. But I was always rather homely looking, and she was a rare beauty. I was also already past the age of attracting beaux, though I had never been very successful at it even as a girl. I was also past the age of having my head turned by a handsome face and a baronet's title. He already had a reputation as a heavy drinker, who could be a bit wild when in his cups. Unfortunately, he also had charm in those days, and he turned the full force of it upon Janette. Our father encouraged him, and when I appealed to him, he accused me of sucking upon sour grapes. Janette accused me of playing too hard at being mother since Mama's passing a few years before. There was nothing I could do to prevent her from marrying him."

"Do not upset yourself, Aunt Edith," Kelliston said when she paused to remove a handkerchief from her reticule and dab it against her cheeks. "It was not your fault."

"Sir Richard was aware of my disapproval," she continued. "I had confronted him with it before the wedding, and he too accused me of eating sour grapes—though he did not phrase it quite as politely as that. I was forbidden to visit my sister at his home, and she came to us only rarely, and always in his company. We were never alone together, Janette and I, though I knew every time I saw her that all was not well with her marriage. I found a way of exchanging letters with her eventually, through a housemaid there who was a niece of our cook. Janette feared for her life and Vincent's. She wrote that she was going to run away to save them, though she did not know where she would go. She could not come back home. On the only occasion she had found a chance to appeal to our father, he informed her that she was no longer his concern. She was the property of her husband and must learn to obey him and avoid

provoking him. When I broached the subject with him, he told me
I must never do so again. A woman, he said, was the absolute property of her father until she married and of her husband after she
did. I helped her run away, Mr. Ellis. We had a governess of whom
I had been particularly fond, though she left in order to marry
when Janette was still very young. She was a widow by this time,
but she lived very respectably in London. She agreed to take Janette
and Vincent in for a short while at least and do what she could to
settle them somewhere."

She paused to dab at her eyes again.

"He caught her as she was gathering up a sleepy Vincent in the
middle of one night," she said. "He beat her terribly, and then he
threw her out of the house before morning came. He would not
allow her to take Vincent and told her he would kill both her and
the child if she tried to return. She believed him. So she went to
London alone and found employment selling flowers from a street
stall until she took your father's eye, Mr. Ellis."

"Ah," he said curtly, getting to his feet to replenish his own
glass, though he left it on the tray after filling it and went to stand
at the window, looking out. It was a bit dizzying to see crowds still
out there, carefree and enjoying themselves at the fete as though the
world had not just wobbled on its axis. Joy was playing what looked
like a game of chasing with a pack of young children.

He was aware that Lady Jennifer was listening to all of this,
though it had nothing whatsoever to do with her. He had dragged
her into it from the start. And much of it was sordid. She was missing part of the fete and the company of others. But it was too late
to do anything about it now. Miss Delmont was speaking again.

"Much of the rest of the story you probably know or can infer,

Ben," she said. "Your father established Janette in a home of her own. I visited her as often as I could, having explained to my father—I lied, I am afraid—that my former governess, who had departed our house in good standing and been respectably married, was suffering from declining health and would welcome my company. I liked your father very much indeed. He was very, very handsome and charming and kind—and he adored my sister. He recognized her as a lady, from the way she spoke, I suppose. He was very young at the time—a year younger than she, in fact—and he was perhaps a little naïve about some of the realities of his life and the expectations he must fulfill. He wanted to marry her. When he knew she was with child—you—he tried to insist upon it. They would brazen out the disapproval of his family, he assured her. It was only then, when she had no choice, that she told him it was an impossibility because she was already married."

She broke off speaking again, presumably to dry her eyes, and Ben turned back to the room and resumed his seat.

"Even then he did not abandon her," Miss Delmont said. "He always treated her with kindness and a sort of reverence. He wept with joy and perhaps a little grief too when you were born. He held you in his arms for a whole hour before he would give you up to me. He always treated me with unfailing courtesy. The time came, though, when he had to bow to reality. He was no ordinary man, after all. He married the eligible daughter of a family close to his home here, though he kept Janette until she died trying to give birth to your sister."

W-H-A-T?

"After that he brought you here," she said. "He explained to me that there could be no further communication between us, that it would be best that way for all of us. The first child of his marriage had been born a week before Janette's death."

Devlin.

"I wished afterward that I had at least tried to persuade him to write to me occasionally to give me news of you," she said. "But I did not think of it at the time. I was too devastated by the death of my sister and my niece. I tried writing a few times and even came here once, but the ban, it seemed, was absolute. Your father folded you into his other family and loved you, I am sure. You are still here."

"I have my own home, Miss Delmont," he said. "I am a widower. I have a young daughter."

"Oh," she said, her hand creeping to her neck, an agonized look on her face.

Kelliston cleared his throat. "After I had found Aunt Edith and become acquainted with her and introduced her to my family," he said, "I was content. The other Delmonts my wife found, including the second cousin with whom Aunt Edith now lives, were more distant relatives and showed no interest in making my acquaintance. But there was someone of my own on my mother's side as well as my aunt and uncle on my father's side to balance my wife's rather large and boisterous family. I was able to learn more of my mother's story, even the fact that when she left my father she had tried to take me with her but had been forced to leave me behind on the threat of death—for both me and herself. I was able to forgive her. I would have left it at that. I confess that I had no wish to establish any contact with *you* when I learned of your existence from Aunt Edith. But my wife believed I should pursue my search to the bitter end. She pointed out to me that it was something I could do for my newly discovered aunt, who very obviously still grieved the loss of you from her life. Hence my letter to you, which I must confess I half hoped you would ignore."

"Oh, Vincent," his aunt said.

"You have Lady Jennifer Arden to thank, at least in part, that I did not ignore it," Ben said.

"I cannot see that suppressing certain realities from our lives, or having them suppressed by others, is anything but harmful," Lady Jennifer said. "Even if those realities are painful or sordid. And even if those who hide them from us are well meaning. Our lives are surely intended to be a full expression of who we are and where we have come from and what we have experienced in our lifetimes. How can we express the fullness of our being if we do not know or cannot face all the facts? If we do not know who we are to the depths of our being?"

All the facts.

His father really had loved his mother. He would have married her before Ben was born and thus legitimized him—just as *he* had married Marjorie and legitimized Joy. His father had had—or almost had—a second child with Janette Kelliston. A daughter. *A sister.* He had brought Ben to Ravenswood because he *adored* him, because Ben was the child he had had with the love of his life—*as he had always told Ben.* He had sheltered his firstborn son within the respectability of his legitimate family and had fiercely protected him from all the more sordid elements of his mother's story. Wrongly, of course. But surely from the best of motives.

All this, of course, was true only if Miss Delmont's interpretation of those few years of his mother's life was correct. She was undoubtedly not lying, but we all see life through the lens of our biases, Ben thought. She had loved his mother, her younger and only sister. But surely she would not be painting his father in such a favorable light if he had not loved her sister totally.

"You are absolutely right, Lady Jennifer," Miss Delmont said. "I could never—"

But she was interrupted by the library door opening abruptly to admit Devlin.

CHAPTER TWENTY-ONE

B en had missed the heats of the log-splitting contest, including the third, to which he had been most looking forward. Cam Holland had won in the second-best time of the six. He would be in the final bout later—against the man who beat him eight years ago.

Ben's long absence puzzled Devlin. It would not have been for any trivial reason. What had Jenny wanted with him that had kept him away so long?

"I am a bit worried about those two," he said to Gwyneth as they made their way, arm in arm, to the front of the house.

"They are both adults, Devlin," she said with a sigh. "Jenny is my age. Ben is older than you. He is in his *thirties.* I love Lucas dearly, and of course he is absolutely *perfect* for Pippa. But does he perhaps take his ducal responsibilities a little too seriously at times?"

"In objecting to a romance between his sister and my father's bastard?" he asked.

"Devlin—"

"It is what is at the crux of this whole thing," he said. "We might as well call a spade a spade. Luc loves Jenny, Gwyneth. I am sure he would love her under any circumstances, but her condition has made him more than ordinarily protective of her. We must not hold it against him. And you must not hold it against me that I wish to protect Ben from hurt and insult. He is my *brother*, as dear to me as Nick or Owen. Except that he is not *really* my brother, is he, and I have always feared that that one difference between us would come to be a problem. He is the most stable and sensible man I know. Except, perhaps, when his heart is engaged. I am not sure that has happened before, even with Marjorie. Maybe it has not happened now."

"Oh, Devlin," she said, "I am very much afraid it has. And I am afraid it will end badly. But I am off to the courtyard to watch the judging of the contests. You are going to see if they are still in the library?"

"It seems unlikely," he said. "But yes. He is not out here with Joy, is he?"

Joy was with a crowd of other young children on the front lawn, playing some game that involved a great deal of shrieking.

Devlin had also noticed a plain chaise that had been pulled off the driveway onto the grass to the east of the house. The driver was standing by the horses in conversation with one of the Ravenswood grooms, a glass of something in one hand. Devlin went to have a word with the men while Gwyneth continued on her way.

His own groom drew himself to attention. "I hope you do not mind that I fetched a glass of ale for the coachman while he waits, my lord," he said.

"I am very glad you did. It is a hot day," Devlin said. He turned his attention to the other man, who was a stranger to him. "If you are expecting a bit of a wait, would it be more convenient to take the chaise back to the village inn?"

"I was told to wait here, your lordship," the man said.

"You have come some distance?" Devlin asked.

"Just eight miles today, your lordship," the man said. "Sir Vincent was unaware that anything special was going on here today, but he decided to come up to the house anyway."

"Sir Vincent?" Devlin raised his eyebrows.

"Sir Vincent Kelliston, your lordship," the coachman said. "And Miss Delmont."

"Ah," Devlin said. "Yes, of course. Enjoy your ale, then."

He strode off toward the front doors. Ben's half brother. He had come in person instead of answering the letter Ben had written him. And he had brought a lady with him. So he was *Sir* Vincent Kelliston, was he?

He let himself into the library a minute or so later.

"Ah, here you are, Ben," he said. "You missed seeing your champion cut through his log as though it were butter. But you will see him again later in the final bout. And here you are, Jenny, out of the glare of the afternoon sun. A wise move. And looking very festive, I see, decked out in the best jewelry the village has to offer. Present me if you will, Ben."

Ben was on his feet. So was Kelliston. And good God, they actually looked a bit alike—same height, similar build, same coloring, though Ben's hair showed no sign of gray yet. There was some indefinable similarity of feature.

"Aunt Edith," Ben said, "may I present Devlin Ware, Earl of Stratton? Miss Delmont, Dev. My mother's elder sister. And Sir Vincent Kelliston, my mother's elder son."

"Miss Delmont," Devlin said, striding toward her and taking her hand in his. "I am Ben's brother. I am delighted to make your acquaintance. Welcome to Ravenswood." He bowed over her hand.

"Thank you, Lord Stratton," she said. "Oh, but you do not look one little bit like your father."

"I favor my mother." He smiled and turned to offer his hand to the other visitor. "Kelliston?" he said. "I am delighted that you have chosen to come in person to meet my brother rather than merely write again. He has been anxiously watching the post every day. Welcome to Ravenswood."

Kelliston shook his hand gravely. "Thank you, Stratton," he said. "If I had known today was a festival day here, I would have chosen to wait a day or two."

"But your timing is perfect," Devlin assured him. "You must join us for tea outside on the lawn in a while and meet the countess and the rest of Ben's family."

"We do not plan to stay long," Kelliston said.

"Your coachman has informed me you came eight miles today," Devlin said. "From a coaching inn, I assume. Did you plan to return there tonight?"

"We do," Kelliston said. "My aunt will need to rest before we begin our journey home tomorrow."

Devlin crossed to the bell rope beside the fireplace next to the chair on which Jenny sat and pulled on it.

"I shall have your coachman sent back now to bring your bags here," he said. "And any servants you brought with you. You must stay for a night or two as my guests. Where else would Ben's brother and aunt stay?"

It looked as if Kelliston was drawing breath to argue the point, but his aunt spoke first.

"How extraordinarily kind of you, Lord Stratton," she said. "I do want to meet Ben's family and get to know him a little better before I go back home with Vincent. I knew Ben as an infant before Janette died."

Janette, Devlin assumed, was Jane Ellis's real name. Janette Kelliston. Or, more probable, Lady Kelliston. How was poor Ben feeling at this moment? Elated that he had discovered two members of his mother's family and perhaps some stories to fill in the missing history? Or horribly bewildered, as even the little he had known of his mother proved to be inaccurate?

"Janette named him Reuben for our father," Miss Delmont said. "But she always called him Ben. So did his papa. Oh. *Your* papa too."

Reuben. Good God. And Ben had had no idea? "Our eldest brother has always been Ben to us," Devlin said with a smile. "The rock upon which our family has always depended. You will stay, then, Kelliston?"

"If my aunt wishes it," Kelliston said stiffly. "Thank you."

A servant came at that moment in answer to the bell, and Devlin sent him with the message for the coachman and also with the request that the Countess of Stratton, who would be found in the courtyard, come to the library when it was convenient to her.

"Ma'am," Devlin said, bowing to Miss Delmont. "My wife will take you in a short while to a guest room and allow you to freshen up before taking you outside to enjoy some company and refreshments and introducing you to some of the Ware side of Ben's family. I must warn you that both she and they will be surprised. Ben confided the contents of his letter from Sir Vincent to me and, I believe, to Lady Jennifer Arden, but he did not wish to speak of it with anyone else for fear it might prove to be some sort of cruel hoax."

"It was no hoax, Lord Stratton," she said. "I have longed for years and years to see my nephew again."

"And now your wish has been granted," he said. "Kelliston, what sort of interest do you have in archery? There is a contest about to begin in the poplar walk east of the house. I would like to watch it myself. Will you accompany me?"

Kelliston inclined his head.

"We will see you in a short while, then, Ben," Devlin said. "You will wish to see Jenny settled somewhere comfortable."

"I will," Ben said, giving Devlin a hard look.

The door opened again at that moment to admit Gwyneth, who looked curiously at the two strangers. Devlin gave her a brief explanation after introducing them.

He hoped with all his heart, as his wife led Miss Delmont off to the guest floor of the east wing a few minutes later and he set off for the poplar alley with Kelliston, that he had convinced the newly discovered half brother and aunt that Ben was not just an illegitimate adjunct to his family but an essential, central pillar of it. The stigma of bastardy would always hang over Ben, but as long as he, the Earl of Stratton, had breath left in his body, Ben would be his *brother*, and as dear a member of the Ware family as Nick and Pippa and Owen and Steph. As dear to himself as the beating of his heart.

And if Sir Vincent Kelliston in particular was going to need some convincing of that, then by God he would do it.

The library seemed unnaturally quiet after everyone had left. Everyone except Lady Jennifer Arden, that was. Ben looked at her, sitting with bent head and hands crossed, palms down, on her lap. His head buzzed with so many racing thoughts and images that it was impossible to sort them into any order. But he was going to have to postpone doing that until later. There was something of greater importance to be done now.

He approached her, went down on his haunches in front of her and then onto one knee, and gathered both her hands in his. It occurred to him that anyone coming into the library at this moment would get quite the wrong impression.

"I am so very sorry, Lady Jennifer," he said. "I have ruined at least an hour of this special day for you and embroiled you in a tale of sordid doings that in no way concerns you and is quite inappropriate for a lady's ears. I have been nothing but trouble to you since we both came here, and I have allowed my daughter to burden and embarrass you with her make-believe world. I will make plans to return home tomorrow or, more probable, the day after, since my relatives are to spend the night here. I will keep both of us out of your life forever after. Tell me now where I may take you. Upstairs to your room? Outside to find your aunt or Pippa? I will—"

"Mr. Ellis—Ben," she said, interrupting him. "Sometimes you speak a lot of nonsense and fustian. And I am growing quite weary of hearing *Lady* attached to my name every time you address me. I am Jennifer."

"Jennifer," he murmured.

"I am so happy for Miss Delmont, who has finally found both her nephews again after so many years of being cut off from you," she said. "Poor Sir Vincent is not at all sure he is happy, but I believe his wife was probably right that he needed to pursue his search for his missing past just as you did. I would be willing to wager on it that she will insist upon meeting you and wish to draw you into her family. Their children will probably wish to make your acquaintance too. But at the very least you have an aunt—your mother's *sister*—who adored you as a child and longs to be a part of your life. And Joy's. Aunt Ethith-ith."

He looked up into her face. She was laughing down at him, and he smiled. He was aware of the rings on her fingers, digging into his own.

"What was the most wonderful thing you heard?" she asked.

It was hard to sort through the jumble in his head to find one thing. "I think that my aunt was part of my mother's life in London and part of mine," he said. "She—my mother—had family there with her, even if not all the time. She was not such an isolated figure as I have always assumed she must have been."

"And what was the most surprising thing?" she asked.

He closed his eyes briefly. That was not hard to answer even though almost everything had been surprising. "I almost had a sister," he said. "But she died with my mother. And there is a memory—of my father holding me so tightly in his arms that I was frightened rather than comforted. I could not breathe. He was sobbing and sobbing. Have I just invented that memory?"

"No," she said softly.

He released her hands and got to his feet. He ran the fingers of one hand through his hair. "I think perhaps my father has been restored to me too today," he said. "I believe I can let go of some of the disillusionment that has blighted my memory of him for the past eight years. He cannot be fully excused for having both a mistress and a wife at the same time and getting a child upon each of them almost simultaneously. But if my aunt is to be believed, he truly loved my mother, as he always told me he did, and would have married her if he could. Perhaps it was only later that he became . . . promiscuous and hurt his family here so irretrievably. But here I go burdening you again."

"Ben," she said. "I felt incredibly privileged when you told me earlier that you wished me to stay. I am very happy to know that the missing half of yourself is no longer missing. Some parts of the story are sad, and my guess is that your father made a conscious decision to keep them all from you in the hope that you would identify wholly with his family here and be happy. It was almost certainly a misguided decision, but it is understandable neverthe-less. Your aunt is going to be able to tell you so many stories."

"Like the ones I tell Joy," he said.

"Oh, and please, please, *please* do not discourage Joy from liv-ing in her make-believe world while we all remain here, whether it is for another day or two or another week," she said. "It can surely do no harm. And I love her."

He scratched the back of his neck and gazed down at her. "Lady—" he said, and stopped. He tried again. *"Jennifer."* But then he could not recall what he had been about to say. "You look terri-bly pretty in your beaded splendor."

She lifted her arms and fluttered her fingers and shook her wrists at him as she laughed. He smiled back at her until she lowered her hands to her lap again and they simply gazed at each other.

"Where do you wish to go?" he asked.

"To my room for a short while," she said, "and then back out-side for tea and the prize-giving ceremony. I would hate to miss either. But I will have you summon Bruce, if you would be so good. You must go and find your aunt and your brother. Have you ever seen Devlin so completely transformed into earl and lord of the manor?"

"Very rarely," he said, grinning. And it was perhaps that trans-formation that had touched him more deeply than anything else in the past hour or so. For Devlin had done it for *him*, to demonstrate to Kelliston that he, Ben, was a valued member of the family here, that he belonged at Ravenswood. That he was *loved*.

And it was his *father*—their father, his and Devlin's—who had done this for him by boldly bringing him here when it might have been easier to have found an adoptive home for his mistress's son or even to have left him at an orphanage.

Ah, Papa, he thought as he rang the bell to summon Bruce.

Jennifer had Bruce take her to her room and leave her there for an hour. By then, she estimated, both the archery and log-splitting contests would be finished and the baking and handicraft contests judged and it would be time for tea. After that there would be a lull for a couple of hours before the ball and banquet to end this fete, which appeared to be bringing so much pleasure to so many people. She felt privileged to be a part of it all.

She washed her hands and face after removing her rings and beads and bracelets, made herself comfortable, and then stretched out on the chaise longue after propping her crutches beside it. She did not plan to sleep, but it was a marvelous luxury to relax in a cool, quiet room for a while and think back over the day.

Such an eventful day.

Her spirits soared and her heart ached. What a peculiar combination of feelings, yet both were true.

The morning had been magical—it was the only word that suited. The prayer outside the church, with the village green and the roadways that surrounded it crowded with people; the youth choir, so well trained that the unaccompanied young voices sang as one, and the one voice, Stephanie's, rang out with such purity that one's throat ached with unshed tears; the maypole dancing; the breakfast on the green while adults talked and children played; the brightly decorated stalls selling their wares and doing a brisk business. If there had been nothing else, Jennifer would have thought it a wonderful morning.

But there had been Joy coming to ask for money to shop at the jewelry stall, just as though Jennifer were her real mama, and Ben appearing from nowhere to take them there and laugh with them as he helped them select matching sets of garish rings, necklaces, and bracelets. And then the stall with its throwing contest, which was not easy to win. But Ben had won a stuffed dog for Joy and the cloth doll with the bright red hair for her. She had it now on the chaise longue beside her—and knew she would have it within sight in her private apartments for the rest of her life. And then there had been that half hour or so inside the church with Ben sitting at the end of the pew beside her chair, holding Joy while Jennifer held her ankle and Ben's hand rested on her bracelets and the organ played.

The magic.

She was even thinking of him as *Ben*, she realized. And of Joy with that soreness about her heart. For the child was not hers and never would be. Make-believe would end within the next week or so, perhaps sooner.

And they had come, his relatives. They had come on surely the best of all days, though they had been inclined to think it was the worst. They had come with their stories, which were heartbreaking in many ways but surely had the potential of ending happily for them all. The aunt had lost her beloved sister and her two nephews all within a few years of one another, but now both nephews had been restored to her, and it seemed to Jennifer that she would cherish them for the rest of her life—along with their wives and their children. The brother, *not* a fortune hunter after all, had been a bit stiff and unhappy this afternoon, but he seemed to be a thoroughly respectable man, and a baronet, no less, and it sounded as if he had a long-standing and sound marriage as well as five children. His wife sounded promising. It was she who had urged him to search for any family on his mother's side and any word of what had happened to his mother when she ran from home all those years ago. Sir Vincent's wife obviously valued family. She came of a large and boisterous one herself.

It was unlikely, perhaps, that Ben would ever be as close to this new brother as he was to his Ware brothers and sisters, but there would surely be a relationship of some sort. Joy would have another aunt and uncle as well as cousins and a great-aunt. And the memory of her own mother would be kept alive through story.

How important stories were. They linked families and generations and communities and shared values and civilization itself. They created history and identity. At their best they perpetuated love.

Love.

There were so many, many kinds of love. Including the kind that inspired some of the world's finest poetry and everyone surely yearned for and sometimes . . . Ah, and sometimes found. Even if only fleetingly.

Jennifer drifted off to sleep.

CHAPTER TWENTY-TWO

It amused Devlin to play the part of Earl of Stratton with full deliberation. It was also something he did today with all seriousness, however, for it was clear to him that Sir Vincent Kelliston had come here at the bidding of his wife and to humor his aunt, but that he was not at all convinced he wished to acknowledge Ben as someone worthy of his notice. And really, why should he? Ben was, after all, the illegitimate son of the mother who had abandoned him for a life of ruin under the protection of a noble lover.

But Ben was not just the sordid product of a sordid affair. He was also the acknowledged and beloved brother of the Earl of Stratton.

They walked out to the poplar alley together, but only after Devlin had stopped to introduce Kelliston to his mother and Lady Catherine Emmett and Lady Rhys, all of whom stared after them, no doubt with a flood of questions Devlin gave them no chance to ask. Doubtless Miss Delmont would answer them all when Gwyneth brought her outside.

Ever the gracious countess, poor Gwyneth must be bewildered and bursting with questions too.

At the poplar alley, where the archery contest was about to begin, Devlin made the introductions to Pippa and Lucas, whom he presented as His Grace, the Duke of Wilby, and his own sister, Her Grace, the duchess. Lucas inclined his head. Pippa reacted with predictable enthusiasm, clasping her hands to her bosom and regarding Kelliston with a glowing smile and sparkling eyes.

"You are Ben's *brother*?" she said. "How marvelous. You even look a little like him." And she stretched out a hand toward him.

Pippa was a ravishing beauty. Even her brother was aware of that. *And* she was a duchess. Kelliston looked a little dazzled as he took her hand and bowed over it.

"Your Grace," he murmured.

Nicholas, when he was introduced, looked every inch the military officer. He took Kelliston's hand in a firm clasp and turned on the full force of his considerable charm. He reminded Devlin more than ever of their father in that moment. And he must have sized up the man in a glance.

"Ben's brother?" he said. "So you searched and you found, did you, and we can no longer keep our brother all to ourselves? Ben will be pleased, however. I recall his telling me once when we were both out in the Peninsula that he had not a single lead that would help him find his mother's side of his family. He found that fact somewhat frustrating, I believe, since family has always been important to him. Come to watch the archery, have you? Our youngest brother, Owen, is over there, waiting to participate. He is the fair-haired one."

Stephanie was in a group with Mari Howell, Clarence Ware, and

Brad Danver. She slapped both hands to her mouth when Devlin explained who Sir Vincent Kelliston was and then opened them like double doors and gazed at him wide-eyed.

"How exciting to discover when you are already grown up that you have another *brother,*" she said. "But do you belong only to Ben? That is not fair. Can you not be our brother too? Ben is our brother and you are his. Does that not make you . . . ?" She paused to work out a possible relationship.

"No, Steph," Clarence said drily. "But I say, this really is rather exciting for Cousin Ben. Where is he? Recovering from the vapors?"

But Kelliston seemed to be unbending at last. He was smiling at Steph. "Perhaps we can claim an honorary relationship, Lady Stephanie," he said. "My eldest children must be close to you in age. Thomas is eighteen and Henrietta is sixteen."

"Then I am between them in age," Stephanie said. "Does this mean I am honorary half aunt to them?" She laughed and so, incredibly, did he.

"We are about to miss the archery," Brad Danver said, and they all turned their attention to it.

Matthew Taylor won, but that was no surprise to anyone. Bertrand came in a respectable fourth. The best that could be said of Owen was that he did not disgrace himself, and at least he had not turned craven at the last moment, as Brad and Clarence had done, and withdrawn from the competition.

But Stephanie wanted to share today's most spectacular news with Owen before anyone else could get to him first. She darted over to him and told him about Sir Vincent Kelliston. He was suitably impressed and strode off to be introduced before Devlin led the man back to the house.

And Stephanie realized that she had trapped herself, far from family, friends, and safety, beside Bertrand Lamarr, Viscount Watley. And good manners dictated that she not charge off in pursuit of her brother and leave him all alone when he was a guest at the house.

"Congratulations," she said. "You did really very well in the contest. You only just missed winning one of the prize ribbons."

From a distance she had watched avidly and fearfully and willed his arrows to find their way to the center of the target. It had been agonizing to see him get so close with his final arrow but not close enough to raise him into third place.

"I shall cry myself to sleep tonight," he said, and startled Stephanie into laughing.

"I do hope you are not too devastated," she said. "There is still the picnic tea to enjoy and the ball tonight."

"You did very well this morning," he said. "You have a truly beautiful singing voice."

"Oh, it is nothing," she said, and it was too much to hope that her face and neck were not all blotched with red patches. She could never blush gracefully, as Pippa could.

"On the contrary," he said. "It is something."

Stephanie made that sound with her lips that she was trying not to do any longer now that she was almost grown up. Owen had told her not so long ago that it made her look and sound like a bullfrog, which was, of course, absurd. But even so . . .

"It is time for tea," she said, and hoped she could lose herself among the departing crowd and not have to walk all the way back to the house with him. He must surely, beyond the shadow of a doubt, be the most handsome, most gorgeous man in all England. Include Wales in that too. And Scotland. Not to mention Ireland.

"Lady Stephanie," Bertrand said. "Is it too much to hope that you do not already have a partner for the first set of the ball this evening?"

Stephanie lost her breath and took a moment to recover it. "I have promised it to Clarence," she said. "My cousin."

"Lucky Clarence," he said. "Do you know the steps of the waltz? Will you dance the first waltz of the evening with me?"

That was when she made her biggest blunder since he arrived at Ravenswood to plague her. Instead of lying and pretending she had never even *heard* of the waltz, she chirped up with the truth. "Oh yes," she said. "I learned to waltz two years ago for an assembly here after Devlin and Ben came home from the wars. We all learned together—Gwyneth and Pippa too. And we waltzed at the assembly even though I was only fifteen at the time."

Owen and Nicholas and Mari were waiting for them to catch up. But it was far too late. Bertrand was looking at her, his eyebrows raised, awaiting her answer to his second question. And she could not be outright rude, could she? It was not in her nature—or her upbringing. Miss Field, her long-time governess, would deem herself an eternal failure.

"Thank you," she said, and told an outright lie at last. "I would like that."

Clarissa, the dowager countess, with Lady Catherine Emmett, Lady Rhys, and the other ladies of her committee, had just finished shaking hands with the judges of the contests when Gwyneth found them. She introduced the older lady she brought with her as Miss Delmont, aunt of Sir Vincent Kelliston from Kent, who had just arrived at Ravenswood in search of his half brother, whom he had never met before.

"He is *Ben's* brother," Gwyneth explained. "And Miss Delmont is Ben's aunt, his mother's sister."

For a moment Clarissa felt dizzy again, as she had earlier when Devlin had introduced Sir Vincent Kelliston before whisking him off almost immediately to watch the archery. Ben's mother had always been someone she had quite determinedly not thought about. Her memories of Ben himself began with the three-year-old little boy with wide, frightened eyes who had clung to Caleb's hand but then had come to her when, numb with shock, she had opened her arms to him. He had killed her outraged determination to reject a whore's spawn by snuggling into her and crying himself to sleep on her lap. Sometimes in the months and years following that she had felt guilty for loving Ben as much as she loved Devlin, her own newborn son. She had never quite been able to explain that love to herself. She had been content to let it be.

Now Ben had people—strangers—to pull him over to the other side, strangers who had had nothing to do with the raising of him or the loving of him. Clarissa felt jealous and annoyed—and instantly guilty over thinking of *herself* more than of Ben.

She gathered both the older woman's hands into her own and smiled with a warmth she made genuine by sheer force of will. "Miss Delmont," she said, "how wonderful that you have come, and today of all days. How wonderful for *Ben*. You will be staying here for the rest of the day, of course, and tonight. Gwyneth will have seen to that."

"The countess has been most kind," Miss Delmont said. "You cannot know how it soothes my heart, Lady Stratton, to know that Ben grew up here, surrounded by love during the long years when

I was cut off from him. He was such an adorable baby and little boy."

Clarissa smiled.

"You will be able to tell Ben many stories about those years, which I daresay he does not remember," Kitty, Lady Catherine Emmett, said. "And stories about his mother too."

"And I want to hear stories about *him* and the thirty years since I saw him last," Miss Delmont said. "He told me he was married and then widowed, and that he has a child."

"Come," Clarissa said after the other ladies had greeted her too and Charles and Marian Ware had come to be introduced as well as Eluned Rhys and her sister-in-law. "We are finished with our work here. Let us go and find some empty chairs out on the lawn. Tea will be served after the final bout of the log-splitting contest."

"You are incredibly kind," Miss Delmont said.

Clarissa hoped all the promised stories of Ben's early years would be told out of her hearing. But she had been raised as a lady, and ladies endured without protest or complaint when they must. She had had years of practice. She could do it again. Though really it was not hard to like Miss Delmont—*sister of Ben's mother*. Ah . . .

They sat out on the lawn with Miss Delmont—Clarissa, Kitty, Bronwyn Rhys, and Marian Ware—relaxing and chatting until Ben came out of the house and looked somewhat dismayed when he saw them and all the other people who had gathered around to be introduced to the stranger. Poor Ben. He hated to be the center of attention. If he could go about his business invisible, he would be quite happy to do so, Clarissa had always thought. He probably did not even realize in how much respect and affection he was held in the neighborhood.

"This has been a busy day for you, Aunt Edith," he said after he had approached them. "I hope you are not overtired. If you are, I will be happy to escort you to your room. Though there will be a quiet time for everyone after tea before the ball begins."

"A ball. Oh my!" she said. "It is many a long year since I attended a ball, Ben."

"I hope you and Vincent will come to this one," he said. "It is a community event that very few people will miss. But you must feel free to withdraw to your room whenever you wish. We will talk at some length tomorrow—just you and I."

"Where is Lady Jennifer?" she asked.

"You have met Jenny, Miss Delmont?" Kitty asked.

"It was she who had us taken to the library when we arrived," Miss Delmont explained. "She stayed with us while her servant went to find Ben, and then she stayed at his request while we spoke with him. She seems to be a very kind young lady."

"She went to her room to rest for a while," Ben explained. "She will be down for tea, though, I expect."

Joy came dashing up to them at that moment, flushed and disheveled and adorned with bright beads on her wrists and fingers and about her neck. She launched herself upon Ben while relating a barely intelligible tale about a little girl who did not play fair in the chasing game but always went down on one knee just as she was about to be tagged with the excuse that she had a stone in her shoe.

"But was the game fun?" Ben asked.

She nodded vigorously. "I don't mind being tagged," she told him, "because I like being *it* and catching the boys. They always think the girls can't run fast like they do. They are silly."

"Yes, sometimes we are," he agreed. "I have someone special for you to meet."

He introduced Great-Aunt Edith, who beamed at her and admired her jewelry.

"Lady Jennifer Arden was wearing beads just like yours," she said. "You both have very good taste."

"Yes," Joy said. "Papa helped us choose them, but Mama paid for them because she said it was all her idea. But really it was mine."

Mama. Joy had taken to calling Jenny that lately, and neither Ben nor Jenny herself seemed inclined to correct her.

"Well, it was a very brilliant idea," Miss Delmont said, and Clarissa noticed that she was gazing at Ben with shrewd eyes.

The archery contest must be over. The lawn was becoming crowded with more people, and Devlin was coming toward them with Ben's half brother. Clarissa had often tried to see something of Caleb in Ben down the years, but there was very little, only enough to convince her that he really was Caleb's son. He must resemble his mother, though. There was a certain likeness between these half brothers.

Sir Vincent Kelliston conversed with them with some reserve of manner though with impeccable courtesy. Clarissa guessed that coming here to find Ben was not all his idea. But he seemed fond of his aunt. And two things occurred to her. Ben's last name had been constructed from Kelliston. And his mother must have been a married woman. She must have been *Lady Kelliston.* Clarissa really, really did not want to know.

"We are on the way to watch the log contest," Devlin explained. "Do you wish to join us, Ben?"

Ben looked at Joy. She wrinkled her nose. "I stay with Grandmama," she said, and clambered onto Clarissa's lap.

"Aunt Edith," Ben said. "Perhaps you would like me to remain with you."

"What I would really like," she said, a mischievous gleam in her eye, "is to go with my nephews to watch these two hefty men chop through their logs. Are women allowed?"

"They are," Ben said, grinning at her. "They are even allowed to cheer. Both my sisters will be doing just that."

"*This,*" she said, sliding her left arm through Ben's and her right arm through Sir Vincent's, "is something I have dreamed of for years."

"Dear Ben," Bronwyn Rhys said as they walked away. "His head must be spinning on his shoulders. In a very good way, though, surely."

The youngest Howell girl from Cartref came dashing up to claim Joy at that moment, and she wriggled off Clarissa's knee after raising puckered lips to be kissed.

Kitty got to her feet. "Who feels like a stroll down to the lake?" she asked.

For a moment it seemed that no one did, but Clarissa agreed that it might be a good idea. "Maybe not all the way," she said. "But a little air and exercise would be very welcome."

Kitty linked an arm through hers and they soon left the lawn and the crowds behind and breathed in the blessed peace of the park itself.

I believe my life is about to change again," Kitty said. "And I think I am happy about it."

"What?" Clarissa asked.

"Jenny has informed me that she is going to live at Greystone with Luc and Pippa," Kitty said. "It is a big step for her. She has always lived at Amberwell and loved it. It is home to her. She has friends and neighbors there of whom she is fond."

"And she has you," Clarissa said.

"Yes." Kitty sighed. "Widowhood left me very lonely, Clarissa. Beatrice married young and went to live in Ireland. I was determined not to cling to Gerald. I always pity young men who have possessive mothers to deal with. When my brother died so unexpectedly just a year after my sister-in-law, and my father demanded that I move to Amberwell to care for Jenny, I did not fight him, even though I knew it would probably be a long-term commitment. I have come to love her as dearly as a daughter. We are best friends, if that is possible between two women of different generations."

"But?" Clarissa looked curiously at her.

"But when Mama and Papa died earlier this year," Kitty said, "and I realized I would not after all be staying at Greystone but must return to Amberwell with Jenny, I felt that the whole course of the rest of my life had been set whether I liked it or not, and . . . Oh, I was *not* unhappy about it, Clarissa."

"But." Clarissa did not make a question of the word this time.

"Yes. But," Kitty said. "I think Jenny may have made her decision largely because of me. I know she loves me."

"Love can be very painful," Clarissa said. "And hopelessly complex. It is very selfless of her to have understood the situation. What will you do?"

"Gerald has always kept the dower house ready for me," Kitty said. "It is the sweetest place imaginable. I can be happy there. I would not move in with him. He is of an age at which he must surely have an eye out for a bride. I will also be able to go on more frequent visits to Beatrice and enjoy my grandsons before they grow up. I will be able to come and go whenever and wherever I please. There is something quite exhilarating about the prospect, though I suspect total freedom is not everything one expects it to be. Maybe . . ."

"Yes?" Clarissa said, looking curiously at her.

"I know we are dear friends," Kitty said. "And I know you are extraordinarily fond of your brother, Clarissa. But perhaps you would not really like seeing us . . . Well."

"You and *George*?" Clarissa had stopped walking.

"Do you have more than one brother?" Kitty asked, looking horribly embarrassed.

Clarissa smiled slowly. "I have noticed that he has been coming here more often than usual," she said. "I have noticed that the two of you seem to enjoy each other's company. I have even thought . . . But—"

"I do so hate sentences that begin with *but*," Kitty said. "I have explained to him that it is an impossibility, that I cannot possibly abandon Jenny, and that it would simply not work to try to add him to the mix. I would be too selfish to share him, and I hope he would be unwilling to share me. But now things are about to change, and I have told him so."

"*Kitty!*" Clarissa exclaimed, grasping her friend's hands.

"It is not at all settled," Kitty said. "He has not asked yet. Not formally anyway. And I have explained that I am older than he by a few years. You must not say a word to him or anyone else. I feel embarrassed that I have even mentioned it. But I did not want to risk losing you as a friend."

"In order to gain me as a *sister*?" Clarissa said, and laughed.

"But I actually wanted to talk to you about something else,"

Kitty said. "I was hoping you would come walking with me and no one else would."

"Jennifer and Ben," Clarissa said.

"Yes."

They resumed their walk. Neither spoke for a while.

"They are so very *right* for each other," Clarissa said at last, pain making her voice almost vibrate.

"Ben Ellis," Kitty said, "is a man in a million."

"And Jenny has the strength and courage of a thousand women and the will to radiate happiness to all around her when she could quite justifiably be pouring out complaints and woe," Clarissa said.

"To Joy she is simply Mama," Kitty said. "Those beads they are both wearing all over their persons! Are we fools, Clarissa?"

"To take one minor fact of Ben's identity and give it greater prominence than all the others combined?" Clarissa said. "To take one minor fact of Jenny's person and make it count for more than any of the others?"

"But could they find *lasting* happiness together?" Kitty asked. "Conventional wisdom would say a resounding no."

"Who can predict the future with any accuracy?" Clarissa asked. "I have come to be of the strong belief that neither of those two would allow themselves to be anything but happy with each other for the rest of their lives."

"*Not* that the decision is ours to make," Kitty said a little sadly.

"It is not," Clarissa agreed.

"Is it my imagination," Kitty asked, "or is the lake farther away now than it was when we started out?"

Clarissa laughed. "I think it is time to turn back," she said. "What a tragedy it would be if we were to miss tea."

CHAPTER TWENTY-THREE

❧

Somehow, even after such a busy day, people found the energy to attend the ball during the evening, surrounded by banks of flowers and greenery so that the Ravenswood ballroom, the French windows along one length all opened up, seemed like a fragrant piece of the outdoors. And almost everyone danced. The Greenfields, Clarissa's parents, did not, claiming old age as their excuse, as did a few other elderly people. Most of the young children did not, though they were allowed to attend until ten o'clock and dashed about, indoors and out, excited and, in most cases, overtired. The Duke and Duchess of Wilby and Lady Catherine Emmett did not dance, as they were in mourning. Lady Jennifer Arden did not. Nor did Sir Vincent Kelliston, who claimed a total inability to feel the rhythm of any piece of music—ask his wife.

But everyone was there, and everyone appeared to be enjoying the occasion.

Devlin opened the ball with Gwyneth, as the Earl of Stratton had always done with his countess. Nicholas danced with his mother, Owen with Ariel Wexford, and Stephanie with her cousin. Ben danced with his aunt, though she protested with pleased laughter that it was something she had not done in years.

Ben danced each set with a different partner, though he was always aware of Lady Jennifer, seated close to the ballroom doors, looking beautiful in black, a stark contrast to the whites and pastel shades worn by most of the other women. She was, as usual when in company, smiling and conversing with everyone who stopped to talk with her. He took her a glass of lemonade between two of the sets, and they smiled at each other as she thanked him. But she was with Lord Hardington and Sally Roberts at the time, so he did not linger.

At half past nine he saw that Joy was sitting on her lap, looking sleepy, while Lady Jennifer talked with her aunt on one side and Uncle George on the other. Ben approached them.

"Tired?" he asked his daughter.

"I don't have my cat," she said a bit crossly. "Or my doggie."

"I think," he said, "they would be bothered by the noise and the bright candlelight if I were to bring them here. How would you like it if I took you to them?"

"Yes." She yawned and reached for him.

"Say good night?" he murmured against her cheek as he lifted her into his arms.

"Good night, Uncle George and Great-Aunty Kitty," she said. "Good night, Mama."

Ben smiled again at Lady Jennifer, and she smiled back. It was precious little communication for such a festive, essentially romantic occasion. It was frustrating.

Joy snuggled into her bed not long after, the new stuffed dog beside her, the cat in her arms. She did not want to stay up for the children's supper, which would soon be served out in the nursery. She did not even ask for a story.

"I was proud of you for giving your first-place ribbon for the egg and spoon race to the little boy who came in last," Ben said.

"Yes," she said. "He was crying."

She yawned, pressed the cat's ear to her mouth, and just like that she was asleep despite the excited yelling and screeching coming from other tired children in the nursery.

Ben missed the banquet. He was neither hungry nor feeling particularly sociable. He sat with his sleeping daughter instead and let his thoughts roam. He had a new brother, with whom he would probably never be particularly close, though he suspected that his new sister-in-law and nephews and nieces would want to meet him at least. He had also acquired a new aunt today. He liked her. He might even come to love her—as she loved him. She was a gentle, kindly soul, who had known much sadness in her life and doubtless a great deal of loneliness. She still lived in her girlhood home with the cousin who had inherited the property from her father, though it sounded as if she spent most if not all her time in her own rooms. He must be a sort of cousin to Ben too, of course, though from what his aunt had said of the man, Ben doubted he would wish to acknowledge the relationship. Ben did not mind. But he minded about his aunt. He was going to try to make sure she was never again left to her loneliness.

And there was Lady Jennifer. No, just *Jennifer*. She did not like him always using her title before her name. In a few more days they would each be leaving Ravenswood, she to move to Greystone to live with Lucas and Pippa, he to go home to Penallen to . . . No, *not* to marry. Not yet anyway. His heart was going to need time to heal.

Though he must not allow that process to take too long. He needed a wife. Penallen needed a mistress. Joy needed a mother.

Ah, good God, this was all madness. He had shaped his whole life to be lived on an even keel. Chaos had rarely threatened him, and when it had—as had happened eight years ago—he had dealt with the disorder with steady efficiency and set up a new order. Now chaos threatened again. No. More than that. Chaos had happened, and this time he did not know how to deal with it.

He got to his feet, bent over his daughter's bed to kiss her, and returned to the ballroom—just in time to hear the announcement Devlin was making before the dancing resumed. It was a betrothal announcement—Uncle George Greenfield's to Lady Catherine Emmett. Good God! Though perhaps he ought not to be surprised, Ben thought. Uncle George had been at Ravenswood more frequently than usual lately, and he had often been in company with Lady Catherine, sometimes with Mother, sometimes just the two of them. He wondered if Jennifer's decision to move to Greystone had made the betrothal more possible than it had been before.

Ten minutes were taken up with congratulations while everyone wanted to shake Uncle George's hand and kiss Lady Catherine's cheek and wish them well and ask about the wedding. It could not take place just yet, of course, because Lady Catherine was still in mourning. Ben was delighted. George had always been a favorite uncle at Ravenswood. He had been widowed a long time ago, as had Lady Catherine, apparently.

The newly betrothed couple could not dance. They stepped outside into the moonlit night while a waltz was announced—the first of the evening. Devlin led Gwyneth onto the floor. Lucas, Ben noticed, took Pippa outside, out of the glare of candlelight from the ballroom and even slightly away from the lanterns that had been strung up along the terrace outside. They were going to waltz out there, their mourning obligation notwithstanding. Mother was going to dance the waltz with Matthew Taylor, and Stephanie, interestingly enough, with Bertrand Lamarr, Viscount Watley. Poor Steph. Her stomach was probably tied in knots as she imagined that the man was dancing with her only out of a sense of obligation or—worse—out of pity. Seventeen was not always a comfortable age to be. When one had no confidence whatsoever in one's looks, it was worse, for to a young person, looks were often everything.

Ben did not waltz.

Jennifer was alone for the moment, and Ben strode across the ballroom toward her before someone else could. She smiled when she saw him coming.

"I cannot ask you to dance, ma'am," he said, taking one of her hands and bowing formally over it. "Because I have two left feet, alas."

She laughed. "I have only one," she said. "The requisite number. But no one has yet decided what the other is. It is unique. That makes me very special."

He chuckled. "I do not suppose you have walked today," he said, letting go of her hand.

"No." She pulled a face. "There has not been an opportunity."

"Your shoes and your crutch are in your room?" he asked her.

"Yes," she said.

"Then let me send someone up to the gallery to light a few candles and then to your room to fetch the shoes while I carry you and your chair up there," he said.

"Now?" she said.

"Now or three o'clock tomorrow morning," he said. "It is all the same to me."

"Now, then," she said, and smiled again. "But not me *in* my chair, I hope. That would be showing off a little too much, Mr. Ben Ellis."

J ennifer had stayed until after supper because Aunt Kitty had come to her room before the ball to have a word with her, and *of course* Jennifer had had to remain for the announcement that so delighted her.

How happy she was now that she had made the decision to go to Greystone to live, largely because she had wanted to give her aunt more freedom. And she liked Mr. Greenfield exceedingly well. She would stay to watch the waltz, she had decided when all the fuss that followed the announcement had died down a bit, and then she would send for Bruce and return to her room. She had been feeling very weary and a little depressed too if the truth were to be told. Ben must have stayed in the nursery with Joy. He had danced with a variety of partners until he took her up there. He had brought her, Jennifer, a glass of lemonade once but had not stayed to talk. He had come to take Joy, but he had not spoken to *her* or even looked at her.

But he had then come back, and he had come to speak with her. He was going to take her walking in the gallery. All that exertion after such a long and busy day. Yet suddenly, miraculously, she was no longer tired. Or depressed.

Bruce was not far from the ballroom doors when they left the room, and it was he who went up to the gallery ahead of them to light the candles in the nearer wall sconces and then go fetch her shoes and her crutch from her room. And it was he who brought up her chair from outside the ballroom. Ben had already carried her up and settled her on the comfortable sofa where she had sat yesterday.

"Thank you, Bruce," she said. "I will not need you again tonight. Mr. Ellis will take me back to my room."

"Perhaps," Ben said when Bruce had gone back down the stairs, "I will make you *walk* back to your room."

"I would have to take giant steps," she said. "My daily quota is fifty."

He knelt before her then to remove her evening slippers and fit on her walking shoes, his hands sure yet gentle. But when tears threatened as she gazed down at him, she pressed them inward until her throat was sore and her chest ached.

There was so little time left.

He helped her to her feet and handed her the crutch, which she settled beneath her arm after sliding it through the leather straps. He placed her left arm over his right. His arm was rock solid, just as he was.

And they walked while she silently counted her steps and the music began again in the ballroom below them—a lively tune this time—and Jennifer wanted time to halt. If only one could do that, stop time and start it at will. Dash over the hard times, linger over the good, freeze the very best. Though *freeze* was not a good word. *Immortalize*, perhaps? Make a heaven of moments like these?

But time marched on, almost literally in her case.

"Twenty-five," she said. "Time to turn."

They turned and stopped for a few moments. They were beside one of the long windows. The candlelight in the gallery was dim.

The night beyond the window was dark, but the moon must be up. There was a band of light across the lake in the distance.

"Do you sometimes wish you could capture a moment and hold it forever close to your heart?" she asked.

"It is called memory," he said.

"But memory is of things past," she said. "I would wish to hold some moments eternally present."

"This moment?" he asked.

"Yes, this," she told him. "This perfection. But it cannot be held eternally present, alas. Memory will have to suffice. I'll always remember. *This*."

"Jennifer," he said, tenderness and pain all mixed together in the single word.

"Tell me you will always remember too," she said. "Even after you . . . are *settled*." She could not *bear* the thought of him being married. She could not *say* it. When it happened, she did not want to know about it—an impossibility since she was going to be living with his sister. But she would not be able to bear it. And she would hear when he had children . . .

"Has it occurred to you," he said, "that we are mad? That we have meekly accepted our own misery because the world has decreed that only misery is right and proper for us, that happiness is unthinkable? Why should we not decide to be *sane*? Why should we always have to *remember* when we could be living every present moment together for as long as we both live?"

"Ben," she said. There were all sorts of rational answers to his questions. But was reason also insanity? The whole world order would collapse, though, if one began to think thus. Nothing would be what one had always thought it was.

"My mother fled misery and abuse and violence," he said. "And it seems she found a certain happiness with my father. It appears he found happiness with her—if what he always told me is correct, and if what my aunt has told me today is. Their happiness was all too brief, alas. She died in childbed. And even before that he had bowed to the demands of society and his position in it by marrying someone else. But they *were* happy, Jennifer. Were they then punished for flouting society's rules? Or was the love and the happiness they knew for all too brief a time worth everything? I would not exist if they had not loved."

"And I would hate that," she said. "I would never have known love, even fleetingly. Romantic love, I mean. *Passionate* love, pure love through to the very soul. Yes, it *has* occurred to me that we are mad. But only because the world is. Because the world rates societal order above love. Love so nearly resembles chaos. But perhaps only love really matters? I mean real, deep-down, rock-solid, unshakable love. Why are there no words for the big realities?"

"Because words confine them," he said. "The big realities know no bounds. They simply *are*."

"I *will* always remember," she told him. "But I will not be able to bear it."

She slid her arm free of the straps on her crutch and let it clatter to the floor. She wrapped both her arms about his neck and rested her forehead against one of his shoulders. Both his arms came about her waist, and they stood thus for a long time while music played merrily beneath their feet and their families and friends and neighbors celebrated a festive day of carefree happiness.

"Penallen is not a hovel," he said eventually. "Or a cottage. It is not even a large house. It is nothing compared to Ravenswood or Greystone or, I daresay, Amberwell, of course. But it is a sizable manor. There is a farm. A rather large and prosperous one."

"And a view out over the sea," she said.

"Yes."

Silence stretched between them as the music came to an end.

"I do not have a fortune to compare to Devlin's," he said then. "Or, I would be willing to wager, to Lucas's. But it is a more than respectable competence nonetheless."

"With a steady income from the large and prosperous farm," she said.

"Yes."

Silence again. Jennifer tested her feet. They still felt comfortable in the shoes. Of course, she had walked only twenty-five steps in them. She loved being upright. She loved the fact that she was only a few inches shorter than Ben. She loved the warm, solid, dependable feel of him all along her body.

"I am the son of an earl and of the estranged wife of a baronet," he said. "A bastard, in other words."

"You are Ben Ellis," she said. "Not Reuben Kelliston. Not anyone else but who you are. There is no better man in the world than you."

"There may have been a bit of hyperbole in that last sentence," he said.

"Not even a jot," she said.

"And then," he said, "there are your brother and your sister and your aunt. And my relatives. Who love us. Whom we love. And society at large. And reality, Jennifer." He heaved a great sigh, and she felt it all the way through her own body.

"Ben." Did he not have the courage, then? Did she? But *was* it courage they lacked? Or was it insanity?

The music began again in the ballroom. Another waltz, a slow, lilting tune this time, perfect for the end of an evening. For surely the ball must be near its end. Dances in the country, Jennifer knew, never went past midnight at the very latest. Country people had morning chores that could not be neglected or even pushed back late into the following morning.

"I love the waltz," she said in an agony of pain. "It is the loveliest, most romantic dance ever invented."

"Waltz with me, then," he said, and she lifted her head at last and gazed into his eyes. He gazed back, not a glimmer of a smile on his face.

How could wisdom and insanity be so indistinguishable from one another that one really did not know which was which?

Incredibly, wondrously, and clumsily, they waltzed. Oh, not keeping pace with the rhythm of the tune being played, slow as it was, but in time nonetheless. They waltzed at one third the speed of the music and barely moved from the spot where they had started. But he held her right hand with his left and kept his right arm firmly about her waist while she rested her left hand on his shoulder. And they did waltz with shuffling feet and swaying motion until she was sobbing and smiling all at the same time, and his eyes in the candlelight were fathoms deep and focused entirely upon her.

But time could not be stopped or even paused. It moved inexorably onward. The music came to an end.

"Let us give it a little time," Ben murmured.

And he kissed her.

Life at Ravenswood did not become quiet and uneventful in the coming days just because the fete was over.

Ben's visitors stayed for two days and seemed rather touched by the warm welcome they were given and the interest everyone took in them and the stories they had to tell. Ben almost had to vie with his brothers and sisters for time alone with them, in fact. He was touched. His family—or what had been his only family—was genuinely delighted for him. His wife, Vincent told Ben before he left, was going to want to meet him and Joy. Ben could expect to hear from her within the next week or so. As for Aunt Edith—well, she did not take too much persuading to agree to spend a few weeks at Penallen after he had returned there.

"I have so much to tell you of your mother, Ben," she said to him just before he handed her into the chaise.

"All of which I wish to hear, Aunt Edith," he said. "But I also want to hear all about *you*."

It was going to take him a while to realize fully that his mother was being restored to him, that he now had two halves to his family background.

Ravenswood also buzzed with the news of the betrothal of Uncle George to Lady Catherine. There was to be a banquet within a few days at the home of the Greenfields to celebrate the news. There was also the news of Gwyneth's second pregnancy, announced by Devlin at the late breakfast that followed the fete. They were expecting the child to make her appearance sometime in February, he told the family and guests.

"Or his," Gwyneth said, smiling. "And we really do not mind which it is."

For the rest of that day and the days following it everyone drove poor Gwyneth crazy—her words—by rushing to do everything for her and constantly producing chairs for her to sit upon and assuring her that if she needed to go upstairs to rest they would understand and not be offended at all.

And on the Tuesday morning following the fete, Matthew Taylor and Cam Holland brought Jennifer's new chair to Ravenswood, and everyone, including even a few of the servants who could dream up an excuse, crowded onto the terrace to have a look at it. Apart from being a lovingly carved work of art, it was also functional and hugged Jennifer's body more cozily than her other chair. The wheels were just large enough that she could turn them with her hands and move herself forward and backward with relative ease. There was a lever she could pull to stop the movement, and a button to press to lock and unlock the brakes. A contraption beneath the chair, largely Cam's handiwork, enabled her to maneuver it so she would not be confined to moving only forward and backward.

There was a great deal of oohing and aahing as well as some laughter as Jennifer sat in the chair and tried out all the moves while Matthew Taylor instructed her and Cam described the intricacies of the turning mechanism to Lucas and Nicholas and Bertrand. Pippa was holding Joy, who was clapping her hands. After a while Owen jumped in front of the chair and pretended to have been knocked over. He rolled from side to side on the terrace, moaning and clutching one knee and demanding that the chair be declared a deadly weapon and Jennifer a dangerous driver.

"I kiss it better, Uncle Owen," Joy cried as she wriggled down from Pippa's arms.

There were visits to Cartref and to Colonel Wexford's and Baron Hardington's. There was a puppy to be called upon every second day. There were children for Joy to play with, either at their homes or at Ravenswood.

But there was, Ben felt, a distinct end-of-summer feel to that week, though it was only early August. For apart from those who actually lived at Ravenswood, everyone would be leaving within the next few days. It was time to go home or, in Nick's case, back to work.

Let us give it a little time, Ben had said to Jennifer after they had waltzed—or nearly waltzed—in the gallery during the ball. He had lost his courage or regained his sanity—he still did not know which—and pulled back from where their conversation had been leading.

A little time.

But there was so little. He and Joy would be returning to Penallen within a few days. Jennifer would be going to Amberwell with her aunt and, soon after that, to Greystone to live.

Let us give it a little time.

He asked Lucas after breakfast on Wednesday morning if he might have a private word with him.

"Of course," Lucas said, and they left the house together and strolled in the general direction of the lake.

Ben took some time to gather his thoughts, but it was Lucas who spoke first.

"When Phil and I met, or rather *remet* last year in London," he said, "we both agreed quite firmly that any sort of relationship with each other, especially marriage, was an absolute impossibility. I will not explain exactly why that was, but it was a very powerful reason. Even as we fell in love and even as my grandfather pressed a match on us we were both quite adamant that it was not going to happen, that it *could* not. Yet here we are, married to each other. And she is heart of my heart, Ben. I am heart of hers. One cringes a bit from such extravagant language, but it is the truth. Sometimes what seems impossible reveals itself as the only real possibility."

"Except," Ben said, "that sometimes one does not have only

one's own happiness to consider. Sometimes there is not a grandparent to push one into doing what one wants more than anything else in the world to do."

"Will a brother do instead?" Lucas asked.

They stopped walking a little past the hill and the temple. Ben frowned at him.

"My father was an earl," he said. "My mother was wife of a baronet. But I am nonetheless a bastard."

"My sister is nobly born, wealthy, beautiful, charming," Lucas said. "She is also twenty-five years old and unmarried, partly because she is more or less a cripple and partly because she will not settle for a marriage in which her position and her wealth are the main attractions."

"I love her," Ben said. "I would love her if she were a pauper or . . . a washerwoman."

"I know," Lucas said. He looked a bit bleak for a moment. "And she loves you. It would be somewhat absurd to doom the two of you to a lifetime of misery—I do not believe I exaggerate—when you are eminently worthy of each other except in one way, which society deems more important than anything else."

Ben nodded slowly.

"I take it," Lucas said, "that it was not something else entirely about which you wished to have a word with me?"

"No," Ben said. "I wished to ask you if you were adamantly opposed to Lady Jennifer Arden marrying me."

"And if I had been?" Lucas asked.

"Then I would not have asked her," Ben said. "Her family is of fundamental importance to her. She would not be happy for long if she had to choose between it and me and chose me. Love is not a single thread in life. It is a vast web, all of it necessary to lasting contentment."

"I am glad your brother and your aunt have found you," Lucas said.

Ben nodded. "Me too," he said.

CHAPTER TWENTY-FOUR

J ennifer," Ben said after dinner that same evening, when there
was still some daylight remaining. "Would you care to take a
drive in the gig?"

"May I drive it?" she asked, brightening.

"But of course," he said.

He had spoken in the hearing of everyone. And he had deliberately mentioned the gig, a vehicle for two. It was surely a broad
enough hint that he was not suggesting a general excursion for everyone's amusement.

He need not have worried. He had had a word with Mother and
with Devlin during the day, and since he had not enjoined strict
secrecy upon either of them, he did not doubt that word had spread.
Neither had voiced any objection. Dev had merely wrung his hand
and wished him luck and happiness, in that order.

"You deserve happiness more than anyone else I know, Ben," he
had assured his brother. "So does Jenny, actually."

Mother had teared up and hugged him. "I am *not* going to warn you that you may have chosen a difficult path ahead, Ben," she had said. "You will be fully aware of that, as will Jenny. But I am confident that neither of you will be daunted by that fact. Just be happy."

"I have not asked the question or been given an answer yet," he had reminded her, but she had waved a dismissive hand at him.

"A mere formality, I am sure," she had said. "Ben, your father would be *very* pleased for you. He loved you dearly."

It had been his turn to tear up.

"It is a lovely evening for a drive," Mother said now, smiling from him to Jennifer. "Go. Do not waste what remains of the daylight."

"Daylight is not always essential to a drive in the park, Mama," Nicholas said with a grin. "The sky is clear. The moon will be up after it gets dark, not to mention a few million stars."

"Take a lantern," Gwyneth suggested. "Just in case."

"Will Joy's nurse be putting her to bed tonight, Ben?" Stephanie asked. "I will go up first and read her a story."

"Thank you, Steph," he said.

"I would offer to go up too," Owen said. "But I would be sure to be accused of getting her overexcited before she goes to bed."

"Perhaps you would care for a walk up to the temple folly, Kitty," Uncle George said. "To watch the sunset."

"Come with us, Clarissa?" Lady Catherine asked. But Mother waved a dismissive hand.

"I can think of nothing I will enjoy more than a quiet evening relaxing in the drawing room," she said. "I have still not quite recovered from the fete, and we have your betrothal banquet at Mama and Papa's to look forward to tomorrow evening, Kitty. You and George go and enjoy the sunset."

W here are we going?" Jennifer asked as she turned the gig in
the direction of the village.

"The summerhouse," Ben said. "Turn left just down here."

Normally they would have taken the driving path around to
the back of the summerhouse, a longish drive since there was no
direct route there from the house. But this evening he directed her
to turn onto the poplar alley and drive the whole length of it, something that had always been strictly forbidden and had never been
done before as far as Ben knew. But she could not walk it, and he
would be damned before he would deny her the experience.

"Are we allowed?" she asked him.

"No," he said. "But I want you to see it all. Next time you can
walk along here like everyone else."

"You think I will be able to, then?" she asked.

"I do." He smiled at her. He was sitting half sideways in his
seat to watch the pleasure she had in driving. "A few days ago
you walked the requisite fifty steps *and* waltzed with me. You have
walked at least fifty steps each day since. Yesterday it was sixty, and
for half those steps you had only your crutch for support."

"And you close by lest I needed your arm," she said.

"But you did not," he told her. "And this afternoon you took
Joy for a ride all around the drawing room in your new chair. And
then Marged."

"I am going to miss Joy so much, Ben," she said.

"There are a few more days before that happens," he told her.

"Including this evening," she said, looking from side to side.
"This is magical. How can such a relatively narrow stretch of grass

with no view to either side except two lines of tall trees be so breathtaking?"

"Sometimes seclusion and nothing but living greenery are soothing to the soul," he said.

"Yes, that is exactly it," she said. "Our souls are delicate things, are they not? They so often need soothing."

"Even now?" he asked her.

"Especially now," she said. "Oh, Ben, I *wish* I had not come here."

"To the alley?" he said. There was a sudden coldness about his heart. "Or do you mean to Ravenswood?"

She shook her head. "I did not mean either. Forgive me," she said. "Sometimes I can be *so* ungrateful. My visit here has changed my life. For the better. Infinitely for the better. It is just that I hate endings. Sometimes when I am away from home and enjoying other people's company I wish I could just click my fingers and find myself back home and avoid all the pain of leave-taking. I will hate saying goodbye to your mother and your brothers and sisters and the Rhyses. Yet even home will no longer be home. I will be moving within a few weeks."

"And me?" he said. "Will you hate saying goodbye to me?"

"Of course," she said as they drew close to the summerhouse. "But life will soon return to normal. And you kept the cooler head in the gallery during the ball. The wiser and more sensible head. I must thank you for that."

"You said you would always remember," he said. "Will you?"

"Of course I will," she told him. "It has been a wonderful, memorable summer. Are we going to go inside the summerhouse? Can we watch the sunset from there?"

"It is my intention," he said.

The walls of the summerhouse were all of glass. He carried her inside and set her down on a sofa, from where she could look back down the alley and over to the west. He went back outside to tether the horse and fetch the lantern Gwyneth had suggested and the picnic basket he had packed earlier. Then he sat down beside her and set an arm along the back of the sofa, not quite touching her.

"The sky is turning lovely colors in the west," she said. "How sad it is that this time next week we will no longer be here to see it."

"The sky is something we have with us wherever we go," he said. "Besides, we are here tonight. Together."

He heard her inhale slowly. But they did not speak for a while. They watched the sunset take control of the western sky though the sun had not yet sunk over the horizon.

"I suggested we give it a little time," he said.

"Yes," she said. "Ever the steady, sensible Ben."

"Steadiness and good sense define who I am," he said. "And love."

"I know," she said. "I understood what you meant when you said we should give it a little time."

"Strong emotions, *passionate* emotions, have never defined me," he said. "I have always kept them at arm's length. I have always been afraid of what they would lead to. Something I could not readily control. Chaos."

"I understand," she said.

"Or glory," he added. "Perhaps it has been the fear of being hurt irretrievably. Perhaps I have always had unconscious memories of terror from my early childhood, when my world came to an end. Though it did not really end after all. I cannot love you sensibly, Jennifer. If I could, and I have tried, I would send you on your way home without a single plea on my own behalf, and I would go home to choose a bride who would fit into my world order and bring me contentment for the rest of my life. I cannot love you sensibly. I can only love you—" He made circling motions with his free hand.

"Passionately?" she suggested.

"Yes," he said. "But I have never loved that way before, and I am not at all sure—"

"I am not at all certain we ever can be sure," she said. "Of anything. If there is one sure thing about life, Ben, it is that it is forever changing. And we cope and adjust—or not. For years I have desperately clung to Amberwell and Aunt Kitty's companionship and a cheerful disposition to compensate for my total dependence upon others. In the last few weeks, however, it seems almost as though some dam has burst in my life and I have to adjust to a new reality or drown. It frankly scares me and exhilarates me. But I am into it now and am determined to move forward. Ben—"

"Jennifer," he said, interrupting her. "Will you— But no, not this way. Let me at least do something right."

He got up from the sofa and went down on one knee before her. He took one of her hands in both of his.

"Jennifer," he said, "will you take a chance on me and marry me and come to live at Penallen with me? I know we have both dismissed the idea as an impossibility. It *is* madness but—"

"Yes," she said.

He sighed. "I know it," he said.

She leaned toward him, the brightness of the sunset giving her face a warm glow. "I mean yes, I will marry you," she said. "I know this is a huge exaggeration and not literally true, Ben, but I really do not know how I would be able to live without you. My heart has been hurting since Saturday night. I mean really, physically *hurting*, and it can only get worse if I say yes, it is impossible, and yes, it is madness. This is the rest of our lives we are talking about. I will stand up to Luc and hope he loves me enough to—"

"I was given his blessing this morning," he told her. "Devlin's and Mother's too."

"Oh," she said.

"Even Joy's," he told her. "I did not know what your answer was going to be, but I did ask her, before I went down to dinner, how she would feel if you were her real mama instead of just her make-believe one until we go home. She said she would love it more than anything else in the whole wide world. She wanted to find you there and then and ask you, but I persuaded her to wait until tomorrow."

"Oh, is it possible to feel so happy?" she asked him. "When you pulled back on Saturday night and said we should take time to think, I thought you were being your usual noble, sensible self."

"My dull, plodding self, you mean?" he said. "I wanted us both to have time to think and not do something impulsive we might regret. But I have thought, and I do not regret loving you, Jennifer. I will not regret marrying you. And I will see to it that *you* do not regret it."

"I will not," she told him. "You have taught me that nothing is impossible."

"I hate to be the bearer of bad news," he said. "But you will never fly."

She laughed. "Have you heard of hot air balloons?" she asked.

"My intrepid wife-to-be," he said.

"Oh, Ben," she said, leaning farther toward him, her eyes suspiciously bright, and kissing him. "Do get up from there. Your knee will be sore."

"There is one other thing," he said, reaching into a pocket to withdraw a worn leather box from his pocket. "Devlin loaned me this from the collection of family heirlooms. Actually, he is trying to insist that it is a gift, not a loan. Regardless, though, it will be replaced with something new as soon as I have the chance to visit a jeweler. We sent your maid to smuggle out the robin ring you bought at the fete and wore on your third finger. Then we found that this ring in the collection was the same size."

He opened the box, and she gazed at the old-fashioned emerald and diamond ring nestled on a yellowed bed of silk within.

"Oh, it is lovely," she said, clasping her hands to her bosom before tilting her left hand toward him, her fingers spread.

He slid the ring onto the third finger and raised her hand to his lips.

"I love you," he said, and she blinked before cupping his cheeks with her hands and kissing him again.

He sat beside her again, and she rested her head on his arm while they watched the sun go down against a background of fiery oranges and reds and purples. Ben thought he had never been happier in his life. Soon he would open the hamper and pour the champagne he had brought and open the container of sweet biscuits. But not just yet. There was no hurry.

"Just as with Aunt Kitty and Mr. Greenfield," Jennifer said, "we will not be able to marry while I am in mourning, Ben."

Yes, he had realized that. Not until after Easter next year. It was a long age away. Uncle George had announced today that his and Lady Catherine's wedding would be in London next May, when the spring Season would be in full swing. They were going to have a grand *ton* wedding at St. George's on Hanover Square. But Ben was not going to let the enforced delay in his own wedding dampen his spirits tonight. Tomorrow they would work something out and then somehow live through the inevitable lengthy engagement.

"Ah," she said with a sigh as the tip of the sun disappeared behind the horizon. "It is gone. But it will rise in the morning."

"Always," he said, smiling and turning his head to kiss her brow.

She tilted her face to his and they kissed more deeply.

How many times must the sun set and rise before they were free to marry? It was best not to know the number. It would seem impossibly high.

"Make love to me, Ben," she said against his mouth.

She felt him go very still even before he lifted his head away from hers and sat looking out at the darkening sky. And it was a fundamental difference between them, she realized, something they would have to address when they married. Perhaps they would simply learn to balance each other, her impetuosity against his caution and good sense.

She had never thought of herself as an impetuous person, but she was in comparison to him. Those words had not been planned.

"Is it what you want?" he asked her.

She was not at all sure. There were all sorts of reasons . . .

"Yes, it is," she said. "But do *you* want it?"

He turned his head again, and even in the heavy dusk she could see the expression on his face. It quickened her breath.

"I must have a promise from you first, though," he said. "If you should discover after you return home that you are with child, Jennifer, or even if you should just suspect it, you must let me know immediately. No waiting to be quite sure and no hesitating while you fear what my reaction might be. No wondering when exactly you should consult a physician or say something to your family. You must let me know and I will come with a special license and to the devil with waiting until after Easter. I will not have you bear that sort of burden alone for one day longer than necessary. Promise me."

Good sense against impetuosity. And she knew he meant it. He had married Joy's mother the very day he discovered that she was with child. But she did not want to think of his first wife tonight.

"I promise," she said. "I almost hope it happens."

"It will be better if it does not," he said. "You deserve a wedding. Your family and mine deserve it. They have loved us, and they have relaxed their strict adherence to the conventions of society *because* they love us."

Doubts assailed her then. And fears. And near panic.

"Ben," she said. "My leg."

"I will be as careful as I can," he said. "I will do my best not to hurt you. You must tell me immediately if I do."

"That is not what I meant," she said. "Ben . . . It is *ugly*. And unsightly." How could she even have *thought* of marrying him? Or any man?

He sighed. "Logic tells me this," he said. "Your right leg is part of you. You are total beauty, body, mind, and spirit. Therefore your right leg must be beautiful."

"And I am too *thin*," she said. It had struck her as ironic that Stephanie considered herself ugly because she was *fat*, while she, Jennifer, hated her own *thinness*. Yet in Stephanie she saw a healthy beauty. Perhaps those who loved her saw her as *slender*, a far more attractive word than *thin*.

"And your hair is an unfashionable color," he said. "Was that next on your list? Shall I start on my imperfections?"

"You have none," she said.

"Actually, I do," he said. "Thank goodness. So do you. Thank goodness. How insufferable we would be, Jennifer, if we were perfect. Will you stop being absurd?"

"Yes," she said, laughing a bit shakily. "But I *am* ugly, Ben, and I am glad it is almost dark. Not quite, though, is it? There is still a band of color on the horizon, and the moon is up—and almost at the full."

He got to his feet then and took the large cushions off the seats of a long sofa and two armchairs and arranged them on the floor. It was a tight fit. He took a heavy blanket from the back of the sofa and stretched it over the makeshift mattress. He strewed some smaller cushions at one end of it to serve as pillows. And he turned to her, on his knees on the mattress, and eased off her slippers and stockings. He reached behind her to undo the tapes and buttons on her dress and lowered it over her shoulders and down to her waist. She was not wearing stays, only a thin shift as an undergarment. He wriggled the dress off under her and let it pool about her feet.

How could such a large and solidly built man have such gentle hands? Hands that brushed her flesh and made her hum with desire and feel that perhaps after all she was beautiful. His hands reached up into her hair and withdrew the pins with methodical care so that he could set them all on a table beside the sofa to be retrieved later. Her hair fell in heavy waves down her back and over her shoulders. He knelt there and gazed at her.

"I did not bring a brush," she said foolishly.

"Oh, my love," he said. "You do not need any brush."

My love. It was the first time he had called her that.

He lifted her onto their bed after that and disposed of his own clothing until he was naked and gorgeous. He slid his hands beneath her shift and up along her sides and off over her head. She could see him. He could see her. It was not going to be a dark night. She was curiously unembarrassed even when, still up on his knees, his eyes roamed all over her, even her twisted leg. He ran one hand lightly down it, and she blinked tears from her eyes. She refused to feel ugly any longer. He deserved beauty, and beauty was what she would give him.

He lowered his head and kissed her. And his hands, and soon his mouth and his tongue too and even his teeth, did what his eyes had just done, but more thoroughly. They moved over her, caressed her, made her beautiful, *loved* her, and filled her with an ache of such longing that she thought she must cry out with it and beg him and beg him . . . But she did not know how to complete the thought.

She wanted him with a terrible yearning, but though she did not know what to do, she did it anyway, using her hands and her mouth not only to feel his beauty and bring herself more pleasure, but to *love* him. For he was the loveliest, most lovable man in the world, and if he had imperfections, she did not know of any. She loved him with all her heart and wished her heart could expand so there was more love to give.

And she learned something new both *of* him and *from* him. Even while she felt heat and passion build between them, she felt tenderness too. This man, she believed, would be a passionate lover, but he would always be a tender one too. There would never be the fierceness of uncontrol between them. And never any sort of violence. Ben Ellis was defined by a number of attributes he had learned in the course of a life in which he had never felt that he quite belonged. But more fundamental than any of those was the fact that he was a loving and a tender man.

And he had chosen to love *her*.

She would spend her life teaching him that he belonged with her. And Joy and—please God—the other children they would have together. At Penallen, his beloved home by the sea.

His body came over her and onto her then, and he spread her legs with his own, ever gentle and careful not to hurt her though she could feel the heat of a passion in him to match her own. He lifted her with both hands beneath her, and she felt him hard and hot at her entrance and then pushing inside her with one long, slow thrust that was shocking and painful and more wonderful than anything she could possibly have imagined, though she *had* imagined.

She inhaled sharply, tensed, and gradually relaxed about him. He was hard and hot and deep, and he was gazing into her face in the moonlight and the purple remains of the sunset.

"I am so sorry," he murmured. "Let me make it a little better for you if I can."

"It can be better?" she asked. "How is that possible when it is already perfect?"

She saw him smile slowly, but he lowered his face into the cushion beside her and began to show her how it could be better, withdrawing to the brink of her, thrusting inward again, and repeating the movement over and over again until there was a rhythm and an ache and a hotness of need and a yearning and a terrible awareness that he was Ben and he was making love to her and he loved her and she loved him. For all time and perhaps all eternity too. But such thoughts, foolish or otherwise, were soon consumed and silenced by the purely physical act of love and all too soon she was crying out and he was murmuring something against her ear and they were in a place that was not a place and they were one for all eternity.

She did not even try to analyze the absurdity of *that* thought. She was welcoming the weight of his heated body as it relaxed onto her own and resisting the urge to sleep. She did not want to sleep. She wanted to cling to this present moment for as long as it was possible.

He grew heavier. And surely warmer. He was very close to sleeping.

Jennifer smiled.

"Time for a glass of champagne," he said a short while later, his voice still sleepy.

"Is that what is in the hamper?" she asked.

"That and some sweet biscuits," he said.

"I am ravenous," she told him.

"Mercy," he said. "Give me some time to recover first."

She laughed when she realized his meaning.

CHAPTER TWENTY-FIVE

ime has a peculiar quality. Sometimes it can gallop by like a
runaway horse, while at other times it crawls along like a
weary tortoise. The last few days at Ravenswood had the first quality, the following eight months the latter. If only, Ben often thought,
it could have been the other way around.

There had been considerable discussion during those few days
about what would happen during the eight-month period and about
the wedding at the end of it, especially its location. The final, communal decision—the couple concerned, even the potential bride,
was given very little say in what was judged a family matter—was
that because of the huge distances involved, the couple would stay
apart for what remained of Jennifer's mourning period and that the
wedding would take place at Greystone, where there would be plenty
of room to house all the guests and seat them at the wedding banquet.

The eight months were filled with busy activity for both Jennifer and Ben, but somehow none of it seemed to hasten the passing of time.

For Jennifer there was the move to Greystone and the lovely new apartment that had been prepared for her. There was her family to enjoy, including the almost daily development of the twins. There were new neighbors to meet and friends to make. There was the huge relief—and curious disappointment—over the discovery that she was not with child. There was Christmas with muted celebrations since they all still mourned—Grandmama and Grandpapa had still been with them just last year. But there were celebrations nevertheless, for Aunt Kitty and George Greenfield came to Greystone—no one had tried to demand that *they* stay apart—as well as Cousin Gerald and Charlotte and Sylvester with their three and a half children, Sylvester's description of their family when everyone noticed upon their arrival that Charlotte was considerably larger than usual. They were in expectation of a surprise "afterthought," Sylvester explained. Susan, their youngest so far, was already six years old.

There was a wedding to plan and hours to spend with a very excited Pippa. And there were exercises to perform every day come rain or shine—fifty steps daily for the first week, then sixty, then seventy-five, until, at one hundred by Christmastime, she stopped counting. There was her chair to learn to maneuver until she could move almost as freely about each level of the house as she would be able to do if she had two fully functional legs. There was her new gig and horse with which to familiarize herself, sometimes with either Bruce up on his perch behind or Luc or Pippa beside her, but often for short distances alone just because she could.

There were letters to write to relatives and friends. And of course to Ben. And Joy. Eight months was a tedious long time. It would have been quite unbearable, she often thought, if it had not been for the letters, one written and one received every day except on those few ghastly occasions when one of his letters was delayed. Even the fact that the following day would bring two did not make up for the dreary disappointment of no letter *today*.

And for Ben there was the gathering of harvest on his farm as a distraction for several weeks. There were neighbors and friends to visit and be visited by. There was the arrival of Stephanie and Owen in September with a frisky Carrie, who for a time needed more attention than a newborn baby, especially as she could not simply be wrapped up in a nappy but had to be chased about expensive furniture and over expensive carpets and only very gradually persuaded to take her business outside. There was the huge relief and curious disappointment of learning that Jennifer was not with child. In November there was the arrival of Aunt Edith, who brought her beaming happiness with her and a million stories and a huge valise just for all her wools and knitting supplies so her hands would not be idle. She did not need much persuading to stay over Christmas.

There was the arrival for Christmas of Vincent and his wife, Alice, and all five of their children. Ben had sent the invitation, fully expecting that it would be rejected, but it was not. And it was quickly obvious that though Vincent was still not one hundred percent sure that he wanted a close relationship with his half brother, Alice most certainly did. She was a plump, motherly woman, who clearly ruled her family by making herself irresistibly lovable to them. Equally clear was the fact that to her, *family* was the most important institution of the human race, particularly her own family and her husband's.

There was even a brief visit to Ravenswood in early February for the christening of Lady Bethan Ware, born earlier than anticipated to Gwyneth and Devlin but in perfectly good health. Aunt Edith, who went with them, largely because Ben had persuaded her to remain with him until at least after Easter, was in raptures of delight. So was Joy when she discovered that Gareth could walk now and was more than eager to play with her.

And there were letters to write, almost all of them to Jennifer. He wrote every day, sometimes at length, sometimes with no more than a few sentences, but he never missed. And if one of hers to him was delayed and he had to wait until the next day to receive two, he felt a little as though the world might have come to an end while he was not paying attention. He respected the custom of mourning the passing of loved ones. But by God he sometimes wished the old Duke and Duchess of Wilby could have been considerate enough to live a couple of years longer.

His lengthiest letter was one of the first. A couple of weeks before, he explained—on the very day of the Ravenswood fete, in fact—Mrs. Collins, one of the three women he had once thought of as a potential wife, had married a prosperous fisherman from the village, a friend of her late husband. A scant week before that, Miss Green had left her great-aunt's employ to return to her home in Gloucestershire. She had been summoned there by her father to receive the addresses of a longtime suitor who had recently inherited enough money from a deceased relative to support a wife in some comfort. As for Miss Atwell, she had gone off to visit her maternal grandmother while school was closed for the summer, had met a young curate at the local church, and had accepted his marriage offer a fortnight later. Ben embellished his account with details he thought would amuse Jennifer, including a few self-deprecating comments.

So much for the anguish of indecision that drove me to Ravenswood for the summer, he wrote. *And so much for three women pining and languishing as they awaited my return and the hoped-for offer to make them Mrs. Ben Ellis of Penallen.*

Jennifer's reply was one of her shortest. It consisted of a large drawing of a round, laughing face with tears rolling down its cheeks and a few words written beneath.

I feel almost inclined to send all three a personal letter of thanks for driving you to Ravenswood and into my arms. Almost, but not quite. P.S. Someone I know will be happier than she can say to be Mrs. Ben Ellis of Penallen after Easter.

Actually, Ben thought as he smiled at the drawing, she would be Lady Jennifer Ellis of Penallen. She would bring her title with her to their marriage.

Ben's shortest letter was written on Boxing Day, *not* because he was too busy with the Christmas celebrations to write at greater length but because his longing for her was so intense all he could do was clutch his pen, keep dipping it in the ink, and stare at the empty sheet on the desk before him. But he finally put pen to paper.

Jennifer, come home, come home, come home. But I know, I know, I know. After Easter. Then I will have you home with me. For the rest of our lives, my love. Ben.

It was his shortest letter. But it was the one that lived beneath Jennifer's pillow for what remained of the endless months of their separation. Propped against the candlestick on the table beside her bed was the drawing that had come with one of Ben's letters in September of a collie pup glaring defiantly out at the beholder (Stephanie's handiwork) with a puddle beneath it (Owen's) and a neatly written message *Wish you were here, preferably with a large mop* (Ben's) and two words in large capitals: *M-A-M-A* at the top and *J-O-Y* at the bottom, with the tail of the *J* curved the wrong way.

Even tortoises reach their destination in time. Though Easter comes but once each year, it *does* come. And with it rebirth. And spring. And hope. And new life.

And a wedding.

A large number of people converged upon Greystone for Easter. For Lucas's family it was the end of a year of mourning for beloved parents and grandparents and time to don colored clothing again and prepare for the joy of Easter Sunday and the family wedding that would follow a few days later. Lucas and Jennifer's sister, Charlotte, came with Viscount Mayberry, her husband, and their four children. The newest addition, Lucy, a second daughter, had been born less than a week after Bethan. Lady Catherine Emmett came with Sir Gerald Emmett, her son. Her daughter Beatrice and Horatio, her husband, were on their way from Ireland with their sons.

And on Ben's side, Devlin and Gwyneth came with their two children and with the dowager countess and Stephanie and Owen, who was between terms at Oxford. George Greenfield traveled with them. Charles and Marian Ware came separately, with son Clarence. Amazingly, Vincent and Alice and all five of their children had also accepted their invitation to the wedding despite the long distance involved. Ben was more touched than he could express in words when he heard. Both sides of his family were going to be with him at his wedding, and it occurred to him that at last he belonged. He might not be a legitimate member of either family, but that was a mere accident of birth. Both families claimed him. Both loved him.

Greystone, Ben thought as he traveled from Penallen with Joy and his aunt, was going to be packed to the rafters with guests— all of them come for his wedding to Jennifer. It was a daunting thought, but the wait was over at last and he would cheerfully face any ordeal that cared to present itself. It would indeed be an ordeal for a man who had spent his life trying to live in the shadows and remain unnoticed. But he was stepping at last into the full light of day, and he felt no real urge to step back again.

He exerted himself during the journey to keep Joy entertained and to converse with his aunt, though for much of the time they amused each other, counting cows or sheep in the fields they passed, making up stories of what was happening inside isolated farm-houses they passed, and sharing anecdotes of the mischief Carrie had gotten into at various times. The collie had been left behind to the eager care of a young housemaid who adored her.

For much of the long journey to Greystone, Ben thought of Marjorie. It was quite deliberate. He was about to move into a new phase of his life, into a new marriage with a woman he passionately loved. The contrast between his first wedding and the one now be-ing planned could not be greater. But it had been a good marriage, his first. They had liked and respected, even loved, each other. They had been faithful to each other. They had both adored their daugh-ter. She had been the mutual joy of their lives.

He had said goodbye to Marjorie on a bleak, barren hillside somewhere in the Pyrenees. He had not even been sure whether it was in Spain or in France. He said another silent goodbye now. But he would not feel guilty about his anticipated happiness. She was gone and he had lived on. He would always revere her memory. He would remember with tenderness and with gratitude her unselfish, undemanding affection for him and the priceless gift of his child. He would always try to keep the memory of her alive for Joy even though his child was filled with excitement at the prospect of taking her new mama home with her when they returned to Penallen.

But he would now finally let his first wife rest in peace.

Marjorie.

"At last," he said on the final afternoon of their journey. "Here we are, Aunt Edith. This is Greystone."

Joy had been here before. She pressed her nose against the window glass as his aunt donned her bonnet and tied the ribbons beneath her chin. Ben felt as though butterflies were dancing in his stomach. Their arrival had obviously been observed. There was a welcoming committee awaiting them outside the doors of the mansion, including two lines of smartly clad servants.

"Mama!" Joy shrieked, and knocked on the glass and waved a hand and grabbed for her stuffed dog to wave its paw.

And there she was, between Lucas on her right and Pippa on her left, seated on what Ben still thought of as her new chair. Jennifer, wearing pale green, her red hair sleek and tightly braided at the back, her face alight with eager happiness.

A liveried footman opened the carriage door and set down the steps, and Ben descended them first. He was given no chance, however, to turn to hand down his aunt. The footman was already doing it. Jennifer was coming toward him, propelling the chair herself.

Joy hurtled down the steps and past Ben to jump onto the footrest of the chair and onto Jennifer's lap to set both arms about her neck and kiss her lips and start prattling.

Ben laughed.

But Joy had spotted Pippa and Stephanie and Mother, and she was down off the chair and dashing toward them.

Lucas came forward to welcome Aunt Edith, both his hands extended.

But it was all background sound and movement to Ben as he set his hands on the arms of Jennifer's chair and leaned over her, devouring her with his eyes, noticing the healthy color in her cheeks and the fact that surely she had gained a bit of weight and was no longer thin.

"At last," he said. "At long, long last, my love."

And, heedless of the rather large and mainly silent audience, he kissed her lingeringly on the mouth.

Jennifer gazed down at the ring on her finger, a cluster of diamonds in a gold setting, which Ben had given her on the day of his arrival. Her betrothal ring. It gleamed with newness. The light caught it at every angle. It always sparkled, sometimes with a pure white light, sometimes with every hue of the rainbow. She slid it off and put it on the third finger of her right hand instead. Her left hand looked suddenly bare, but it would not be for long. Another hour or so at the most.

She turned her chair to admire her bridesmaids and flower girls, who were standing by her bed admiring *her*. She laughed and held out her arms to them—Stephanie in pale blue, Susan in lemon yellow, Joy in pink. All had their hair piled high, Stephanie's with her usual coiled braids, Susan's in a cluster of curls, Joy's in a topknot. All of them had narrow ribbons of all three colors threaded through their hair.

"Beautiful," she said. "You all look just as I imagined you would. A feast for the eyes."

"And you look *ever* so lovely, Aunt Jenny," Susan said, her voice sounding almost awed. "I have never seen your hair like that."

It was piled in intricate curls on her head. She had decided not to wear a bonnet but to have a flower garland instead. But Luc had fetched three tiaras from the ducal collection a few days ago, and she and Pippa had agreed the least ostentatious of them, the diamond-studded one, was by far the most gorgeous. Jennifer was wearing it now. It would be returned to the collection after the wedding, of course.

"I am so glad," Stephanie said, "that you resisted all the suggestions of bright colors for your gown, Jenny, though it must have been tempting when you wore black for a whole year. You look— oh, what is the word?—*stunning*."

Her gown was ivory lace over ivory silk. At first she had wanted white, but her modiste had set the ivory fabrics over the white and looked at her inquiringly, and Jennifer had taken her unspoken advice.

Joy was bouncing up and down on the spot, threatening the stability of her topknot. "You are going to be my mama, my mama, my mama," she said.

"Are you excited, by any chance?" Stephanie asked, laughing at her.

"Excited, excited, excited," Joy said.

But they were interrupted. Pippa and Charlotte and Aunt Kitty came into the room, closely followed by Gwyneth and the Dowager Countess of Stratton. Lady Kelliston and Miss Delmont arrived a few moments later. All was a flurry of noise and laughter for a few minutes while everyone admired the bride and the bridesmaid and flower girls while resisting the urge to hug any of them and risk creasing their dresses or dislodging their carefully arranged coiffures.

Miss Delmont wiped away tears with her handkerchief and declared that she had never been happier in her life. Lady Kelliston set a comforting arm about her shoulders. Gwyneth said that Devlin, poor thing, was fearful that he would drop the ring at a crucial moment in the nuptial service and have to chase it on hands and knees beneath the pews. The dowager countess, with a significant look at Jennifer's feet on the footrest of her chair, predicted Ben would be knocked over backward when he saw her. Aunt Kitty complained that she was *jealous* since she had to wait a whole month more for her own wedding. Pippa marveled that her dearest friend was going to be married to her brother—and then looked arrested.

"But those are the exact words you said to me on *my* wedding day," she said, and they both laughed and blinked back tears.

"Oh, I say," Owen said from the doorway. "You three girls look as fine as fivepence. You might even outshine the bride. Wait a minute, though. The bride is looking . . . hmm. What is the word?" And then he used the very one Stephanie had used a few minutes ago. "You look *stunning*, Jenny. Ben could very well be the luckiest man in England." He grinned at her. "But I have been sent up to warn everyone that if we do not get ourselves to the church soon, the rector might lose interest and retreat to his rectory to work on his sermon for next Sunday or something dire like that."

"Go away, Owen," Stephanie said.

He went. So did everyone else except the bridal party. But soon after, Luc came to carry Jennifer down to the carriage, while Bruce came to carry her chair.

"Good God, Jen," Luc said as he carried her. "I did not realize how choked up I was going to feel on your wedding day—and I am not even your *father*. How on earth am I going to feel when it is Emily's turn?"

"I think you have a few years to prepare yourself," she said. Emily and Christopher had recently celebrated their first birthday.

"I will try not to embarrass you and start bawling in the church," he said.

She kissed his cheek before he set her down on the carriage seat and took his place beside her. She smiled as Stephanie, Susan, and Joy sat on the seat opposite.

Her wedding day.

At last. Oh, at long, long last.

B ridegrooms were supposed to be horribly nervous. They were supposed to find breakfast impossible to eat. They were supposed to imagine that their cravat had shrunk overnight or their neck had swollen. They were supposed to feel a sick dread that someone would speak up during that brief pause in the nuptial service when the clergyman invited anyone who knew of any impediment to the marriage to speak out now or forever remain quiet. They were supposed to fear that their hands would shake too badly to place the ring on the bride's finger. They were supposed to fear she would not even turn up.

Ben ate a hearty breakfast and knew this to be the happiest day of his life. He had waited long enough, by God, and he was going to enjoy every moment of his wedding day. The old Ben Ellis would have cringed at the thought of a crowded church and a wedding breakfast for so many invited guests that a dining room even in a ducal mansion would just not be large enough. The ballroom would have to suffice instead.

But he was not the old Ben Ellis. He deserved love and happiness as much as anyone else. He deserved Jennifer, and she deserved him. *Not* because of anything to do with their birth or status in society, but because they were close and dear friends and loved each other with the passionate, forever kind of love everyone dreamed of and very few found.

The church was indeed full—with family and friends and neighbors with whom Jennifer had made friends in the past eight months. The back pews were crowded with servants from Greystone. Even though Ben had arrived early with Devlin, the street outside the church was already lined with people come to watch the guests arrive and cheer the appearance of the bridegroom and, later, the Duke of Wilby with the bride, his sister. The crowd would have grown by then, Ben knew. It would remain to hear the church bells peal and watch the bride and groom emerge as husband and wife.

He was going to enjoy it all.

He wondered if Lucas would push Jennifer's chair along the nave or if she would exert her independence and propel it herself while her brother walked beside her. It would not matter either way. She was entitled to do what best pleased her on her wedding day.

He heard a great cheer outside the church. Devlin's nudge to his arm was not necessary. She had arrived. He got to his feet with everyone else and half turned—as he was not supposed to do—to watch her approach. It took a few minutes while expectant murmurs ran through the congregation. Then the organ began to play, only partly drowning out the collective "Oooh" of the members of the congregation as they got their first sight of the bride.

Lady Jennifer Arden, tall, straight-backed, incredibly lovely, was walking slowly along the nave, a crutch under her right arm, her left arm drawn through the Duke of Wilby's. His hand covered hers. Behind them came Steph and Joy and Susan Bonham, a visual delight in pastel shades that complemented one another.

But after the first moments Ben saw only his bride in white or perhaps ivory, a jeweled tiara sparkling in her dark red curls. And on her feet, shoes that looked identical to the ones John Rogers made for her last summer except that these were ivory, gold, and silver.

Her eyes met his as she approached him, walked to him, and her smile lit up his heart and his life. He was hardly aware that he was smiling back. He did not even hear the "Aah" of the congregation.

And then she was facing him, standing, her hand in his, her eyes steady on his, smiling though her face was in repose. And this was it.

Their wedding.

"Dearly beloved," the rector said.

And just a few minutes later, it was done. They were married and there would be no more endless waiting and even more endless separation.

They were man and wife.

"That's my mama. Mama, Mama, Mama," Joy told Susan as she jumped up and down on the spot and the congregation laughed and Stephanie held her hand and bent to whisper something in her ear. Ben winked at her, and Jennifer turned her head to smile at her.

They walked—walked together—slowly back along the nave a few minutes later, after the register had been signed, while the organ played a joyful anthem inside and the church bells pealed the joyful tidings to those outside. Although her chair had been brought, Jennifer declined to use it.

"This," she murmured to Ben, "is what I have dreamed of for months and months."

"Well, Lady Jennifer Ellis," he said, smiling down at her when they reached the church doorway, and what looked like a vast crowd set up a cheer, and a group of young people, led by Owen and Clarence Ware, a few of Jennifer's nephews, and a couple of Kellistons, waited in the churchyard, fully armed with colorful flower petals.

"Well, Mr. Ellis," his wife said, "I would prefer *Mrs. Ben* Ellis."

"We are going to have to make a dash for it," he told her. "Just watch for that crutch."

And he swept her up into his arms and made a run for the flower-bedecked barouche that awaited them outside the wide-open church gates. No one had one iota of mercy on him, thus burdened. Petals rained down upon them, and Jennifer laughed, and Ben chuckled.

He set her down on the seat and took his place beside her. She waved to the crowd as the coachman started to shut the door. But a little pink ball of pink lace and muslin hurtled past him before he could complete the action, scrambled up the steps and onto the seat, and burrowed down between the bride and groom. They both looked down at her and across at each other and smiled.

Joy had been bubbling over with excitement and happiness until she saw that that barouche was going to take her mama and papa away without her. That was when panic had set in, and she had broken away from Stephanie and Susan and gone running. But now she had wriggled her way between Mama and Papa and she was safe. Even when the barouche moved away from the church gates and a terrible noise startled her, as though all the pots and pans in the world had been tied under the carriage and were being dragged along the road, she merely clapped her hands over her ears and burrowed deeper and felt as safe as safe could be with the warmth and solid bulk of Papa on one side of her and the warm, fragrant softness of Mama on the other.

The terrible metallic din drowned out both the church bells and the cheers of the crowd. Jennifer turned her laughing face to Ben's, and he laughed back. What else could they do? Any sort of conversation was out of the question.

Well, actually there was *one* thing they could do, and Ben, not being a slowtop, did it.

He set an arm about her shoulders, leaned across their daughter nestled in between them, and kissed his wife.

They were blissfully unaware of the roar of renewed cheering behind them.